69 **Sn** Sam Nolan Post Transition Metal	70 **La** Los Angeles Post Transition Metal	71 **P** Porsche Non Metal	72 **Mc** Annie Noble Gas	73 **Dr** Mike Noble Gas
79 **N** Nadine Non Metal	80 **Bo** Bowie Non Metal	81 **Cn** Cosa Nostra Heavy Metal	82 **D** Digital Urban	83 **Ah** Narcissism Carbon
89 **Ps** Plastic Inert Gas	90 **Tv** Media Inert Gas	91 **Dp** Depression Metalloid	92 **Xx** Xanax Metalloid	93 **L** Ashley Metalloid
99 **M** Marchesi Carbon	100 **Lm** Le Monde Carbon	102 **Os** Oscar Non Metal	103 **Sc** Scalpel Non Metal	104 **C** Clash Heavy Metal
110 **M** Molecule Post Transition Metal	111 **O** Oxygen Post Transition Metal	112 **Am** Atom Inert Gas	113 **H** Hydrogen Inert Gas	114 **U** Uracil Urban
120 **H** Hilton Heavy Metal	121 **Sz** Schizoid Heavy Metal	122 **Ni** Lithium Heavy Metal	123 **R** Ramone Post Transition Metal	124 **Rx** Clozapine Post Transition Metal

Digital DNA®

by Alan J Hampton

for
Brett, Dexter, Ethan & Blaine

Sunnydene 2020
ISBN 978-1-5272-6148-8

Chapter 1
Tinseltown

Somewhere a rock song floats on the air. Nothing heavy, just a soft-rock anthem, punctuating the dawning realisation of waking from another hangover. As he opens his eyes slowly, Sam Nolan stares at the closed curtains with the sun creeping round the edges. It's a Monday. It's another sore head, dry mouth Monday.

He pulls his aching body out of bed, stepping over the strewn clothes and fast food wrappers, pulling back the tired curtains to reveal a picture postcard view – palm trees, heat haze, and the bluest of blue skies.

Negotiating the debris on the floor, he heads to the bathroom to flush himself clean and prep for the day ahead.

The warm shower brings life; the razor shave brings a deep clean, and as he completes his routine, his confidence surges, and the hangover starts to fade. By the time he spits the mouthwash and pats the aftershave, Sam Nolan is ready to rock.

The Porsche fires up first time, and he smiles, reflecting on one of the few reliable constants in his life. The garage door creaks to the final stage of opening, and he guns the car out onto the sunny street. Two left turns and he slips effortlessly onto the freeway, only to slow to a crawl almost instantly. He curses the traffic and flicks the radio onto a rock classic station. As a song from his youth creeps into the car, he starts to weigh up his situation. He's been doing this more and more, a sure sign of the dreaded mid-life crisis. Forty-five, slightly greying, still fit. Good (but not great) plastic surgical practice, and a few bucks in the bank.

So far, so good. Now the negatives. A failed marriage, a daughter that can't stand him, manageable but mounting debts, and a string of broken friendships.

- Hmmm. About a draw - he thinks to himself.

The song ends just as the traffic eases and he starts to pick up the pace until the road flows clear. Junction 46 signs loom up and he slips the car onto the off ramp and round the long sweeping curve he had taken every day for the last twelve years. Stopped at the red light, he glances across the top of the steering wheel to the billboard advertising 'professional dating' where apparently singles who are 'too busy to date' smile down at him. He makes a mental note of the web address and speeds through the green light. Two blocks down Sunnyside Clinic sits back from the road flanked by a couple of palm trees that have seen better days. A white frontage with a cheery sign and frosted windows exude a confidence that's just slightly tinged with neglect.

The car pulls into the premier parking slot, and Nolan slides out, slipping on his jacket and locking the door all in one smooth move. He feels the sun eat into his back in the eight steps to the door, then the wall of cold air slams into him as he steps through the front door.

- Morning Courtney – he pronounces striding forcefully towards his office, eliciting only a mild grunt in response from the bored receptionist.

He closes the door behind him, and slips behind his desk. A neat, ordered office, small but functional with the latest Apple computer dwarfing the contemporary beech wood desk. Horizontal blinds give a cool, measured feel, and there are few hints to a personality, medical diplomas and industry recognition taking precedence over personal photographs or memories. A water dispenser occasionally gurgles in the corner and the gentle hum of the air conditioning gives a comforting backdrop.

Nolan flicks on the computer and removes his diary from the worn leather briefcase, which was a graduation gift from his parents, back in Edinburgh, a million years ago.

As he stares at the briefcase, he remembers his parents, smiling, bursting with pride, as their son, Sam Nolan, not only the first Nolan to go to university, but here he was graduating with honours in medicine, and about to embark on a career as a surgeon.

The briefcase was from Masterton's, one of the oldest Department Stores in Edinburgh, by appointment to Her Majesty the Queen. A fitting graduation present from his proud parents.

He remembers their joy when he married Jane, a pretty but dull daughter of a family friend, and when their grand-daughter Sarah was born, they all could have died of happiness. A few happy years followed, with a nice house in the Edinburgh suburbs, an excellent posting to St John's Hospital in Edinburgh, where a varied but not too taxing workload allowed for the boredom to creep in. A regular 9-5 routine with little variation, predictable nights in, and boring weekends with vapid friends or work colleagues soon had Nolan longing for more. A knock on the door broke his stream of memory, and Annie, his nurse, friend, confidant, and general organiser came striding into the room carrying two takeaway coffee cups and a folder under her arm.

- Well if it isn't Doctor Do-little – she grinned sidling up to his left placing one of the cups in front of him.

- Something to get you ready for the Garcia facelift at mid-day – she quipped.

- Anaesthetist is in at 10.30 and Mrs Garcia is due in at eleven - She flopped the folder onto his desk.

- I'll leave you to review your notes……..don't forget the latex allergy!

- She laughed as she headed out of the room. Nolan mumbled a thanks but she had already left the room and closed the door.

He flipped open the folder revealing photographs of a middle aged Hispanic woman.

- Not unattractive - he mused - but going to be a lot better when I'm finished - he thought to himself, laughing inwardly. He supped on the coffee and sat back in the chair gazing at his own untidy, scratchy handwriting in the folder.

Unable to concentrate on the task at hand, he picked up his mobile phone and scrolled through the contacts. Finding the correct one, he calls and leans back in the chair.

- Not a good time for you – the other end on the line laughs. Dan Phillips is Nolan's bookie.

- Could be better – Nolan spits through gritted teeth – Where are we at? – he quizzed.

-With last night's debacle, we are at 77k…..now you know that's a

3

good bit more than even I'm comfortable with, right? -
- Oh come on, I can make that in a couple of weeks if I'm really on the case -
- Well further up the line is taking a bit of an interest in your case, if you know what I mean, so either get some cash into me soon or start winning! -
- Put 5 on tonight. Home team. I surely can't lose that! -
A knock at the door interrupts, and Annie's head pops round the door to announce the anaesthetist's arrival.
- I gotta go - He hangs up the call and puts the phone on his desk.
A careful read through of his notes is then followed by a Google search of today's suture and sedative, just to make sure there are no new FDA guidelines or bans.
He strides over to the cupboard, opens the door and takes out his scrubs. Slipping off his shoes, he dons his surgical wear. He picks up the folder, his stethoscope and heads out to the reception, where he can hear Mrs Garcia and Annie's laughter. The door closes silently behind him.
Three hours later, Nolan eases into his office, removing his cap and gown. He slumps into the chair, satisfied that another patient's dream of eternal youth is another step closer to reality.
Annie enters the room carrying two mugs of coffee in Pharmaceutical Company corporate branding.
She hands one to Nolan as he reclines into the leather couch.
- Another job well done, Captain! – She toasted him.
- One or two wee issues but overall I think she's going to come out great. Good starting point and no weight issues. She's from money, right? -
- The Aston Martin at the door says yes. She paid bank transfer on Thursday last week the minute I emailed her too. Address is Calabasas – Annie recited.
- Maybe she'll tell her friends -
- You mean to say they won't ask why her face is swathed in bandages?-
They both laugh and just for a moment Nolan feels a glimmer of

4

genuine happiness. Then it passes.

A knock on the door and the bored receptionist enters with a takeaway lunch box which she drops on Nolan's desk in her inimitable uninterested style.

- Thanks – Nolan mutters glancing and rolling his eyes to Annie who rises from the couch and follows Bored Receptionist out.

The lunchbox is brown and clearly made from recycled cardboard.

- Oh good – he thinks to himself - More rabbit food -

He opens the box to reveal various unknown salad items; some green, some yellow, but mostly brown. He opens the little fork and water carton and tentatively starts to eat his unknown lunch.

He flips on the computer screen and opens his digital diary.

4.00pm Consultation Jan Redmond – Breast Enlargement

5.00pm Follow Up #2 Sandra Henderson – Tummy Tuck

6.00pm Consultation Andrew Jones – Rhinoplasty

He switches over to email and starts to scan through the seemingly endless list of messages. One name jumps off the page – Sarah Nolan. An email from his estranged fifteen year old daughter, containing a highly impersonal message inviting him to attend some dance thing at her High School. He checks the date. A week on Wednesday. He can make it, but the thought of a stultifying boring two hour dance routine with ex-wife Jane and her do-no-wrong boyfriend of the moment, is more than he can bear.

- Sorry honey I have surgery that night otherwise I would love to go. I trust Mum will be there so you aren't alone? – He reads it a couple of times to make sure it isn't too sarcastic. He sends the email and discards all the other messages of cut-price car loans, discounted office furniture and clandestine sexual encounters.

He clears the desk of all debris, and hears the muffled chit chat from the reception area which heralds the arrival of the flat-chested Jan Redmond.

A pretty, petit dark haired woman in her late thirties, Jan Redmond confidently enters the room and shakes Nolan's hand.

- Dr Nolan, I presume? - She smiled, lowering herself onto the chair.

5

- Yes…..Mrs Redmond/ Miss Redmond? - He queried well aware that her flirty nature and blushing cheeks on her entry signalled a single woman - And let's not forget her desire for bigger tits - he thought to himself.

- Miss Redmond - she playfully offered.

- So we are looking to increase your bust. Any idea where you would like to be?

- Well I am a rather disappointing 32B, and as I have been on a strict diet and yoga plan for the last two years, I feel I have everything else right, but there seems to be a lack of balance in the chest area -

- Okay, can you please remove your top and bra so I can get a proper look? Nolan rose up from his desk and pulled the cord on the window blinds instantly shutting out the Californian sun. He walked over and locked the door as the patient removed her blouse and shot a checking glance at Nolan as she reached around and unclasped her bra.

It was at this moment that Sam Nolan was grateful that he had stuck in at school.

They were indeed in need of some va-va-voom, he thought to himself, but she had clearly kept herself in shape.

- Have you ever nursed? - He enquired in a matter of fact tone, peering closely at her left breast.

- No. No children -

He examined her methodically and popped over to the desk every couple of minutes jotting notes and squiggles on his notepad.

- You can pop your clothes on again - he said whilst pulling up a file on the computer.

Once she had dressed, he opened the blinds and unlocked the door.

He swivelled the computer screen round so she could see a 3-D image of a digital woman of similar proportion to herself.

- Here we are at 32B, and then he started to tap the space bar, and as he did so every tap saw the breasts increase on screen.

- Stop! She excitedly shouted. –That's it! That's perfect!

- That's 36D – perhaps a little too big in one go? -

- No, that's what I want – she said a little indignantly.

6

Nolan then bent down to his right lower desk drawer and produced a breast implant.

- This is the size you want to insert into your chest? -

She gazed at the implant, almost hypnotised, before taking it from him, kneading it through her fingers, studying every mark, every millimetre of its being. She held it to her chest.

- No, this feels good. This is what I want – she added forcefully.

- You're the boss – he smiled, accepting the implant back.

He then went through all the paperwork and disclaimers, finally showing her the price on screen. He stared at her face looking for reaction.

- Fine she said, let's do this – She smiled.

- Right – He stood up and headed to the door and held it open for her.

- Annie will check the diary with you just now and get you sorted out. The next time I'll be seeing you is on boob day! - He grinned.

How she laughed. She shook his hand, pecked him lightly on the cheek, and headed off to reception still laughing as he closed the door.

He filled a cup of water from the dispenser and sat back behind his desk all ready for his 5pm. A second follow up appointment on a nervous, fluttery sort of woman, he recalled. He had performed the tummy tuck six weeks ago, and although he hadn't been the happiest with it, the woman was ecstatic.

His thoughts were interrupted as Annie walked into the room.

- So I'm getting a pay rise? - She stood with her hands on her hips.

- I beg your pardon? -

- Pay rise. Me. Annie. -

- It's August. I hadn't planned it? -

- Well I've just checked our previous four breast enlargement procedures, and it appears Miss Redmond is paying an extra $1000. Therefore I can only assume you wish to reward your loyal employees? -

-We've been the same price for ages…………I've got stuff going on………..We need to start making more profit…..all that business stuff you're always preaching at me…. – he feebly countered, no real

7

conviction in his voice.

- I'm well aware why you've done this. You need to be careful Sam, gambling is not a good look on you -
- I know, I know – he looked sheepishly at the floor.

The front door opened and a chatter of voices caused Annie to turn around and head out. He let out a long sigh.

Sandra Henderson slightly stooped; looking left and right, enters Nolan's office.

- Sandra! - He boomed out rising from his chair and offering his hand.
- Hello – she feebly replied and limply shakes his hand.
- Please sit – he points toward the chair, and she gingerly eases down onto the chair.

Her eyes dart around the room. - This is one nervous bunny – he thought. She crosses and uncrosses her legs several times as Nolan returns to his desk.

- So how are we feeling?-
- Great Doctor Nolan. I've been following your instructions to the letter, and the scar is already starting to fade. Look! - She joyously pulls up her cream blouse revealing a neat scar across her abdomen.

Nolan rose from his chair and crouched beside her, gently running his finger along the scar. She flinches under his initial touch with a sharp intake of breath, and then relaxes as he pats her knee in reassurance. He takes his magnifying glass from his pocket and begins to study the scar in detail. He switches on the penlight on the top and slowly scans across the wound.

- There's a very light inflammation to the right side, but other than that, I think we are on the right path. I'll give you a script for some antibiotics that'll settle that down. Otherwise, everything else OK? -
- Very much – she beams – In fact, I've felt so much happier since the operation, and I feel my confidence coming back again -
- Confidence? Back? – Did she ever have any? - He thought to himself.
- It's even given me the nudge I need to think about dating again. Ever since Jeff ran off with his business partner, I've lacked confidence. I've lacked a basic desire! - Her eyes came alive with that small outburst.

8

- Well I like to think, Sandra, that I'm more than just your surgeon, and that not only with professional advice, but also advice as a friend. I mean I've known you now for about ten weeks, and think this little 'journey' which we've had here together has been a learning curve – Nolan was off now, playing the part of the concerned professional, with the personal edge – You see, I see myself as more than a surgeon, more than the degrees and diplomas, - he waved his hand in the direction of the framed certificates on the wall - I'm a counsellor, a confidant, a friend - His eyes met hers as he emphasised the 'friend'– I've advised many patients throughout the years on their problems and issues, above and beyond the call of duty, sometimes in the middle of the night, sometimes in the middle of my holiday! But you see Sandra, - he said straightening up and taking her hand in his, - I've been through this before with female patients, where their partner has upped and away with the pretty gym bunny or the maid, in fact, in my own personal situation,……. -
- Jeff's business partner was a man – she interjected.
- Sorry what did you say? – A surprised Nolan leant back, irritated at this interruption of his pitch.
- Jeff's business partner was a man - she said tilting her head slightly and gazing at the floor.
- Oh. Right. Wow. Well I can see now how that may have given rise to certain, how shall we say, self-doubt? -
- I'm over the worst of it now, and our daughter also finds the whole episode distasteful. In fact, she won't even acknowledge any of his calls, emails or letters. The whole thing is just so sordid -
Nolan shuddered thinking of his own daughter situation.
- So what steps are you taking about dating again? – He interjected quickly; keen to get the subject off daughters.
- Well I've joined a web dating service here in Los Angeles for busy professionals -
Nolan's mind immediately went to the billboard he'd seen that morning.
– That one will not be getting a subscription, not from Sam Nolan, or

any of his other online aliases – he thought to himself.

He imagined Sandra's photographs and spiel. Semi glamorous photographs taken ten years ago, cropping Jeff out, naturally. No doubt she likes dogs, beach life and long walks. Boring and predictable. Probably 'too busy' to find a partner, and 'doesn't like the bar scene' in West Hollywood. Looking for a nerdy, quiet, but outgoing partner, probably to make up for her complete lack of personality, but no doubt caring, and liking quiet nights in with a glass of wine.

- I've viewed a couple of prospective matches - she states brightly, interrupting Nolan's harsh self critique of her imaginary dating profile.

- But I really wanted to wait until the scar had really gone down before I went out on a date, you know, in case things developed quickly - She looked down at the floor again.

- If you don't mind me asking, Sandra, what do you do for a living? – he quizzed.

- Clerk. Book-keeper. Something really pointless and boring – he thought to himself.

- I have a dog-grooming business – she perks up at the mention of her career.

- Bingo – thought Nolan.

The rise of the Metro sexual lifestyle in California had brought with it a massive increase in the amount of designer dogs, and with that, all the frippery and pointless businesses associated with said dogs. Walking services, gourmet dog foods, dog dieticians, dog psychologists, dog accessory boutiques, and of course dog grooming. He recounted a previous girlfriend who had one of those little carry–in-a-bag dogs, always kissing it, speaking to it. Used to make him sick thinking of that overgrown rat getting all the attention once his star had fallen. It had been a promising relationship, her, a divorced wealthy socialite, him playing the part of the successful Hollywood (not Beverley Hills) surgeon. His Scottish brogue always worked a charm here in Los Angeles, and whenever he could, he laid it on Shaun Connery style, thicker than a weightlifter's arm. But all these LA socialites were all the same, vapid, insecure, needy types, and when they turned on you, boy,

10

they turned.
- So, you seem to be well on the road to recovery Sandra - he said changing the narrative and looking to wind the appointment up.
- Yes, is there anything else I should be doing? -
- No, you seem to be doing it all, keep moisturising the area around the scar and don't hesitate to call if there's anything out of the ordinary -
She rose from the chair with her head slightly bowed and straightened her clothes before looking up.
- Thanks again Dr Nolan – she offered her limp wrist in handshake.
- No problem Sandra, I hope the dating thing works out for you -
She blushed and headed out the door.
When his own marriage had finally broken down, Nolan's relationship with his girlfriend now seemed pointless and worthless, like the three-way relationship with himself, his wife and Nadine had in some way validated her part in his life. It was like once he had finally got what was once unattainable, what he desired, he no longer wanted it. Once Jane had left and he had Nadine all to himself, he started to dislike her attitude, her dress sense, and then the little things started to annoy him, like the way she called her handgun 'Frankie'. In their early courtship, she kept going on about 'Frankie' and Nolan had thought it was a child or a dog, but then discovered whilst rummaging in her Mercedes glove box, it was her pearl handled Glock 9mm pistol.
When he first met Nadine, she was a pretty would-be socialite, recently divorced.
She spent her days at the gym, the tofu bars, shopping for lycra, and generally driving round looking for anything to break the routine of her mundane boring routine. Nolan had been squaring away his losses to Phillips over lunch at Sunset Plaza, and was drinking a cool glass of Pinot Grigio staring into space whilst Phillips rambled away about odds and chances and other nonsense. His glaze diverted left to a slim blonde in a very, very tight dress on one of the high stools which looked out over Sunset Strip. She was smoking a cigarette and had two empty martini glasses in front of her. She had a slightly damaged look, and despite the fantastic figure, was definitely the wrong side of thirty.

Some nip and tuck had been done around the eyes, he reckoned, and those bra-less breasts were just a bit too perky. A small perfect nose and rich, full red lips set off her slightly punky demeanour. She reminded him of someone, but he couldn't remember, then it came to him - Cyndi Lauper in her prime - he thought to himself. He left Phillips with promises to be in touch, and then glided over in his best confident Shaun Connery Hollywood Plastic Surgeon way.

She immediately turned as he approached, and offered up a chair. Introductions were made, drinks were drank, and within two hours, Nolan was in her bed. A tempestuous two-year affair followed, with highs such as the Plastic Surgeon Conference in Las Vegas, where they had a week of lovemaking and drinking as Nolan lived as a single man again, to the lows of her needy desperate phone calls to his house at 2am. He was always torn with Nadine, he knew he had no future with her, but the sex and the sense of adventure were like a drug, and he kept going back for more. It was as if her longing for him amplified how little his wife thought of him, Jane had never come to any work conferences, never wanted sex other than at regimented times and dates. She had never shown any interest in his work. He started to notice how Jane belittled him in front of company, and jealously guarded their daughter from him, like a prize. More and more he came to the realisation that his marriage was dead, he no longer loved his wife, and was indifferent to his daughter, but Nadine probably wasn't the answer. Nadine however, had brought his sexual mojo back. Even Annie had noticed his swagger and his rediscovered confidence.

The clandestine meetings and secret trysts at Nadine's condo were getting more and more frequent, and Nolan had been getting sloppy with his excuses and diversions. One minute he pictured a new life with Nadine, whilst sitting bored at a typical LA cocktail party with his wife, the next lying naked with Nadine after a marathon two-hour sex session, longing to be anywhere but there.

Nadine adored Nolan, seeing both the perfect older lover, and the financial meal ticket that would allow her to live in the style to which she had become accustomed.

They would have long conversations about a life together, and initially, Nolan would be enthused and dream up the most elaborate scenarios and fantasies about taking her back to Scotland to see where he grew up. As time went on, she became disillusioned with his promises, and came to the conclusion that he was simply using her for sex. This was probably true.

As their relationship deteriorated, they had drink-fuelled arguments, usually ending with Nadine threatening to call his wife and expose the affair, after which they occasionally came to blows, but always ended up in bed.

Then one Saturday afternoon, Jane was gone. Nolan had been down at the clinic on a consultation basis from 9 until 4, and he'd argued with Nadine by text over lunch. He drew the Porsche into the garage, and even before he opened the door into the hallway, he knew something was wrong. The babble of TV's or voices wasn't there. He edged gingerly into the house calling her name – Jane! Janey! You there? - The house seemed cleaner, neater. He then realised some of the pictures were missing from the wall. He slowly turned into the lounge with its panoramic view of downtown in a haze way off in the distance. His Eames chairs were there, but that was it. No TV, no stereo, the leopard chaise lounge which they bought in Santa Barbara, all gone.

He ran up the stairs to Sarah's bedroom. Empty. He could see the faded rectangles on the wall where her posters had been.

- Jane! – Jane! – What's going on? – He shouted into the hallway.

His voice echoed in the house, and he knew she was gone. He knew this was it. He had prepared for this mentally, but it was always going to be on his terms. When *he* decided to leave. It was not supposed to be like this.

He dialled her mobile number only to go straight to answer phone. He hung up. He dialled Sarah's number. It rang out. No voicemail option. He text them both asking where they were.

He searched through the house until he found the letter in the kitchen. Jane's neat handwriting stood out on the crisp white paper on the speckled kitchen worktop.

13

He opened the letter forcefully, ripping it with unnecessary haste. The single folded letter inside looked mercifully short, and he read through what he had been dreading inwardly for several months now. Yes, she was aware of Nadine. No, she wasn't available to talk. Yes, their American Dream was over. Yes, he would be hearing from her lawyer. A loud car horn on the road outside the clinic brought him back into the present.

The bleep of an incoming text message broke his consciousness, and he opened the message. Philips. It's a short message. 'Another bad day Sam'

- Shit – Nolan checked the football scores on his computer. His worst fears have been realised as the Tennessee Titans defy all the odds to pull off the shock result of the season against the Jacksonville Jaguars.

- Damn Damn Damn – he slams the mouse onto the desk, rueing his luck.

He texts Philips. - UK soccer. Arsenal tomorrow home win 2k- He puts the phone face down on the desk.

He can hear the opening of the front door and the exchanging of pleasantries. This will be Mr Andrew Jones, a consultation on Rhinoplasty.

Annie shows him into the office, introducing Nolan, and when sure Andrew Jones was looking at Nolan, widened her own eyes in exclamation to Nolan.

This guy had a really big crooked nose. Completely hooked and a prominent bump.

- Easy money- he thought.

Dr Nolan – Andrew Jones began – you were very highly recommended to me by a colleague of mine, Shane Price…..you know him? He works with me at the Astoria……you performed some anti-ageing treatment to him last year? -

- Yes, yes, yes – Nolan remembered Price, vain little creep who ran the Astoria nightclub up on Sunset. Nadine had introduced them on one of their many nights out there. Once Price found out Nolan was a Plastic Surgeon, he began to pester him for special treatment. At first Nolan

14

simply agreed and vaguely promised to see him sometime, but then every time they went to the Astoria, there was a private table with his name on it and complementary Bollinger was sent over. Inevitably Nolan and Nadine would grudgingly accept, and inevitably Price would appear with some young floozy and gush over Nolan as if they were best friends. He wanted to stop going there but a mixture of laziness, Nadine's insistence, and the copious amounts of free champagne was just too much for Nolan's ego, and eventually agreed to give Price a medium level facelift on the house.

- How is Shane? I haven't seen much of him these days. I'm not much at the Astoria these days -
- He's fine Dr Nolan – says to pass on his regards -
- I must pop in again some night. I don't remember you, though, and I'm pretty good with faces. Or you had better hope I am – he laughed.
- I just started as accountant there three months ago. Shane just needed a guiding hand through these recessionary times -
- I bet he does – Nolan thought to himself. Price was a real shark, involved in everything. Bit of low level dealing, late night lock-ins, entry level prostitution (guys and gals) and definitely tax avoidance. Which would probably mean this poor clown would be doing time in the next few years.
- Are you enjoying working at the Astoria? - Nolan interjected.
- Well that's why I'm here Dr Nolan. As you are well aware, the Astoria is one of Hollywood's premier late night establishments, and attracts some of the most gorgeous and desirable women in Los Angeles. I'm not *too* bad looking, I have a nice house & car, a few dollars behind me, and a dream job in a Sunset Strip nightclub. But to be blunt, I also have this – he pointed at his misshapen nose. - This – he pointed again – is stopping me from living the dream, Dr Nolan, *living the dream!* If you could just do something to take the focus off my nose, anything, to take the focus off my nose, I could start making the most of my situation -
He looked painfully at Nolan, almost pleadingly.
- Right – let's have a little look. Nolan put the latex gloves on and

began to gently caress Jones's nose, carefully tracing around the edge, running his index finger repeatedly up and down the ridge of the offending area.

- Tilt your head back please – he gently cradled his head with his left hand then lit his penlight and shone the light up each nostril. He lifted his left hand from behind his head and pulled a pair of tweezers from his breast pocket and pulled out several nasal hairs blocking his view. Jones winced as he did this.

- Jesus! How the hell are you going to put up with the very real and immediate pain once I've chiselled that abomination off your face? – he thought to himself.

He shone the light up again revealing the location of immediate blood vessels then looked from the outside, the penlight illuminating his veiny skin. The dark shadow of the oversize bone was apparent.

Nolan returned to his seat placing his tools on the desk.

- This is indeed a major piece of nasal reduction – he offered - In fact, Andrew, maybe one of the largest I've had to deal with. However, I can do something for you though - his face breaking into a smile.

-Thank you! Thank you! - gushed Jones.

Nolan began to sketch on a Pharmaceutical Company notepad. He drew a vague approximation of Jones's nose side on.

- This - he began and paused - is what I'm looking to do – he drew a line back and forth creating a straighter line, back and forth until the paper began to tear.

- Perfect – whispered Jones.

- And this – as he wrote $9,000 below the sketch – is what you're going to give me so you can then start having the pick of the talent at the Astoria – he purred looking up at Jones.

Jones burst out into nervous laughter, to which Nolan joined in, aware that Jones was eyeing him to see if this was acceptable.

-You, you, you – Nolan wagged a finger at Jones like a schoolteacher, which sent Jones into hysterical laughter.

- Annie will schedule you in Andrew, should be in about two to three weeks, so in about two months you can be holding court on a Saturday night -

Jones continued laughing as he shook Nolan's hand and retreated out into the corridor. Nolan followed him right up to Annie's desk and casually shot her a glance.

- Mr Jones has consented to a Rhinoplasty, Annie, and is looking to book in as soon as possible -
- Alright Mr. Jones, let's have a look – Annie mumbled as she began to scroll through her computer screen – The earliest we have would be Friday 13th at 1pm. Not superstitious are we? - She enquired playfully.
- Not at all - he countered, still giggling and glancing at Nolan for his approval.
- Has Dr Nolan taken you through the pricing for the procedure Mr. Jones? -
- Yes – interjected Nolan quickly – We have agreed a reduced rate of $9,000 for our good friend here, as he is an associate of Shane Price. Do you remember Mr. Price Annie? -
- Hmmm – I think so – Annie said looking over the top of her glasses disapprovingly at Nolan.

Bored Receptionist got up from her desk and wandered past the group at Annie's desk heading for the canteen, her shoes scuffing as she walked. It always annoyed Nolan how the stupid girl didn't lift her feet when she walked, always dragging and scuffing as she walked, emphasising her boredom and general apathy.

Nolan noticed Jones's gaze shifting from Annie's neat small cleavage to bored receptionist's youthful derriere.

Jones's eyes then met Nolan's and they smiled conspiratorially.

Annie printed out the various disclaimer and allergy forms.

- Right – I'll leave you guys to sort out the boring stuff, and I'll see you on Friday the 13th Andrew! -

He shook Jones's hand and headed back to the coolness of his office.

He checked his watch. 6.45pm.

He hit the off switch to the computer and turned to the outside window. Cars were trundling down the street outside and the sun was just setting on the top edge of the valley. He pulled the blinds shut in a single motion causing them to swing left and right. He arched his back pointing his right arm into the air easing into his jacket rather ungracefully.

He heard the door closing heralding the departure of Andrew Jones, and then the inevitable visit from Annie.

He was not disappointed as she swung into the office, folder in hand.

- $9,000? – *Reduced* rate? – What are you playing at? He could get 2 new noses anywhere else for that! –

- He needs the work of two noses Annie! - Nolan countered, causing her to laugh.

- Relax. He thinks he's getting a deal and he's a mate of sleazy Shane Price. He's not going anywhere else -

- Sam….This rate hiking and random pricing flies in the face of all the price lists, all the organising and all the stability I'm trying to bring and maintain in this practice. The last thing we need is unprofessionalism and your gambling throwing everything down the toilet! I'm not stupid Sam, I can see the losses. I know your face when you've lost. And I'm seeing that face more and more – she scolded.

- It's OK Annie – honestly. Just a wee lean spell. A few more Jan Redmonds and Andrew Joneses and we'll be on top of the world -

- Just cool the gambling, Sam. Get yourself straightened out with that and everything else will follow. Look at you. You're wasting away. Getting through the day here, then off to the bars on the strip to medicate your losses, falling into bed in the small hours, then up the next day and do it all over again? -

- Steady on…..that's a bit harsh? -

She was right of course. It was like some Groundhog Day. Not like the film though. That was fun.

- It's OK, everything is in hand. I'm just working through some things. Look how busy we are. Plenty work and opportunity. All the pieces will fall into place. Just you wait and see – he said unconvincingly.

- Well go have a good think to yourself Sam. It's not just you if this ship goes down…..- Her voice tailed off and she turned and closed the door behind her.

Nolan waited until he heard Annie and Bored Receptionist leave together. He pushed his finger in between two blind slats and watched as they both entered Annie's car and drove off.

Puffing his cheeks he slowly exhaled a sigh.

He stepped smartly through the office and punched in the alarm code, pulling the now bleeping door closed behind him.

Slipping out of his jacket and into the car, he gunned the engine and rapidly sped out onto the street. It was that strange half-light at dusk, where everything looks clean but surreal. The car headlights picked out his route as he headed into West Hollywood.

He didn't feel hungry but knew he had to eat something. After negotiating a myriad of back streets and short cuts, he turned up the steep hill at the Le Monde Hotel. Le Monde was a cosy little Hollywood boutique hotel, familiar with visiting rock stars, Hollywood insiders, and a little bit off the bar circuit.

The Porsche pulled up sharply at the doorway, and the valet jumped off his stand to take Nolan's car.

Nolan headed straight for the bar, a post-modern, slightly garish vision that always gave him the impression of an art student's failed installation. Blue lights, dressmaker's torsos, zebra rugs and multiple vintage cathode ray TV sets made up this hellish cocktail of décor, but he felt sadly a little bit at home. Several tables held various couples deep in conversation and perhaps two or three business deals underway. Four suited business men were all standing drinking Scotch at the bar, comparing credit cards.

He found an unoccupied corner booth and slipped in. Almost immediately a young waitress appeared, proffering a black metal menu. He took the menu and ordered a beer and a Canadian Club over ice. Staring at the several TV screens he saw an old black and white film he recognised, but couldn't remember its name. He drank the cold beer intermittently with a sip of CC – What is the name of that film? – He thought to himself, cursing his failing memory. There was some big moral message. He remembered that. That was when they knew how to make proper films in this town. No sex, violence, or special effects. Just

19

a good storyline with a kicker at the end, and a patriotic message or some feel good moralising.

The heroine was on screen, close-up, and a tear on her cheek. Camera was on soft focus filter – Still doesn't hide that wonky bottom lip – he thought to himself - or that slight blemish on her Adam's apple - Just as he prepared to consider his surgical options back in 1944, the waitress stood in his line of vision, electronic notepad in her hand. – Ready to order? – She enquired vacantly.

Without looking at the menu he asked for a burger – Well done, no salad and some mayo for the fries – he handed back the menu – And another round of drinks – he added impatiently.

Before he could revisit the TV screens, he felt the vibration of his mobile phone. He pulled it from his pocket, his face illuminated with the faint glow.

PHILLIPS

He accepted and put the phone to his ear.

- It's a no on the Arsenal tomorrow Sam -
- Eh? What do you mean? -
- It's a no for anything now Sam, until you can do something about your outstanding. I mean I told them you were good for it, but they're getting pissed off now. My excuses don't cut it and I've been told in no uncertain terms you gotta stump something up -
- Jesus Dan......I do not need to hear this kind of negativity just now. You aware how much I've given you guys over the last year? – He started to do the mental calculation himself, but as soon as he began to realise the total figure, he shook his head and dropped the idea.
- It's not negativity, Sam, its economics. You gotta pay something. A gesture. Some goodwill -
- Well how much? I have five procedures in the next seven days, and I can pitch up maybe $10k? -

Phillips stifled a small nervous laugh and then with a sharp intake of breath said – They want $30k now Sam, and a firm payment plan for the rest. No more until you're up to date. They're not messing about this time Sam, and it's not just you. Tightening up on everyone. Yes indeed -

20

- Jesus! Where am I meant to turn up 30 grand in a week? – He felt a light sweat on his brow, and suddenly thought the room was really warm.

- There's no week Sam, it's like tomorrow, day after at best. They know where you stay. Nice house. They know you're a Surgeon with his own clinic in Hollywood. You drive a Porsche for heaven's sake. You look like a wealthy guy, Sam -

The waitress put another beer and CC in front of him and took the empties away.

He waited until she was out of earshot, following her with his eyes until she was back behind the counter.

- Really? Where did all this come from? All these things are worth good money, yes, but it's not cash in the bank. Cash flow. That's what it's all about. I've put thousands and thousands of dollars into you guys pockets over the last year, and you never hear me complain? It's just a shitty spell. You know?.......I've had these before and I'll inevitably have these again. Jesus. Thirty grand? -

- Look - go speak to your banker, your stockbroker, I don't know…..just whoever will front you up just to keep everyone happy. We don't want any scenes. I'll text you tomorrow and we can sort out a meet up. Don't do anything silly now…….These people do not get messed about -

Phillips hung up.

- Goddammit – he thought to himself, rubbing his hand over the back of his neck, feeling the light moisture on his skin.

The burger appeared in front of him open faced with the fries in a little trendy wire basket. He realised what minuscule appetite he had earlier had now deserted him.

He downed the beer and the CC and waved to the waitress for a repeat.

Chapter 2
Dude Ranch

The intermittent ping of the mobile alarm penetrates through the murk. Nolan slowly opens his eyes focusing on the chink of bright sunlight cutting between the curtains. He notices the tiny specks of dust floating in the light, down, down, and then disappear forever. Slowly he reaches out and picks the phone, silencing the shrill alarm tone with one touch. As he puts the phone back on the nightstand, he realises he is hung-over again.

- No, no, no – he thinks to himself -Why did I drink last night? - The mood of regret is soon dwarfed by the heavy headache and churning stomach.

He lies quietly for a few minutes on his back, fighting the inevitable. He tries breathing through his mouth and focussing on the ceiling, but the bile rises in his throat and he sprints through to the bathroom just in time to be violently sick in the wash-hand basin. After retching several times he pauses for breath, breathing heavily. It's not over. Another wave of nausea and he throws up again. Each painful retch bringing more burning bile from his deepest being out onto the brilliant white porcelain. This repeats several times before he finally feels the ache subside, and he slumps on the cool tiled floor.

He works out that he has spent at least 20 minutes of his grooming and commuting routine being sick and is now running late.

The power shower fires into life, and as he completes his shave and begins to brush his teeth, some semblance of normality begins to return. Pouring through his memories of the previous night, he can't remember coming back into the house, but the car keys by the bed indicate he managed to drive home OK, despite the alcohol.

He remembers the endless Canadian Club and beer, and the casual conversations with fellow barflies and bar staff. In fact, he vaguely remembers trying to convince the barmaid to come home with him, but the lure of the Porsche and the 90210 Zip code didn't cut it this time.

It's then as he descends the stairs to the garage he remembers the call from Phillips.

Phillips actually sounded serious this time. Not his usual creepy, jokey, self.

Slightly more concerned than he looked, he took the phone from his pocket and called Phillips. Straight to answer phone. He hung up.

The garage door clattered up letting in blinding sunlight, causing Nolan to lift his hand to shield his eyes. He throws his jacket and briefcase onto the passenger seat and gets into the car. As he starts the car and hears its faithful growl, he notices a big dark blue BMW parked on the opposite side of the street.

- Odd place to park - he thought.

He hit the garage door closer and gunned the car out onto the street. As he sped away, a short glance in his rear view mirror confirmed what he thought was two occupants in the BMW.

The first left turn loomed up and the car vanished from his mirror.

He flicked on 98.5 FM just in time to hear the opening riff of 'Welcome to the Jungle' – Indeed – he thought.

Still feeling a bit sleepy, but secretly proud of how little hangovers affected him nowadays; he took his second left turn, noticing an identical blue BMW heading in the opposite direction.

- Must have been a sale on those - he laughed to himself.

He slips onto the freeway and within minutes has slowed to a crawl. According to the sat nav it's only a fifteen minute delay today. Weaving and lane hopping cuts this down to about ten minutes, and before long he is up to seventy and before too long the familiar Junction 46 sign gleams in the sunlight directing Nolan to his destination.

- The gods are with me today – he thought to himself as the lights almost magically turned green allowing unimpeded progress.

He swings the car aggressively into his parking space and strides forcefully to the front door checking his watch as he opens the door.

- Only ten minutes late today – Nolan announced

- That I take it goes down as an improvement? – Annie observed from the reception.

- Bloody traffic…….you know how it is Annie? – He queried, smiling. Bored Receptionist looked on abjectly then returns to her catatonic state.

He nods in acknowledgement to Bored Receptionist but she doesn't move.

- Well it's a good job we have a nice easy day today – Annie collects her files and shoos Nolan toward his room.

He stumbles forward into his room tossing his jacket onto the coat stand and drops the briefcase on the floor at his desk.

- Is that the latest John Paul Gaultier? – She asks impudently, sniffing the air.

- Paco Rabanne - he states confidently.

- I would have said that but there seems to be a little too much *alcohol* about that scent…………..-

- Oooooo – a little below the belt, Miz McDonald. Just because I happened to have the odd glass of wine with dinner last night doesn't mean I should be subjected to this level of scrutiny and abuse? – he playfully retorted.

He sat down and switched on his computer as Annie stood in front of his desk, files held tight to her chest shaking her head.

- What? – He held his palms upright.

- I said yesterday Sam that this couldn't go on. Drunk every night. Surgery the next day. Flirting with the trade. Back out get drunk again and repeat. Damn it Sam! Start thinking of others and not yourself! You know, something is going to go wrong......You're a good surgeon, and I'm certainly not going to criticise your work, but sooner or later because of the lifestyle, you're going to make a mistake. And you should know more than anyone, that mistakes in this game can be fatal….for both you and the patient –

Little did she know how prophetic this was.

- I know, I know - he said looking down at the floor shaking his head.

- It's just I've got some other issues right now, and having a couple of drinks makes it all seem a bit more………..*manageable* – He looked up at Annie with sad dog eyes.

- Right – I don't want to have this conversation tomorrow, especially given the workload. So tonight Sam, for God's sake, just have a coke or go to the movies or something – she looked imploringly at him.
- Sure – Movies, coke, yep. Got it -
- Right. He clapped his hands together and rubbed them. Who is on the table today? – He tilted his head and gave an exaggerated grin.

As Annie started into the details of that morning's procedure, out of Nolan's office window, a dark blue BMW crept into the neighbouring car park, 'Crumbles' an upscale cupcake shop that Nolan detested. He looked away.

After three hours in surgery pinning back the ears of a Hollywood socialite's spoilt youngest son, Nolan wearily treads back to his office, thinking about an ice cold coke in a glass bottle to sate the hangover thirst that had plagued him all morning.

Bored Receptionist unusually stuck her head round from her desk and mumbled something Nolan couldn't make out.

- What's that? – He queried striding up the corridor – I can't hear you – he added with a touch of impatience.

As he turned into the reception he became aware of two men casually seated in the waiting area, both with their eyes trained on him.

- There are these two men here………..- she started.
- Dr.Nolan – shouted the shorter of the two men rising from his seat, his hand extended for a handshake. - Evan Williams, Dr Nolan, and this is my associate Frank DaLuca - The second man also rose from his chair. Williams was a squat, athletic, man in his fifties, lightly perspiring in the LA heat, but wearing a $3000 Armani suit and year-round tan. DaLuca was a taller, more menacing presence with slicked back jet black hair, and also immaculately dressed.

- I'm sorry, - Nolan started – Do you have an appointment? - he queried, knowing full well they didn't.

He shook each hand in turn suspiciously, narrowing his eyes as he looked at them.

- Not exactly Dr Nolan, but we do need to talk to you with regard to a very personal, private issue - he stated righteously.

25

- I'm afraid I have a very busy schedule and I simply just can't see anyone that hasn't made an appointment............. - his voice trailed off as he spied the blue BMW out the window. Clearly one of the BMW's he had seen at his house that morning.

- This won't take very long – DaLuca added in a matter of fact tone, smiling.

- We have a small matter to discuss which I believe Dan Phillips brought to your attention yesterday – he continued – So if we could just have five minutes of your very precious time, we'll be on our way – he smiled and tilted his head.

- Yes, of course, of course, - Nolan muttered nervously pointing them toward his office, but Williams extended his arm toward the office door making sure Nolan went in first.

As he entered the room, he went over to the window and closed the blind, again staring at the blue BMW.

He saw Annie quizzically staring in behind the two men as they entered the office and he closed the door on her look of bewilderment.

- We'll not keep you Dr Nolan – Williams began, continuing to stand as Nolan sat back in his chair.

- I believe Dan Phillips made the position of our business very clear, and I would be grateful if you wouldn't mind confirming when you would be able to settle your account? We fully understand getting cash together at short notice can be a bit troublesome, so we're thinking, maybe tomorrow about this time? – He smiled.

- I'm, I'm sure you must appreciate that drawing large cash payments attracts the wrong kind of attention.....- he stammered – And I'm not quite sure how much I can lay my hands on in a day.....– his voice reducing in volume.

- Your current balance is now at $81k, however, we know you're good for it, but there comes a time when you have to step back, re-assess, and be prudent with credit control. We're thinking about thirty tomorrow, then another twenty a week later, then a round off thirty the week after that. Let's say the last thousand is on us. Once you've settled, we can go back to business as usual -

Nolan felt the colour drain from his face – I'm not quite sure I can meet those terms – he offered meekly.
- Oh I'm sure you can Dr Nolan. A nice business like this, Beverley Hills Zip code, Porsche in the drive? Oh, you have it Dr Nolan, believe me. Now that's what's going to happen. Myself and Mr DaLuca are going to come by here tomorrow at 3pm, and you are going to have a nice bag with thirty thousand dollars inside it – He tilted his head slightly – Understand? – He delivered with just the correct amount of menace.
- I'm…. I'm…. I'm……Nolan stammered breathing heavily.
- In full agreement – Williams added – Excellent. We'll be here sharp at 3pm tomorrow – He shot Nolan a steely look and nodded his head as he turned and headed out the door. DaLuca followed glancing left and right as he closed the door behind him.
Nolan sat breathing heavily in his chair. - $30k? Tomorrow? Jesus - He flipped on the browser on the computer and hit the 'bank' shortcut. Typing in his password, he tried to remember the last time he looked at the business account. Never really needed to. Annie saw to all that.
The checking account showed $27,512, and the investment account showed $11,000.
He flipped the page to 'personal'.
The checking account showed $614.29, and the investment account showed $78,000.
His brief happiness at the $78,000 soon evaporated as he remembered the lock put on that account by the divorce judge and that the money was locked in.
He grabbed his phone and searched for Jane's number. He stabbed the dial button and waited for the response.
- Hello - A clearly irate and bored ex-wife was on the line.
- Hi Jane, how's it going? – He enquired optimistically.
- What do you want Sam? – She continued in the monotone voice.
- Well now that you mention it, I seem to have a small cash flow issue and need access to our joint savings account. It's just for a couple of weeks, I have so many appointments just now, I'm running out of my

credit at the suppliers, and the last thing you would want is my, sorry, *our* income to dry up -
- Oh really – she drawled - Well perhaps you could get Annie to draw up a list of amounts and recipients, email it to my lawyer, and I'll see what we can do, no promises though - she smugly replied.
- Oh come on Jane – he pleaded.
- Thought as much. No doubt needed to pay bar bills, gambling, your nightclub buddies, or maybe the next Hollywood starlet whose career you've promised to bankroll. Not a chance! – She hung up.
- Jane! Jane! Jane! – he shouted into the phone. He hung up and redialled. Straight to answer phone. He tried Sarah's phone hoping she was there too, but again, straight to answer phone. He clattered the phone down on the desk.
- Everything alright? – Annie enquired peering round the edge of the door.
- Yes – he said looking down at his desk.
- Okey-dokes – she turned and headed back into the corridor – Didn't like the look of those guys……. – she shouted back as she walked away.
He picked up the mobile and called Phillips.
- What the hell Dan? – He turned the chair away from an imaginary witness, half shouting/whispering as soon as Phillips answered.
- I told you Sam, they are not messing about. Marchesi, their boss, was down here last night, told me in no uncertain terms to let you and others know the credit facility was withdrawn and there were new terms to be put to you, and basically you'd better pay up -
- Yeah they made their 'new terms' very clear – Nolan sighed.
- Sam, I don't want to stress you out any more, but this time I felt they are kinda serious, and I think you gotta go to your Plastic Surgery piggy bank and square these guys away -
- That's the problem Dan. I have a small cash flow issue at the moment, and twenty four hours is not long enough for me to resolve this -
- Don't run away from this Sam, you gotta face it head on and deal with it – he gasped – they made out I'm liable too ! -

28

Nolan laughed nervously, imagining Phillips' discomfort.

- Nothing to laugh about! We're both gonna end up in an unmarked grave outside Vegas if you don't deal with this! –

- Right. Let's calm down and decide how to deal with this. I can get probably the $30k for tomorrow, then plan to stall another 2 weeks when I can.........-

- You don't understand Sam! This is it! No negotiation. No Stalling. $30k tomorrow, $20k a week later, $30k the week after. Just like they said. That's it! -

- Well I don't think I can do it – he slumped back in his chair. – Perhaps if I spoke to this.....Marchesi? – He enquired.

- That guy is not for speaking to Sam. He's a psychopath. Seriously. No talk -

- Let me think – He hung up the phone. Leaning forward he held the phone against his brow –

He placed the phone inside his desk, and composed a short email to his ex-wife Jane.

Please get in touch. Urgent. Sam.

He heard the front door of the clinic open and close, followed by the babble of conversation that heralded the arrival of his 4pm.

When he had concluded his appointments for the day, he ducked out of dinner with Annie & Bored Receptionist, making his excuses.

Annie berated him, suspecting an evening of drinking ahead. Nolan reassured her he genuinely was tired, and was heading straight home.

He pointed the Porsche in the opposite direction and headed south toward Santa Monica. He weaved through the traffic until his exit, and then headed down towards the beach. Two blocks back from the beach in a dimly – lit residential area, he pulled up outside a two-storey beach house, whose fading paintwork was matched by the fading light. All the houses looked the same, but the fluttering Scottish Lion Rampant flag on the roof confirmed he was at the right house.

He looked up to the upstairs lounge window where a warm glow revealed the inhabitant was in.

He locked the car and approached the front door.

He pressed the doorbell twice then knocked twice as in some pre-ordained code.

The outside light came on and the door was answered by a middle-aged pony-tailed man with a craggy face.

- Sam? Is that you? -
- Bruno – how are you? Long time no see! -
- Come in, Come in – he gestured.

Bruno was an ex-university friend also from Edinburgh who had been out in LA since the late eighties, attempting to craft a career in Rock & Pop Merchandise, but ultimately ending up crafting a career selling a completely different type of merchandise.

They climbed the stairs together and stepped into the lounge which had a beautiful view of the now setting sun.

Nolan was temporarily speechless as he drank in the beauty of this spectacle.

- Gorgeous, isn't it? – Bruno stated comfortably – Forced to watch that every day – he joked.
- Isn't it just………….. - Nolan's voice tailed away.
- So my friend, what can I do you for? – Bruno dropped himself into a large armchair. – Our usual 'weapon of choice'? Or something just to blot out the pain? -
- Strangely, not this time – started Nolan – I'm needing money, Bruno. Just for a couple of weeks. I've loads of work but I need something to go away – He bowed his head raising his eyes to gauge the response.
- Sure, sure, I can help you out. – Bruno started, - I have a few thou here in the safe and a couple of grand next door…………….
- I need $30k. I'm $80k in a hole, but need to hand over $30k tomorrow, then the rest over the next two weeks. I only have about $30k -
- What? I don't have it Sam. If I did, I would give you it, but I don't have it. – He looked imploringly at Nolan.
- But when I brought you all those Tuinal you paid over $30k? – He snapped back.
- That was with notice Sam – he laughed – and I had known a month in advance!

30

- So what are you doing with all the money you make? – His voice getting noticeably louder and more impatient.
- Calm down Sam. This – he gestured to the room - is $8,500 per month. I don't work. That motorcycle outside. The wee drug bunnies who show up here wanting their drugs for free. This life Sam…..like everything in Los Angeles….. it's not free -
- You're telling me – Nolan slumped into another chair, wiping his brow – what the hell am I gonna do? -
- No nice way to tell you Sam, you are gonna have to deal with this. Right or wrong, it's gotta be dealt with. If I were you, I'd give the $30k tomorrow and go negotiate something. That stupid car of yours. That's worth $100k? That watch – he pointed to Nolan's wrist – that's another $30k. Pawn that stuff to get them off your back, and when you have the money, pay them, then get your stuff back – he held his hands open.
- You're right – He sat up in the chair. It sounded so much more reasonable and plausible when somebody else said it. What good would it do beating him up or worse? He was good for it. They knew that. So what if he had to slum it in a rental car for a few weeks. Yes, this was the way.
- I know I'm right – Bruno winked at him and rose from his chair and went to a retro styled fridge sitting on the balcony.
He opened it and pulled out a couple of bottles of beer.
- A wee toast? – He suggested.
- One won't hurt – he laughed and grabbed the beer bottle.

A dull ache behind his right ear woke Nolan. It took several seconds before he realised where he was. The sunlight was again splitting a crack in the curtains, and as he moved onto his side, he felt the ache and protest of what he thought was every muscle in his body. He was in Bruno's lounge stretched out on the floral settee. There was no air conditioning, and he felt the damp patches of sweat at his underarm and groin.

He pulled the curtains back, wincing in the light, and then studied his crumpled self in the full length mirror. Not much point in looking for Bruno. He wasn't a 'morning' guy.

-Jesus – he muttered to himself as he stooped to pick up his car keys. He let himself out of the house and hopped into the Porsche.

The clock read 7.20am.

He started up and drove off to find a McDonalds, get a coffee then head off home to change for work.

Once at work, Nolan went through the motions of the morning workload, reviewing two post procedures, always conscious of the time, zeroing in on the 3pm deadline.

1pm. He called Carlo at Porsche of Hollywood.

- Hey Sam, how's it going? – The affable Porsche salesman had sold Nolan a number of cars over the years, although Nolan was always a little suspicious of the attention he gave Jane - Creepy bastard – he thought.

- Hey Carlo, yeah it's good – he replied with mild impatience.

- Look, I'm in between transactions just now Carlo, and need some cash pretty quick. I was just wondering if you guys would like to take my car back? You know, like for a few weeks or so until this sorts itself out? - Carlo laughed on the other end of the phone, irritating Nolan intensely.

- Sam, Sam, Sam.......we're not a pawn shop bud. We would definitely like your car back, in fact, could give you quite a tidy sum. I have 2 or 3 customers who have seen it going about Hollywood, and I think I could definitely move it on. But we can't give you cash and hold it for you. We're a business. Maybe we could take it now and you could trade up to a new one when you're ready? -

Nolan knew the smarmy git would love to get his hands on Nolan's car. Then pass it off to some rich idiot as something Carlo had specified and put together himself. Through gritted teeth he said – would you give $100k for it?

- Woah! Straight to the point my man! Maybe as a trade, but around seventy-five for cash. You come back within three months and I'll do the trade at $100k, and give you the extra $25k against a new one? -

- You know that car is $120k all day long – he stated quietly.
- And you know I gotta turn a profit. Look I can go eighty, then dock you another five when you pick a new one. How's that? -
- That's bloody robbery but I guess beggars can't be choosers. I'll just head over – he resigned.
- Woah! What, like now? - Carlo questioned.
- Well, it'll take me twenty minutes to get there – Nolan shrugged.
- No, no, no – bring it by next week, and I'll get our guys look at it, and if it's hot to trot, I can cut you a cheque then -
An exasperated Nolan shook his head and spoke softly – I kinda need it now, Carlo -
- That's not gonna happen Sam. What the heck do you need to sell your car in twenty minutes for? -
- My funeral - Nolan hung up.
He couldn't eat the featureless swill Bored Receptionist put on his desk. He opened the Diet Coke and gently sipped away, feeling the gnawing hunger and nerves in his stomach. He stood up and closed the blind.
He picked up the phone, searched pawn shops on his computer, and punched in the number.
#1 – Hello West Hollywood Pawn – answered a bright young girl.
- Ah yes. I was just wondering if you guys would be interested in a 2005 Rolex Submariner mint condition with papers? – He authoratively enquired.
- I'm sorry, Mr Sanders who appraises our watches is on holiday today……….
Nolan hung up.
#2 – Hello – Bel Air Pawn – lazily drawled an older woman.
- Ah yes. I was just wondering if you guys would be interested in a 2005 Rolex Submariner mint condition with papers? – he once again authoratively enquired.
- Not at the moment Honey, we are moving premises this week and……………
Nolan hung up – he sighed.
#3 – Good Afternoon, Beverley Jewellery & Pawn – an officious man answered.

- Hello. I was just wondering if you guys would be interested in a 2005 Rolex Submariner mint condition with papers? – he once again authoratively enquired.

- No problem sir. If you would care to bring it down we would certainly be interested-

- Excellent. Would you be able to give me an idea of what it was likely to be worth? – Nolan enquired.

- If it's mint, boxed, papers and totally legitimate, we would be looking in the region of five to six thousand dollars -

Nolan hung up.

#4 – Goooooood Afternooooon, Eyyy and Teeee Pawn – a Pakistani man answered.

Nolan hung up.

#5 – Afternoon, you're through to A1 Jewellery. Press one for sales. Press two for……

Nolan hung up.

This was not going to happen.

2pm.

Looking up the business bank accounts online, he hoped that some magical transaction would occur, and money would have somehow appeared in the account, but there was nothing since a utility bill deduction the day before.

He checked his private banking but alas, nothing new there either.

2.30pm

He called Phillips. Straight to answer phone.

He called Jane. Straight to answer phone.

Then something happened. He rose from the chair and gently parted two of the blind slats with his pen. In the adjacent parking lot sat the blue BMW. DaLuca was outside the car smoking a cigarette.

Nolan felt a twinge of panic. They were here. Early. Maybe they thought he would not show up today, or perhaps bunk off early.

Williams was slowly walking round Nolan's Porsche, looking intently at the car. He sat back down and started to rehearse his lines………. -

Ah yes, Mr DaLuca, Mr Williams, good to see you again. You know, a funny thing happened to me on the way here……..- he nervously giggled to himself. – I'll offer up the cash I have first, then top up with the watch if need be. All else fails, give them the car key. He was still muttering to himself and imaging various scenarios when he heard the door open and male voices.

A couple of minutes later, Annie struck her head around the door nervously.

- Those guys who were here yesterday to see you again? – She looked crestfallen.

Nolan felt the thin bead of perspiration on his brow.

- Yes, yes, no problem Annie, show them in – he said with absolutely no conviction.

As Annie turned around to go and fetch Williams & DaLuca, she gasped as they were standing right behind her.

- It's OK Miss, Sam is expecting us – Williams smiled and stood back to let Annie retreat.

She stepped backwards slowly, anxiously looking at Nolan, who dismissed her with a nonchalant wave of the hand.

Williams and DaLuca stepped into the office and closed the door behind them.

- Right guys – started Nolan – I've had a wee look at everything I've got available at the moment, and I can cut you a business cheque for fifteen thousand dollars just now, along with this splendid Rolex which is easily worth ten thousand dollars, as I paid over fifteen thousand for it over ten years ago, and that would sort things just now, right? – He was aware he was talking at a hundred miles an hour and that any rehearsed calm was now gone.

Williams and DaLuca looked and each other and said nothing. They then looked back at Nolan.

- Look – he implored, turning the computer screen toward them - I have $78,000 in this account, but it needs seven days notice to withdraw, and I went this morning but the guy who deals with these type of accounts is on vacation until tomorrow but I'll go back ……………. -

- Dr Nolan – started Williams very quietly and very deliberately – Did

35

myself and Mr DaLuca not make ourselves perfectly clear yesterday what was to happen? We need to walk in here, and you were to hand over $30k in cash. You can't point to computer screens or cut cheques or bank transfers. We only deal in cash. C-A-S-H - he spelled out -You know that. We know that. Now what do you think my boss would say if I go back to him and say that Dr Nolan had written us a cheque or was about to do a bank transfer? - He gestured towards Nolan.

- I, I, I don't know what to say, what to do, you gave me an unrealistic timeframe to get cash of that magnitude to you, and I simply couldn't do it – He breathed his answer, the fear palpable, and the sweat on his brow now very real.

Williams glanced at DaLuca then Nolan gave a sharp intake of breath as Williams reached into his coat, but only to retrieve a mobile phone.

- Relax Dr Nolan, I just gotta make a call – he soothed but with a crooked smile.

He dialled the contact then stood up, walking into the corner of the room quietly speaking at a level where Nolan knew he was talking, but could not make out anything he was saying.

He turned then put the phone in his pocket.

- I hope you have no appointments this afternoon, Dr Nolan – Williams stated matter of factly, - As you now have an appointment with Salvatore Marchesi right now in Beverley Hills. Shall we? – He opened the door and gestured for Nolan to go first.

- I'll just get my coat – he stammered, knocking the remnants of the Diet Coke over his desk.

- Steady Doc – joked DaLuca.

Nolan headed out the door his jacket over his arm sheepishly.

He straightened up as he approached Annie and Bored Receptionist. – I'm afraid something rather important has come up and I have to make an urgent house call. Can you please call Mr Bradley and reschedule as soon as possible? – He gave an air of nervous confidence.

Bored Receptionist didn't even look up, still staring at someone's Facebook profile on the screen – Yes of course Dr Nolan – Annie replied cautiously.

Williams and DaLuca flanked Nolan as they walked across the lot to the blue BMW. DaLuca held the back door open for Nolan, and he entered the car sheepishly.

- This car is very comfortable – Nolan nervously thought to himself.

They cut through half a dozen streets of housing before heading out onto Sunset and the short drive to Beverley Hills. It was a beautiful afternoon with the bluest of blue skies, but Nolan could only look at the back of the two men in the car, neither talking to each other. As they started up the hills, Nolan remembered driving Jane around these very streets when they first came to view Los Angeles. How carefree it all was back then. How beautiful she was. How young they felt. How he promised her one of these gilded Hollywood Mansions, or one of the sleek, flat topped ultra modern homes with the deck level infinity pools. How happy they were. Rich, successful, and a world of potential, all in front of them. How the hell had he let it come to this?

Just at that, the car turned sharply to the left, and stopped at a set of black metal gates. The gates slowly began to open, revealing beautiful landscaped gardens and a narrow winding steep driveway.

The BMW glided up the drive silently, until it stopped underneath a port-cochere, with huge planters full of exotic plants and a small Koy pond at the end.

The drive and frontage of the property was immaculate, with nothing out of place.

Williams and DaLuca exited the car then opened Nolan's door.

He eased out of the car, nervously taking in all the splendour all around him.

DaLuca motioned for him to follow, and Williams headed off in another direction.

Stepping through the hallway of the house it was a short distance to the large open glass doors poolside where white curtains gently shifted in the breeze, and Nolan could see a man sitting casually dressed smoking a cigarette.

- Dr Nolan – the man exclaimed with a huge smile, rising from the chair and shaking his hand enthusiastically. – I'm terribly sorry we have to meet under these circumstances, but my name is Salvatore Marchesi. Please take a seat – he gestured to the beautiful wicker woven poolside chairs.

- Thank you – whispered Nolan as he sat in the poolside armchair, feeling slightly more at ease – This guy seems OK – he thought to himself – Reasonable -

- Dr Nolan, my associates have informed me that you were unable to meet your side of our recent proposal, and as a consequence of that, we are sitting here – he adjusted his position in the chair.

Marchesi was fit, athletic, tanned. Younger than Nolan himself he thought, but classic quality clothes, casual but classy. Maybe a little too much jewellery, and that watch is a real taste holiday. A bit like an older Leo DiCaprio, he thought. Maybe a wee hint of nip and tuck around those eyes too.

- Now before you even start to explain, Dr Nolan, please have a drink - He gestured toward the table beside Nolan where bottles of San Pellegrino chilled in ice buckets.

He took a bottle, opened it and poured it into a long glass with ice and cucumber.

The liquid was heaven to his parched mouth. He let out a sigh of relief.

- Mr Marchesi……… – He started before he was cut off.

- Please, call me Salvatore – he offered.

- Salvatore, I am so sorry and embarrassed about what happened today. As I explained to your colleagues, Mr Williams and Mr DaLuca, I have money in the bank but the account is a notice account and……..- he noticed Marchesi was slowly shaking his head.

- Dr Nolan. That account you speak of is a joint one with your wife, and as such is currently the subject of a legal action, and although half of that *may* be yours, it certainly isn't something that you can access anytime soon – he adjusted the sunglasses on his face.

Unable to see where his eyes were looking through the sunglasses, Nolan continued regardless – I have money in an alternative account that I can access tomorrow and make sure that I bring it to you here? – He tentatively queried.

- You see I don't think you can, Dr Nolan. Let us just say for argument's sake that you withdraw your thirty-six thousand dollars from your checking and your investment account. That's way short of our $80k debt. Now let's also assume that Carlo manages to front you $80k for your Porsche. And maybe some poor pawnshop ends up with your battered and bruised Rolex after parting with five thousand dollars. You've $120k max. That's it Sam. Everything. Maybe once the divorce is settled, some of that cash from the sale of the house and the joint account makes its way to you after the lawyers and the alimony people take their cut. Let's face it Sam, you're on a road to nowhere – he lifted the sunglasses up onto his head to study Nolan's reaction.

He let Nolan stare awkwardly at the ground for another twenty seconds.

- However, I did not bring you all the way up here to simply rubbish your financial position. There is an alternative, Dr. Nolan -

Nolan looked up sharply.

- My good lady Marianne desires some corrective facial surgery, Dr Nolan, and I think we can bring all this unpleasantness to a speedy conclusion. I have decided that you will perform the necessary work this evening, and in return for this, and any subsequent follow up treatments as required, I am prepared to write off all your debts, in total, Dr Nolan. You will be well aware that this is way in excess of your normal rates, or other practices' charges, but as the work, and our arrangement is a little 'unusual', I am prepared to make this accommodation – he smiled.

- Tonight?.......muttered Nolan......I'm not sure......maybe.......- he mumbled

- Yes tonight. Dr. Nolan. I suggest that you contact Miss McDonald at the clinic and instruct her to prepare – Marchesi crossed his legs and sat back.

- Yes, yes, of course – muttered Nolan, slipping the phone from his pocket and dialling the clinic.

- Sunnyside Clinic – answered Bored Receptionist.

- Courtney, put me through to Annie please – he was cut off to insipid hold music – Must get that changed – he thought to himself.

- Sam! Where are you? What's happening? – A nervous Annie jabbed questioningly.
- I'm fine, Annie, now listen carefully. Prep for a facelift straight away. Don't let the Chinese anaesthetist leave. I'm coming in the next hour or so with the patient. Get your scrubs on and book in for a 2-3 hour session. This is an emergency, and most importantly, don't give me any grief. This has to be done, and it has to be done right. Okay? -
- But Sam………….she implored.
- Annie, just do this, please – he hissed.
- But Sam……..alright. Is this anything to do with these two men you left with? -
- No, completely unconnected. I will tell you the full story later, let's just make this happen – Without waiting for her reply he hung up the call, and looked up to Marchesi.
- All set. Now, can I meet the patient and see what I have to do? – He cracked a thin smile.
- Of course, Dr. Nolan. – He turned to DaLuca and nodded. DaLuca headed back into the house. Minutes later, he heard the sound of high heels cracking on the marble floor, until a well-dressed, tanned woman stepped onto the patio and walked right up to Nolan and stood over him.
- You must be the famous Dr Nolan? – She enquired playfully.
Nolan drank her in. Definitely Hollywood, easily ten years younger than Marchesi, very nice figure, expensive clothes, expensive jewellery, breasts very pert, so no stranger to the knife. Something very familiar though, although he couldn't quite put his finger on it.
- Infamous – he quipped, whilst standing up and kissing the back of her hand.
- My wife Marianne – introduced Marchesi – who I'm sure you will agree is a very attractive woman, Dr. Nolan.
Nolan nodded meekly, wearing a forced smile, unsure if any complement would be too much or not enough.
- However, despite my best efforts to re-assure her, she is not happy with her nose, Dr.Nolan, and she is also experiencing some ageing under her eyes – Marchesi stopped, allowing Nolan to tilt his head from

side to side whilst examining her face.

Nolan recognised the small tell-tale incisions behind the ears where a previous face lift had taken place, - May I? - He gently pulled the loose skin under her eyes sideways with his thumbs, giving the desired effect.

-Let me see, let me see – squealed Marianne.

DaLuca stepped forward and turned his phone camera so she could see her face.

- Yes, yes, yes, I like! She excitedly chattered.

Nolan began to examine the nose. Nothing was untoward at all with the nose. Fine form, firm skin, and if anything had a little turn up at the end that older women in particular pay Nolan to re-create.

- I can see the issue with the eyes, but your nose seems perfect to me? - He quizzed gently.

- Dr Nolan, I'm not quite sure if you can tell, but I'm a look a like of someone. Someone famous -

Nolan looked puzzled and shook his head. Then the penny dropped.

- You look a little bit like........Cyndi Lauper? – He asked astonishingly.

- Yes, Yes, Yes! – She clapped her hands – He is the right surgeon, Salvatore. He sees where I want to be! We girls do just want to have fun! -

He could see it. The hair, the clothes, with the tightened crow's feet around the eyes, she *did* look like Cyndi Lauper, and yes, she had done her homework. The paring down of the nose and reshaping into a smaller, neater affair would complete her look.

Meanwhile Marianne had looked up photographs on her phone and began showing Nolan photographs of Cyndi Lauper's face through the ages, whilst giving a running commentary on the fashion, makeup style and personal issues the star had faced when these pictures were taken. No wonder his interest had been piqued. She also looked a lot like Nadine. No wonder she seemed familiar. They could be twins.

In the early days of their relationship he used to call her Cyndi much to her chagrin. Nolan always had a thing about look a likes.

Genetics had always amazed him.

- Do you have an older sister? – He enquired.

- No, should I? -

- It's just you remind me of someone – not Ms Lauper though – he laughed nervously, clearly relived this was not Nadine's sister.

Marchesi signalled to DaLuca to get the car.

- Right Dr Nolan, Frank will take you and Marianne back to your clinic and he will drop you both off. If you would be as good as to call me as soon as the procedure is complete on this number – he handed Nolan a small business card – and we'll take things from there – He walked over to Marianne and kissed her lightly on the cheek, whispered in her ear, then walked off into the house followed by Williams.

Marianne took Nolan's hand and led him back to the house and to the waiting car.

- Give me five minutes to get dressed and put my face on – she purred.

- Thought that was my job – quipped Nolan, causing her to giggle.

Twenty minutes later, the BMW was gently creeping down the Marchesi driveway.

Nolan gazed out the side window, the large property gates slipping past, slowly at first, then more rapidly as they descended the hill, and the property values dropped like the altitude.

Marianne sat with her compact mirror examining her face from every conceivable angle.

After a silent drive, DaLuca duly dispatched them at the clinic entrance. Although the sun was setting, it was still half-light, and the clinic's illumination made it look clearer than ever.

Nolan held the door to let Marianne enter, as the BMW crept away.

Bored Receptionist barely looked up before looking back to her phone.

- This way, Mrs Marchesi – he pointed down the hall toward pre-op.

Annie had heard the voices and stepped out into the corridor with a worried look.

- Hi Annie, this is our patient, Mrs Marchesi – he beamed enthusiastically, shooting Annie a pleading look.

Annie shook her hand unconvincingly, tilting her head to the side – You look like….-

- Call me Marianne – she interrupted.

- If you could prep Mrs Marchesi, and I'll be through in just a minute, once I have all my notes – Nolan wheeled off into his office and shut the door behind him leaning back against the closed door. He closed his eyes and breathed out heavily. After a few seconds, he opened his desk and lifted out the Ipad and began to search for photographs of Cindi Lauper, storing those which detailed and profiled the neat, tidy nose best. After selecting about half a dozen, he changed into his scrubs, stepped into his slip ons and headed through to the pre-op.

.

Chapter 3
Chasing Shadows

It was dark outside, but the lights of the Sunnyside Clinic were still burning.
- What just went on in there? – shouted an angry Annie, throwing her clipboard onto the desk, as she followed Nolan into Post Op. She stared impatiently at him.
- What are you playing at? – She shouted even louder this time – You are going to get us sued, you selfish idiot! A simple Rhinoplasty. You can do that in your sleep! So what's the problem this time? Christ, I could have done a better job than that, Sam!
I just hope you have a great excuse for when you're trying to explain to those guys why she looks like Mrs Potato Head! – She stormed off into the bathroom.
Nolan couldn't believe it. The crow feet tuck was perfect. No issue at all. But trying to match that nose……..Annie was right. The kind of procedure he could normally do in his sleep. But this time he had several passes at the bone and simply couldn't get the angle right, until he realised he had taken too much. Now he was looking at reconstructive work, and in the meantime was going to have to explain why a straightforward nose job was now a two stage reconstruct. And that's assuming he can get it right this time.
He dialled up Marchesi's number.
- Hi there. That's stage one of Marianne's work completed, Mr Marchesi -
- What did you say? -
- That's the first stage of her procedure completed, I've tucked around the eyes and prepared the bone and nasal cavities for the second stage which I would expect to do next week? - He tentatively suggested.
- I don't recall any mention of two stages, Dr.Nolan? – He growled threateningly.- I …..I….I assumed that you would have known that? You appeared fairly knowledgeable of the process surely you knew

this?.... - his voice tailed off.

- No, didn't, Dr Nolan, however as a professional, we are at your discretion, and therefore will follow your instructions to the letter to ensure a satisfactory outcome for everyone. When will my wife be ready for collection Dr Nolan? -

- She will probably come round in about an hour, but I would like to administer her pain relief personally, and I would recommend that she stay with us tonight. I will stay here with her to ensure everything is fine, and perhaps one of your associates could collect her tomorrow morning around ten o'clock? -

- Will see you then Dr Nolan -

Before he could answer, Marchesi had hung up.

That could have gone better, he thought, but at least he was off the hook. For now.

Meanwhile Annie shuffled about the clinic in silence, clearly upset.

- Annie........- he pleaded.

- Forget it! – She snapped back – I don't know what's going on here Sam, but there's something not right -

He decided to leave sleeping dogs lie and retreated to the safety of his office. He knew Annie would deal with the patient coming out of anaesthesia as she had done a hundred times, but what now? Even by his own self-bullshitting confidence, this was a new low. Somehow he had to get his mojo back. He leaned back in his chair, put his feet up on the desk and closed his eyes, letting out a wearied long, sigh.

The next thing he felt was a sharp poke in the ribs. Annie stood over him. He face seemed more relaxed, less pained.

- C'mon cowboy, she's coming round – and with that, she turned and headed to recovery. Nolan glanced at his watch. He had dosed off for the last hour and hadn't even noticed.

Pain relief was administered to Marchesi's wife and she slipped back into a semi conscious state, mumbling nonsense and random words. Annie checked her drain and drip. Satisfied all was good, she turned to Nolan.

- I trust I can leave you now Sam? Just call if you need me – she turned and left.

Nolan waved but she had already left. He slumped in the seat next to the patient.

He looked at her bandaged features in the dim light. He gently pushed the hair off her face and began running the back of his finger down the profile of her cheek, carefully avoiding his most recent work. He studied her neat tight neck, and the lightly tanned décolletage.

- No, no, no ………………Tony…..don't kill her…….don't kill her….- she slurred loudly causing Nolan to jump back. He sat there, transfixed as she continued to mumble, than again, clearly, - It wasn't her…..it wasn't her……- She was now almost sobbing. He leaned over the bed and pumped the morphine drip a couple of times.

Sitting back down, he reached forward and held her hand lightly, all the time cooing and shooshing her quiet. She continued to mumble quietly for a couple of minutes then drifted back to an uneasy sleep.

Nolan exhaled and sat back in the chair. There was no doubt she has witnessed some pretty horrible things on a day to day basis, and he was in no doubt unless he could get this sorted, he was going to be one of these unfortunate incidents.

He drifted off to sleep, but like his patient, it was an uneasy, restless sleep. He kept snapping awake, aware of some horrible nightmares or thoughts, but couldn't recall what they were. Continuing to doze in the chair, he became aware of light around the edge of the room curtain. His watch read 7.20am.

Rising from the seat, he pulled back the curtains, and then adjusted the blind to let in a wash of light, cleansing the room of its dark secrets revealed the previous night.

Nolan suddenly realised it was one of the few mornings in LA that he hadn't woken with a hangover. He laughed to himself, the irony not lost on him.

Just then he heard the front door open.

- Just meeeeee – Annie cheerily shouted through.

Marianne Marchesi began to stir in the bed, groaning and moaning and slowly moving. Annie came into the room and began comforting her just as she started to fully come round.

Nolan retired to his office where Annie had left a Starbucks and a bagel on his desk. He ate hungrily, supping the milky coffee, realising it had been quite some time since he last ate.

- Go home Sam, I've got this. Courtney will be in shortly if there's anything. I'll hand her over and explain you need to rest…….honestly its fine. Go! – Annie made the shooing motion with her hands – Remember appointments start at four so you go put your head down for a couple hours.

She was right, of course. He grabbed his jacket and briefcase and stepped out into the morning LA sun. It was amazing how fresh and new everything looked with just a wash of sunshine and that morning feeling. Maybe it was the Scottish psyche of persistent dark, dull, wet environments that had conditioned him to appreciate any sunshine, any kind of hospitable weather. Despite almost eight years in LA, he still loved the sun, the heat. The thought of returning to Edinburgh's dark, dingy, damp streets made him feel sick.

He gunned the 911 out onto the Interstate and headed back to Nolan Towers.

As he headed along the familiar road home, Nolan's mind started to replay the events of the last twenty-four hours and it was now starting to dawn on him that this was indeed a serious situation. The confident swaggering Nolan style was now in serious jeopardy.

The garage door retracted and he drove inside. He exited the car and hopefully checked the mailbox for some kind of good news, but it was all junk mail - Yes, maybe I do need a new mattress - he thought to himself, scanning the lurid cheap flyer, - but Mattress World would probably be my last port of call! -

A seductive bespeckled attractive girl adorned the Vision Express flyer – I'd remove those glasses and tell her I was Brad Pitt – he chuckled to himself, casting the bundle of leaflets into the trash.

Once in the house he checked the answer phone. No flashing light. He stumbled through to the bedroom, suddenly realising how tired he actually was, then slumped fully clothed on the bed, kicking his shoes off in a high arc. He closed his eyes – How the hell did I get here

…………………- and fell asleep.

The intermittent ping of the phone alarm causes Nolan to sit up abruptly. Nolan slowly opens his eyes focusing on the chink of bright sunlight between the curtains. He notices the tiny specks of dust floating in the light, down, down then disappear forever. Slowly he reaches out and picks the phone, silencing the shrill alarm tone with one touch. Once again he realises that he is not hung-over.

- This feels good – he thinks to himself and makes a pointless mental note to stop drinking which he will instantly forget.

Showered, shaved and re-booted, Nolan breezes back through the doors of Sunnyside Clinic, winking at Bored Receptionist and striding to his office.

Annie was already seated in his chair, her feet on the desk as she aimlessly flicked through a celebrity gossip magazine – Too bad Cindi Lauper is in Europe – she held the magazine triumphantly above her head showing a beach photograph of a trim figure walking hand in hand with a younger man – Otherwise you could get her to pop in and model for you while you try to shape that nose – she added sarcastically.

- Did the patient get collected OK? – He queried matter-of-factly.

- Yes she did Sam, but these guys are really serious? They even asked me how common it was to do a nose job over two sessions.

- I hope you told them it was? – he added with a bit more urgency.

- I told them it was completely routine, and that there was nothing to worry about, as she was in the hands of one of the best Plastic Surgeons in Los Angeles -

Nolan was unsure if she was being sarcastic or helpful.

- Hmmm. Anyways, who is our delightful contestants today for the Sunnyside game show? - He smiled broadly.

Annie jumped out of the chair and pointed to his computer screen, then walked out of the room, blowing him a kiss as she left.

Nolan sat in the chair and flipped on the computer screen to reveal his digital diary.

4.00pm Consultation Alex Reed - liposuction

5.00pm Follow Up #1 Steve Carerra (Lead Singer of Black Mass) –

liposuction

6.00pm Consultation Annette Grey – Facelift

7.00pm Consultation Demon Daniels – Possible Gender Re-assignment

- Hmmm. Interesting set - he thought to himself.

The muffled voices and stilted laughter in the background announced the (early) arrival of Alex Reed.

Reed tentatively craned his neck around the door, then locking eyes with Nolan, pushed it fully open and proffered his hand in a limp handshake.

- Sit down, sit down – Nolan gestured to the chair.

Reed was a ratty, greasy-haired individual. Slightly podgy, nothing too bad thought Nolan, but it was a John Paul Gaultier suit, and they can work magic on some pretty freaky bodies.

- Now Mr Reed, your notes here tell me that you are looking for a little bit of liposuction to reduce your stomach and overall waist girth. Is that correct? -

- Yes Dr. Nolan – he began to remove his jacket, shirt and tie, revealing indeed a very bloated and swollen midriff.

Nolan got up and began to examine Reed's pasty white torso.

- Yes this area here – as he pointed to the hairy belly button – is a doughnut shape of visceral fat. This is the area we will mainly focus on – he circled the pen on Reed's stomach. –We will then also work on these love handles – he grabbed a handful of hairy man – and get these removed pretty much completely. We are looking at a single day appointment, where you will be unconscious for approximately two hours. You will be discharged later that day wearing a very tight girdle around your midriff, and with a pain killer script. You should desist from any activity at all for about seventy two hours, and even then take it easy for about two weeks, at which point we shall have a follow up meeting to check all OK and everybody happy. This will cost $7,800 – he rattled off.

- Thank you Dr Nolan. I've been using an 'Ab-Belt' for the last six months and trying hard not to eat bad stuff, but it's LA…….. you know what I mean? Nothing seems to work and I simply don't have the time anymore to exercise – he puffed out.

- What line of work are you in that reduces your exercise capability? -

- I'm an agent Dr Nolan, with a very, very demanding clientele – again he puffed out the reply as if under duress.

- Well as a physician, I suggest that you adapt your lifestyle to incorporate some physical exercise at some point every day Mr Reed – Nolan proffered.

- Oh I get daily physical exercise, if you know what I mean Dr Nolan? – he winked lecherously – All these young starlets thinking they're gong to be the next big thing? – He laughed a filthy, coughy laugh.

Nolan pictured the helpless, poor beautiful girls being lured into this fat, greasy slob's office and forced into horrible sexual acts in the vain hope of advancing their career.

- I see – Nolan also laughed conspiratorially.

- I'm sure you must get the same offers all the time here Dr Nolan – he gazed all round the room, peering at the framed Diplomas and Certificates on the wall before fixating directly at Nolan – with all your surgery and Diplomas? – Again he laughed.

- Strangely no, they all leave once I make them pretty – quipped Nolan causing Reed to convulse in overly enthusiastic laughter.

Reed regained his composure – You're a real live one you - he pointed at Nolan, and Nolan could see that there was some food residue on Reed's front bottom teeth.

- Well if that concludes our consultation……..- Nolan stood up, now desperate to avoid Reed's mouth with the white foam and assorted foodstuffs on display – Annie will schedule your surgery day, and get you in the system -

Reed now stood up and shook Nolan's hand bowing his head and walking backwards toward the door.

- Thank you Dr Nolan, thank you Sir - and with that he closed the door behind him and made his way down the corridor to the reception area.

Nolan sat back in his chair slowly shaking his head in disapproval. He switched over to look at the emails on his screen, curious if there was anything from Jane, but there was nothing. He apparently could have any woman he wanted, according to the title of a junk email, and he was also apparently pre-approved for a $50k loan. Pity it wasn't $150k loan, he chuckled to himself.

Out of the corner of his eye he noticed a chauffeur driven Bentley cruise into the car park outside. It pulled up to the visitor parking and out stepped Steve Carerra, the lead singer with heavy metal legends, Black Mass. He turned and looked around the car park scanning his surroundings. Carerra was a tall, muscular man with long curly black hair. His stubble and sunglasses hinted at a hangover, and he winced in the sunlight as he removed his sunglasses and headed for the door.

Carerra's entrance even managed to excite the unexcitable Bored Receptionist, as Nolan heard her squeal with delight as Carerra entered the clinic. Black Mass were an iconic 80's band, drenched in excess and faux outrage, and after a couple of platinum selling LP's had faded into 90's obscurity. The use of their main song 'Séance Party' in a Calvin Klein advertising campaign, re-introduced them to a new audience, and with reunion tours and a new LP, they found themselves back at the top again. Scarcely a gossip magazine or entertainment TV channel failed to feature Carerra and his band mates, or their celebrity girlfriends/wives/ex-wives.

Annie knocked on the door and opened it to reveal the rock star standing behind her –Steve Carerra is your five o'clock Dr Nolan – and she retreated sheepishly with a slight blush to her cheeks as Carerra strode in the room, and reached over to shake Nolan's hand.

- Pleasure – he muttered then sat on the visitor chair. He fidgeted in the chair, rubbing his hands, unable to look at Nolan.

Nolan surmised that due to the nervous fidgeting he was probably a coke head, as he was clutching a water bottle, drank the recommended weekly alcohol allowance in a day, and the yellowed fingers on his left hand indicated a forty-a-day cigarette habit.

- Steve, if I may call you Steve? - Carerra nodded his agreement.

- My notes here suggest that you were looking for some sculpting of your midriff? – He glanced down at the paunch currently concealed beneath a Jack Daniels T-shirt. - Mmmm yeah, I've uh, not been working out or keeping my diet healthy, uh, so you know, I was like, wanting you to get rid of this – he grabbed a healthy handful of Steve Carerra stomach and shook it.

Nolan looked at the tattoos on his hand as his various bangles and bracelets jangled as he shook his gut.

He stood up and took off his blazer, then pulled the t-shirt over his head revealing a tired, worn, muscular torso decorated with random colourful tattoos of birds of paradise, Chinese lettering, crucifixes, and clichéd quotes. Nolan's eyes then gravitated to the swollen belly, with light stretch marks to the sides, and even Popeye's left arm and can of spinach seemed to be perversely stretched and oversized.

Bizarrely, the fat was all centred in the front of the stomach, making Nolan's job so much simpler. Nolan felt the area, probing and squeezing, kneading and spreading.

–Yes this should present no significant problem – Nolan joked as he returned to sit back behind his desk, Carerra pulling his T-shirt back on.

- I'm going to be $9000 for this – Nolan continued, wilfully hiking his rate again.

- Um, yeah that's cool, you know, eh…when do you think I can um, get this done? We have a tour rehearsal starting early next month, and um, I kinda want this out of the way, you know? – His eyes darted around the room, again unable to look at Nolan.

- Our diary is generally four to six weeks in advance Steve, however for a *fee*, we could maybe squeeze you in two weeks? – he reclined back in his chair, smug faced, fully aware he could now get another $5k – I'm not guaranteeing that you'll be fully recovered by the start of the month, but you will be able to work. The compression top I have for you will fit under your t-shirts and no-one will be none the wiser -

- Wow, um, yeah that would be great, eh, um I also need you and your staff to sign a confidentiality thing, you know? Just so that none of these celebrity magazines find out, you know? I mean, um, eh, they paid my ex-housekeeper $20,000 for some pictures he took of me by the pool, um you know, and I was with the girl from the new Mission Impossible movie, and we were like, um just hanging out, so you can

just imagine what they would pay for dirt on this um.......situation –
Nolan's eyes and ears perked up – Twenty thousand just for pictures of
the two of you? Was she topless? Were you intimate? – His rapid
questioning caught him off guard, and caused him to tilt his head
backward.
- Woah man, nothing like that, you know, maybe a little dry hump, but
nothing at all. It was shitty for her to do that to me. Miss Mission
Impossible binned me after that too – he stared down at the ground.
Nolan shot a sideways glance. This was one job he was definitely
taking.
He dialled Annie's extension – Can you put Mr Carerra in for 1pm two
weeks today, Annie, with a two hour window –
- But there's a meeting scheduled with the reps from Ethicon at 1 pm? –
- Cancel it. Mr Carerra's health is priority – he looked up and winked at
Carerra, who gave him a thumbs up – And besides, these Reps can
come anytime. Set us up for a little lipo – he hung up the phone and
beamed at Carerra – That's us set up now Steve, all you have to do is
show up on time here at 1 pm. Nothing to eat twelve hours before, and
we will have you ready to go about 2.30-3pm –
He stood up and offered his hand, which Carerra shook enthusiastically.
Opening the door he leant out into the corridor and shouted for Annie.
- I'll leave you in Annie's capable hands, and she will get all the
paperwork sorted and emailed out to you along with the bank details etc
–
Annie leaned into the office, and again took a red face.
- Just this way Mr Carerra – Annie simpered, as he lazily lurched out of
the room.
Nolan reached into his pocket and pulled out his phone.
He looked up Phillips' number and dialled. Straight to answer phone.
He hung up - Nothing to say anyway – he thought, but slightly curious
as to what Phillips knew about his situation with Marchesi.
He reached into the under desk mini fridge and pulled out an Evian. He
leaned back in his chair and sipped the ice cold water.
He slowly opened his eyes and looked over at the appointment notes on

his computer screen for his 6pm.

Annette Grey (51). Requiring a re-assessment of her facial skin. Nice Hollywood Hills address, personalised phone number, and 79 credit rating. All good. He read on. Marital status left blank - Possibly under review - he mused. No allergies, distinguishing marks, special diets, or specific information – A first time for everything – he laughed thinking of all the stupid inane crap he had seen on these forms over the years. 'Allergic to hair' 'Allergic to water' 'South American diet' 'Eskimo diet' Distinguishing marks…. 'Small mole to left shoulder' The stupid clown neglected to mention he had a giant eagle tattooed on his back, but mentioned a 3mm standard mole on his shoulder. Distinguishing marks…..'confident appearance' which is apparently hipster for shaved head, tattooed face and more metal in her face than Argentina's silver export market. Aside from all the predictable 'cool' and 'awesome' and 'incredibly driven' comments under specific information, there was some very dark 'uncomfortable in this life', 'does not mix with other humans', and 'I see evil in everything, including this procedure'.

A gentle knock on the door broke Nolan's train of thought, and Annie ushered in a very neat, trim short-haired woman in a grey business suit.

- Dr Nolan – she offered her hand.

Nolan shook her hand and sat down. Immediately he had assessed a considerable amount of sun damage to her facial skin, and some heavy sagging below the ears and eyes. She was very neat otherwise, and she was wearing high quality make up.

As she placed her handbag on the spare chair alongside, Nolan spied the Chanel make-up bag and smiled quietly to himself.

- Your notes here tell me that you are looking……- he was interrupted by a light knock on the door.

Annie swung the door wide to allow an older man to hobble in.

- My husband Hugh - announced Annette Grey.

Nolan hated this. Spouses, partners, best friends and general hanger-ons were a constant source of irritation to Nolan, always chipping in with their stupid comments and observations. Worst of all, he had to indulge them.

Nolan stood up and shook his hand. Annette Grey moved her bag to the floor and let her considerably older husband to flop down in the chair. He gave out an exasperated sigh as he flopped backwards, clearly surprised by the Hag Chair Company's patented suspension back system.

- Careful – Joked Nolan, secretly wishing he had fallen backwards in the chair, or at very least, hurt his back.

- Now then, Mr & Mrs Grey, you are looking to have some surgical tightening of the facial skin? – Nolan enquired.

He then had to listen to a twenty minute tale of holidays, lifestyle excess and youthful bad choices which now led the 51 year old Annette Grey to Sam Nolan's surgery and the 72 year old Hugh Grey here to pay for it.

He left his chair and began to fashion Annette Grey's loose skin into a pleasing, more youthful position, all the time subjected to Hugh Grey's halitosis. His teeth hadn't been cleaned in a while, judging by the cream coloured fur coating the gaps between his teeth, and this was delightfully combined with a $30 Tuscan Tuna Macrobiotic Salad which he had for lunch. Hugh Grey now insisted in inspecting every aspect of Nolan's surgical intentions to within a couple of inches, due to his failing eyesight.

Once they were satisfied with the explanation of the procedure, Nolan quoted them the standard facelift fee, but with an added 20% bad breath tax. A date was agreed and Nolan could finally get rid of the foul odour now inhabiting his office.

As they left the office in Annie's charming company, Nolan ran to his private bathroom where he brushed his teeth thoroughly.

On returning to the office, Nolan drew the blinds open and pushed out the ventilator hoppers at the top of the window, letting fresh, but clammy air pour into his room. He saw the Greys both entering a gleaming white Bentley convertible. He shook his head in disbelief, and sat down to study his notes for his 7pm.

Demon Daniels. A 26 year old music producer from West Hollywood who had 'major unusual surgical gender requirements' - Of course you do – thought Nolan – But you're not confused, you're just an idiot. He read on. Address was a c/o Record Company. So this was a tax break too. He internet searched the name. Up popped a bizarre looking individual with a giant horn on his/her head, and a rainbow coloured pony tail looked to be coming out of his/her ass.

- Jesus Christ - He flicked onto YouTube and selected the most popular track he/she/it had produced…..'You don't know what it is' Nolan laughed and imagined the song was autobiographical. Apparently the song was also 'Featuring Cammy D' who Nolan worked out was the fat ginger white kid dressing in African Tribal gowns and bouncing around squealing like a stuck pig.

- Oh oh oh oh, someone with impeccable music taste – minced a voice from the open door, as the bizarre Demon Daniels strode into the room – I do like it when we're all singing from the same page – he suggestively remarked before convulsing into hysterical laughter.

Nolan was taken by surprise and slowly rose offering his hand in handshake, to which Daniels simply waved it away – Not for me my good man – and the offered the back of his hand for Nolan to kiss.

- Eh, well please sit down Mr Daniels - mumbled Nolan, completely ignoring the outstretched arm.

- Not Mister for much longer, if you're anything of the surgeon I've heard you are Sam Nolan – answered Daniels, tilting his head back and baring his teeth.

Daniels was head to toe in shiny black PVC, with a thin sliver of toned stomach visible between trousers and tunic. Large black oversize boots with clumpy heels were adored with shiny chrome spikes and studs. His hair was centre parted, one side bleached blonde, the other jet black. Various nose rings and a veritable array of metal jewellery was spread across his face and head. A tattoo of what Nolan thought was a Pink Flamingo peeped out from the top of his tunic. Several rune-type symbols were tattooed across the nape of his very thin and turkey-like neck. Bright green John Lennon penny-round sunglasses were just dark enough to conceal his eye movements.

- Thank you very much, you've clearly done your homework as to my success rate in this type of procedure. I have conducted over 12 of these here in Los Angeles with no revision work or significant follow up surgery, and in fact, can confirm that one of the most famous Trans-Sexual presenters on cable TV in Los Angeles today, was one of my clients – Nolan leaned back in the chair, back in command, reeling off his spiel has he had done many times before. This type of surgery was intricate and very expensive. Especially with his LA record company footing the bill.

- Oh I think you maybe slightly misunderstand, Dr Nolan – Daniels half spoke/half whispered – Is he trying to sound like Marilyn Monroe? – Nolan wondered.

- I don't want to be a woman, I want to be asexual. No genitals. No sex drive. I want to be the most unique and original individual on the planet. I'm going to remove all the tattoos, all the jewellery; I'm going to create my own style of clothing, my own style of outward presentation, *my own style of living* – He breathed the last comment. Nolan looked surprised and leaned back in his chair exhaling as he did so.

Daniels leaned forward - I want no penis. I simply want to be able to pass water normally through a small opening. I want to be completely smooth and flawless – he looked straight at Nolan – like a dolphin.

Nolan couldn't tell if he was staring at him or not. He looked deep into the sunglasses but couldn't make out his eyes. This made Nolan very uncomfortable.

- I've taken the liberty of having one of the designers at CBS Records draw up these images of what I'm after – he handed Nolan some A4 sheets with artist-sketched fantasy drawings showing the sleek, smooth, future Demon Daniels like some alien.

- I see – said Nolan, shuffling the drawings then arranging them in front on his desk. He poured over the details and the fine artistry – It is not beyond my capability to do something like this, however, with unchartered territory comes great strides, but also great risks. I will need to analyse this further, and perhaps involve a colleague of mine whose field of speciality is more of the post-trauma nature, in terms of reconstruction, however I think something could be done to accommodate your wishes. This will be expensive though – He stared right at the sunglasses for any movement or variation as he said this. There was none.

- We could be talking two or possibly three stages, each carrying significant risk, and possibly a final price tag of six figures – again he started intently looking for any kind of reaction.

Daniels looked indifferent - If I say yes, when can you start? – It was now his turn to study Nolan's face.

The thought of $100k in short notice immediately caught Nolan off-guard, and he knocked over his empty glass in his haste to consult his computer screen.

- Let me see – he peered at the screen over his glasses.

He scanned the next two weeks of appointments. Nothing was free. He eventually came to his Pro-Bono slot 'for the community'. He hit the delete button.

- Yes, we can move aside a couple of appointments I have and start the process a week on Friday at 10am – his eyes widened as Daniels considered this.

Daniels suddenly stood up abruptly, causing Nolan to start – Then it is settled Dr Nolan, I shall present myself at 10am – he turned and marched out of the office.

Nolan buzzed Annie.

- Stop his highness and give him the pre-op prep pack would you? And remind him – no eating 12 hours prior!

- Goodbye - Nolan shouted after him as he heard the clumpy boots banging down the hallway. Maybe the risk would scare him. Maybe the *price* would scare him. Maybe he was just a weirdo. He laughed to himself again. – *Maybe* he was just a weirdo? He's a complete lunatic. Nolan stared at the ground and exhaled a long breath, mentally exhausted.

Annie craned her head round the door – what or who was that??? -

- That my dear Annie, is a rapping Trans-Sexual who wished to have all his/her/it's sexual organs removed and become a space alien dolphin –

he said stoically, without a hint of sarcasm.

Annie laughed as she turned to leave – just another day in Paradise, Sam – and her footsteps carried down the corridor.

Five days had passed since the Marchesi surgery. He had been tempted to call to check on the patient, but the thought of a negative outcome was too much for him to bear. It had been a stressful few days and now he was hungry. He said his farewells to Annie & Bored Receptionist, and headed out to the car park.

He started the car, taking a few seconds to reflect that his Porsche was the most reliable thing in his life, before pointing it downtown and headed to the Strip.

Easing into his familiar night time territory, he decided to leave the car at the 24 hour garage, which was half way between his house and the top of Sunset Strip.

He left the car with Joe, an aspiring actor from Wisconsin, who was merely filling his time between auditions, working as a valet parker. Nolan asked him to keep a particular eye on his car, and left him with the keys, twenty dollars, and a promise that he could take care of the small birthmark on his left cheek.

He folded his blazer over his arm and headed down the leafy street, taking in the beautiful sunset which was unfolding before him, and remembered the horrible dark nights back in Scotland. Sometimes he wished he had stayed, and sometimes he wished it had just worked out better here in LA. He knew he was flawed, imperfect, unreliable, but he also had a massive self confidence, and in California, confidence is everything.

His first port of call was the Tropicana Bar & Grill, where he had a steak with fries, and a not too shabby glass of house Malbec.

Remembering his earlier promise to himself, he declined a second glass of Malbec, opting for a mineral water. Settling his check, he smiled and winked at the pretty young waitress, leaving a healthy twenty dollar tip.

As he ambled further down the Strip, the sun was now set, and the street lights flickered into life. A stretch limo flashed past, darkened completely out, concealing it's mystery celebrity occupant.

His next port of call was Gee Gee's Cosy Corner, a legendary LA rocker hang out from the 60's which had fallen on harder times, but Nolan loved the LP records on the walls, and knowing he was in the favourite bar of some of his musical heroes.

He ordered a draught Budweiser, then spied the glass of the drinker next to him at the bar, noting the smeary, dirty marks around the rim.

- On second thoughts, make that a bottle of Peroni – he shouted to the barmaid, who pushed the beer tap back aggressively and let out a long sigh.

- Bang goes your tip - thought Nolan, smiling as the grumpy barmaid thumped the bottle in front of him.

- Sammy boy……Samoid……..Nolanski – a ponytailed Bruno came striding through the crowd at the bar, grabbing Nolan by the shoulder – How have you been? – He asked, not waiting for a reply, before continuing into a tale of debauchery involving the grumpy barmaid and a bottle of tequila.

- So how did that thing work out for you……you know the money thing Sam? – He asked with genuine concern, waiting for a reply this time.

- Well I'm still in that situation – he cursed Bruno under his breath for reminding him.

- But I'm sure it'll get resolved one way or another -

- Sounds like a song to me – Bruno quipped, convulsing with laughter, his unsteadiness on his feet confirming Nolan's suspicion, that he was drunk. Or high. Or both.

Sensing Nolan's irritation, Bruno put his arm around him – C'mon Sam, lighten up man! – He looked left to right and scanned the whole bar before slipping a discreet package into Nolan's left hand – On the house, buddy. Make you forget your cares. But be careful, there are four in there. One at a time Sam, you wouldn't want to get comatose yet! – He sniggered conspiratorially.

- Woo! Jonesy! Chicky-Boy! Woo! – Bruno waved and shouted as some of his coterie of friends/customers entered the bar.

Another round of drinks appeared and Nolan felt increasingly detached from the company, not wishing to hear tales of drunken and drug excess, besides, he was now on a bit of a downer, with Bruno reminding him of the Marchesi situation.

He took everyone's order and got a round of drinks in. He toasted with them, and then when Bruno was fully holding court, he headed to the men's room, and darted out onto the street, confident his presence would not be missed for some time.

He walked past several bars, but wary of being dragged into company, decided to opt for somewhere he had never been in before.

Catatonia fitted that bill, but as he approached the door, it became apparent that this was a lesbian bar. A myriad of rainbow stickers covered the glass at the side of the door, and the chunky bouncer on the door was indeed female. He turned on his heels and headed further down the strip.

Eco Bar was also another venue he had noticed previously, but the imitation tree bark on the exterior always put him off. He tentatively entered the bar, and seeing it was relatively quiet, headed to the bar and ordered a Peroni.

- We only stock our own beers here - announced a shrill voice belonging to a pink-haired, nose-ringed, Dr Marten wearing elf – All organically produced and ethically sourced ingredients- she continued her spiel.

Nolan looked at the drinks menu.

Triple A - Argentinean Artisan Ale. Boomer – A wheaty golden ale made from an authentic 60's hippy recipe. Tinseltown – Hollywood's own Craft beer.

- I'll have a Tinseltown -

A beer swiftly appeared before him. It tasted awful. He laid a twenty on the bar and left.

He spat on the pavement as he carried on down the street, eager to remove the taste of Tinseltown. The irony was not lost on him.He needed a drink quickly to get rid of the taste, and next up was Radio

Stars, a frontage he had never noticed before, particularly with a name like that.

He went straight to the bar, and to his joy, saw the labels of regular beers in the coolers. As the barmaid got his drink, he noted the excited babble in the bar, and wondered why he had never heard of this place. Just as the beer came, loud music started up, causing him to turn around.

There was a small illuminated stage, on which two drunken women were beginning to screech out the opening words to Hotel California. Nolan's heart sank. He hated Karaoke. But the beer was good, and cold. He turned back around then glanced down the bar. He could not believe his eyes. At the end of the bar, as if framed in a golden light, there was Nadine.

As beautiful as ever, her hair perfectly coffered, wearing a tight, ribbed black dress, sipping a Martini.

He negotiated the busy bar, walked up behind her, and even before he had a chance to say anything, she spun round, a look of shock on her face.

- Sam! How are you! Where have you been hiding? – She leant toward him and kissed him lightly on the cheek.

Nolan found her familiar scent intoxicating and just like that, all the good memories came rushing back, and the bad ones cast aside.

He ordered them drinks, and just as luck would have it, another couple rose from the darkened booth at the back of the bar, and they nestled into their cosy retreat.

They spent a couple of hours reminiscing, laughing, and for a short while, Nolan was happy. But he kept looking at that nose. That perfect sweet nose. If only it was as simple as to take hers and pop it on Marianne Marchesi. Even though he had only couple of drinks, he began to assess the work of a full nasal graft. He had performed a full face once before, but he shook his head, trying to remove the image in his head.

Nolan stood up and headed to the men's room, but not before having to promise to Nadine that he would return. He gave her his jacket as collateral, which amused her no end. She had drank heavily, and was definitely tipsy, he thought inching his way through the crowd, as a Texas elementary school teacher struggled manfully with George Michael's Careless Whisper.

- Hey Sam, you be careful there – boomed a voice in his ear, suddenly breaking his train of thought. He looked up and there was DaLuca. The room suddenly felt very claustrophobic, as Nolan muttered pleasantries to DaLuca, all the while edging toward the men's room. DaLuca grinned and toasted his glass – See you around Dr Nolan! - Nolan splashed his face with cold water in the sink.

- Did he follow him there? Was it just by chance? Do mafia guys like Karaoke? -

He finished up then headed back the long way round the dance floor, skirting the edge of the now busy bar, keeping DaLuca in view out of the corner of his eye.

He slid into the booth alongside Nadine. – I think we should go now. Maybe a drink somewhere else? – He offered his hand.

- Sure. I'm in the mood for a few – she winked at him and gathered her belongings, stumbling as she exited the booth.

Outside Nolan hailed a cab – take us to the Montrose – he told the driver, keeping one eye on the doorway to see if DaLuca was following. The taxi sped away as he continued to watch the doorway through the rear window until it was out of view.

A few minutes later they pitched up at Montrose, Nolan and the bellhop helping a clearly drunk Nadine out of the cab and into the hotel.

- Aw Sam......- she slurred – not this place? –

- It's all good – he ushered her past the reception and into the lift to the bar. The bellhop looked over as the lift doors began to close, Nolan over exaggerated a roll of the eyes just as the doors closed.

Once in the quiet bar, settled with drinks, Nadine's mean drunk began to materialise. Nolan then remembered this side of her.

- You needn't think I'm sleeping with you tonight – she bellowed, causing the other two customers to look round.

- Ssssh! - He put his finger on her lips. She bit him hard causing him to wince.

63

- What the hell was that for? – He clutched his coiled hand to his chest – These hands are my living! –
- Living? You pathetic, useless clown – she took a large mouthful of her Martini.
- Don't start – he implored.
- You don't wanna see me start. I've nobody……Sam Nolan……Nobody. And it's your entire fault……- she spilled the remains of her Martini on the table.
Nolan was aware of the bar staff whispering and discussing their situation. He signalled to the waitress and asked for a cab, all the time making apologetic faces and gestures.
- Come on, dear, let's get you home – he said loudly helping Nadine to her feet.
- You make me……sick – she stammered.
He was now well reminded why their relationship ended.
Again the bellhop helped Nolan manhandle her into the cab.
- Sunnyside Clinic 2928 Melrose – he whispered at the driver.
Nolan was sweating. He felt his brow and then looked to see if there was damp staining on his armpits.
The cab drew into the clinic car park.
The meter read $19. Nolan gave the driver a twenty which he studiously examined, clearly hoping the tip had been more.
Nolan leapt out of the car and ran round to help a drunken Nadine stagger out of the car.
- Where's this, Sam…….is this The Rainbow? Victors?.......... -
They entered the clinic, Nadine draped over his arm as he manfully punched in the alarm code with his free hand. They headed into his office, and she slumped into the leather chesterfield. He turned on the lights low, slowly, one at a time, finally leaning over her to turn on the last one. She reached up and grabbed his shirt pulling him toward her, and she kissed him fully on the lips.
- You know you really treated me like dirt – she began with a slight slur pushing him away cursing - He pulled away – A drink perhaps? – She nodded lazily, muttering under her breath….– Where the hell is this? -

She looked around the dimly lit room.

Nolan opened the drink cupboard and produced a bottle of Canadian Club and two glasses.

- Let me go check for ice – he smartly moved around the furniture and ducked out of the room, returning almost immediately.

He felt his jacket pocket for Bruno's drugs and dropped all four small pills into one of the glasses, swirling it to dissolve.

– Do you think it was fate that caused us to meet again tonight? – enquired Nolan, still swirling the drinks, one corner of his eye checking there were no tell-tale residue or bubbles.

- You know I don't believe.........in fate Sam, it's just stuff that happens......we live within ½ an hour of each other......not beyond the realms of possibility we would run into each other......- her words drunkenly tailed off.

Her complete inebriation was now in stark contrast to Nolan's measured calm through his inebriation.

He inspected the drink then handed her the glass of golden liquid.

- Thought you went for ice Sam? There's no ice in this – she stared at the glass almost cross-eyed.

- Your good health – he toasted her, clanking their glasses together.

The noise of the colliding glasses seemed to galvanise her and she started sipping.

- Yeuch. This crap must be old, it tastes a bit funny.....or cheap! – She screwed up her face.

- Maybe it is Nadine. Maybe it is. But it's all we've got - he smiled and winked at her.

- I'd never party with you again Sam Nolan….. – She slurred into her drink – You picked me up and you threw me away! – Tears began to run down her cheeks – You promised Sam, you bloody promised.......- she drunkenly tried to rise from the couch, but Bruno's downers were kicking in hard and she fell back – You're a filthy pig Sam Nolan…..A filthy, stinking pig. What was I even thinking about getting involved with you when I could have had a *real* Doctor, not some inbred Scottish failure.......you and your wife......you disgust me.........take me home....take me home...... -

- Drink up sweetheart – he encouraged with a grim smile, cursing under his breath, and she downed the remaining contents of the glass, dropping it on the wooden floor.

- I don't feel too good.......maybe too many........her voice tailed off as she closed her eyes.

- There's the ice, Sam......there's all the ice......there's no ice.......- her voice tailed off as she passed out.

Nolan looked at the crumpled form in front of him. He took a deep breath, lifted a pillow from the examination table and forced it down onto her face, smothering out her life with minimal resistance.

Chapter 4
Rock Candy Line

Nadine's lifeless body was now lying directly on the operating table. The merest flicker of regret passed over Nolan's eyes, but was gone in a nanosecond.

This was the answer to all his problems. He had one hour, possibly ninety minutes, before the loss of blood flow would damage the nose. He darted about the room switching on equipment, adjusting, all the time focused on the job in hand.

He donned his surgical robes, pulled on his gloves, and lifted his scalpel; He held it to the light as he always did, checking the purity. It glinted majestically in the pure, cool surgical light.

He breathed in, and began to cut.

Thirty minutes later, he gently detached the central section of Nadine's nose and surrounding facial tissue, and lowered it into the cryogenic storage. He closed the lid and checked the temperature.

Gently he lifted it on to the work surface, and then turned to what was left of Nadine. A large gaping bloody hole in middle of her face contrasted sharply to the cool, white sleek surroundings of the operating theatre.

- What a great album cover – thought Nolan as he paused before covering the body. He manfully struggled to fit her remains in the body bag himself, noticing that Nadine had perhaps gained a few pounds since their time together.

Eventually the bag closed at the top and Nolan took a few seconds to catch his breath.

Moving to the freezer store, he punched in the alarm code and entered the dimly lit store, carefully checking the auto close was off on the door alarm.

He returned to the theatre and carefully lifted the cryogenic case and put it on the first shelf inside the store.

The largest compartment was on the floor running the full length. He pulled the door down releasing a blast of cold air and vapour. He checked it was completely empty, then returned to the theatre and gingerly lifted the body and carried it into the store. He dropped it on the cold tiled floor and pushed it into the confined space, then after a couple of attempts, managed to get the door to close.

- She's not going to fit in the 911 in one piece – he mused, considering his dissection options. He stood up and closed the door of the lower freezer store and punched in a new code to prevent anyone else from inadvertently discovering Nadine.

He reached into his pocket and dialled Marchesi's number. At first he thought of the inconvenience of a call this late, but then concluded that a Mafioso's peak hours would probably be through the night.

Marchesi grunted into the phone.

- Good evening Mr Marchesi - he began – I do apologise for the timing of my call, but something very important has come up, and I'm calling to ask that you bring Mrs. Marchesi into the clinic as soon as possible to conclude her surgery. There was some specific material I require to finish her work, and I have just taken a rather unexpected delivery, and rather than prevaricate or delay for an alternative delivery, I thought I would call and see if this was possible? -

- It's almost one in the morning Dr Nolan. Are you drunk? – Marchesi said without a hint of emotion.

- I am aware of how strange this must seem, Mr Marchesi, but this will genuinely ensure a satisfactory outcome to your good lady's procedure – Nolan sounded slightly nervous.

No reply from Marchesi.

- I…I…I've done many surgeries at inopportune times and at all times of the day….in fact when Cher came to see me about…….- he continued.

- We will be there within the hour – Marchesi barked and hung up the phone.

Nolan breathed a sigh of relief then dialled Annie's number.

- Hello……. A clearly sleeping Annie answered the phone.

- Annie, don't get mad, don't ask questions, just get dressed and meet

me at the clinic in half an hour.
- Sam? What's going on……..- her voice tailed off, half asleep.
- Annie! Annie! Just do as I say. Get your scrubs on and meet me at the clinic as soon as you can. I need you there. No questions, no grief, just do it – Nolan's voice became more pleading.
- Oh Sam……. – She hung up.
Nolan now busied himself prepping the anaesthesia. He had done many minor surgeries with just Annie to assist, but this one was a bit more involved and there was absolutely no room for error. A mess up here and he would have to pack his bags and run tonight.
Twenty minutes later, he heard a car draw up into the car park. Its high-pitched engine note was not that of the Marchesi BMW, rather the impudent whine of a budget Ford. Annie was here.
She came bustling into the clinic, scowling and petulant.
- Come now, Annie, immediately – she mimicked Nolan's voice – All I say is that better be worth it Sam….who's the lucky patient? -
- It's Marianne Marchesi - Nolan looked downward fiddling with the gas taps.
- Really? Just like that you decide to take on one of the hardest jobs you've had at two in the morning? Are for real? – She was genuinely shocked.
- Annie – you have to trust me on this - he held both her hands in his - I had a donor……and the nose structure and cartilage is perfect. I couldn't wait – he continued adjusting the gas.
Annie stood there open mouthed and eyes wide – You've been at that creep Watson's place haven't you? That sick bastard at the Morgue! I should have known. All very well him stealing jewellery or personal effects, but body parts? How much did you pay him this time Sam?.....Jesus!....After the time the newspapers had all the evidence on him selling kidneys and hearts to that Quack up in Santa Barbara! -
Nolan had forgotten about Watson. A dull, slow-witted individual with dubious hygiene, Watson was the caretaker of the morgue on Wilshire. There had been a scandal a few years back where an undercover reporter had posed as a client and Watson had attempted to sell him

69

vital organs from recently deceased John Does brought into the morgue. Paperwork was manipulated as if they hadn't existed and Watson made a pretty penny selling on the vital organs to low-grade transplant quacks willing to exploit desperate people. Nolan had bought blood bags from him before but nothing as radical as body parts - Good cover though - he thought.

- Yes I know, it's not the most ethical, but I'm in a hole, Annie. I have to get out of it, and some poor woman just wound up in Watson's room and she just happened to be a literal dead ringer for Cindi Lauper. I don't know. Maybe God wants to help me out for a change instead of having a good belly laugh at my misfortune. Anyway, I've acquired her nose, and checked it dimensionally with a digital reading - He turned away sharply and began laying out his tools.

Annie muttered under her breath and began helping him.

The front door of the clinic opened announcing the arrival of the Marchesi's.

Annie scuttled through to greet them as Nolan went into the freezer room to retrieve the nose.

Nolan smiled and nodded to Marchesi and DaLuca as he put his arm around Marianne Marchesi and guided her into the prep room.

He heard the door close behind them and the sound of Annie locking up.

- Now there's nothing different to the last time Marianne, I'm now just going to finish off what we started – Nolan smiled noticing her slightly glazed expression, indicating previous moderate alcohol intake - Usually a no-no before surgery- he thought - But tonight, needs must.

Nolan gestured to the gown neatly laid on the trolley and left the room. He went into his office and checked his phone. No messages.

Returning to the theatre, Annie was asking Marianne to count backwards from ten, having administered the anaesthetic.

Nolan picked up his scalpel, lifted his eyes, and briefly locked gaze with Annie.

- Let's rock – he muttered and began to cut.

Two and a half hours later, he finished applying the final dressing across Marianne Marchesi's face.

- That is your best yet, Sam, I have to admit – Annie said shaking her head.

- I don't know if it's pressurised situations or the time of day, or just your general unreliability, but sometimes you surprise even me. You knocked this one out of the park, Sam. Treat all this as a warning. Stay away from Phillips, the gambling, and most of all, people like this – she pointed at the patient.

- I know, I know – he nodded like a scolded puppy.

- I do genuinely see this as an epiphany; I have to cut my ties with this unsustainable lifestyle. Need to sort myself out with Sarah and be someone she could be proud of. Need to see if there's anything left with Jane, and if not, make it all right so we can all get on, and all have a good life – he looked earnestly at Annie before cracking a smile.

- Sometimes I don't know if you mean it or are taking the piss Sam – she looked straight at him unsmiling – I guess if you keep away from the floozies and hangers-on like that Nadine......... – She visibly shuddered and made the uuurgh sound.

Nolan glanced sideways at the patient's bandaged nose.

- Closer than you think – he thought to himself.

- I am being genuine Annie.......I know I need to change. It's not fair on you guys here either. You deserve an honest, hardworking boss. And that's what I am going to be. Now wrap it up in here while I go phone Marchesi - he headed back to his office, pulling off his robes as he walked.

Washing his hands in the small wash hand basin in his room, he let out a huge sigh.

- That was very, very close – he thought to himself – That could have gone so wrong, but ended up so right! Apart from the murder.

He dried his hands and dialled Marchesi's number.

- Mr Marchesi. You will be delighted to know that your good wife's surgery is now complete and I am 100% satisfied with the procedure. She will be ready for collection tomorrow morning about 10am, and I personally will stay here with her until then, and in two weeks time we

71

shall have a check up to ensure the healing is progressing all as planned. With all being well, I would expect your wife's face to be fully healed in approximately six weeks once all the swelling has reduced – Nolan enthusiastically reported.

Marchesi grunted into the phone and moving his mouth away from the phone, barked instruction for DaLuca and Williams to collect Mrs Marchesi at 10am.

Returning to the phone, Marchesi continued - I hope for your sake Dr Nolan that Mrs Marchesi is happy with the results – he said quietly, with just a hint of menace.

- Oh I'm sure she will be, Mr Marchesi. I have taken the liberty of taking a few photographs at various stages of the procedure, and on a professional level am very proud of the work done, and on a personal level, totally relieved that I have managed to meet your expectations - Nolan breathlessly continued.

- We'll see about that Dr Nolan. Goodbye. – He hung up the phone.

He slouched back in the chair letting out a long sigh.

Annie looked in the slightly ajar door – I'll go get some shut eye and be back for lunchtime -

Nolan nodded in agreement –What would I do without you – he smiled – I'll stay here until she's collected then come back tomorrow lunchtime -

Annie waved at him and left his office, her heels clacking down the corridor.

- Thanks Annie – he shouted after her.

The pee-poh of the door closer indicated she had left the building, and he heard her car start and head off.

He lifted his glass and the remains of the Canadian Club bottle and headed into Post-Op to sit with Marianne Marchesi.

He pulled up the chair next to her bed, and before long had nodded off.

====0====

The banging and clattering through in the reception roused Nolan from his slumbers, Bored Receptionist going through her opening routine. He rose gingerly and crossed the room to open the blind slightly, letting the daylight flood into the room. After a cup of coffee, the noises in the reception now indicated it was ten o'clock, and DaLuca had arrived. They helped a groggy Marianne Marchesi into a wheel chair, then out and into the dark blue BMW at the door. Any conversation with DaLuca was met with guttural grunts, so he didn't bother. As they drove off out of the parking lot, Nolan turned to Bored Receptionist – Keep a note of all calls......I'm off home for a shower and some sleep. Annie will be in at lunchtime for a couple of small check ups later in the afternoon. I'll be back in tomorrow lunchtime. See you later – He grabbed his jacket, hopped into the car and headed home.

He woke around eight pm, after a fitful sleep, punctuated by memories and thoughts of Nadine and the night before.

He had a quick shower, a glass of red wine, and then drove down to The Montrose.

He tossed the keys to the valet and headed into reception, pausing only to nod in acknowledgement to the bellhop from the night before.

He entered the lift and headed up to the bar. He needed a drink badly.

The sound of the phone alarm penetrates through the murk. Nolan slowly opens his eyes focusing on the chink of bright sunlight cutting between the curtains. He notices the tiny specks of dust floating in the light, down, down, and then disappear forever. The constant bleeping of the alarm brings him round. He realises he is hung-over. Again.

He lay back in the bed exhaling loudly, which in turn emphasised the dryness of the inside of his mouth. He tried to organise a timeline of events in his head from the previous night. There was the red wine at the Montrose.........Bruno was there. Being a pest as usual............ there was shots at the Montrose.........one of Bruno's druggy friends was buying.......Karaoke at that bar where he met Nadine the night before...........Singing some Johnny Cash song at

Karaoke with Bruno…….Throwing up in the car park outside the Rainbow……..Couldn't remember much after that………Some god-awful nightclub at Sunset Plaza that bizarrely was a pizza restaurant downstairs, and an 80's nightclub upstairs. He vaguely remembered ordering pizza and sharing it with someone………Just at that moment he was startled by someone in the bed beside him rolling onto their side. The realisation someone was in his bed snapped Nolan to life. He looked down at a young beautiful face, still wearing makeup. He noticed the perfect skin, the California tan, the immaculate white teeth…….Her eyes popped open. Nolan startled back.

- Hey… Sam……how's the head this morning? – She enquired softly.
- Eh……..fine…..em…..um……sure……- he mumbled unconvincingly.
- You don't remember though, do you? – She giggled.
- I remember having pizza with you at the end of the night? – He enquired tentatively.
- Not bad, Sam…..now how about my name? – She laughed, pulling the sheets up to just below her eyes.
- I confess. I simply don't know – he hung his head in mock shame and turned his eyes upward, affecting his best sad puppy face.

She threw the sheets off, exposing a fantastically athletic, toned body which made Nolan's eyes widen – Did I? – he thought to himself.

- It's Madison, Sam. Like the Avenue. Madison Scott - She pulled herself close until their noses were touching.
- Well that's handy. I won't forget that now. Madison the Avenue, and Scott like my nationality. We're simply meant to be – He mocked with more than a hint of irony.
- And now I have to get to my work sweetheart – he said leaping out of the bed and into the en-suite bathroom in one swift motion, hoping she didn't see anything she didn't like.

Inside, Nolan was brimming with pride that he had attracted such a youthful, gorgeous creature, but alarmed that he could not remember if they had sex.

He showered quickly, feeling the murk and hangover fall from his body

74

and down the drain where it belonged.

After drying himself, he checked his body's reflection in the Art Deco mirror.

- Still not too shabby - he thought, changing position from right side to left side.

He brushed his teeth, then doused him self a little more liberally with cologne. He opted for Chanel's 'Allure Sport'. Someone had once complemented him on wearing that particular fragrance, and had said that 'It was the smell of money'. That ticked all the right boxes with Nolan.

He walked through the bedroom with the towel round his waist, stopping to briefly kiss Madison gently on the forehead before proceeding to his dressing room, where he selected a Hugo Boss shirt and tie with an Calvin Klein dark grey business suit.

Returning to the bedroom, dressed powerfully, his hair immaculate, he stooped to gather his Rolex watch from the night stand.

Madison looked up at him, the contrast between the drunken mid-life punk of last night and the sleek, cool, LA Surgeon standing before her now, was written on her face. And Nolan knew it. Her initial confidence now put back in its box by the sheer presence of Samuel Joseph Nolan.

- Stay as long as you like Madison, the door alarm key is coded, so you can leave whenever and it'll lock behind you – he removed a business card from his breast pocket and laid it on the nightstand, tapping it gently – And this is me, my cell, office, and generally how to get in touch. I would personally love to see you again – he bent down and kissed her gently on the nose.

She breathed in his cologne and gave a little gasp as she fell back onto the pillow.

Nolan left the room, giving the pistol shot mime to her as he left.

The Porsche fires up, and as the garage door opens to reveal the bright sunlight, Nolan realises he is very happy.

He guns the car out onto the street, just as KRQR 97.3 FM plays the intro to The Clash's 'Magnificent Seven'.

- Now that's more like it – he thought to himself. Sun in the sky, Clash

75

on the radio, babe in the bed, and Sam Nolan in the pink.

He edged the Porsche into the clinic car park, pausing to let two leggy girls cross in front of him, they both turned to look at the sports car whilst sucking on the straws of their Jack-In-The-Box sodas. Nolan smiled and saluted as they crossed. He then crawled into the prize reserved spot outside the clinic, ensuring in his wing mirror that they were still watching him.

He exited the car and strode up to the clinic door giving a little foot shuffle as he opened the door.

Bored receptionist didn't even look up and slapped the mail and some memo notes on the counter – Afternoon Dr Nolan – she mumbled in a monotone.

-And what a fine day it is too Courtney! – he picked a flower from the display on the counter and buttonholed it on his suit, picked up the mail and headed down the corridor to his office, whistling as he went.

As soon as he sat at his desk, his phone pinged.

He hurriedly grabbed the phone, but it was an unknown number. Opening the message, it was a photograph. Here was Madison in his kitchen, wearing one of his shirts toasting him with a cup of coffee. Again he puffed up with pride. He sent back a heart emoji, then set about installing her number into the phone memory.

Annie strode into the room without knocking, causing him to bolt upright and drop the phone.

- Ah-ha! Guilty secrets no doubt? – She laughed and laid a pile of folders on his desk.

- Em, yes – he laid the phone inside his top drawer.

- So, who do we have today? – He ventured enthusiastically.

- Mmmmm………you do smell good today, Sam…..what's that aftershave? – Annie cooed.

- That is the smell of money, Annie – he laughed.

She turned the computer screen toward him – there's today's aftershaves – she swaggered out of the office laughing.

4pm Follow Up #2 Jamie Lee – Reconstructive Facial Surgery

5pm Follow Up #1 Jane Valentine – Tattoo Removal Correction

6pm Consultation – Astrid Wilders – Breast Enhancement
7pm Surgery - Demon Daniels - Stage 1 Surgery Penis Removal
- The fun never ends – he thought to himself, his previous happy state
now ebbing away with the realisation he now had to work.
The murmur of voices in the hallway indicated the arrival of Jamie Lee.
She was (or had been) an attractive mid-forties Hollywood housewife
who had been involved in a serious car accident about three years
earlier. Although strapped into the vehicle, the force of the collision was
so great that a freakish turn of events had seen the entire dashboard
wrap itself around her head. Several months and a great deal of
reconstructive surgery at Cedar Sinai had kept her alive, but
unfortunately had failed to keep her marriage going, and her Set
Designer husband had absconded to the Hills with an aspiring 22 year
old starlet.
A couple of years of expensive pointless psychiatry had since gone by
before she realised that a positive outlook, good lawyer, and fantastic
Plastic Surgeon were what she really needed to get back to normal.
Having experienced her attitude for himself, and having conducted
several small reconstructive procedures on her, Nolan assumed that she
also had that high-profile lawyer.
- Hello Jamie – he rose up and lightly holding her shoulders kissed her
gently on each bandaged cheek.
Her voice was muffled by the tightly wound facial dressings. She began
to mumble.
- No, don't strain yourself. We'll be hearing you in full chorus shortly -
he beamed.
He leant over and hit the intercom to Annie – Can you pop in to assist
with Mrs Lee's dressings please Annie? -
- If you can just remove your jacket and sit upright on the chair? – He
gestured to the examination chair.
Meekly she took small steps over to the chair, Nolan running a price tag
on her clothes – Jimmy Choo heels - $1,000, Chanel Skirt $450,
Burberry Cashmere Sweater $1,500, Cartier gold wristwatch $9,000.
Looks like the lawyer was doing his job.

Now to confirm Nolan was doing his.

Annie entered the room pulling on surgical gloves.

- Oh Hi Jamie.......- she began, to which Jamie Lee began to mumble again.

- Don't answer – Annie laughed, eyes closed shaking her head from side to side.

Nolan pulled the overhead light directly over her bandaged face and then began to gently cut the crepe bandage up the right hand side of her face.

Annie looked on intently.

Nolan paused and looked directly at Annie.

- Suspense killing you, Miss McDonald? – He asked sarcastically.

Annie just smiled and stared at the crepe bandage.

- Now please keep still and don't worry – he cooed whilst gently cutting the bandage.

He peeled the cut edges away with only a slight adhesion to some light blistering on each cheek, but Nolan knew it was good.

Annie dabbed at the slight abrasions with a pad between tongs.

- There – Nolan pulled away the last traces of the dressing. He then pulled the overhead mirror on the light stand out from behind the light to allow Jamie Lee to view the result.

- Oh Dr Nolan.......she sniffed......you truly are a miracle worker........I could never have believed I could look like this again.........-

Nolan looked up and winked at Annie.

- Oh.....oh.....oh....- she wailed.

- I bet you would cry if you had any tear ducts left – Nolan quipped causing Annie to stagger backwards and Jamie Lee to convulse in fits of laughter.

- Oh Dr Nolan........you are terrible - she mock punched him in the arm.

- If it makes you this happy, then it's all worthwhile. Now I'll just write a small list here of moisturisers and emollients I want you to apply for the next week or so, but with the skin now exposed to the air, healing

will rapidly accelerate. But you must keep out of that sun. Understand?
– He mock punched her in the arm. As he turned back to his desk, he
noticed her rubbing her arm, and realised he had punched her too hard.
He handed the note to Annie, and Jamie got up, kissed both of his
cheeks, and left with promises to invite Nolan and Annie to all manner
of celebrity Hollywood fund raisers.
Annie ushered her down the hall, all the time nodding and agreeing
with Jamie Lee.
Nolan checked his phone. A text message from Phillips. He opened it.
- Sam my man – glad to hear you worked the little problem out with
your credit. Believe all OK – you want any action gimme a call –
So. It would appear Mr & Mrs Marchesi would at least on the surface
be quite happy with what he had done so far. His word was good again.
His *credit* was good again.
Before he could even contemplate the outcome of West Bromwich
Albion's home fixture against Liverpool FC, Annie craned her neck
around the door.
- That really was a good job you did there, Sam. She's always been
quite fragile in all the time she's been coming here, and that's the best
I've seen her. Good on the inside, and now on the outside too – She
mimed the gunshot at him and turned and headed down the hall.
- Five minutes until your 5pm Jane Valentine - she shouted her heels
clacking down the hallway.
Nolan checked his phone again. Nothing.
He twisted the control stock on the blinds moving them to a slight
horizontal position and squinted out into the car park. The sunlight
suddenly glinted on the windscreen reflection of a beat up Ford as it
thundered into the lot before stopping aggressively in the visitor bay.
The door opened as a tall, dark haired girl emerged, casually dressed,
but with style, in complete contrast to her car. All in black with tight
pants and a blazer, she adjusted her sunglasses; causing Nolan to duck
down thinking she had spied his voyeurism. She grabbed her bag from
the car, slammed the door and headed for the clinic.
Minutes later she was ushered in by Annie to Nolan's office. Casual

indifference simply oozed out of her. Nolan couldn't help but admire her attitude and appearance. – Please take a seat Jane. Now I believe my notes here state you are looking to have a tattoo removed? – He smiled and tilted his head.

Without saying a word, she whipped off her blazer, and pulled down the corner of her blouse to reveal not just a delicate floral bra strap, but a huge black ugly tattoo of Steve Carerra and the Black Mass logo.

Nolan had an inward snigger, thinking of Steve Carerra sat in that very chair several days ago, a million miles away from the athletic rock god depicted so graphically on the left shoulder and arm of Miss Jane Doe.

- I'm guessing that Jane Valentine is not your birth name, and I'm also guessing that this tattoo is fairly old? – Nolan queried.

- Right on both counts, Doctor. Abigail Baumgardner wouldn't really cut it in the world of rock groupies, and neither would a tattoo free torso. This abomination was fortunately my only foray into the world of 'ink'. It worked well enough with the band in question, but now I'm all grown up and I'm sick of seeing this in the mirror everyday –

Nolan gently pulled the blouse a little lower and moved the bra strap with the end of his pen.

- Hmmmm. A very solid dark ink has been used, however I can possibly neutralise the ink with a laser and by injecting some skin tone dye just under the epidermis. A skin graft would be too noticeable so I think the laser and dye is the way to go - Nolan returned to his seat and turned the computer monitor toward her.

- I have some footage of a similar procedure I carried out last year for a leg tattoo of Motley Crue. Not as dark as Black Mass, but a significant job nonetheless – He tapped the keyboard then looked up as the video started showing an amply proportioned woman's leg adorned with the Motley Crue Dr Feelgood logo.

In segmented sections of laser treatment the image got fainter and fainter until the final section showed Nolan injecting the leg before the image was completely erased.

- That's a brilliant job Doctor. Several people had recommended you. 'You must go see Dr Tatt-off' – she smiled.

- What a great name – thought Nolan. He pictured the billboards on the freeway showing him along with Jane Valentine before and afters and a giant 'CALL 1-800-TATT-OFF'
- You might have given me an excellent business idea Jane – he humbly mumbled.
- I'm not blowing smoke up your backside, Doctor. You have a real good reputation not just for tattoo removal, but for celebrity look a like surgery –
- Really? – Nolan was genuinely surprised. Then he started to think about all the clients who had been in to consult who wanted to look like Hollywood celebrities. Mrs Campbell who had her nose altered so she looked like Cher, The stupid Polish girl who had the facial injections to look like Angelina Jolie, a man called Kim who had the pectoral implants so his chest matched Schwarzenegger's exactly. He realised he did do a lot of look a like stuff. Hard to do, but extremely well paid. Maybe that was the area to specialise in – If I had a good reputation before for that, just wait till Marianne Marchesi/Cindi Lauper is spotted in Hollywood circles! – he thought to himself.
- So how much will I be for this Doctor? – She pointed at the computer screen.
Momentarily distracted by his new business dream, Nolan now was back in the room.
- I can do this over three visits at $1200 per visit – he asserted.
- Great. She opened her handbag and offered Nolan a white envelope.
-There's $1000 in there and I'll bring the balance on my first visit – She beamed at him as she swung her blazer over her shoulder and strode out of his office. – Thanks Doc – she shouted as she left.
- Annie will schedule your first visit - he shouted after her.
He felt the vibration of a text message on his mobile phone in the drawer. He opened the drawer to reveal 'Madison' He tapped the message – Wanna meet up tonight? Le Monde @ 9.30pm x M – he closed the drawer.
Things were indeed on the up.
His eyes had already alighted on his next patient's file on his desk. An

81

overdone brunette with huge breasts had been photographed from several angles. He started to scan through the notes. Apparently she had handed the photographs in to show her current state. Maybe 45-50, overweight top half, exaggerated by the oversize breasts, too much make-up, dyed brown hair, although a decent job, which indicated a good stylist, always a sign of someone willing to spend on looks. Her legs were spindly and veiney, definitely that of an older woman, and a bizarre juxtaposition with her upper half – A real cut and shut – Nolan sniggered to himself. He imagined somewhere else in Los Angeles there was a slender flat chested woman with huge thick tree trunk legs making an appointment with another surgeon.

Reading through the notes, it turned out she had previously worked in the Adult Film industry, and although no dates were given, Nolan assumed it had been quite a while ago. She lived in one of the better lower avenues of the Hills, so had either been quite good at her 'acting' or had possibly married into money. Either way this was going to be another winner for the Sunnyside Clinic. Turning the page, he realised that in her surgical objectives, she wasn't coming in to have the balloons deflated, and rather she wanted to increase her bust.

- Jesus Christ – he leaned back in the chair then forward again to study the Polaroid photographs of her side on. Despite wearing a very tight top and no bra, it was difficult to ascertain how good a job they were, Nolan shuffling the photographs like some weird deck of cards looking back and forth.

Hearing a car door close in the car park, he looked out just to see Jane Valentine's beat up Ford accelerate out of the lot passing an incoming Mercedes SUV. The Mercedes was gleaming in the sunlight, looking like it was brand new, and coasted to a halt. There was no doubt that this was Astrid Wilders. All Nolan could see was a huge chest, magnified by a blue and white horizontal striped top pulled tight. Her hair was in pigtails and underscored by large black Jackie O sunglasses. She tottered out of the car in heels too high for a weekday, and began the arduous task to walking the twenty feet from her car to the Clinic front door. Like a newborn baby deer she ungracefully staggered across

82

the car park.

- Fashion over comfort. My kind of client – Nolan thought to himself. Annie introduced Astrid Wilders with wide eyed aplomb, clearly unimpressed with the overdone ex-Porn Star. As she tottered into the office, her assorted bracelets, necklaces and chains jangled and chimed as she moved.

- Doctor Nolan – she whined in a Bostonian accent – I've heard so much about yoooouuu – chink, clang as she offered up her hand for a handshake to which Nolan lifted to his lips and lightly kissed whilst looking directly at her. That always broke the ice.

- Ohhhh – clink, clang, chink as she lifted her other hand to her ample chest.

- That's so gentlemanly. They don't do stuff like that no more, do they? – She directed at Annie.

- No indeed – said Annie looking at the floor and backing out of the room, closing the door as she left.

- Well I must say Doctor Nolan you're even better looking than your website photograph – she drawled as she backed down into the consultation chair.

- Flattery will get you everywhere – Nolan dryly retorted, looking over the top of his spectacles.

This sent her into a laugh cycle, possibly the most irritating laugh he had ever heard.

He made a mental note to keep the quips and jokes to a minimum.

- Now my notes here tell me that you want to *increase* your chest, Mrs Wilders? – He diverted his gaze to her stretched top.

- Please call me Astrid, Doctor. Yes, I have an exciting career opportunity that depends on it –

Nolan thought about asking what possible 'career opportunity' could depend on having size 44K breasts, however thought the better of it.

- You see I've heard of this procedure where you can fit an inflatable device that allows me to pump them up or down as required – She reached into her handbag and presented Nolan with a sheaf of paper.

- I printed that off the internet…..you're bound to have heard of it – she

83

relaxed back in the chair.

- This is a system for reconstructive surgery Astrid….like for someone disfigured in a car accident, or after breast cancer mastectomy….it's not designed for……well, *recreational* surgery –

- Look at the article Doctor. That girl hasn't had any of those things. And she's making a fortune! There's no reason why I can't get those, in fact, I'm a prime candidate – she cupped her breasts and smiled.

- Astrid…….it's on a moral plane as well. I wouldn't be doing my job if I was to agree to a procedure that possibly could have a negative impact on your quality of life….-

- Quality of life? Quality of life? – She interjected quite forcefully, causing Nolan to start back.

- I'm fifty-four, Doctor - Really? I was thinking sixty-four - Nolan thought to himself - All I've been able to do in life has been in the Adult film industry. I can't suddenly decide to be a secretary or a nurse. I've been fortunate this far, and now I have get something that sets me apart. Having the Biggest Breasts in LA would allow me to get another couple of years out of it. Who knows, maybe a husband! – She started her irritating cackling again – I'm aware this type of work is very specialised, and after doing my research, your name and clinic kept coming up again and again. I know as well that I could probably get this done in Mexico for under $10,000, maybe even in this town for under $20,000, but I have all my money here Doctor – she produced a large brown envelope bulging and brimming with cash.

Nolan's eyes lit up.

- I have $25,000 here Doctor. It's all I have, but I'm putting all my money and all my faith in you Doctor Nolan –

In the nanosecond it took him to agree, he remembered to inform her that she would be personally and exclusively liable, and that she would be required to sign disclaimers to this effect.

Once she had finally regained her composure, and stopped thanking him, Nolan ushered her towards the door, she tottered Bambi style over to him to cuddle him, tears in her eyes, and he felt the full 1,000 millilitres of saline in each breast squash against his chest.

- Goodbye Doctor, I won't forget this – she tearfully blubbed heading down the corridor.

Letting out a long sigh, Nolan opened the next file on his desk.

- Oh good. The freak who wants his dick off – he gently shook his head from side to side.

- But he's paying sweetly for it – chimed Annie at the door.

- Did I say that out loud? – He asked, genuinely shocked.

- Yesirree – Annie bounced around the room looking for something.

- Can I help you? – He snapped with a hint of irritation.

- Have you seen the Ethicon rep's business card? I appear to have misplaced it – she ditted about looking high and low.

- Yes it's here in the bin – he reached under the desk and brought up a waste bin brimming with trash – Along with your dignity if you're chasing after younger guys like him – he winked at her.

The pee-poh of the door opener sounded heralding the arrival of Demon Daniels.

Annie snatched the bin from him and headed off to greet the patient.

Nolan sighed, stood up, and lifted his scrubs and headed for pre-op.

- I'm not in the right frame of mind for lunatics today – he thought as he heard the clumping of Daniels' oversize moon boots approaching the room.

Sporting a purple Mohican wig and 80's wrap around black shades, Demon Daniels entered the small brightly-lit room.

Annie proffered greetings and stilted introductions.

Nolan shook his hand and pointed to the changing cubicle and asked him to undress.

- Please take everything off, Demon. All rings, piercings, jewellery, 'attachments'.......his voice tailed off.

After what seemed like an inordinate amount of time, a completely unrecognisable small boy child emerged from the cubicle. Lean, shaven headed, and without a hair on his body, it looked like he was on his way to his goal.

-I'm afraid the underpants must come off too, Demon – he jokily instructed before looking back at his notes.

Nolan then noticed out of the corner of his eye that Annie was staring at the patient.

- Annie, perhaps you could prepare the pre-med? – He asked politely. Her gaze still didn't avert.

- Annie. Annie – he hissed.

He then turned to a naked Demon Daniels standing nervously looking at the gas canisters fixed to the wall.

Nolan was not often shocked, but his eyes alighted on Daniels and went down to his groin, where one of the largest, most perfectly formed penises hung perfectly on his small frame.

Annie's face had reddened and she muttered her excuses as she pulled on her latex gloves and began turning the gas canisters on and checking the gauges.

Nolan pulled over the inspection lamp from the ceiling and shone it onto Daniels. Dropping to a crouched position, he gently held the magnificent specimen of manhood gingerly in his gloved hands. Turning it over and from side to side, it was clear there were no imperfections, no stain on this model of masculinity.

- Are you sure about this Demon? That really is one hell of a huge……..-

- Completely sure Doctor Nolan – he interrupted - Even two of our female roadies tried to talk me out of this at the weekend, but my mind is made up – he haughtily folded his arms and strode over to the operating table and lay down.

Nolan was already wondering if he could preserve this thing, hell, he would love to graft this onto himself!

- No, no, no - he thought to himself – must stick to the surgical plan! - He could see the pain in Annie's eyes as the anaesthetist walked in and offered the mask to Daniels and asked him to count backward from twenty.

He slipped into unconsciousness and Annie wheeled the bed through the swing doors into theatre.

- Nolan waltzed through and flicked on the music. Malcolm McLaren's Blue Danube Waltz began to immerse the room. Nolan began marking

86

the body with black marker lines.
- What a waste, eh Annie? – He joked.
- See when I saw the little freak without all the crap on his face and without all the leather and clumpy boots, just naked and stripped back, I wanted to mother him, to look after him. He looked so *fragile*.......but when *that* fell out of his pants......Wow – her eyes widened.
- I could fancy him you know? I could. But just like everything else in my life, it's going to get taken away from me – she turned away.
- Oh come on Annie. If you're a good little helper today, I'll maybe let you take the dick home with you – he laughed heartily – And you could inject a little Botox if you felt it was a bit on the small side – He giggled closing his eyes tightly.
Annie's face broke into a grin as even the anaesthetist turned her face away, her body heaving with laughter.
- Right. Let's get it on. Or in this case, let's get it off – he lifted the scalpel, examined its flawless edge and began to cut.
Four hours later, Annie wheeled the bed through to post op, and Nolan stripped off his bloody scrubs and headed to the shower.
After a long cool shower, he towelled himself dry then applied some Armani Original.
The lemony fragrance was the perfect re-invigorator after four hours of complex intricate genital surgery.
He checked his phone to discover several missed calls from Marianne Marchesi. His blood ran cold. What had happened to warrant so many calls? What was the problem?
There was a text.
- Calm down - He said to himself. If it had been bad, those hoods would have barged their way in here and dragged him up to the Hills. He opened the text.
' Please don't get angry.....I took the dressings off a little bit to have a look Sam, as my husband was very keen to see the end result. I tried calling several times but you must be busy making other women beautiful too. We are so happy with this Sam. So, so, so happy. Salvatore and myself want to thank you personally, and we would love

to take you to dinner next Saturday at Courtesan – Please give me a call when you can – Marianne xxx '

Courtesan was the coolest, hippest restaurant in Beverley Hills and it was rumoured to have a six-month waiting list for bookings – I guess the Marchesi's frighten them too – he thought to himself, imagining himself striding out of a limousine up the little red carpet and rope fences at Courtesan.

He popped the phone into his pocket, and headed off out to meet Madison at Le Monde, absolutely brimming with confidence.

Chapter 5
Waiting For A Miracle

Dry mouth. Dull ache behind ears. Another hang-over.
As he lay on his side in bed peering at the chink of light between the curtains, Nolan began to forensically piece together his movements of the previous night.
There had been the few après surgery drinks at Crumbs down on Sunset, where he had fallen in with a couple of med students who recognised him from the clinic website. He had managed to get fleeced for several rounds of drinks before he had to split to meet Madison at the Le Monde. He wanted to be cool and turn up fashionably late, but unfortunately, Madison was more fashionable than he was, causing him to have several drinks before she arrived almost one hour later.
Then he remembered the tight turn to the Valet at the Le Monde and he had clipped a small Volvo parked outside as he made the turn. Acknowledging that the smell of those Canadian Clubs on his breath might get someone nervous enough to call the police, he had given the Valet and the Bellhop $200 to hide the Porsche in a darkened spot in the garage and blame some hit and run.
Madison had been her usual gorgeous self, and after a meal and drinks they had taxied back to Nolan's where he had cracked out the Vintage special occasion Champagne.
He couldn't remember how the night had ended………
He turned round in the bed to come nose to nose with Madison. He was startled and pulled back suddenly causing her to rouse from her slumber.
- Sammmmm…………hey……- she sleepily opened her eyes. Some hair fell across her face.
- Hey sweetheart……how you feeling? – He leant under the bed and produced a bottle of Evian and offered it to her.
They shared the lukewarm water and Nolan felt the hangover start to lift.

- C'mon. Shake your tail and I'll take you to this little hipster breakfast place – she teased jumping naked out of bed and then a hop, step, and jump into the bathroom.

She finished up in the shower and emerged in neat bright sportswear.

- I took the liberty of leaving an overnight bag here. I hope you don't mind? - She coyly half-whispered, standing framed in the doorway hand on hip.

- No, no, no, not at all…....- Nolan was stammering and stuttering. She was definitely one of the best looking women he had ever been involved with.

He stumbled into the shower holding his shirt from the previous night over his groin.

She laughed and started to make the bed.

Once he was ready, he remembered the car was at the Le Monde with probably some scratches over the front wing.

He called a cab and within minutes they were on their way. At the Le Monde garage, Alphonse the Valet was listening to music with his headphones in. Nolan noticed the Volvo was no longer at the front door. Alphonse coolly took his headphones out as Nolan and Madison approached.

- Hey Doctor Nolan. I'll just go git your car – He winked conspiratorially at Nolan.

Nolan pulled Madison close to him with his arm round her waist. The sun was shining through the Cherry Blossom trees on the Avenue, and Nolan felt in control.

The roar of the flat six engine up in the garage caused the birds on the trees to fly off,

and the Porsche stuck its sleek nose out of the garage entrance.

Alphonse got out of the car and held the door open for Madison all the time keeping eye contact. Nolan wandered round to the driver's side, casually checking the handful of small scratches on the wing and the light damage to the alloy wheel. With Madison safely inside the car and the growl of the idling engine, Alphonse confirmed that he had applied paint remover to the damage, however Porsche dealership work was going to be required to bring the car up to Nolan's immaculate standard. He slipped Alphonse another $50 and they drove off.

- Okay Madison, where am I going? I am starving, so this better not be one of those hippy Vegan eco ethical nut-only restaurants –
She laughed – No Sam, its hipster, but it does have the best Bacon and Avocado open breakfast sandwiches I've ever tasted. Head over to the Convention Centre area. It's near there –
As they slipped onto the freeway, they were immediately slowed by Saturday traffic.
Forty minutes later they were crawling the streets nearby the Convention Centre.

- I'm sure it's about here......- her voice tailed off, looking left and right.
- What's it called? – He asked.
- Seven Grand –
- That better not be an indication about the price – he retorted.
He turned the corner and found the restaurant. There was fortunately parking at the rear. Once parked they headed round the block to the front door.
Hand in hand they strode along the wide leafy avenue, when suddenly something on one of the billboards took his attention.

- I don't believe it.......I simply don't believe it.......- He let go Madison's hand and ran over to one of the many neatly framed posters lining the road announcing events and attractions at the Convention Centre and the Staples Centre.
-.........It can't be.......surely......-
Madison came up behind him and put her arms around his waist.

- Whatcha lookin' at Sam? – She playfully asked.
- I don't believe it.......Doctor Mike! My old room mate and pal from Edinburgh University all those years ago! He's giving some talk here today on Molecular Regeneration Therapy.......'the power to heal from any damage if so much as one cell remains'.... Wow. We have to go. We must go. It doesn't start till 2pm, so let's go get breakfast first.......Jesus, Dr Mike! –

They headed off with Nolan still shaking his head and smiling – Dr Mike……Dr Mike…..-

After a genuinely magnificent Bacon and Avocado open sandwich just as Madison had promised, a couple of espressos to straighten them out, they left the restaurant, fortunately the check not living up to the establishment's name.

Crossing the road in the sun, they headed for Convention Centre. There was a small queue outside the auditorium where the talk was taking place.

Two attendants stood issuing lapel badges and checking off a sheet.

- Ah yes. Two spaces for Dr Nolan of the Sunnyside Clinic – he asserted.

Madison gave a suppressed giggle at the blatant lie.

- There doesn't appear to be your name on this list Dr Nolan? – The small Chinese guy began running his pen up and down a fairly small list of attendees.

- I can assure you that my secretary booked these a number of weeks ago – he sounded more impatient.

Looking at the attendee list upside down, he counted 28 names.

- For goodness sake - You have 28 attendees in a 1000 – Seater auditorium. I don't think we're taking anyone's seat – he impatiently snapped.

The young girl attendant was also very flustered. Nolan slipped her a $20 note.

- You kids run along now and get yourself a couple of Chai soy decaf lattes or whatever floats your boat –

He pushed his way past them and into the auditorium.

Nolan was surprised to see the giant photo of Mike on the stage screen background.

- Is that him? – enquired Madison.

- Yeah……he's not aged well. It must be twenty years since I've seen him. He was a good mate, soft, but a good mate - He reflected mournfully.

- So what happened to you guys? – She leant over to him.

92

- Just grew apart. He was my best man at my wedding in Edinburgh, but he never sent an Anniversary Card each year as you would expect a Best Man to do. He was always more absorbed in his work. We were thick as thieves at University, and right up to the point when I got married.......After that, any gigs I would go to with our other friends, I always invited him, but he always had an excuse not to go. After a while, I guess I stopped asking, and he stopped answering......He came to Sarah's Christening, but just showed up, dropped off a present, and I noticed a short while later he had left. When I left to go to the States, we had a small farewell party to which he was invited, but he didn't show. I don't know if he's married, or if he has kids, or what's he's doing. I figured he didn't want to know me, or that I had massively over valued our friendship. But here he is! – Nolan pointed to the stage as the lights dimmed and Dr Mike tentatively edged onto the stage. Gingerly he began to address the small audience, and introduced himself as Dr Michael Richardson of The Ingleside Institute, Edinburgh, Scotland.

- Good Afternoon. When I left University in Edinburgh, as a keen twenty-four year old, I had a vision of what could be done when I had seen the DNA Double Helix of Watson and Crick.

Here were the very building blocks of life, and yet we had only begun to imagine what possibilities were out there. Many of you out there will have followed my career which such blockbusting papers as '*Discovery of Western European R1b1a2Y Chromosome Variants in 1000 Genomes*' and '*A Novel Multiplex for Simultaneous Amplification of Chromosome STR Markers*' – he announced sarcastically, causing a murmur of laughter in the audience.

However, it was not until I took up residency at the Roslin Institute near Edinburgh in the capacity of mad scientist in residence, that I was given free reign to follow my dream. That dream as you know, was realised on 5th July, 1996, with the birth of Dolly the Sheep, the first living creature to be cloned from genetic material. My patented procedure of Somatic Cell Nuclear Transfer was now on the front page of every newspaper in the world. This truly was the Premier League. As a poor student in Edinburgh in the 80's, I had imagined a method by which we could replace imperfection, faulty DNA, and recreate genetic material from a desired host.

My celebrity, however was not to last. The Institute wanted to rest on its laurels, take it easy, after the hard work had all been done, and we could all dine out on this for the rest of our lives. My attitude was that this was simply the first step. I had much grander plans and theories to test out and experiment. This was making the Patrons and Directors of the Institute very nervous, and within 12 months of the ground breaking birth of Dolly, I was unemployed. Regarded as a Quack, a Renegade, and a Maverick. Sure, I had offers. Minsk, Pretoria, Buenos Aires. But that just wasn't going to cut it. So, I built a custom-made facility myself, outside Edinburgh to rival Roslin. Every grant, lottery fund, potential donor was hunted down and shaken down for their cash. Between their donations and my family's not inconsiderable wealth, we opened The Ingleside Institute in 1998. Along with my team of Dr Blair and Dr Stevens, we have now developed the subject of today's presentation.

I must warn you, that before I continue, you must ditch all of your pre-conceived notions and establishment concepts of right and wrong, moral and immoral.

This is not playing at God. This truly is *being* God –

There was a small smattering of applause which he acknowledged with a small bow. He turned around and began fiddling awkwardly with a remote control.

He gave up and reached over and started a film clip on the large screen which began with fields of cows and sheep.

- Once we had the technology to clone food cycle animals, we had then turned our efforts to reduce birth and genetic defects in the same field, thus eradicating imperfections, disabilities, and undesirable elements. In addition to this, the animals themselves had a better life cycle and maximised the financial value of the species in question. This of course, was of massive interest to the farming community, as this would maximise their potential for profit. This was achieved in early 2000;

however it was a small accident within the confines of the laboratory that truly changed my world. As with most major discoveries, they happen by accident, not design. We had started to develop small creatures who would host the desired DNA structures up to the point where they could then be transplanted to the subject. For instance, we would propagate bovine kidney cells in a mouse, and at the correct term of maturity, transfer these to the cow with the deficient kidney. In true mad professor style, a number of subjects were left to longer terms, and we discovered that the organ in question would physically start to grow on the subject as an independent organ. When it was obvious that these small carrier mice were struggling under the burden of a cow's liver growing on their body, we would then euthanize them by means of a fatal dose of microwave radiation. It was decided to do this at intervals to establish the optimum period of support for both donor and donor organ. We did not establish this, however. When the first specimen was due to be euthanized, Dr Blair had set the incorrect level of microwave radiation, and the specimen in question did die, but the organ became fully formed and functional, as if basically freshly removed from a donor cow. A six-month development of the organ had taken place in minutes. The organ was immediately stored and later transplanted successfully. This then led us to experiment with other creatures and to cross mix interspecies. After two years of intense work, we now have the most developed molecular regeneration therapy from donor DNA. No longer do we have to think of cell restructuring and modification as long-winded analogue algorithms.

We are now truly linear. We are now truly in the future. We are now truly digital. We call this 'The Digital DNA' – Mike stepped backward to applause from the crowd, as images of oversize mice and rats with cow's tails and pigs' noses grotesquely growing on their backs filled the screen.

Mike hushed the audience down and continued his lecture regarding industry ethics, the need for regulation, and the endless possibilities of food chain animal replication on an industrial scale. Then came a pitch for funding. It was obvious at this point that the majority of the audience were specially selected funders from California's Biotech community. Nolan however was blown away.

At the end of the lecture, Dr Mike made his way over to a group of medical research types standing the coffee bar in the foyer. They patted him on the back and toasted him with their soy lattes.

Nolan approached the group huddled around Dr Mike.

- Could you top mine up with some stem cells please? – Nolan shouted over the hubbub.

Clearly irritated by the tone and poor choice of subject matter, Dr Mike turned around indignant. The scowl however, quickly turned to a wide smile as he recognised his old friend.

- Oh my days. Sam! How the heck are you! – He nudged some bespeckled undergraduates out of the way to grab Nolan's hand and shake it enthusiastically.

- How long has it been Sam? God…….I heard you had moved out here with Jane…….- his voice tailed off as his eyes noticed that Madison had her right arm around Nolan's waist.

- That's right Dr Mike. It was maybe '93/'94 that we made the move. And no, this isn't Jane – they all laughed politely.

- Listen I have to go meet with a couple of funder groups in the suites upstairs, but if you guys were free for something to eat later, I'd love to have familiar company and a catch up. I'm not enjoying the antiseptic Holiday Inn environment. But only if you guys are free? – Dr Mike looked at them pleadingly.

- Well Doctor – he lifted the name tag on Dr Mike's shirt - …..Richardson…..that seems like an offer we couldn't possibly refuse. Could we Madison? – Nolan looked at Madison, his head cocked.

- Madison. What a lovely name – interjected Dr Mike.

- Damn. Sorry. In all my excitement of seeing you again, I completely forgot introductions. Madison Scott, my girlfriend of 48 hours, I give you Dr Mike Richardson, my friend of 36 years – Nolan split a wide smile.

- Delighted – Dr Mike shook Madison's hand – And now I really must go earn my corn. Where will I meet you guys? – He started to slowly pace backwards.

- We'll come find you at the Convention Centre Holiday Inn. Say 7.30? – asked Nolan.
- Perfect – Dr Mike turned and waved in the air as he walked away, excited young under graduates scampering after him.
- That is so incredible – Nolan stood, hands on hips, shaking his head.
- I know. Twenty odd years since you've seen him – Madison chimed in.
- No. That a dork like him, with zero personality, and average grades could come up with something so brilliant...... – he grabbed Madison's hand and they headed out of the building.
Later, as dusk fell, Nolan's Porsche crept up into the Entrance Foyer. Dr Mike was standing waiting at the door, hands in pockets wearing what looked like to Nolan charity shop cords and a hideous tweed blazer. He clocked it was Nolan in the car, and waved frantically as he ran over.
Nolan lowered the passenger window and leant over - Taxi for Dr Mike? –
Dr Mike laughed and hopped into the car, looking all around at its cool, sleek interior.
- It's apparently the perfect symbiosis of man-made and natural materials in a celebration of speed and triumph over adversity..........or so the Porsche salesman said – Nolan grinned.
- Gluing bits onto ageing celebrities must pay well out here –
- It certainly does -
- Madison not joining us? – Dr Mike enquired innocently.
- No she's got some *thing* on.......- Nolan waved his hands absentmindedly – But I thought it better we had a good old catch up ourselves bud – he playfully punched Dr Mike on the upper arm, but judging by the look on his face, it had maybe been a little too hard.
Nolan laughed and floored the accelerator causing the Porsche to leap out of the foyer unloading area, and the bellhop to jump back onto the pavement.
- I thought we could just hang out and have a few beers at one of my favourite places in Hollywood – Nolan offered, as they sped along the freeway.

Dr Mike nodded in agreement, his low voice possibly useless in competition with the Cult's 'She Sells Sanctuary' blasting out of the car stereo.

- It's called Le Monde – Nolan stated.

- What is? – Dr Mike looked puzzled.

- The hotel where we're going. It first attracted me because of the name, thought it might remind me of home, but it turns out it's the polar extreme of home. Makes you forget bloody Scotland! – Nolan laughed again.

This time as they approached, Nolan kept a considerable distance from the other vehicles outside the Hotel. As he stopped the car to give the keys to the Valet, it was obvious he was blocking the road, as the SUV behind them honked their horn.

- I see your driving hasn't improved – quipped Dr Mike exiting the car. The valet swapped over with Nolan and gingerly eased the Porsche into the garage.

The driver of the SUV rolled down his window and shouted obscenities as Nolan casually strolled towards the lobby with Dr Mike. Nolan smiled and waved at the SUV. They continued to walk in the front door, catching just a brief 'asshole' shouted way in the distance as the SUV roared off.

- Now that part is very similar to Scotland! – Dr Mike laughed shaking his head.

They headed to the Bar & Grill on the first floor, and before long were seated in one of the candle lit booths with beers and steaks.

Every time the lithe young waitress walked past or checked on them, Dr Mike paused mid sentence and followed her with his eyes.

- Why are they all so good looking here? – He shook his head in disbelief.

- I'm a great believer that our miserable climate, miserable upbringing, miserable attitude and ultimately miserable existence in Scotland, all eventually expresses itself physically in our exterior – Nolan casually remarked.- That's very easy for a Plastic Surgeon to say. So why didn't you stay in Scotland where there is clearly a bigger market for you to ply your trade? - Dr Mike retorted.

Nolan made the thumb and forefinger rubbing gesture.

- Money. Moolah. Spondoolicks. Dough. Cash. I can perform one procedure here for the right client that can keep me for three months. Back home they would rather stay ugly than pay. I did some low-grade cheap work before we came out here, but patients too moany, too cheap, too bloody desperate, Mike – Nolan looked down at the table – But what about you? I listened to that talk today, and you know what? I was sold. Me. The most cynical disbelieving son of a bitch you could meet. What you are doing Mike, is genius. And I don't use that word lightly. Genius – he sat back and stared at Dr Mike.

- A toast – he offered up his bottle of Peroni – A toast to one of my oldest mates and his brilliant work – Dr Mike sheepishly lifted his bottle to clink with Nolan's, conscious that the drunker they had become, the louder their voices had become, and the other customers in the bar were looking over at their table, with a couple of guys lifting their bottles too shouting 'Cheers'.

They shot the breeze for another several beers, going over relationships, music, common acquaintances, etc.

Still every time the waitress freshened their drinks, Dr Mike goofily followed her with his eyes.

- Seriously though Mike, it is great to see you again……..and well, you've humbled me with your fantastic work – Nolan sat back.

- Goodness. I had no idea my work was of such profound interest to you. As you will have heard in the speech, it's been a bit of a struggle financially, and getting people to take you seriously. I do believe, - Dr Mike's eyes were drooping slightly and he was slightly slurring his words after six Peronis – That life will offer you one huge opportunity, more if you're lucky, but that one huge opportunity you must grab with both hands and run like mad with it. I had mine, and I like to think I've done pretty well – Nolan leaned forward - Mike, you are spot on. But this is where your second huge opportunity is about present itself to you – Dr Mike looked puzzled and leaned in conspiratorially.

- When are you going back to Edinburgh? – Nolan enquired.

- My ticket is for the day after tomorrow, but it's an open ticket. I can hang around a bit longer if you're up for it? Not as if I've anything to hurry back for – he looked mournfully to the side.

Nolan grabbed his shoulders. – I've had the most fantastic idea. It came to me when I was listening to your speech. How do you fancy getting the band back together Mike? I mean like really go for it here. Me and you. Me and you – he pointed at them in turn.

Dr Mike looked puzzled. – But I'm not a surgeon……..in fact the sight of humans being operated on makes my knees go funny……Dr Mike's voice tailed off.

- Let's just say, for argument's sake, that we set up your Digital DNA laboratory here in Los Angeles – Dr Mike brightened up instantly – That's why I'm fund raising, Sam, to keep my own lab back in Edinburgh going –

- Why the hell would you want to go back to the drizzle and all the unhappiness? –

Just as Nolan asked him, the young waitress sashayed past their table, Dr Mike's eyes immediately attaching to her bottom.

- Just think of seeing her every day – he gestured in the direction of the waitress – and the weather! This is your chance, Mike. What do you have waiting back home for you except a tax bill and a heap of grief. Out here we could make *history!* Let's just imagine that we get your lab up and running here in L.A., and between your ability to create micro – millimetre exact body parts and characteristics, and my surgical ability, we could be millionaires! – Nolan's voice was now getting excited.

Dr Mike tilted his head to the side in slight drunken puzzlement.

- You want to farm DNA? – Dr Mike looked shocked – I mean, never mind all the ethical arguments and complications, that wasn't what I wanted this used for. I wanted this to be used for the betterment of humanity –

- And what betterment than making rich people feel and look better whilst getting paid phenomenal money for it! Listen Mike; there are literally thousands of Plastic Surgeons here in the greater Los Angeles area. Every day I have to fight for my scraps. My place in the queue.

Granted we get our share, and hell, yes sometimes I make a good few dollars, and maybe have a steak. But once you have something so new, something so desirable, and so goddamn sexy, then you can charge what you like. There are no morals here, Mike. No scruples, no ethical argument. That all goes out the window. This place is a money factory, Mike, and we have the keys – he sat back in the chair and swigged on his bottle of Peroni.

Dr Mike was rubbing his hand on his brow.

- I don't know Sam. This……this…..this scheme just feels like I'd be taking a different turn in my life –

Sensing a slight warming, Nolan moved in for the kill.

- You're spot on Mike. You'd be taking the turn down Dr Mike Boulevard. A Boulevard paved in gold where the only cars were Rolls Royce's and all the women had butts like little Julia there – he waved over at the waitress – this is soooo do-able.

Just like Lennon & McCartney, Jagger & Richards, Rotten & Matlock, opposites coming together for the greater good. It happens in all great teams and partnerships. It's the sparks that start the fire. No use if we're all the same. This can, nay, will be huge –

- You sure, Sam? As much as you may want it to be, it's not 1986. I've been on my own a long time, devoting everything to my work. I mean, you've at least got something here – He looked pained.

- Yes I do. And now it can be yours too! Like you said, these opportunities only come along once or twice in a lifetime. This isn't just for you, Mike, it's for me too. I've been running on empty for a while – his head bowed – Since Jane and Sarah left, I've been rudderless, filling my time with drinking, going out, having meaningless sexual encounters with vapid, beautiful women –

Dr Mike let out a whimper.

- It's this place, Mike. When things are good, it's great. When things are bad, they're awful. I know it sounds corny, but I have been waiting on something like this happening to me. It was fate, Mike. I'd never have gone to that poseur's paradise for brunch. It was Madison who wanted to go there, a girl I met a couple of days ago. If I hadn't been going to that restaurant, I wouldn't have seen your poster, and I wouldn't have met you again. You see? It was meant to be! – he implored.

- It does sound appealing. I've nothing back home. My Dad's dead, my ninety year-old Mother is in a Senile Dementia ward, and hasn't opened her eyes or spoken for three years. The change *would* do me good. Like you, I've been in limbo. No friends, no relationships, just work – He sat back and looked up at the ceiling.

Nolan grabbed his hand - That's why it's time –

- You sure this works financially? You think there's enough people in Los Angeles who would come? – he quizzed.

- Are you kidding? For what we can offer? The accelerated recovery time alone would have us the top place in the city, never mind the flawless look-a-like surgery. It's all I hear in consultations – 'Give me a nose like so and so' and ' Give me boobs like what's her name' and 'Make me look like Marlon Brando in The Wild One'. It is literally all these people think about – he looked around the bar.

- Listen – He gestured to the waitress who sexily strolled up to the table.

- Another round guys? – She smiled, lifting the empty bottles.

- Yes, another two please Julia. I hope you don't mind me asking you a personal question? - Nolan enquired.

- Depends – she smiled directly at Dr Mike causing him to blush slightly.

- Have you ever had any work done? - Nolan quizzed directly.

- Wow. You mean like surgery? - She looked slightly taken aback by Nolan's directness.

- It's OK. You don't have to answer, it's just my friend here……..We're both Doctors and we're thinking of a new business -

- So, well back in 2010 I had just come out of a relationship that wasn't very good for me, so I went on a diet then had these – She cupped her own breasts – Given a little help against our enemy, gravity – she giggled - And then I had a little eyelid tuck to freshen my face up – she leaned on towards them to let them see, almost causing Dr Mike to fall off his seat – and I guess that's about it – She flashed a smile at Dr Mike directly again.

- Beautiful – cooed Nolan, nodding his head.

- So, do you see yourself having any future surgical adventures? – Dr Mike now asked.

- If my numbers come up I would looooove to get some other work done….maybe some anti cellulite treatments…… - she then looked up at the ceiling, deep in concentration.

- Is there anyone that you would want to look like? – Nolan interjected.

- Oh my God yes! I've always thought I look a bit like Demi Moore back in her 'Striptease' days…..not her 'G.I.Jane' days – she paused – But their daughter is so cool, so yeah probably Demi……or see when I was reading some of the Hollywood magazines, there was this British girl who's dating the James Bond guy? Well, turns out she's like Royalty or something but didn't find out till she was 30 or something? She has the most beautiful face………if only I had some of that Royal blood………..-

- Just some of that Royal DNA? – queried Nolan.

- Oh my god yes – she fired back.

Nolan shot a 'told you so' look at Dr Mike.

Dr Mike re-arranged himself in his seat – I think I'd better get off to bed…..I'm feeling a little light headed – he sidled out of the booth slightly staggering as he exited before holding onto the edge of the table.

- I guess that'll be the check then, Julia – Nolan reclined back as the waitress headed off to the bar.

- So, Mike, do you have a shopping list for what you would need for you to set up here? –

- I have the wish list I paraded to the sponsors at the event today, which I suppose would be the starting point. I'd have to get some of the equipment shipped over from Scotland, but I could get everything together in a couple of weeks. All I would need to get going is about $50k and 250 square metres – Dr Mike drunkenly smiled.- The space is no problem at the Sunnyside Clinic – Nolan looked thoughtful - the

103

$50k might take a little bit longer.......You have any money? –
- Maybe $25k at a push in some crap Bank Account back home.
Certainly not enough to get us going. I thought you were the hot-shot
celebrity surgeon? –
- Funny you say that. I have a surgery tomorrow afternoon at 1pm. It
may just be the answer to our situation. You free to observe? –
- What type is it? I couldn't stand a full-on blood and guts job – Dr
Mike laughed.
- It's just a little Lipo on a middle-aged guy. Nothing heavy. But it
might just get us the extra money we need – Nolan rose from the booth
putting a handful of dollar bills into the check.
- Wow. You must be too well paid if you're getting $25k for a little bit
of Lipo? – Dr Mike looked incredulous.
- You'll see – Nolan put his arm around Dr Mike, winked at the
waitress and headed down to the waiting taxi.
They arrived at Nolan's house 30 minutes later, Dr Mike clearly
impressed with the
Tesla electric taxi that made no sound. As they entered the vestibule and
the discreet lighting came on all around the house, Dr Mike gasped in
astonishment and drank in the view of the interior of the house. Quiet
music began to play in the background, and the TV screens sprang into
life.
 He was truly speechless as they ascended the open plan stair to the
mezzanine level lounge where the extensive glass doors framed the
twinkling lights of Los Angeles off in the distance.
- You have come a long way from our little student flat in Leith – Dr
Mike muttered, looking around in all directions.
 - Yeah, well this is the material side, Mike, unfortunately this lifestyle
has a price out here, and it's not just in money. I'm now not so sure I
was ready to pay that price – he reached into the fridge and pulled out
two cans of Pabst Blue Ribbon – a wee nightcap? - He held them up in
the air.
They reclined back in the sofa, side by side, sipping on their beers.
- You know I saw Bruno the other week? – Nolan offered.

- That stoner from University? Where on earth did you see him? – Dr Mike drunkenly exclaimed, his eyes half shut.
- Being a stoner – laughed Nolan – No, really, he has a lovely beach apartment, does nothing all day but deal and smoke drugs. He occasionally allows young nubile girls to settle their debt with him sexually, but yeah, that's Bruno. He made being a waster a career choice. I'm actually quite envious sometimes – he looked along at Dr Mike, who had fallen asleep, his head off to one side, but still clutching his beer can.
Nolan lifted the can from his grasp, turned out the light and headed off to bed.

Another morning, another hang-over.
Easing out of bed and over to his night-before discarded crumpled blazer, Nolan fished the bleeping phone from the pocket and silenced it. He showered then headed through to the spare room where Dr Mike was standing in the middle of the floor in his underpants looking confused. Clearly sporting a raging hang-over, Nolan guided him to the shower, turned on the water, and pushed him in.
- I'll go get you a hang-over breakfast – he shouted into the steamy room as he closed the door and switched on the extractor fan.
Twenty minutes later Dr Mike tentatively crept into the kitchen.
- Jesus Christ! – Exclaimed Nolan – Creeping Jesus! Don't give me a fright like that! – Dr Mike lifted his hands in acknowledgement and sat at the breakfast bar and began drinking the fresh orange juice laid out for him.
- Now here's a Full Californian for you – quipped Nolan, pushing a plate full of food in front of a distinctly queasy looking Dr Mike.
- Basically it's the same as a Full Scottish, eggs, bacon, sausage, beans, toast, but I add a wee bit of avocado on the top and it becomes a Full Californian – Nolan did a tah-dah gesture causing Dr Mike to giggle.
- Get that down you and we'll head to the clinic for today's surgery.

The surgery that's going to pay for the Digital DNA! – Nolan started tucking in enthusiastically to his plate, over emphasising his chewing motion, a la Clockwork Orange.

Half an hour later they were in the Porsche speeding along the freeway, with both windows down, the soft Californian air cosseting their hair.

- You still haven't told me why you think this small procedure is going to be so well paid today, Sam? – Dr Mike enquired, the hair blowing all over his face.

- At ten am today, Dr Mike, we are going to perform a gentle liposuction and abdomen resculpting on a famous musician. He has already deposited the $14,000 surgical fee for this two hour standard procedure, and by the time we're done and dusted, we can be at Crumbs at Sunset Plaza for the late lunch special at 3pm – Nolan flashed his teeth and raised his Armani sunglasses to wink at Dr Mike.

They pulled up to the clinic, and Nolan strode through the door purposefully, Dr Mike tentatively following.

- This, - He gestured to Annie, bent over deep in conversation with Bored Receptionist, - is Annie. Annie keeps me right. Annie makes me tick. Annie does not find me attractive in any way, shape or form - Dr Mike managed an awkward smile and shook her hand – And this is……..eh…..eh…..thingy…… – he pointed at Bored Receptionist.

- Courtney – corrected Annie impatiently – Never mind sweetheart – she cooed at Bored Receptionist who looked wounded.

- This is my best friend in life, Dr Mike. No surname, just Dr Mike. A colleague and fellow student of The University of Edinburgh, Scotland – Nolan strode on toward his office, Dr Mike making apologies whilst walking backwards and nodding – Yes….yes….lovely to meet you…..yes –

- Take a seat – Nolan indicated to Dr Mike.

Annie entered the office clutching a sheaf of papers and closed the door behind her.

– Li Ping will be anaesthetist today……- she began.

- More appropriate if it had been Li-Po – quipped Nolan sending Dr Mike into spasms of laughter. Nolan grinned at Annie.

Annie tutted and turned to Dr Mike – Has he always been like this? Please tell me he was better back when you knew him? –
- No, he was worse – joked Dr Mike, wiping a laughter tear from his eye.
- Now this document here, - began Annie, laying a small part of the paperwork in front of Nolan – Is the confidentiality agreement from Mr Carerra's lawyer regarding his procedure today. Li Ping has signed her copy and I've signed mine, all we need is for you to sign here, here and initial here – she turned the page over.
Nolan hurriedly scribbled his name and initials as requested without bothering to look. Annie shuffled up the papers and headed for the door – I think that's Mr Carerra's Bentley coming into the car park, Sam – she peered over the top of the blinds.
Nolan swivelled round in his chair and parted the blinds with his pen. A black Bentley crept into the 'visitor' designated space.
- Showtime! – exclaimed Nolan, shoo-ing Annie out of the room.
- Right Mike, if you head to the theatre and scrub up but stay in the changing room until I come and get you, OK? – Nolan instructed as he headed out the door, noting the familiar chime of the door alarm, heralding the entry of one Steve Carerra.
He strode purposefully down the corridor, firmly shaking his patient's hand as they met in the reception area.
They exchanged pleasantries, and Nolan then handed an obviously high Steve Carerra onto Annie for prep and pre-med – He'll not need much – he quipped.
A gushing Annie led Carerra away and Nolan headed into the changing rooms to put on his scrubs.
Dr Mike was already suited and booted and washing his hands in the sink trough.
Nolan quickly popped on his scrubs and hat, kicked off his shoes and slid into his surgery mules. He opened the small locker with 'Sam' and a little magnetic Scottish flag on it, reached inside, and pulled out a Nikon digital camera. Switching it on and pressing buttons to make the lens go in and out, he then handed it to Dr Mike.

- Big red button on the top. One press for one photo, keep it pressed for a burst. Take as many as you like, we can sift through them later. – Nolan went over to the trough and began to wash his hands.
- So these are for your case notes, Sam? – Dr Mike enquired nervously.
- Hell no. These will be the $25k we need to get our laboratory going - He gave Dr Mike a cheesy grin.
- What do you mean? –
- That slightly podgy gentleman through there – he nodded his head in the general direction - is a certain Steve Carerra, the singer with Black Mass – you've heard of Back Mass, right? –
Dr Mike shook his head in bewilderment – You mean a big rock group? –
Huge. They were one of the biggest bands in the world when we were at University, remember? That Kate Smith you fancied had their posters all over her flat when we went to those parties there – do you not remember? –
Dr Mike's face blushed red – I remember Kate –
Well that Mr Carerra who is currently being administered a General Anaesthesia cocktail of drugs and gas to top up the current cocktail of drugs and alcohol in his bloodstream, is a very famous guy. In fact, so famous that a previous employee of his recently sold intimate photographs of him to the press. Now wouldn't it be amazing if some pictures of him undergoing surgery at an exclusive private Hollywood clinic got into the public domain? -
- Didn't you just sign a confidentiality agreement back in the office? – Dr Mike looked puzzled.
- Yep. I did. You did not. I do the surgery, you take the pictures. Simple - Nolan dried his hands.
- But….but….but….I don't want to get in any trouble…….- Dr Mike mumbled whilst turning the camera in his hands.
- Trouble? There won't be any trouble. Nobody knows you're here. Provided you take the photos standing on the stepladder I've positioned in the corner of the theatre, I'd say if anyone asks that we must have been broken into and a hidden remote camera was used. I've got this all

sussed – he tapped the side of his head several times.
- I…..I….I….don't know…….what about Annie? What about Li-Ping?
– Dr Mike looked anxious.
- Don't make it bloody obvious, they'll be too busy working. And they
both have their backs to you, so creep in quietly, take a few snaps then
come out here again. Two minutes. No problem. Even if they see you,
make sure the camera is hidden. I'll just tell them you're popping in to
see how it looks. Here – he leaned over to the camera – this is the zoom
button. So zoom right in and make sure that you get his face in real
good. I've done a couple of test runs so the height etc is perfect. Do a
good job now – he patted Dr Mike on the arm, pulled up his face mask
and strode through the door into theatre, leaving Dr Mike standing
staring at the camera.
Nolan strode into the theatre where the patient was laid out
unconscious, Annie and the anaesthetist busily maintaining the
equipment. He reached over to the remote control, bizarrely sitting
among his surgical instruments, and hit play.
He looked left at Li-Ping, then right at Annie – Showtime! – He
grinned.
Dr Mike's daydream was broken by the sound of The New York Dolls'
'Stranded in the Jungle' blaring from beyond the door.
After five nervous minutes, Dr Mike crept into the theatre, the blaring
music covering any trace of his movements. He gingerly ascended the
ladder and turned to sit to the top step, and then produced the camera
and zoomed in.
An almost sixth sense caused Nolan to glance out of the corner of his
eye and spot Dr Mike. He moved slightly backward and off the patient
to give the best possible shot.
Dr Mike quietly crept around the theatre, the small orange blinking light
occasionally confirming his presence. He skirted around behind Li-Ping
and Annie, popping the camera up and down. Their faces were fixed in
concentration, unaware of his proximity.
- Creeping Jesus indeed – smiled Nolan to himself.
Dr Mike gave the thumbs up, confirming the deed was done.

Nolan moved the suction wand to a new area of Carerra's bloated gut and then looked up, but Dr Mike was gone.

Chapter 6
Ninety Eight Point Four

The cocktail music in the bar was beginning to irritate Nolan. Dr Mike's constant questioning was beginning to irritate Nolan. The lateness of Miles DuPrey was beginning to irritate Nolan.

He looked up to the waitress and lifted his empty glass and shook it from side to side. – Another two Canadian Club please - Dr. Mike was away to let him know his wasn't finished, however the steely pissed-off look on Nolan's face made him think twice.

Just as he was about to inform Nolan that the National Enquirer agent go-between was now almost ninety minutes overdue, a hawkish, ruddy faced man in a cheap business suit entered the bar sheepishly and began looking all around.

- Bingo! – Nolan stood up and shouted over – Miles! Miles! Over here! – Miles Du Prey looked over the top of his glasses and scuttled over to their booth.

- Sorry about the delay. I thought you might have gone. Car had a flat so I Uber'ed over, but Mohammed took me miles away before I realised he was taking me to Santa Monica – he mopped his brow and laid his briefcase on the seat between himself and Nolan.

- So do you have the images we discussed? – Miles DuPrey conspiratorially asked under his breath.

- Straight down to business eh? Of course – Nolan replied, carefully selecting the images on the digital camera and then handed it to him. His eyes widened as he flicked through the images. – That's Steve Carrera alright......have you cropped these down Dr Nolan? – Yes I have – replied Nolan confidently – I had to make sure I wasn't having a supporting role, and that the theatre was not instantly identifiable. Other than that, they're as fresh as the day – He sat back and swigged on his drink.

Miles DuPrey kept scrolling back and forth, zooming in and out.

- So you said a couple of National Papers have offered over $15K? – He casually enquired.

- Well I don't want to name names, Miles, but yeah. But you're here. Now. And we can sort this now – He leaned forward looking directly into his eyes.

Dr Mike kept sipping his drink and looking straight ahead, clearly nervous.

- Well my boss has only authorised me up to $10k............- Nolan's eyes lit up.

- But these are so good; I can go another $2k myself on top. How does that sound? – He shifted in his seat.

- I think you know that if you let these get away from you, and other publications are running this when it could have been 'By Miles DuPrey' on every TV station and every front page, you'll find that extra three thousand to get us over the line – A thin bead of sweat was apparent on Nolan's forehead.

Dr Mike started tapping Nolan's foot under the table, and making a light whimpering noise, trying to get him to wind back and simply take the $12k.

There was a tense silence which seemed like ages.

- Okay. You got me – Miles DuPrey fished his iPhone out from his pocket – What are the bank details? – He looked enquiringly at Nolan then Dr Mike.

Nolan stood up – I'll leave Dr Mike to give you the details, Miles. Nolan started off to the restroom, took three steps then returned to the table, reaching over to grab the camera and popped it in his pocket.

- Safety first, eh guys? – He winked at them both and headed off to the restroom.

In the restroom Nolan splashed his face with cold water, and he leaned forward on the sink, staring at his own reflection. He paused, then giggled, and headed back to the table.

His phone pinged. Nolan pulled it out of his pocket to see the confirmation from his bank that $15k was now nestling in their account.

- Superb, Miles - He fished the digital camera out of his pocket and handed it to him – A pleasure doing business with you –

He nodded to Dr Mike and they left the bar.

Out in the parking lot they got into Nolan's 911 and headed out onto the freeway.

- Now I think you should go pack and we'll get a flight back to Edinburgh tomorrow so we can start packing up what we need there. We can order from your list this afternoon, and hopefully that can be waiting for us when we get back. It's probably a good idea not to be around when the Carerra story hits the papers anyway – Nolan gunned the Porsche towards home.

The next morning, the Uber driver deposited Nolan and Dr Mike at LAX departures. A sullen Pakistani driver unloaded their bags kerbside and got in and drove off without a word.

- Bang goes your tip buddy – Nolan spat as he pulled out his phone and rated the driver 1 out of 5.

Dr Mike laughed and wheeled the cases inside to the British Airways desk, his eyes scanning the massive board of destinations.

- I hate cattle class – Nolan said as they joined a lengthy check-in queue. Glancing to the right he noticed the Executive Club check-in was empty. He grabbed Dr Mike's arm and pulled him over into the vacant line, and they strolled right up to the desk. A pretty young girl in British Airways uniform tilted her head to the side and asked for their passports.

- Well, 'Amber' – crooned Nolan, staring at her name badge – I hope you can ensure a safe and happy transition from Los Angeles to London for Dr Mike and myself? – using his thickest Scottish accent.

She smiled and scanned the passports – It appears you gentlemen are flying Economy today, and the check-in for Economy is over there – she made a pained expression and indicated toward the large queue.

Nolan turned to Dr Mike – What the hell are you playing at booking us in Economy? – He thundered. A clearly shocked Dr Mike began stuttering excuses and shaking.

– Don't you know the importance of this trip? – He bellowed winking at Dr Mike.

Dr Mike caught the hint and began placating Nolan and asked him to stand back from the counter.

113

Dr Mike approached Amber and whispered in her ear. She lifted her hand to cover her mouth – Oh my god. I am so sorry. Let me see if there is first class available – she began tap tap tapping the keyboard furiously – Yes, here we are. 6 A and 6 B. Will that be alright? – She looked pleadingly at the two men.

- That's perfect – said Dr Mike lifting the luggage into the loading area. She printed the Boarding cards and directed them toward the executive lounge.

A bemused Nolan put his arm around Dr Mike and they left the counter.

- "I am so sorry, and I am so privileged to have met you" – he cooed, imitating the young hostess, whilst rubbing his arm.

When they entered the lounge, Nolan ordered two double Canadian Clubs, then turned to Dr Mike.

- What the hell did you tell her? – He looked incredulously at Dr Mike.

- I said you were Sam Nolan, the World Famous Neurosurgeon who had recently been given three months to live due to cancer, and that you were spending your final days performing as many life saving procedures as possible all over the world for charity. She immediately said she'd heard of you and the wonderful work you were doing – Dr Mike grinned.

- That's…….that's…..that's…..incredible team work! Nolan hugged Dr Mike.

Out of the corner of his eye he saw Amber standing at the counter looking over at them hugging, and wiping a tear from her eye.

The flight was boring and uneventful. Two blockbuster films and a less than blockbuster meal had only been made bearable by the complementary generous serves of red wine. A two-hour layover in London before the toy flight up to Edinburgh did nothing to calm Nolan's clear indifference to his homeland.

The plane deposited them into a bleak, dull, rainy afternoon in Edinburgh, in what seemed to Nolan like a million miles away from the life and sunshine of California.

A mixture of the red wine wearing off and the foul weather, now weighed on his back. Nolan paused at the top of the stairs exiting the plane - Glad to see the weather has never changed – he shook his head and descended the steps.

A text message pinged on his mobile phone and he urgently fished it from his pocket, but it was only the mobile provider's notice of intention to charge as much as humanly possible while he was out of the US.

They caught a cab outside the airport and headed to Dr Mike's flat. Nolan had no time for the particularly inquisitive Edinburgh taxi driver, giving only cursory one-word answers to his interrogation of himself and Dr Mike.

Dr Mike was far too polite and engaged the driver in pointless chat about the weather, traffic conditions, and his bowel regularity. Unfortunately once he established that they were both Doctors, the detailed analysis of his toilet habits, frequency and content increased drastically, forcing Nolan to focus on the endless grey drab landscape speeding past behind a cold, water flecked side window, whilst Dr Mike attempted to offer diagnosis and possible respite cures for the driver.

- This is it! – Proudly exclaimed Dr Mike as they pulled up outside a grand Victorian terrace in the Centre of Edinburgh. They exited the cab, Nolan looking up at the faded grandeur of the building. Dr Mike leapt ahead and opened the communal door, Nolan noticing most of the other occupant's names on the intercom were of foreign extraction.

They made their way up through a modest tiled hall with dying indoor plants to the green door on the first floor. Dr Mike twisted the key and they were in.

A small dark hallway gave way to a sparse, generous lounge with several pieces of antique mismatched furniture.

- No wonder you were in a hurry to get away from LA – Nolan joked gently punching Dr Mike's arm, again Dr Mike wincing as if he had punched him too hard.

He showed Nolan into a spare bedroom which lacked any warmth or personality.

Nolan threw down his luggage and straightened his jacket. He looked around the room which depressed him.

- Right. Let's go eat and grab a drink, early night, and then we can get over to the laboratory tomorrow morning nice and early, and start the packing. Sooner we get out of this place, the better –
Dr Mike looked hurt.
- I meant Scotland – Nolan followed up hurriedly, Dr Mike cowering back, expecting another punch to the arm.
Ten minutes later Nolan and Dr Mike entered one of the numerous faceless corporate bars in Edinburgh's Grassmarket. The smell of the soiled carpet, irregularly cleaned bathrooms and general body odour made Nolan wince as he entered, and teenage memories of such places came flooding back.
Dr Mike ordered up two local ales and pointed to a small vacant table in the busy bar.
As they took their seats, Dr Mike picked up the dog-eared menu, littered with garish pictures of multicoloured, perfectly served (and photographed) food.
- If you think I'm eating anything in this toilet, you're sadly mistaken – Nolan sipped at his beer.
- It doesn't look too bad – Dr Mike flipped the menu back and forth.
- I gave up eating all that fried garbage when I moved to the States. And look at me now! – Nolan lifted his sweater to reveal a neat trim torso. He poked Dr Mike in his flabby paunch. – Now that's what a Scottish diet does for you. And you should know better – he scolded.
Dr Mike flushed with embarrassment.
Just as Nolan went to console him, a fight broke out, and a pint glass flew through the air narrowly missing their table.
- Right. Enough of this. Nolan grabbed Dr Mike's arm and they headed out the door as various customers came running in to get involved. The melee of swearing, breaking glass and women's screams all reminded Nolan why he had left this godforsaken place. Nolan wanted to head back to the flat, but Dr Mike convinced him to give another pub a chance.
They walked up towards the town, and alighted upon the 'Hangman's Noose'.

- Here we are – Dr Mike enthusiastically chirped as he held the door open. Nolan was aware as soon as they entered the bar, the majority of other customers turned to witness their entrance. Nolan spun 180 degrees on his heels to leave, but ended up walking straight into Dr Mike.
- C'mon it's not that bad – he pushed Nolan towards the bar. A multiple tattooed and face pierced approximation of a female with dyed pink hair approached him with an air of casual indifference.
- She has to be related to Bored Receptionist – he thought.
- Yes? – She began.
- Hello. I'll have two pints of Guinness please – He pleasantly replied. She grunted and moved off to pour the drinks. He looked both ways, conscious that his every move was being studied by the clientele. Dr Mike had squeezed into a small table with only two small seats, with a crowd of fat, loud, women on a hen night on one side, and two drunken down and outs on the other.

Nolan cursed his choice of seating, and carried the drinks over. The drunks barely acknowledged as he sat down, however the screeching and cackling from the bridal party grew in intensity as he sat down. He could barely hear Dr Mike, as the drunken men began to argue, their voices rising, only to be shouted down by the pink-haired barmaid. As they quietened reluctantly, the babble from the women picked up. They would mutter and whisper conspiratorially, only then to burst into Hyena-like hysterical laughter.

He had given up on trying to listen to Dr Mike's soft mumbling, when one of the fat women turned to him.
- Take our picture, would you? –
- When a fair maiden such as yourself asks so nicely, who am I to refuse? –
- Eh? – She looked completely baffled.
- Yes – he nodded, taking the mobile phone and standing up and stepping back to frame all their not inconsiderable bulk into the camera screen.
- Say cheese – he shouted, as they all proceeded to shout at once, a flash

117

mob of hair dye, too tight clothing, and various sizes of inflatable penises. One girl lifted her top to reveal large, white flabby breasts, as the rest of the crowd egged her on.

- Here….you could get lucky tonight…….she's getting married next week and is desperate for a final fling – slurred the owner of the phone as he handed it back.

He smiled and leant over to lift Dr Mike by the arm, past their half finished beers, and out of the bar.

Within the hour they were spread out across Dr Mike's leather couches, beer in hand, munching on takeaway pizza, watching old Top of The Pops re-runs.

Nolan made a mental note – Never, ever, ever go out in Scotland again - The following morning was unsurprisingly grey and overcast as Nolan and Dr Mike exited the taxi at a bleak industrial park on the outskirts of the city. Nolan looked unimpressed as Dr Mike bounded to the front door and punched in the entry code.

Once inside, Dr Mike switched on all the fluorescent lights, and they flickered to life, one at a time, working their way up the large clinical room, revealing more and more gleaming new heavy medical equipment. Nolan's initial disappointment at the dismal entrance was all gone, as banks of computer screens jerked into life, and the hum of energy filled the huge room.

-I must say, Mike, this is pretty bloody impressive. Very impressive – he scanned the room slowly, taking in the sheer volume of equipment.

- Yes it is, isn't it? I thought it best we come at the weekend when neither of the other Doctors or staff would be here – he stated whilst adjusting dials, and flicking switches.

- What will they do when they realise you're gone? – Nolan enquired.

- I'll come up with something. Probably best to keep them working away here anyways, I mean Blair is doing some excellent work on interspecies DNA compatibility, and determining the common building blocks, and as for Stevens, he's a capable guy, he'll keep the place running smoothly. His father's a millionaire, so he doesn't really have to work; it's more like we are a very expensive babysitting service. His father thinks investing money here every year is a small price to pay to keep him out of bother somewhere else – He said, whilst pressing a switch causing two large doors to open slowly, revealing a small gyroscopic device suspended by wire in what looked like a slightly oversized microwave oven. Large radioactive warning symbols were on each of the three static walls.

- Ta-dah- Dr Mike presented the device in the style of a game show hostess.

Nolan, ever wary of the radioactive warnings - Christ, should we even be in here without lead suits? – joking aside, he was clearly impressed by the scale of the room.

- No we're fine. This is the very centrifuge that spun Dolly's DNA. A complete accident. When we spun the DNA at a very specific rate, we found that the host material began to expand. We then found that the point microseconds before the material imploded, that the molecular activity was incredibly frantic, but if we applied gentle small microwave rays, it would stabilise in that condition at many times it's original mass. This obviously has connotations in the regard that we could theoretically produce oversize animals, thus creating a solution of scale for world hunger hotspots. We had made significant developments at this time, however it was a freezing cold Sunday night last November, when Blair was helping me prepare several bovine strain DNA for this process, he had a bit of a cold, and impatient to get away home. Two hours after he had left for the evening, I noticed that the centrifuge was still spinning, and more alarmingly, he had left the sample exposed to a prolonged dose of microwave radiation. Cursing his incompetence and lack of professionalism, I removed the sample from the sealed room, and I checked that the equipment was not damaged. Needless to say the machinery was fine, however, it was when I examined the sample, which I expected to have been fried, had been replicated several times in varying degrees of perfection, alongside the original. There were of course, two that were of aesthetic duplication, although on analysis, this proved to be only visually, so we had initially thought that we were at the start of a long journey.

That was until you pointed out in your own inimitable way, that aesthetic perfection was all you needed in cosmetic surgery! – He tapped the side of his head with his index finger knowingly.

- Do you realise the life we are about to have, Mike? – Nolan beamed – This is absolutely amazing. We are truly going to change the world! – He spun around the room finally resting his right arm around Dr Mike's shoulder.

- Right. We had better get measuring all of this stuff to see if it fits in a container – Dr Mike busied himself with checking calibrations on the computer while Nolan began to list each piece of equipment with its physical dimensions on his notepad.

Nolan's mood was improved. He checked his mobile phone. No messages.

=====0=====

Three weeks later, a bronzed Nolan was organising unloading of the medical equipment from the containers in the car park at the Sunnyside Clinic.

A painfully sunburned Dr Mike in shorts and short sleeved shirt was attempting to keep inventory and slow down the Mexican removal men busily marching in and out of the clinic, all the time geed up and egged on by Nolan.

- You have to keep on at them. Otherwise they'd just laze around and take forever – asserted Nolan, hands on hips.

Just at that, one of the removal men dropped a box containing glass Petri dishes, the glass smashing on the hot tarmac.

Dr Mike looked pained.

- Chop Chop Amigos – Nolan pushed the worker back into the container – Keep going. I'll clean this up – as he strode into the clinic, carefully dodging the melee of immigrant workers scuttling in and out.

- Annie! Annie! Annie! – He shouted down the hallway. Just at the third call, Annie stuck her head out from the staff recreation room.

- See if you can get whatshername to clean up some broken glass in the car park that Pancho Villa just dropped – He carried on striding forward into the new laboratory, where the main elements of Dr Mike's Edinburgh laboratory now sat polished and positioned. He looked out the half shut blinds to the car park, where Dr Mike stood with his clipboard desperately trying to read and check off the boxes by their catalogue numbers as the army of workers carried on regardless. Meanwhile Bored Receptionist was crouching down sweeping up the broken glass.

He re-arranged a couple of smaller wheeled trolleys then leant back against the wall, taking in the layout of the room, as boxes and strange looking pieces of tubing and metal stands were brought in and laid out on the floor.

A sweating Dr Mike entered the room – Nearly there – he gasped through his apparent discomfort and fatigue, a complete contrast to Nolan's neat, unfazed demeanour.

Just at that moment, two Mexican removal men were banging a pallet truck with an obviously overweight crate delicately perched thereon, swaying from side to side.

- No, No, No, you idiots – Dr Mike exclaimed pushing them away from the crate – Sam, come and help me with this before these clowns wreck twenty years of development! - He turned to the removal men – Cuidate Mucho, Cuidate Mucho! – He put his arm around the crate which had 'FRAGILE' written on every side. He turned his head and scowled at them – Come on Sam! – He grunted as he pulled the pallet truck into the room.

- What's so special about this? – Nolan eyed the crate up and down, hands on hips.

- This is the most important part Sam. Think of it as the 3D printer that formulates the host DNA into the desired body part or cell structure. This is what will make Cameron Diaz's breasts, or JFK's cheekbones, or David Bowie's eyes, or……. –

- Sam Nolan's penis – interjected Nolan, causing them both to laugh.

- All we do then is transplant the organ in question, pop in a few steroids and a wee digital DNA injection to promote growth of the damaged area, and then after that, should just be like any other transplant surgery, but in a fraction of the time! -

- I'm going to leave you get on with this, while I go meet the guys from the LA Times about our new advertisement – He pointed his finger at Dr Mike and made the shooter gesture before heading out the door.

A few days later, as Nolan's Porsche sped along the freeway, he studied the roadside billboards looking for their one. Online Dating was still the advertising king, accounting for at least 25% of the ads he had passed that morning. Just as he passed the Calabasas exit, there it was. A young girl crying with her head in her hands, a celebrity gossip magazine open with a myriad of glamorous stars' red carpet photographs. 'Don't settle for second best – Sunnyside Clinic now offering ultimate surgical perfection' GUARANTEED written in red stamped diagonally in the corner.

- A little cheap and tacky – he thought to himself, lifting his camera phone to take a photograph – Perfect for here – he purred, speeding up as he passed the sign.

The Porsche eased into the car park and he hopped, skipped and jumped up to the front door of the clinic, swinging his jacket over his shoulder as he opened the door.

- Many calls? – He asked Bored Receptionist.
- Many what? – She replied, with a studied degree of disinterest.
- Calls. You know, what we employ you here to do – he held her gaze – whilst making the phone gesture to his ear.
- Oh. No – She then looked back to her magazine.

Slightly taken aback, Nolan carried on down the hall and into his office. Annie breezed into the room, clutching a wad of files to her chest.

- Are we ready to hear today's motley crew? –
- Yeah sure. Wait. What time did you come in today? –
- About 8.30 as usual. Why? – Annie looked puzzled.
- No calls? – He was genuinely shocked.
- Not unless you count the fantastic savings we could make by changing our Electricity provider? Why? –
- Oh nothing. Just spent $5k on some advertising and thought we might have had some response –

- When did the ad start to run? – She quizzed.
- Today – he looked dejected as she burst into laughter.
Annie sat down shaking her head. – Oh Sam………-
- So never mind all the mid-lifers and the tummy tuckers, Annie, find
me someone we can use our new toys on……..someone *interesting!* –
He threw his hands up in the air.
- Well…….- Annie opened the first file – No – she moved on to the
second file – No – then the third, fourth and fifth - I don't think any if
these are suitable…..unless instead of pinning back this girl's ears you
could graft new ones on? – She laughed.
- Yeah. You name me some famous ears – Nolan shook his head.
- Hold on Sam, what about that girl that dresses like Madonna and
drives about in that old 50's car? I still have her file from last year.
Remember you said you wouldn't have anything to do with making her
uglier than she was? –
- Yes I remember her. She's a fruitcake – Nolan reclined back in his
chair.
- A rich fruitcake Sam. She wanted you to put the gap between her eye
teeth, deform the nasal bridge and make her ears more prominent. I
think there was also some tucking around the lower eyelids too? –
Annie hurried off to the reception to retrieve the file.
Breathlessly Annie rushed into the room and handed the file to Nolan.
He pulled his seat forward and began to study the notes.
- That's her right enough. She was quite pretty. And young. Why the
hell would she want to look like Madonna? – He continued studying his
notes.
Annie suppressed a laugh.
- Her parents manage *both* the Armani and the Chanel franchise
boutiques over on Rodeo. So, no problem with funding……..maybe a
problem with angry parents once they see her physical appearance on
the 'Borderline' – he laughed.
- She can always say 'Papa don't Preach' – joked Annie joining in.
- Yes…..and he'll be saying 'Who's That Girl?' – said Nolan causing
them to burst into hysterical laughter.

Their laughing stopped as Bored Receptionist opened the door and stood staring blankly at their hilarity.
- Yes Courtney? – enquired Annie tilting her head in annoyance that their fun had been interrupted.
- Steve Carerra is in reception to see Dr Nolan – she droned.
- Shit – Nolan slid the chair backwards across the floor to the window and tilted the blind just enough to see the black Bentley in the car park.
- Did you tell him I was here? – asked Nolan.
- Your car is right at the door – she answered with a studied boredom, before turning and walking back down the hall.
- I thought Steve Carerra's follow up was in about 2 weeks......- Annie mumbled, flicking through the pages of Nolan's diary on screen.
- It's not his follow up Annie. Did you not see a newspaper or a television the whole time I was away in Scotland? I was four thousand miles away and even I heard! – He asked impatiently before rolling back to the window and looking out.
- Well no, you see my sister Janice had just broken up with her boyfriend.........-
- I'm sorry Annie; I really don't have the time for a potted history of your sister's romantic entanglements. Needless to say, Mr Carerra out there is going to be pissed off, because while we were away, someone leaked photos of him getting his liposuction treatment here, and almost every tabloid and TV channel ran with it –
Annie covered her mouth with her hand.
- How embarrassing for him. Who could have possibly done such a thing...........- Her eyes widened and dawning of realisation swept over her face.
- Sam! -
Nolan shooed her away. – Show Mr Carerra in – He stood up and ran his fingers through his hair and exhaled heavily.
He heard Carerra's heavy boots clumping and scuffing as he walked very deliberately towards the office.
- Lift your bloody feet – thought Nolan nervously.
A light knock on the slightly ajar door and Steve Carerra craned his head around into the office.

- Steve! Great to see you – Nolan gushed over-enthusiastically, whilst getting up from his chair.

Carerra entered the room confidently, still scuffing his feet on the polished wood floor.

- And look at you – Nolan excitedly pointed at the now reduced midriff of the aging rock star – Looking more like that second album cover now eh? Come, come, and take a seat. As it happens, I'm just back from the UK, and you were most definitely on my to-call list. It's just terrible what happened, Steve – he slid back into his chair and reclined gently.

Carerra sat impassively.

Nolan felt anxious, unable to see the eye movements behind the $600 Gucci sunglasses Carerra was sporting – You know, I've had Annie interview all the staff with access to the clinic, and my intention is to get that emailed over to you later today Steve. Between us, I think we can figure out who was behind this terrible, terrible, act. You know we have about 10 clinicians and technicians, and about five cleaning staff all with access. But, by golly, that's now changed – He nervously took a breath – you want a Pellegrino Steve? A Coke? Can always get you a Coke –

Carerra shook his head lightly.

– It has been one of the singularly most embarrassing things to happen to me in my life Dr Nolan, – he spoke quietly – Sure I've had the naked pictures when I was 22, or even the notorious two guys ones in my early thirties –

- Two guys ones????? – Nolan thought.

- But that was when I was on meth, and didn't eat except on weekends, so I was about nine stone. Even the divorce photos in the Enquirer, I could explain to my Mum & Dad. But this…….this….. – He began shaking his head.

Nolan quietly sat anxiously looking at the door, wondering if he could make a dash for it.

- Terrible……..awful…….so sad………- Nolan was aware he was muttering and making sympathetic noises.

Carerra stood tall and squared up to Nolan as he gingerly rose from his chair.

- Is the best thing to ever happen to me! - He grabbed Nolan and hugged him tight, rocking from side to side.

He laughed in Nolan's ear, his hot breath carrying the merest hint of garlic and beer.

- You see, my management felt I was too aloof; too Hollywood, over the last few years. With a new solo LP in the can, and the tour about to start, the ticket sales were less than impressive. They were worried that I was on the wane, and that no-one other than the die-hards would be interested. But you know what they say…..'Any publicity is good publicity' …….and it turns out I got a lot of sympathy from the public, who it turns out, are mainly overweight, out of condition slobs too! – He laughed loudly again, this time releasing his grip on Nolan.

- You see they felt *empathy* with me. Or something like that. And now, my new LP is already gold on advance orders! – He jigged over to the chair and sat down.

- Now there is still a slight trust issue with all this Dr Nolan, I came to you because you have, or should I say had a reputation for confidentiality. Now it's worked out fine this time, but maybe someone else might not get the same result or be quite as understanding – he lifted his sunglasses and gave him a wink.

- Now I know you say you've interviewed all the staff, etcetera, etcetera, etcetera. But I would like to ask you if you were involved in this Dr Nolan. Just give me a straight answer yes or no – he leaned in toward Nolan, his sunglasses in his hand, his eyes firmly focused on Nolan's face.

- Of…of….of course not Steve….. I take the code of ethics and Doctor/Patient privilege very, very, seriously – He leant back in the chair, hoping his reply whilst sincere, carried a slight tone of offence.

- No, of course you didn't, Doctor, please forgive me for asking. I just had to hear it directly from you – Carerra now looked at the ground.

- Success – thought Nolan to himself.

- Although Steve, I have had this nagging doubt ever since I found out about all this……..-

- Go on, - said Carerra, shifting forward in his seat.

- Are you familiar with Salvatore Marchesi? – enquired Nolan.
Carerra nodded his head slowly.
- He's a, how shall we say, connected type Italian businessman? –
Nolan now took the turn to wink at Carerra, who nodded knowingly.
- His wife was in for some small procedure maybe a couple of days
before you, you, know, a bit of facial, a nip here, a tuck there, well, I
don't mean to sound paranoid or anything, but I had a feeling
something wasn't right when she was here. You know there were like
blacked out cars driving past every fifteen minutes or so, strange cars
parked up in the lot, phone calls that hung up when answered, that sort
of thing. Then I remembered that the alarm company called me the
night before her procedure, to say the alarm had been activated. I came
down, no sign of forced entry, nothing missing, and put it down to
maybe vermin or a fly in the building. So the week after she left, I
notice some equipment in the theatre not in its correct place. It's clearly
been moved.
So when I saw your photographs on the news, I knew that was the angle
in the theatre.
So I concluded that Marchesi had installed his own CCTV in my place
to keep an eye on his good lady, and then had inadvertently caught your
work in amongst several other procedures that week. I reckon that's
what's happened Steve, but for God's sake, keep it to yourself, okay? I
don't want to end up in the foundations of the new Apple headquarters
– he looked pleadingly at Carerra.
Carerra removed his sunglasses and looked thoughtfully out of the
window.
- No, that's gonna stay with me Dr Nolan. I think you nailed it right. I
know him alright. That slimeball was banging my guitar player's wife a
few years back. Nothing came of it, but there was some unpleasantness,
and he will definitely bear a grudge against anyone from or connected
to Black Mass. You know, it all makes sense. You're right. He's got my
images by accident, and the thought of making a few dirty dollars
whilst sticking it to me, just proved to be too much of a temptation.
Thanks Dr. Nolan – He rose from his seat and shook his hand.

127

Nolan could scarcely believe his luck. It had all worked out just fine. Carerra in gratitude, and full confidence, whilst turning the Black Mass machine against the Italian scumbag who tried to intimidate Sam Nolan. Perfect.

- There's no answer from Angela Rimini's cell or home phone, but I left a message – Annie leant in the door opening to impart.

- Angela who? – Nolan looked up, puzzled.

- Madonna! – Annie rolled her eyes and turned to leave, only to walk directly into Dr Mike.

- Jesus, Mike! Make some noise when you creep up on people –

- Always thought he was 'light on the loafers' – chuckled Nolan.

Annie slammed the door behind them, leaving the two Doctors to greet each other.

- Any potential hits off our new advert? – enquired Dr Mike jovially.

- Surprisingly not – shot back Nolan, instantly deflating Dr Mikes' demeanour.

- However, we've had a wee look through the outstanding client base, ongoing patients and retainers without much luck, but in the reject pile, we've hit pay dirt. All the loony tunes and crackpots we had to turn away due to the inability to meet expectation, well, they're ripe for this kinda stuff – Nolan reclined in his chair.

 - What about the mentally unstable ones? – enquired Dr Mike.

- Especially them! – Nolan handed Dr Mike Angela Rimini's file.

Dr Mike pulled his glasses from his pocket, put them on and began to scan through the file.

- Interesting……and no doubt do-able……and it shouldn't be too hard to get some of Madonna's DNA…….- he looked over the top of his glasses at Nolan, causing them both to start laughing.

The phone began ringing.

- That's Angela Rimini for you Dr Nolan – Bored Receptionist put the call through.

Nolan pointed at the phone, then the file, then made the spinning finger gesture to the side of his head to indicate to Dr Mike who was on the phone.

- Ah hello, Angela. Thank you so much for calling – He flicked the phone onto speaker.
- Well thank you, Dr Nolan. To be honest I was a little surprised when I received a message from your clinic, as I was sure you had made it clear you were unwilling to perform the work I had required – she said rather haughtily.
Nolan shot Dr Mike a glance at the use of the past tense.
- Had, Miss Rimini? You already had the procedures carried out? – Before he had a chance to continue, Angela Rimini eagerly chimed in.
- No, not at all. You see, everywhere I went after I had tried your clinic, suggested that I required a psychological assessment, and none of them would proceed without that, regardless of the money that I offered. I had thought that you had blackballed me in your little Plastic Surgeon community….Do you need my psychological assessment, Dr Nolan? -
- No, Angela….may I call you Angela…….of course not on all counts. I have little contact with my peers as they are all so jealous of the reputation of the Sunnyside Clinic.
I would certainly never go out of my way to obstruct someone's dreams of aesthetic artistry…..in fact, I'm sure the only reason we could not accommodate you last time was due to an illness on my part, so I must profusely apologise if I have come across anything other than professional and onboard with your hopes and dreams – he winked at Dr Mike who sat in amazement.
- Dr Nolan, am I to believe that you are now willing to perform the necessary procedures I originally requested to realise my lifelong dream? – They could hear a light sob in her voice.
- Angela, we would be honoured and privileged to carry out anything necessary to help to achieve your goal. It just so happens that I have the expert assistance of a visiting eminent Doctor, who has much expertise in the field of aesthetic reproduction. It also just so happens, that due to a cancellation, our diaries have Theatre space next Tuesday. Now I know it's short notice, but if you wouldn't mind coming in tomorrow afternoon, say around 2pm, we could get you prepped and ready for next Tuesday?-

- Dr Nolan, you have no idea how happy I am. Of course. I'll be in tomorrow at two – see you then, and thank you, thank you, thank you…… - Nolan hung up the phone.

- I guess we'll see how this all works then, Dr Mike – Nolan said, reclining in his chair and folding his arms.

- Right, so let me get this straight. A moderately attractive woman in her early forties, with no more than a passing resemblance to Madonna, wants to be transformed into 1982 pop Madonna? Interesting – Dr Mike leaned over to Nolan's computer and searched 'Madonna Images'. Alighting upon several, he saved each one in turn. He then clicked on Facebook, and typed in 'Angela Rimini'

- Well it's not you – laughed Dr Mike highlighting an overweight woman in lycra.

Scrolling past several more, they found a waif-like creature in a typical 80's pop star pose – Mmmmm…..a 'Dancer'…….lives in Los Angeles…….that's got to be her – Dr Mike clicked on the 'photos' section and they began to browse through Angela's most intimate online photographs.

- I suppose it's do-able – Dr Mike tilted his head 90 degrees while flicking through her 'Summer of Love' photo album.

- Imagine breaking a perfectly aligned nose to re-set crooked – he flicked between the online Madonna photos and Angela's, zooming in and out on the nose.

- Imagine prising in between those eye teeth and creating and unsightly gap – he furiously flicked between various photographs, the zooming in and out getting more frantic, the noise of the mouse wheel clearly beginning to irritate Nolan.

- Imagine…. – began Dr Mike, only to be interrupted by an impatient Nolan.

- Imagine it quietly in your head Mike. Imagine it tonight just before you close your eyes and slip gently into slumber. But most importantly, imagine $20,000 for just a few hours work –

- So what's the plan? – Dr Mike carried on scrolling.

- I believe – began Nolan, clamping his hand firmly over Dr Mike's to prevent further mouse activity – that we are looking at starting with the rhinoplasty, followed by the tucks under each eye, then on to the ears. A small cut here – he zoomed in on a celebrity magazine photograph side view – And we insert a small grommet to cause the ears to protrude maybe 10mm, then a couple of small sutures where the lobe meets the cheek, I think maybe two Ethicon Vicryl about 5mm. Her jaw line is pretty close, so after that I reckon a 250ml turbo shot of some Ciccone DNA? – He looked sideways to Dr Mike.

- I think that covers it pretty well. I suspect the root DNA is fairly dominant, given the strength of the subject's features, and will easily assist with our surgical procedures of getting to where we want to be. If we expose it to about 500 millisieverts for about 20 minutes I suspect that it will be nice and active when injected, and speed up the healing and adoption of our measures. It's worked out well that this patient isn't requiring any actual transplanted material – Dr Mike paused for a moment – This is so amazing, Sam.....although........what happens if it doesn't work? – He looked painfully at Nolan.

- I had thought about that......for a nanosecond! She's a fruit loop, Mike. These people have far more money than sense. She's been waiting all her life to be told what we're telling her....she said that herself. Even if it doesn't take as well as we think, between my surgical hand and the power of suggestion, she'll be happy enough. Up Sunset with her denim twinsuit, skipping along the pavement. The difference is, Mike, she *wants* it to work more than we do. We can't lose. You've done this loads of times before, you're surely not having a crisis of confidence? –

- No Sam, but I've only ever done this with Horses, Sheep and Mice....... - he looked nervously at Nolan.

- And they all looked like they were supposed to – right? – queried Nolan.

- You know we never really studied the visual characteristics? Just the genetic material....just the makeup.....but now you say it.... - a broad smile broke out over his face – they did look

131

identical…..yes…..yes…..this is going to work! – Just then his smile suddenly dropped from his face – so where do we get Madonna DNA within a week? – Dr Mike looked pained.
- Relax. I might just go meet her – Nolan smiled.
- And what? Shake her hand? Steal her gloves? Swab her cutlery? *Seduce* her? Dr Mike mocked.
- Nah. Like a virgin – They burst into laughter.

Chapter 7
Overnight Sensation

- Why are we queuing here Sam? – a clearly perplexed Dr Mike asked. Nolan and Dr Mike were in a large queue outside the very touristy Chinese Theatre in Hollywood. The sun was beating down, and it was uncomfortable, even at 9.30am. A busy cavalcade of tourists, hustlers, street performers and pimps filled the small courtyard, the sound of ten boom boxes all at once all merging into a slurried beat.
The queue was slow moving and predominantly Asian. They began inching towards the hole in the wall kiosk.
- This, my dear man, will give us a little downtime to relax and take in the sights, as well as providing some valuable information - He winked at Dr Mike as their turn came round.
- Two please – Nolan paid, lifted the tickets and headed out of the shade and into the sun, Dr Mike trailing behind.
- There's our ride – he pointed at an open topped minibus, half full of Chinese tourists, busily snapping their cameras at anything that moved. They boarded the bus, nodding to the driver, and took seats right behind him.
Nolan opened up a large map and spread it over his lap.
- When stuck in traffic yesterday on Highland, this kid was going from car to car with these discount vouchers for this tour. 'Homes of the Stars'. I took the voucher, but just as I was about to toss it, one name on the list of celebrities stood out. Madonna.
There she was. Sandwiched between Matt Damon and Jerry Lewis. Bet she would like that! - He nudged Dr Mike painfully – So I thought we have to see where she lives, and maybe we could come back later and maybe rake through her garbage, or steal something out of the drive, or I dunno......something –
The bus lurched out of its stop and began the slow crawl through traffic toward Beverly Hills. The driver began his oft-repeated commentary in a low drone.

133

- Ladies and Gentlemen, we have just left the world famous Gaumann's Chinese Theatre, home of the world famous Oscars – he carried on in a monotone as the bus lurched and swerved it's way through the morning traffic like a ship in choppy water.

Nolan began tracing his finger along the map until he found the property with Madonna's name on it. Unfortunately it was toward the end of a two hour tour.

The bus had now turned into the leafy sun-drenched side streets of Beverly Hills, as the driver droned on about Marilyn Monroe and John Wayne. The bus struggled manfully up the small winding streets and avenues, occasionally stopping and reversing to let other bus tours through, the drivers grudgingly acknowledging each other in the dog eat dog world of Hollywood bus tours.

Nolan had found when he made playful quips to the driver's monotonous commentary, others on the bus laughed heartily, whilst the Chinese looked straight ahead.

Ever the showman, Nolan's observations became louder and louder, playing to the ready made audience behind them.

Dr Mike noticed the driver's mounting irritation in the rear view mirror, catching an unhappy grimace, as his companion joked about the sizes of property gates in relation to said property owner's manhood, causing a flurry of laughter.

Dr Mike nudged Nolan and whispered to him that the driver was unhappy with this unofficial, bootleg commentary.

By now, Nolan was in full flow, and a pissed off tour guide? That was a bonus.

As the bus snaked round the corner into the more urbane Rodeo Drive, the glare and glamour of modern Hollywood was laid out before them. The Rolls Royces, Bentleys, Lamborghinis, and assorted other automotive pornography, elegant, slim well-heeled women, delicately negotiating the spotless pavements with their tiny dogs, fat businessmen with oversize sunglasses, their ill shape softened by $5000 tailoring, the immaculately groomed palm trees, the subtle shop frontages with their even more subtle guards just inside the doorways, and the little

134

sparkles, the fairy dust that just seemed to glisten on everything in this street.
- Now Mr smart guy Scotsman, this is the world famous Rodeo Drive – drawled the bus driver in a confident tone – The most famous street in the whole of the United States. Gucci, Chanel, Armani, Dior, they're all here. Betcha got nothing like this where you come from –
- Well actually, - began Nolan, causing Dr Mike to put his head into his hands – As a matter of fact, we do. We have a street with all those designers. It even has a chip shop. And a Poundland. As well as the prestigious Muirhouse Neighborhood Centre. You might have heard of it? – The driver looked in puzzlement at Nolan in his rear view mirror.
- The West Granton Access in the delightful Edinburgh district of Pilton -
This caused Dr Mike to convulse in fits of laughter, thinking of the notoriously crime and drug-ridden area of Edinburgh close to their student flat.
- It's a world famous destination in Edin-bo-ro. It's where all the major celebrities visit when in Scotland – Nolan confidently continued.
- I think I heard of it – the driver nodded to himself sincerely – I heard of it……Pilton – Edin-bo-ro…..- he muttered hesitantly.
Nolan shot a smile at the now eye-watering Dr Mike.
The bus lumbered around for over an hour through narrow, leafy streets, all with giant gates and private security signs. By this time they had learned the Hollywood homes of several B-listers, talk show hosts, and dead sportsmen.
Eventually they turned into Bel-Air.
Nolan studied the map carefully. They were approaching the Ciccone residence.   - Apparently Hugh Grant rented the neighbouring property during his prostitute years in L.A. The property across the road was at one time owned by the silent movie star Buster Keaton – Dr Mike read from the map. The bus slowed down as it approached the target.
- Ladies and Gentlemen, I know I've said it a few times already on this tour, but get your cameras at the ready – the bus crowd groaned - The

135

electric gates to the Madonna residence are opening, and you may just get a glimpse of the Material Girl herself! – excitedly chimed the driver. As they slowed to a halt, the big black wrought iron gates completed their arc, and 22 cameras/phones on the tour bus lifted in unison. Nolan squinted through the sunlight, staring intensely at his own mobile phone.

The anti climax was complete as a large panel van slowly inched out of the drive, an elderly Mexican woman at the wheel.

- Aw shoot – cursed Dr Mike, amplifying the collective groan from the bus.

-Sorry folks, better luck next house – optimistically chimed the driver as the bus now lurched up the hill.

Dr Mike noticed that Nolan was continuing to take repeated photographs of the van as it crawled away.

- You studying trucks now, Sam? – He laughed.

Nolan was reviewing the photographs on his phone, when he eventually zoomed in on the logo on the side of the truck.

'Merry Maids Cleaning Professionals' with a telephone number underneath.

- Bingo – Nolan exclaimed.

The remainder of the tour was fairly uneventful, and as the bus pulled into the parking lot behind Gaumann's Chinese Theatre and parked up, Nolan stood up and prepared to leave. However the driver was now almost blocking the exit, obviously looking for tips, given the home-made paper sign held around a Starbucks cup with an elastic band with 'TIPS' in bright coloured child's writing.

Dr Mike struggled to extract a couple of dollars from his back pocket, and deposited in the cup while Nolan sneaked past with his hands firmly in his pockets.

Any animosity the driver had for the pair dissipated as a gaggle of Chinese from the rear of the bus advanced waving $20 bills in the air.

Back at the clinic, Nolan spread the map out on the table and Dr.Mike noticed the loose, illegible scribbled notes Nolan had made on it.

Nolan had checked online for Merry Maids Cleaning Professionals, and was now on the phone.

- Ah yes, good afternoon. My name is Robert Smith. I have just rented a property up on Cascadia, and was recommended your company by my neighbour. I was wondering if it would be possible for me to meet with your cleaning staff who actually operate in this area? –

- I see. No, I would not like to meet the 'Team Leader' or any other members of the management team. My neighbour is at 1520 Cascadia, and I'm sure if you check your records, you'll know exactly who I'm talking about. It is important for me, as a Hollywood executive to have a completely hands-on approach to anything to do with my family, and I would simply like to meet the person or persons who would actually perform the cleaning duties –

Whilst listening to the Merry Maids telephonist, he began to internet search the credit records of the Merry Maids business. Important profit information and articles of association sped across the screen until he arrived at the Shareholder section. It appeared a Richard Nadler and George DeBary along with various members of their families were the two main owners of the business.

- I'm terribly sorry to interrupt, but if you cannot arrange this for me, can you put me on to Richard or George please? – The receptionist immediately paused, and asked him to hold.

After a few minutes, a gruff-sounding man came on the phone.

- Ah Richard, how are you doing.......yes, well I can't say I blame you.........yes, yes.......yes, we met at Leo's house a couple of years back? Yes that's right......yes that was me.........- Dr Mike sat staring in astonishment.

- No, that's fine........yes if that was possible? How fabulous. Tell them not to call security at the gate. I'll be at the gate waiting for them. 11am tomorrow? Excellent. Give my best to – he quickly glanced at the computer screen – Irene. Tell her I was asking for her. Yes Thank you. No you too. Bye – He hung up the phone.

- *Did* you know him? – asked Dr Mike.

- No. Just told him everything he wanted to hear – He smiled.

- So you weren't at "Leo's House" – he made the air commas motion.

- Nope. But Di Caprio has so many parties here in Hollywood that Richard Nadler, cleaner to the stars, will have been at one of them. As for the wife – He's probably banging the girl who answered the phone……he was *real* keen to get off that subject! – He choked out a dirty laugh.

- Given that Conchita will be cleaning Madonna's at roughly the time we passed, it's a fair assumption that she'll be there same time tomorrow. We rock up and make her an offer she can't refuse – he winked at Dr Mike.

They high-fived each other and both reclined into their respective seats letting out a sigh simultaneously, which caused them to burst into laughter.

The next morning sharp at 11am Nolan's newly valeted 911 sat gleaming in the entrance driveway of 1521 Cascadia, reversed fully up to the metal security gates.

Dr Mike was nervously glancing over his shoulder at the gates and the two security cameras trained directly on them.

- Are you sure we're alright to sit here? – He nervously asked.

- Relax. If it was a beat up Chevvy or a Station Wagon they'd be out, but they see a $100k Porsche they'll just think it's some lovers tryst or I've stopped to do some Coke or something. Anyone comes to the car let me deal with it – He kept checking the rear view mirror. After several minutes, he stopped to pull his sunglasses down slightly as the large white Merry Maids van crawled up the hill and indicated toward the drive.

He started the car and drove out to the edge of the drive to prevent the van turning in.

- Let's go – he jumped out of the car, pocketing his sunglasses, and approached the Mexican lady in the driver's seat.

- Good Morning. My name is Robert Smith and I'm the gentleman you were to meet regarding the maintenance of this fine house you see behind me – he turned with a sweeping gesture toward the house gates. She eyed them both suspiciously.

- And your name is………? – began Nolan as she reached into her bag and handed him a small business card.

- Julia Lopez – he extended her hand and shook both of them. Dr Mike noticed she was making no effort to leave the driver's seat.

- Well Julia Lopez, this is your lucky day. Believe it or not, we do not want you to carry out the cleaning duties in this fine house, rather, we want to give you the opportunity to make $500 right here, right now. You see, we're both avid Madonna fans – She looked at Nolan intently, then Dr Mike – Really? – She said with a mixture of disbelief and curiosity.

- Yes absolutely. There is nothing more important to us than having something that belongs to the great lady herself.

Now we know that you clean her house every morning and start about 11am, so we figured, let's see if Julia Lopez can get us something.....or maybe Julia Lopez *has* something already that we could buy? –

- Like what? – She opened the door and stepped out onto the road.

- Well anything really, but it has to be hers. I don't want *your* old pants, Julia Lopez – He laughed leaning against the side of the truck.

- I can have a look at what I have in the back - She barged past him and round to the rear of the truck and opened up to reveal a mountain of white plastic bags, various storage boxes and cleaning utensils.

She climbed into the back of the truck and burst open a white plastic bag and began ferreting through its contents on the floor.

She held up a hairbrush. – This any use? Lady Madonna threw this in the trash. I know this – Dr Mike and Nolan looked at each other then at Julia Lopez.

- You are certain this is hers? Not her kids? – enquired Dr Mike excitedly.

- Oh yes. Lady Madonna no share her stuff with no-one. No-one but her at house now anyways – She thrust the hairbrush forward to an excitable Dr Mike who began examining the hair strands on the brush.

- Back up – said Nolan winking at Dr Mike – Anything else Julia Lopez? We need one thing each – he stood on his tiptoes, his eyes scanning the rear of the truck.

She rummaged around the truck until she held up a pair of slippers –

She wear these all the time. She has about twenty pairs. Throws them away even when they not worn. I have six pairs – she beamed.

- Yes. That will do nicely Julia Lopez. Now definitely Madonna's? – She nodded lethargically then climbed out of the truck as Nolan handed her a bundle of notes. This immediately improved her demeanour.

- Now Julia Lopez, do you clean the house of anyone else that we might know? – Nolan stared intently at her. She rattled off a few names of Z-listers and some people Nolan had never heard of. He started to take down the names in the notes section of his phone.

- Okay. Okay. Now Julia Lopez, I'm going to keep your card, and if you can remember anyone good looking and famous whose house you have access to, or you start at someone new who we might know, I want you to keep something, and I'll give you a call, and we can maybe do some business again. Hell, I might even need a cleaner! – He laughed loudly as he headed back to the car waving to Julia Lopez as she stood counting the money outside the truck.

After a celebratory liquid lunch, they arrived back at the clinic.

The bright lights flickered to life and machines began to hum as Dr Mike and Nolan began moving methodically up the lab powering up lighting and appliances as they advanced.

They then donned lab coats and Nolan aimed the remote control at the music system like a pistol. Within seconds the New York Dolls began to flood the laboratory.

They laid the hairbrush and the slippers under bright light. Both Nolan and Dr Mike were using head mounted magnifying glasses and began meticulously examining the items with a delicate sickle probe.

Dr Mike carefully selected two strands of hair from the hairbrush and carefully removed them with tweezers placing each one on a Petri dish. Nolan meanwhile was gently using the sickle probe to drag back the fur sole of the slipper to reveal minute flakes of dried skin. Again, the largest one Nolan lifted using tweezers and laid onto another Petri dish. Dr Mike then began the process of separating the DNA and then onto replicating millions of the PCR. Nolan ably assisted, shuttling between the centrifuges and the two microscopes. Dr Mike then placed two samples of the separated DNA in test tubes and placed them in the cryogenic room, his presence there reminding Nolan that a dismembered Nadine was in there too, barely six inches away from Dr Mike's feet.

He made a mental note to dispose of her in the next few days as activity in the laboratory would intensify.

- Everything OK? – Enquired Dr Mike, aware of the vacant look on Nolan's face.

- Yeah. Sorry. I was miles away. Let's get these samples into the soak - he purposefully thrust two test tubes toward Dr Mike.

Dr Mike began to switch on the centrifuges, their gentle hum and the soft glow of the fluorescent lights creating an eerie calm.

After half an hour, Dr Mike invited Nolan to look into the microscope where he observed the sample on the slide.

- That is pure Madonna – he beamed.

- Sounds like the title of her last album – mimicked Nolan, causing them both to laugh.

Dr Mike gathered up the prepared syringes and kissed them as he carried them into the cold storage.

- Well stage one complete.......it's all up to you now Sam – Dr Mike high-fived Nolan. They removed their lab coats.

- Time for a celebratory drink – said Nolan as he put his arm around Dr Mike's shoulder and they headed out the door.

The next day a confident Nolan and slightly hung-over Dr Mike had the pre-op meeting with Angela Rimini.

- She looks even more like Madonna than Madonna – thought Nolan – This is going to be a walk in the park –

- So Angela, what we are going to do, is we are going to put you to sleep, and then get this nose – he touched her nose with his pen – slightly re-aligned – he pointed to the nose on an image on the computer screen of a smiling Madonna, likely at an award ceremony –

followed by a tiny little tuck under each eye, - He ran the pen tip under each eye - then on to the ears. A small cut here – He gently touched behind her ear - And we insert a small grommet to cause your ears to protrude maybe 10mm, then a couple of small stitches here – He touched the base of her ear where it met the cheek, and then a small incision in your gum line and a spacer inserted to separate the eye teeth. Then I'll package you up nice and tight, so when you wake up, we have your meds ramped up, and you're feeling comfortable –
- When will I be able to see the results, Dr Nolan? – She enthusiastically questioned.
- We are using a brand new technique of cell repair and rejuvenation, which is expected to have you back to normal in a fraction of the time of regular surgery, so we think there will be very little downtime if any. It is groundbreaking work, Angela, and in truth, we're not sure how long you will take to recover. But we can guarantee you it will be considerably less than the normal four to six weeks of regular surgical recovery. That said, I'm sure that you'll love the result – Nolan tapped the end of his own nose with the pen and winked at Angela Rimini.
Angela Rimini stood up hugged Nolan then Dr Mike, sniffing and wiping a tear from her eye.
- I trust you – she whispered.
Dr Mike shot a glance at Nolan as he hugged her causing Nolan to grin.
- And we trust you Angela – began Dr Mike – As you will go down in history as the first beneficiary of the pioneering Sunnyside Clinic Digital DNA – He clicked his heels together and nodded in salute. Angela Rimini hugged him again before being led away by Annie continually uttering thanks and gratitude between sobs.
- See you here at two o'clock tomorrow – shouted Nolan laughing – I need a drink – He started to remove his white coat.
- No! No! No! – Dr Mike barred his path – The biggest moment in our lives, and you want to get wasted the night before? No I won't have it. We need to be calm and focussed. I've done my bit. I've looked over your last work and it is superb. So I need you to be 100% -
Nolan didn't have the heart to tell him he was probably still hung-over

on most of the procedures he referred to.

- Alright. Guess it's just the strip club tonight then – He headed for the door.

Again Dr Mike placed his hand on Nolan's chest – No. We're going for a quiet meal, *then* maybe catch a movie, but no alcohol, and an early night.

Nolan nodded in agreement, and dolefully put on his jacket, and they headed out to the parking lot.

A cheerful, over enthusiastic advertisement for a new car dealership in Downtown LA murmurs in the background, the excited yelps of the announcer punctuating the dawning realisation of waking from another hangover. As he opens his eyes slowly, Nolan stares at the closed curtains with the sun creeping round the edges. Dust particles float in the air caught in the shaft of sunlight. He began to wonder at what point mass defeats gravity. Then it comes back to him….this is the big day. He checked his watch. 10.22am.

He pulls his aching body out of bed, stepping over the strewn clothes and fast food wrappers, pulling back the curtains to bathe himself in light.

He winces back, turning around to survey the previous day's clothes all scattered across the floor. His eyes move back to the bed where the lump under the duvet indicates human form – Madison? – He thought to himself, searching through his memory files trying to piece together random memories from the previous night.

There was the honest intentions of a quiet night, he remembered the meal at Le Monde, they had gone there as they thought it would be quiet……Then he remembered the British rock band that was staying in the hotel. On hearing the British accents they had invited them to join them….then he remembered the 'one beer' line with Dr Mike wagging his finger in disapproval….then the bottles of Red Wine that he recommended to the band……'you must try this'……then the

143

Bollinger……then the shots……but he couldn't remember going home. Couldn't even remember going to bed…..

He gingerly lifted the corner of the duvet and snuck a look. Once he saw the brown corduroy, he yanked the whole duvet off to reveal a fully clothed and clearly suffering Dr Mike, who was now moaning and wincing in the light.

- Thank god it's you, Mike – he flung the duvet back over Dr Mike and his protestations, and headed off into the shower.

Apres shower, Nolan headed to the kitchen and swallowed a cocktail of Ibuprofen, Antacids, and Paracetamol, all washed down with fresh orange juice.

- Even the hangovers are better here – He thought to himself before looking up as a dishevelled Dr Mike ambled into the kitchen, looking very much the worse for wear, despite a cleansing shower – Or perhaps not – He corrected himself.

- Does this always happen with you Sam? – Dr Mike quizzed through slitted eyes.

- Only on days with a 'y' in them – He cracked back – Get yourself a shower, shave, and a……-

- No need for that – interrupted Dr Mike.

- I was going to say shampoo – Nolan grinned.

An hour later, Nolan's garage door creaked upward, and the white Porsche crept out onto Magnolia Drive, and gunned off towards the Sunnyside Clinic.

The beautiful bright sunshine and The Clash on the car radio lifted both their spirits, Dr Mike even cracking jokes as they passed some bizarre looking individuals at the stop sign.

Once at the clinic, they began methodically preparing the theatre. Annie flitted in and out making small adjustments, lifting utensils, carrying pans, re-arranging equipment.

Nolan began laying out his scalpels, neatly in size order. Dr Mike was in laboratory busying himself with his equipment, a mass of tubes and wires all connected but all converging on the oversize microwave structure which was almost five feet tall.

The machines were omitting a comforting hum, as he brought the DNA material through from the cold store.

As he started to agitate material from the syringe into a small Petri dish, he was aware of the arrival of the patient, Annie's ooh-ing and aah-ing only being outdone by Nolan's simpering tone.

- Are you ready to make history Angela? – Announced Nolan – Let's get a few photographs for the 'before' section shall we? – He pulled out the camera from behind his back.

With that Angela Rimini leaned forward giving her best Marilyn Monroe pout, whilst Nolan began snapping away with his camera.

- Beautiful……great…..oh my word……beautiful……. - He noticed Grumpy Chinese Anaesthetist hovering in the background – And here's Li Ping all set to get the show on the road – she stared at him blankly.

Grumpy Chinese Anaesthetist and Annie escorted Angela Rimini into the prep room. After a few minutes, Annie wheeled her out on the bed, in scrubs and hair pulled back into a net. Nolan patted her hand as she went past through the double doors into the theatre.

He stuck his head into the laboratory.

- It's show time – Dr Mike slid his wheeled chair back to the computer screen, tapped in several figures then turned to Nolan as the hum began to increase slightly in intensity.

- About 20 seconds should do it -   He stabbed '20' on the keyboard and it appeared on the screen and began counting down.

When the countdown completed, Dr Mike opened the small door and gingerly lifted the small Petri dish out, and then proceeded to examine it under the microscope. He then drew the liquid up into two syringes, and then placed them on a platter and presented them to Nolan.

- Come on then, Dr Frankenstein……..Let's make our monster – They headed off into the theatre.

Once inside, Angela Rimini was already under, all monitors sat even and ready, and a masked Annie and Grumpy Chinese Anaesthetist looked quizzically at Nolan and Dr. Mike.

The theatre sprung into life as the music began.

Nolan started with a long incision down the length of her nose, and then began to chip gently at the bone. Working steadily and calmly, he moved on to the areas beneath her lower eyelid.

He noticed Dr Mike was sweating profusely.

- Calm down – he looked up at Dr Mike.

- I'm not good with blood……..despite my profession – he muttered – In the lab it's binary, not real….but this? – He recoiled as Nolan chipped off another piece of bone.

Carefully resetting and stitching the nose, Nolan then deftly made small incisions under the eye and then began to tease the loose skin with the suture before completing a series of neat stitches. He then moved onto the lower earlobe, cutting in small, neat, deliberate strokes, before carefully inserting a silicone spacer. Tidying up the ears, he then began to separate the eye teeth with a small silver clamp, turning the screw slowly, causing the teeth to separate. Annie held the clamp while he made incisions into the gum line, and he began to manipulate the teeth into position using a set of dividers. Half an hour later, Nolan laid his bloodied implements aside, and took a long look at Angela Rimini, scanning for imperfection. Even through the disfigured, swollen, and discoloured face, he was satisfied with the work.

He looked over to Annie, his biggest fan, and also his biggest critic. She gave the thumbs up and the 'OK' symbol.

- Okay Dr Mike…..Now it's your turn – Nolan stepped back, as Dr Mike advanced carrying the two syringes on a metal tray. He held the first up to the light and squirted a little out of the end to remove any air bubbles, and then injected the long needle into the area between her nose and mouth. Slowly releasing into her bloodstream, he looked up pensively at Nolan, before swapping the empty syringe for the second one. He then proceeded to inject her in the lower neck – Right in the main line…..- He muttered.

Leaving Annie to dress her wounds, Nolan and Dr Mike headed back to clean up.

Once back in his everyday clothes, Nolan popped into the recovery room to be greeted by Angela Rimini in true Egyptian Mummy mode, her entire head swathed in bandages.

Grumpy Chinese Anaesthetist gave them both the thumbs up, and they turned and headed back to Nolan's office, where Bored Receptionist had left a couple of Starbucks take-outs on his desk.

They sat back and savoured their lattes.

- That went as good as it could have been from my end – began Nolan, looking to illicit response.

Staring out the window, Dr Mike slowly sipped on his takeout cup which had 'Dr Mick' on it. – I think the 2 x 50mls should be right…..But I guess we'll find out. We did trials last year with over and under doses in relation to body mass…..But that was on a rat -

- Well? How did that go? – Nolan implored.

- There was a 20% margin for error. The under dose resulted in mild deformity, and the overdose caused a cardiac arrest. But in 99% of cases, the mass/donor DNA ratio when correct was spot on.

I know this is the first human trial, but the Bovine tests were successful, and we even trialled pure breed dog DNA in a mongrel of the same breed. The host DNA was completely overrun, and even the UK Kennel Club passed the animal as pure breed. We had several members of the team that thought this was a excellent means of fund raising, however I wasn't on board with deliberately trying to deceive people –

Nolan's ears pricked up. – You mean you could turn out a Tibetan Mastiff from a regular bull mastiff? I saw one of those dogs on the news that had changed hands for $1.6 million!!! – he now sat up in his chair.

- Theoretically, yes, but I have a moral issue with deliberate deception like that – He sipped his coffee, looking out the window.

- But if the dog is legit by DNA, the Kennel Club verify, then what's the issue? – quizzed Nolan.

- We would have to falsify the parentage; we would have to lie about its origins – Moaned Dr Mike.

- If it looks like a duck, quacks like a duck, and is worth $1.6 million, to me it's a bloody duck! –

He laughed and sat back in his chair – And you have a 'moral issue' with some creative animal breeding, but not with butchering that woman through there into some circus freak look-a-like? – He laughed. Dr Mike looked uncomfortable, and fished out his mobile telephone and began to study it intensely.

- Oh sorry Mike. It's just I'm beginning to see the opportunities that your….sorry…*Our* technique can open up…..I mean come on…..You don't want to be poor all your life do you? – He looked quizzically at Dr Mike.

- No, of course not……It's just I wanted it not to be all about the money…..- He looked wounded.

- That's always what people with no money say – grinned Nolan - C'mon let's go grab a burger, and we can check back on our wee pop star later -

They headed out of the clinic, stopping briefly to give Annie some instructions, and assurances they would be back by 6pm.

- That's me not eating meat now – sulked Dr Mike as Nolan's Porsche crept into the Sunnyside Clinic parking lot. Nolan laughed thinking about the look on Dr Mike's face when he ordered them the 3/4 pounder loaded burger called 'The Heart Stopper' up at the "Meat 'n' Greet" Burger Restaurant on Melrose. They exited the car, and headed in the front door.

A brief exchange with Annie, which included some less than subtle attempts by Annie to smell Nolan's breath to determine if he had been drinking, and then the two Doctors headed to recovery to check on the patient.

They both bent over Angela Rimini's heavily bandaged head, examining round the edges with the headlight Nolan was now wearing. He gently lifted the edges of the crepe bandages repeatedly with the small metal tongs.

- Why are you persistently lifting those dressings? Leave her be and we'll have a good look in the morning – Dr Mike impatiently announced, removing his jacket and slouching in the armchair, before

148

turning on the TV with the remote.

- Come over here – Nolan peered under the edge of the dressing closest to her ear.

- Look at this pulse maybe 15mm below where the wound is – Dr Mike leant in and observed the small twitching pulse.

- Hmmm. Could be some kind of post operative reaction? – He ventured.

Nolan however, had crossed to the other side of the bed – It's the same on this side too – He nervously held the dressing back to allow Dr Mike to check.

- In fact, look at the nasal area. Do you see that gentle movement? – He hovered the small surgical probe over her nose.

- Dr Mike gently put the back of his pinky finger against the side of her nose.

Then her cheek. Then her forehead.

- Her whole head is moving – Dr Mike urgently swung the heart and breathing

Monitor around on its castors.

- Blood pressure fine…….heart rate fine…….breathing regular……what's going on? You know I think I'll up her meds a smidgeon – He tapped on the morphine dripper and dialled up another notch.

- You ever seen anything like this before, Sam? –

Nolan shook his head slowly.

- I think we should have a sleepover in here tonight, Sam. I've turned up the alarm to max volume, so we'll know of any issue –

The rest of the evening they continued to monitor the patient, whilst simultaneously checking online medical journals for any similar cases of post-operative severe twitching nerve endings.

Several instances of broadly similar instances were found and subsequently discounted. There was no doubt they were in completely unchartered territory.

They re-arranged the chairs so they were facing Angela's bed, and using stands and stools, fashioned a rather uncomfortable looking sleep

149

chair. Nolan pulled the trolley through from pre-op. The spare blankets and sheets came out and they bedded down and prepared for the night ahead.

The following morning, Nolan came to very slowly, at first unsure where he was, before memory kicked in. He noticed his head wasn't pounding; there was no acidic taste in his mouth. He realised it was the first time in a long time he'd woken up without a hangover.

He swung his legs off the medical trolley and crossed the room to open the curtains just an enough to illuminate the room.

He glanced at his watch. 6.20 am. He noted it was also the earliest he had risen, in fact on occasion, gone to bed even later than this. He checked his phone. Two messages from Madison. He speed read them then placed the phone on the bedside cabinet, his movement causing a sleepy Dr Mike to move slowly as he emerged from under a Sunnyside Clinic branded blanket.

Nolan switched on the gentle light above Angela Rimini's bed, and then gently held the back of his hand against her cheek.

- Whatever that was last night, it's stopped – He carried on gently resting his hand on her nose, forehead and under her chin – All vitals are good…. – He glanced at the monitors and then went to re-adjust her drips – Maybe time to bring her back up? – He ventured.

Dr Mike donned a headlight and probe and began closely examining the edges of the dressings, oblivious.

Nolan busied himself gathering up the sheets, folding and straightening, and dragging the furniture back into place. The pee-poh of the door alarm sounded announcing Annie's arrival, and she shuffled into the room carrying a takeaway bag of breakfast goodies, and two brightly coloured smoothies.

- Urgh….this smells like the boys gym at school – She strode across the room toward the windows and opened the curtains and ventilators.

Nolan laughed and turned to Dr Mike to share their hilarity, but he was engrossed, and focused right in on Angela Rimini's left side.

- I think it was Dr Mike who did all the pumping last night Annie – he quipped looking back for his usual riposte, but even through Annie's

150

giggling and his promptings, Dr Mike was intently staring at the side of the patient's face, slowly moving the edge of the dressing, and he had now lifted a pair of elongated scissors and was vey gently cutting at the edge of the dressing.

- I said it was that Heart Stopper Burger that gave you the wind – Joked Nolan, but by this time he could see how serious the look on Dr Mike's face was.

- Come over here a second would you? – Dr Mike said quietly to no-one in particular.

- Now I know you're a good surgeon, Sam…..but this is just amazing…..- Annie peered over from the other side as Nolan now focused right in on the dressing just below Angela Rimini's right ear. Dr Mike gingerly lifted the edge of the dressing which he had previously cut with a pair of small forceps, pulling the dressing further and further back until the small bloodied swab covering the wound fell out.

- Be careful….we don't want any infection! – Nolan began to force himself forward.

Dr Mike stood back to let him through, whereupon the remainder of that area's dressings fell away to reveal an almost completely healed incision.

Nolan stopped dead, staring intently at her lower ear, where only several hours previously he had made a 15mm mid depth incision. This would normally take 2-3 weeks to heal to this extent, but this had apparently happened overnight.

Nolan stood there staring, as Annie and Dr Mike moved round to the left ear, and began gently but urgently cutting the dressing.

- Same here! – exclaimed an excitable Annie.

Annie began raising the bed up to the main examination overhead lamp, and pulled it over the patient's face.

- This isn't right……what is going on here……- Mumbled Nolan, who looked completely shell shocked.

- It's possible that we may have over exposed the donor DNA to the microwaves, and the extra energy has accelerated the healing process –

151

Dr Mike could barely contain himself.

He began gently cutting up the right side of the facial dressing as Nolan snapped into life and hurried through to scrub up in the adjoining room.

Annie began to pull out dressings and swabs from the trolley and laid them on the bed.

Dr Mike looked at her.

- Just in case she's not fully healed – she justified.

Nolan re-entered the room, just as Dr Mike finished cutting up the final section of the facial dressing.

He pulled the overhead right above the patient's face, before steadying himself.

Looking at both Annie and Dr Mike, one after the other intently, he gently eased one side of the dressing mask up and bent over to look inside.

He then leaned over the other side and did the same.

Both Annie and Dr Mike held their breath, as Nolan gently easing his fingers under each side, and slowly lifted the mask off, the remainder of the dressings and swabs falling to the sides.

Miraculously, there in front of them, although slightly marked and not fully healed, unmistakably, was 1984 Madonna.

Chapter 8
My Stars

- Are you aware of what we've achieved? – Beamed an excitable Dr Mike to a clearly shocked Sam Nolan sitting in his office chair, fingertip to fingertip.
- I must confess I had my doubts Sam, but this marriage of your surgical expertise and the Digital DNA..........My God................. – He shook his head and sat down.
Their reflections were pierced by the ringing of Nolan's phone.
- That's your 10.30 here – drawled Bored Receptionist.
- Damn. Forgot we had consultations today......Annie ! Annie ! – He shouted through the door.
An unhappy Annie struck her head round the door – I'm busy making Angela Rimini comfortable. One of you two clowns should probably be in the room when she comes round –
- Where are the notes for today's consultations? – snapped Nolan.
- All three files are on your desk – she glowered and lowered her eyes to the desk.
Nolan looked down and lifted his elbows. He had been leaning on them all along.
- Oh.......-
Annie raised her eyebrows and headed back into recovery.
- Alright Dr Mike, what do you make of our first contender today? John Lennon wannabe Simon Walker has literally spent thousands on Beatle suits, wigs, guitars, etc as part of the Beatles tribute act 'Bootleg Beatles' – Nolan read out – Bearing more than a passing resemblance to John Lennon, Simon was the logical choice to play him in the tribute act, which has led to the boys being engaged by Twentieth Century Fox to play the group in the upcoming TV series 'The Beatles'. Since this engagement, the boys have all quit their day jobs and are currently under contract to 20th Century Fox Studios for a reported seven figure sum. Pre production meetings are underway and shooting starts in three

months, and Simon is keen to have some minor surgical procedures in order to complete his look. It is imperative to Simon this remains confidential, and that the recovery time is factored in any calculations to be complete prior to filming......- Nolan tossed the file over to Dr Mike – I remember taking this one by telephone the day after our ads went up…..he's a Yank that's a complete Anglophile – He picked up the telephone – Show Mr Walker in please –

A tall, thin mid twenties man was shown into the office by Bored Receptionist. Both Nolan and Dr Mike greeted him, and offered up a guest chair. Nolan returned to his desk and Dr Mike leant against the wall.

Simon Walker was dressed in black polo neck, drainpipes and Converse sneakers. Facially, he bore a slight resemblance to John Lennon, but with close cropped fair hair, the illusion probably required a wig.

- How do you do, Simon, I'm Dr Sam Nolan, and this is my esteemed colleague, Dr Mike Richardson – Dr Mike nodded.

They listened to Simon Walker's thoughts on surgery, and then called up a John Lennon image he had selected, which they put side by side with his both front and side profile photographs.

- Your eyes aren't slitty enough, and your nose is too small - began Nolan – I could use the medical terms but thought you want it laid out in black and white.

We can perform a small tuck at each tear duct that would narrow the distance between your eyelids like so – he walked round and pulled his eyelids of his right eye together, then handed him a small mirror to check – and we can then insert some small collagen fillers around the bridge of your nose, which we would then manipulate into that – he pointed back at the John Lennon image on screen. He returned to his seat and sat back.

- That…that…that…sounds incredible Dr Nolan, but can you guarantee all healing completed prior to my filming start date? – He asked nervously.- I think we can indeed guarantee a quick healing time – He shot a glance at a smiling Dr Mike – in fact, I don't think you'll believe how quick you heal – He smiled and nodded his head.

Just at that moment there was a knock on the door.

Annie stuck her head in – that's Angela coming round now! Will at least one of you guys please come and help us? – She darted away.

- I think this could be an opportunity for Simon to have a look at our latest work, what do you think Mike? – Dr Mike nodded and bowed allowing Nolan and Simon Walker to pass before him.

- Do you have a fee in mind Dr Nolan? – began Simon Walker as they walked down the hallway to recovery.

- Let's have a little look at Angela Rimini, Simon, before we talk numbers. I'm sure it will focus your mind – They shuffled through the double doors into recovery where to all intents and purposes, Madonna sat in a reclined position with several pillows at her back.

- Dr Nolan……Where are my bandages? What kind of care do you call this? My face is swollen and painful, and you don't even have the wounds covered! What the hell have you done to me! – It was at this point she noticed the look of absolute shock on Simon Walker's face. Who the hell is this? – She gestured at him - Oh my god…oh my god….oh my god……- She moaned bursting into tears. Annie consoled her.

- Relax Angela – began Nolan – I told you that you were having one of the most ground-breaking, innovative procedures ever conceived. This was not an orthodox procedure. I need you to calm down and take a deep breath – She continued sobbing but her eyes lifted up to Nolan.

- Now, Simon. Can you please tell Angela Rimini what you see when you look at her?

- It is the most incredible thing I've seen……..– He started while shaking his head from side to side – ……If I didn't know better, I would say that I'm either dreaming, hallucinating, or been transported back in a time machine………But I am looking at 80's Madonna……. – He continued shaking his head in disbelief.

Angela Rimini stopped sobbing, and began running her tongue over the artificially created gap in her teeth, then gingerly lifted her fingers and ran them along gently under her eyes, then over the bridge of her nose, feeling the small bump –

I.....I....I...don't understand......wha...wha......I.... - She looked from side to side then up at all the smiling faces in the room before directly at Sam Nolan – Am I still hallucinating? What's going on.........I should be bandaged up........should be doped up......- She looked imploringly at Nolan.

- Easy now, Angela, you've had some serious surgery, and you've been under for longer probably than we would have liked, but we wanted to keep your pain exposure to a minimum........Nolan wheeled over the Cheval mirror backwards right up to the side of the bed – Now please prepare yourself - then flipped it over, allowing Angela Rimini full sight of her upper body.

Angela Rimini just sat staring at her reflection. No-one in the room spoke, all eyes on the patient.

Dr Mike looked nervously at Nolan. Nolan stared intently at Angela Rimini. He then noticed a tear build then fall down her right cheek. Then another, then another, until she was weeping and convulsing.

-.....Oh.....oh...Dr Nolan......Dr Roth......oh....you truly are the hands of god......- She grabbed Dr Mike's hand and began caressing it, kissing it.

- I'm guessing you're happy with everything? – Quizzed a confident Nolan.

This caused her to convulse into weeping and shaking.

Annie moved to console her, as Nolan and Dr Mike took an arm each of Simon Walker and guided him back to the office.

- Now you were asking about price.......... - He began.

A short while later, once Simon Walker had unloaded his credit card details and sent on his merry way, Nolan began flicking through the second file.

- Hmmm. Christina Randolph. 42 years old. Single. Thinks she looks a bit like Angelica Huston. Wants us to complete the look. Biological clock ticking. He lifted the file over to Dr Mike.

- We talking Morticia Addams Angelica or Prinzi's Honour Angelica? – Queried Dr Mike.

- Dunno – said Nolan, spinning round in his chair and internet searching the actress.

- She's kinda cute........- He turned his head sideways looking at an image, zooming in and out – Especially in the Addams Family.......Maybe we better check out our gal now too – He tapped the keyboard furiously.

- Christina Randolph - Heiress to the Randolph Estate. Hollywood Royalty of the thirties. Her father married several different Playboy models throughout the eighties and nineties after her mother died of a drug overdose. Several dalliances with Z-listers along with failed businesses.........Let's check out some images........Well we have our work cut out here, Mike. She's more Grizzly Addams than Morticia Addams – He moved an image alongside the Angelica Huston one. Dr Mike leant over from the side and they began making notes.

The growl of a large-engined car in the parking lot caused both Doctors to turn and look out the slatted blinds. A large red 50's American car pulled up, and a stylish woman in period 50's clothing with headscarf and sunglasses exited the car and headed for the clinic.

- That's her – Nolan glanced back to the computer screen – I think there is some Liposuction required as well – He grinned and minimised the screen.

A few minutes later, Christina Randolph sat before them, removing her headscarf and sunglasses. She looked tired, older than her years, but retained a certain elegance.

They exchanged pleasantries and introductions, before Dr Mike sat back in the chair.

- Why the Angelica Huston thing, Christina? Dr Nolan here can weave his magic on you, a nip here, a tuck there, add a bit here, take a bit there, and easily take ten years off you, and you would look like a sports version of yourself, but to get the technical specifics and genetic characteristics of her face, we may have to dig a little deeper, which is ultimately more painful, and more expensive – queried Dr Mike.

- Oh money and pain aren't the only issues. You see I was in love once. Just the once. The damage done to my heart has prevented me from moving on, finding someone else, doing the things that couples take for granted. You see, I was once in love with Jack Nicolson. He two timed me, and probably half of Laurel Canyon, but I loved him. She didn't want him......She wanted the Hollywood excess, the glamour. She was seeing Ryan O'Neal for heaven's sake. It was all just a bit of fun for her. He must have liked that look, because I was always being told how I looked a little bit like her. So I know you'll think I'm crazy, but I want to look just like she used to. You see her now? – She scowled and pulled a face – I'm going to reflect her former beauty in her current withered old face. You see, he wanted that once.......and you never know......he may want it again........ – She sat back and looked down at the ground.

- Have you seen Jack since? – queried Dr Mike.
- At a few gala fund raisers, but nothing more than a nod of the head – She looked crestfallen.
- Wow - exclaimed Nolan – This is fairly extreme revenge is it not? A woman scorned and all that......Possibly even borderline psychotic – He looked over at Dr Mike who shrugged – But you know what? I love it! –
Her face broke into a broad smile.

- Dr. Mike here will take you through to Annie and we'll get you booked in the next few weeks if that's OK? – Nolan tilted his head and gave a broad grin.
A clearly happy Christina Randolph tottered out on her high heels cooing at Dr Mike and giggling.
By the time Dr Mike had returned, Nolan had the third file open on his desk and an image of a large breasted naked woman on his computer screen.
- I don't think this is the time for looking at porn.......Our next appointment is in reception – Ventured Dr Mike.
- This isn't porn. Our next appointment is Jo Laselles – He pushed the file over to Dr Mike – looking for a breast enhancement.....I was merely having a look at some of my previous work – He scrolled through a number of topless women on screen as Dr Mike leaned in to get a better view.

- That is some very nice work, you seem to have a fair bit of breast enhancement experience? -
- It's the number one procedure here in Hollywood. Every clinic will do this, good, bad, or average. That's why I had to stand out, and make sure that I had a reputation for excellence. I guess it helps that I have a good eye for the female form – He winked at Dr Mike – But you know, you can always improve. I was thinking, maybe this time, instead of the usual cut, stuff and stitch, how about we add the Digital DNA? I'm confident I can get the shape and size right, but to have the wee helping hand, I think we could create the ultimate perfect boob job –
- You see, this is what I was afraid of. That all my work would be reduced to a boob job – started Dr Mike with a pained look.
- Come on. We're making people feel better about themselves….Elevating their self esteem. If we didn't do it, someone else would. If we're helping create a world of better looking, confident people, isn't that something to be proud of? – Nolan opened his palms toward Dr Mike.
Annie knocked and stuck her head round the door.
- That's Jo been waiting ten minutes guys? – Both Doctors nodded.
Jo Laselles was a thirty-two year old divorced Hollywood advertising executive. Tall, elegant, and extremely well-dressed, she cut quite the figure entering the office. She was clearly aware that both of them were eyeing her in a less than medically appropriate manner.
She shook both their hands in turn before taking a seat.
Nolan thought even the way she lowered herself onto the chair was in slow motion, very deliberate, and downright sexy.
They exchanged pleasantries, and then got down to business.
- I am at present a 32 B, however, I have taken the liberty of bringing you these images of what I'm after – she handed over a memory stick, which Nolan fired into the computer. He swivelled the screen around to let them all view.
He clicked through several images of women in swimsuits and Chanel gowns.
- I'm afraid these pictures aren't really detailed enough. I get the

159

general idea you want to be somewhere around a 36 D – he turned the screen back toward himself and began furiously tapping the keyboard. He muttered away to himself, giving a running commentary of searching and saving images. After a few minutes, he turned the screen around again allowing them to view.

- Now these images are of a less glamorous origin Jo, but I want you to tell me if any of these are what you're thinking? – He flicked up image after image of topless women.

- That one. Yes. And that one. No not her. Those are too heavy looking. Yes that one. Definitely not that style –

They eventually agreed on two images of the same woman.

- Her breasts are magnificent – Jo Laselles stated matter-of-factly – The form, the weight, the slightest of upturn…….I am more than happy to entrust this to both of you if you can guarantee that my breasts will look like that – She sat back and pointed directly at the screen.

- Oh I think we can promise you Jo that your breasts will be more like those that you can possibly imagine – He cracked a smile and held out his hand - Dr Mike will take you to Annie to get you scheduled in.

When Dr Mike returned Nolan was scanning through the same images on screen.

- I take it this is some of your past work? – He enquired.

- No. It's The Dollhouse up on Sunset – you know the big strip club? It's their website. – Nolan continued to intently scrutinise the topless women.

- You mean she wasn't looking at casework but at strippers? – He gasped.

- Not just any strippers, but L.A.'s finest. See? It says here – He pointed at the screen – Jo seemed to really like Candy – He tilted his head sideways studying an outstretched Candy on a dancing pole – Yes I think Candy is definitely our template –

- How exactly do you propose to get a sample of her DNA……? – Dr. Mike started then tailed off when he noticed the broad grin on Nolan's face.

- Oh I'm sure I can manage to get some of *her* DNA – Sniggered Nolan.

He then checked his phone, his happy demeanour stopped dead in its tracks.
- What's up? –queried Dr Mike.
- Nothing – snapped Nolan, pushing the mobile phone into his jacket pocket – C'mon let's get a bite to eat before we check out Candy's breast structure close up! –
Just as they were leaving the office, Annie ran into the room.
- Angela Rimini has left! She had asked for a coffee and when I was making it she must have got dressed, packed her bag and left! Courtney's not sure if she went past her – She grimaced.
- I suspect she wouldn't notice a Nuclear Winter. Never mind her…….You saw how quick she was healing….she'll be fine. The money was cleared in the bank last night and she's out being a Material Girl today. What's the problem? Now Dr Mike and I have some serious research to do, and we may be slightly late after lunch – He grabbed Dr Mike's arm and ushered him down the hall.

A couple of days later, Nolan was reviewing case files on computer, whilst Dr Mike poured through the paper files, occasionally lifting a photograph to inspect closer.
Annie burst into the room.
- You're going to want to see this – she leant over the desk and flicked the remote control at the wall-mounted TV.
NBC-18 LA had a clearly excitable Angela Rimini on a daytime chat show being interviewed by an over-done host.
She was in full period Madonna clothing with Beret, striped t-shirt and braces.
- Damn. She's perfect……..that's…….that's…….pretty incredible – Began Dr Mike.
The audience on TV began cheering and whooping loudly as the camera zoomed in on Angela's face and brought up complimentary Madonna images alongside.

Nolan simply stared at the screen. The excited host and members of the audience gushed over Angela's appearance.

- ......uncanny......unbelievable.....miracle.......could pass for twins.......don't believe what I'm seeing here........-

Just at that moment, the camera was on close up of her face, when Angela Rimini turned to look directly into the camera – It was all the fantastic work of Doctors Sam Nolan and Mike Richardson – She began - At the Sunnyside Clinic here in Beverly Hills......and with virtually no recovery downtime – She turned her head back to the host who then continued to query details of the procedure, cost, and pain threshold.

Then, without warning, the phone began to ring, all echoey out in the hall. Annie rushed out of the room, her running steps click-clacking on the polished floor.

A few minutes passed and yet the phone continued to ring.

- Can't hear a damn word they're saying about us – began Nolan – Annie! Annie! Have you got that phone yet? –

There was no answer yet, the phone continued to ring.

It was at that point he looked down at the handset on his desk. All four lines were flashing.

Things were never going to be the same again.

Nolan grabbed the phone and selected a line, motioning to Dr Mike to move to the office next door and grab another call.

A torrent of calls ensued following the TV exposure, and it became very apparent that celebrity look a like surgery in LA was very much a growth market. They took over twenty names and numbers before switching the system over to answer phone.

Over the next few months, both Nolan and Dr Mike worked hard, up to two or three procedures a day, and when not in theatre, they had to spend every available minute on the search for specific DNA samples to satisfy their ever-growing market. They now had an army of cleaners, maids and servants, who all had access to the mansions of the Hollywood elite, occasionally hitting a home-run when huge parties would take place in the Hollywood Hills. The empty bottles, lipstick–marked glassware, cigarette butts, random clothing, and even crack pipes and condoms, would all be surreptitiously collected, labelled and stored by the Sunnyside Clinic's vast array of Beverly Hills service industry staff, all boosting their incomes.

They had also made their way around all the bars and lounges in West Hollywood, engaging the waiters, doormen and kitchen staff, tipping heavily, ensuring a regular supply of celebrity DNA samples. Every night they ate out, systematically touring and rotating the better-heeled restaurants, establishing contacts with the Maître'd, a quiet word when leaving, and a generous tip wrapped around a Sunnyside Clinic business card.

Nolan had now also taken to using two mobile phones, one for business, and one for personal use.

Dr Mike had sectioned parts of the cold store at the clinic, and they had amassed a huge catalogue of material, which they stored and cross-referenced under an elaborate referencing system. Dr Mike had particularly thought this essential, as now they were a headline news business, and the threat of burglary or deliberate vandalism by their competitors was a very real threat.

Nolan had wisely sought the services and expertise of the Perfect 10 advertising agency, which was universally recognised as the best PR on the West Coast. The reclusive Rossi brothers who ran the agency weren't the keenest at first, but once they had listened to Nolan's spiel, and they had thrown in some free work on their wives, they were hooked.

Perfect 10 commissioned a number of TV advertisements and radio jingles in order to cash in on their new exposure, and they were also delighted to see that several chat shows and lifestyle programmes were hosting previous clients, usually replete with before and after photographs, which simply fuelled the Sunnyside Clinic frenzy.

Several magazines and Internet publishers had been in touch, and the agency ensured that 'exclusive' access was given on a restricted level, building hype about the Clinic, and an air of mystique of the two pioneering surgeons, who no-one seemed to know. It was all the good components of a Hollywood story, and boy, did Perfect 10 recognise this. They expunged all traces of Nolan and Dr Mike online, removing social media, previous business internet presences, and all photographic records of their existence.

Dr Mike became somewhat perturbed by this, but was soon reassured by the Rossi brothers as to the necessity of their anonymity. Although most requests for surgery tended to revolve around fairly well-known film stars and celebrities, sample acquisitions were fairly straightforward for the living, but a tad more complicated for the deceased. It was apparent that there were just as many, if not more, dead icons than living, and this created a greater challenge.

One such client had offered up a considerable fee to enhance her Marilyn Monroe appearance. A professional Marilyn impersonator, she was making a decent living from TV documentaries, bachelor parties, and general PR work, however a crowded field of imitators and the ravages of time had made an upgrade inevitable. A basic Rhytidectomy had been the starting point, but having seen the work of the Sunnyside clinic on Good Morning LA, she had decided to approach the Clinic through her friend Madison, who was dating one of the hottest properties in LA, Dr Sam Nolan.

This presented a new problem, however Dr Mike had discovered that there was a visiting exhibition 'The Stage Wear of Marilyn Monroe' currently on at the Getty.

Nolan had suggested they visit the gallery without delay, and had also suggested they meet up with Bruno for old time's sake, as Dr Mike hadn't seen him in more than twenty years.

A few days later, after an emotional reunion in the car park at the Getty, they made their way up to the museum.

- It's in the East Pavilion – said Nolan pouring over a museum map. They headed off in the direction indicated on the giant overhead sign.

- Isn't this great? - began Bruno – I mean, here we are all are, all these years later, in……here – Bruno waved a sweeping arm over the skyline from the Getty.

- It is great isn't it – Dr Mike put his arm around Bruno.- And you guys……..- Bruno swivelled and pointed at them – this surgery thing……..Wow! There's somebody on TV almost every day now with stories about how great you are at mimicking famous folks…….I knew you did alright at your surgery Sam, but did you need this guy……*this guy?????–* He ruffled Dr Mike's hair – To finally make some real money? – He walked backward, laughing.

Nolan winked at Dr Mike – Just lucky, I guess – He shrugged his shoulders.

The three of them made their way into the exhibition. Various display cabinets filled the room, each one individually lit, bathing the couture inside in an almost ethereal glow.

- So why'd you guys wanna come here? Inspiration? Research? Someone wanna look-a-like Marilyn? – He pointed his finger at a huge wall mural of Andy Warhol's most famous work.

- Something like that – Nolan muttered, scanning the security systems in place.

They stopped to look at small neat cardigan within a flat glass case. " Gifted from Anne Baxter after the filming of 'All About Eve' 1950" – No use – thought Nolan - might be more Anne Baxter DNA on that – Several other displays were considered and rejected before he focussed in on the small flat glass displays which appeared to have no alarms.

"How to Marry A Millionaire – Pink Gloves -1953"

They continued through the exhibition, chatting about old times, giggling, but all the time Nolan was scanning the exhibits and the room. Once through the gallery, they retired to the Café Terrace outside, with its views over Downtown LA.

Dr Mike was volunteered by Nolan to stand in the café queue for three beers. As soon as he turned the corner, Nolan leaned into Bruno.

- Bruno, I'm gonna give you the chance to make some easy money – Bruno leaned in – Go on –

- Now I'm not sure if you want to undertake it or if one of your lowlife friends would be the ideal candidate, but there's a reason we're here today, and it's not an appreciation of movie stars of the fifties – Bruno looked interested - I need those pink gloves that are in that flat case towards the start of the exhibit – He fished his telephone out of his pocket and showed a photograph he had taken of exhibit V26 – I've had a good look, and the stuff doesn't look particularly well guarded to me. There's no wiring or alarms on those flat cases. The long windows just to the left of the cabinets look pretty easy to open – He looked up at Bruno who was studying the photograph.

- What we talking about? – His gaze looked up to meet Nolan's.
- For you, 5k. Nice quick easy job, just a pair of gloves, so it's not like the FBI and SWAT teams will get called in, heck no, they'll claim off the insurance, then before you know it, some good Samaritan will find them and hand them in – He leant back in his chair.
- When do you need them? – whispered Bruno.
- No great rush, maybe by the weekend? – He laughed.
- I take it Dr Mike's not in on this? - he continued.
- Of course not – laughed Nolan.

Bruno turned his chair around to face the outside wall of the East Pavilion, and the bank of several long glass windows.

Just at that moment Dr Mike set down a tray of beers – What we saying, guys? –
- Just admiring the Neo-Classicism of the East Pavilion – drawled Bruno, causing them all to laugh.

After finishing up their drink, Bruno insisted they exited back through the exhibition.

- Doesn't appear to be much scope for lifting some samples here Sam, everything is sealed……do you think we could bribe one of the guards to open up a case? – Dr Mike asked as he looked anxiously at the guard.
- No, there's CCTV all round – Nolan looked up at the cameras in each corner.
- Bruno seems very interested in Marilyn's clothing, not what I expected at all – queried Dr Mike as they headed over to Bruno, leaning over the display cases. Nolan put his arm around Bruno, and the three friends made their way to the exit.

Back at the clinic, Dr Mike had busied himself labelling and cross-referencing samples in the cold store, when he came into the office to find Nolan glued to the computer screen, intently focused.

- Brilliant to see old Bruno again….. – Began Dr Mike, when Nolan cut him off sharply – Sssssh! – he angrily hissed.
Dr Mike walked around to view the screen, its glow reflected on there faces.
- It's on a countdown……15, 14, 13, 12……..3,2,1- c'mon, c'mon, refresh for goodness sake – He stabbed at the return key on the keyboard.
- Ah-ha! - Nolan spun his chair around in triumph with is hands above his head – We are now the proud owners of John Lennon's hat! – Dr Mike squinted down at the screen. – eBay? How do you know it's real? – He stood back – and you paid over $3,500????? – He gasped.
- It was actually $3,501.66. And it's real because although it's on eBay, it was a live auction carried out by Rock Collectibles inc. of Las Vegas who have a 100% feedback rating from over seven thousand transactions – He sat back smugly in his seat.
- No, seriously, how do we know it's real? – Dr Mike genuinely quizzed.
- It'll be here in twenty-four hours. Excellent. – continued Nolan ignoring Dr Mike's concerns.
- Simon Walker is scheduled for Wednesday, so that gives us a few days to get the samples taken off. Right. Back to eBay…….look Mike…….Jennifer Aniston's jacket from the famous 'Friends' episode……..apparently given to the seller by his cousin who worked on the set…….yeah that'll be right……..- He continued scrolling – ohohoh…….Kurt Cobain's stage worn sweater……..aw….he can't guarantee authenticity…….-
Dr. Mike turned away shaking his head – Right, c'mon Sam. We need to get all these – He pointed to a bizarre array of everyday items arranged on a lab bench – Sampled, tagged and referenced tonight. We can do beer and eBay tomorrow night –
Nolan rose up, donned his white jacket and headed out of the office – Okay, okay, let's get this all done…just don't nag – as the door closed behind him.
The following morning Nolan opened his eyes. Again, he was stunned

by how good he felt. No sore head, no furry tongue, no acid stomach. He realised his surroundings were different. He realised he was on the small couch in his office. Dr Mike was on the office chair fast asleep with his feet on the desk. He looked at his watch. 6.30am.

- Christ, this no drinking is really agreeing with me – He thought to himself, again conscious that he usually only experienced 6.30am when had been up all night.

He headed through into the kitchen and made coffee for himself and Dr Mike.

The sun's rays punctuated the room through the small gaps in the blinds. He put the mug of coffee on the desk in front of Dr Mike, pushing his feet off the desk and then opening the blind to let the full sunlight flood into the room.

Dr Mike shook his head, rubbing his eyes – Jeez Sam, that's a brutal start to the day – he leaned over to caress the coffee mug.

- Busy day today. A facial reconstruction in the style of Jean Claude Van Damme this morning, followed by a working lunch with the Ethicon rep (no drinking), then a 3pm Bing Crosby 'ear job' on a 60 year –old Paramount Studios executive. Did you know they glued his ears back on all his films until 1930? No, me neither. I just found that out yesterday. Never mind. We can 3D print some new ears after lunch – Nolan laughed as he picked up the remote control and took aim at the wall mounted TV – Better see who's bigging up the Sunnyside Clinic today –

The TV flickered to life – 'Police are on the scene this morning with forensic experts looking for clues – the newsreader monotoned – but bizarrely the thieves only took the one item from the exhibit, ignoring, or unaware of the considerable value of neighbouring items –

Dr Mike looked up to see the Getty Museum on the TV screen viewed from an overhead helicopter. He looked open-mouthed at Nolan. The TV then switched to inside the East Pavilion, where lines of yellow and black Police tape zig-zagged the room, and several policemen milled about.

- Don't ask – began Nolan, who then switched the channel to an early

168

morning chat show, with the audience cheering and clapping.

- So how does this all tie in with our little trip yesterday? – He asked angrily.

- Bruno – whispered Nolan.

- What was that? I didn't quite hear! – shouted Dr Mike.

- Bruno – again whispered Nolan.

- So that was our little trip yesterday. Scope the place out. Then get a clearly destitute and desperate Bruno to go and steal the gloves for us! – He glowered.

- If I'd told you, you would have found some way to scupper it or try and make me feel guilty – replied Nolan.

- So now we're fugitives from the law? – He pointed at the TV screen – they'll be checking all the people who visited recently on CCTV……..Oh my god! We're foreigners here too…….They'll chuck us out! Just when it's all coming together! – Dr Mike's impassioned rant came to an abrupt end as there was a banging on the front door.

- Oh my god. They're here! – Dr Mike slouched on the chair head in hands.

- If it is the police, leave the talking to me. We were at the museum yes, but don't know anything about anything. Okay? – Nolan pointed at him then headed down the hall. Dr Mike rose up and peeked round the door frame as Nolan went to answer the door.

When he opened it, he was met with a dishevelled Bruno, clutching a sports holdall.

- Alright chaps. Got a wee delivery for you here – he held the bag up. Nolan grabbed him by the shoulder and pulled him into the clinic, looking left and right outside afterward.

Bruno meandered behind the bored receptionist's desk and took a seat. He threw the sports holdall to Nolan who caught it first time.

Dr Mike had come wandering through at the sound of Bruno's voice. Nolan removed the pink gloves and handed them to Dr Mike – Get what we need off these ASAP –

Dr Mike scuttled off down the hall mumbling his displeasure.

- Now just the matter of five thousand George Washingtons….

169

– began Bruno.

- Steady, Bruno, our clients who pay in cash wouldn't bother with chump change like that……..it's Benjamin Franklins for you – he opened the locked drawer in the reception desk and picked out a key.

- I'll be two minutes – he disappeared into the safe cupboard, re-appearing shortly after and threw Bruno a bundle of notes.

They chatted for a few minutes, and then Dr Mike came down the hall with the gloves and handed them to Nolan, who stuffed them back into the sports holdall – Now go drop them outside the Wilshire Police Station – Bruno laughed, jumped up from the chair, and bid them farewell.

Nolan checked his mobile phone. No messages.

They headed back into the office, just as a David Bowie clone was being interviewed on Jessica, a morning chat-show. An incredulous host fawned over Bowie, the TV camera zooming in on his profile as the audience clapped.

- That was only Wednesday we did him, and look how well that's come out – began Dr Mike staring at the screen. Nolan flicked the TV off.

- I think we should go freshen up. C'mon let's get set for the day ahead! – He put his arm around him as they headed down the hall.

They drew up at the palatial downtown offices of Perfect 10, the valet taking the car as they exited.

They both looked up at the towering structure, possibly one of the highest in downtown LA.

The rush of cool air enveloped them as they strode to the busy reception desk where an attractive blonde greeted them.

- We have a ten o'clock with Mike and Tony Rossi– began Dr Mike, conscious of the digital clock on the wall that read 10:09.

- Oh, actually you do, Dr's Nolan and Richardson? – she said looking at her computer screen – It's just we get so many people showing up here just expecting to be seen by the brothers - She picked up the phone – Hi Julia…..Yes both of them are here…..Yes lift two… - She hung up – If you'll just follow me – She headed away from the busy bank of lifts in the atrium, and round the corner to a small insignificant corridor, where

170

she leaned inside the door way and summoned the lift. Dr Mike noticed Nolan appeared more interested in the receptionist's derriere rather than the surroundings.

- Julia will get you at the top – she smiled.- Has anyone ever told you that you look like Kim Wilde? – began Nolan, just as the lift opened and Dr Mike grabbed his arm and pulled him inside.

The lift opened at clearly the top floor, where they were met by another attractive girl who bore more than a passing resemblance to Pamela Anderson.

- I bet you get this all the time, but....... - Started Nolan before a dig in the ribs from Dr Mike prompted him to stop. She smiled and showed them into a large glass office with spectacular views over downtown. They both sat down in the Eames chairs diagonal to the large metal desk which bore the old fashioned name plates with 'Mike Rossi' and 'Tony Rossi'.

The two brothers then entered, both in immaculately cut business suits, highlighting the casual attire of the two Doctors.

- Guys, guys,…..- They all hugged each other, and retired to their respective seats.

- Well, well - began Mike Rossi – Our two intrepid Doctors are now the names on everyone's lips all over America – Tony Rossi nodded in agreement – and I guess our job is now to get your faces on everyone's eyes in America – he continued.

Nolan sat back in his chair smiling and nodded. Dr Mike's composure was decidedly uneasy.

Tony Rossi leaned back in his chair – you know I think it could work so well for you guys. You're both not unattractive, no major deformities or disabilities, – His eyes ran all over them – And you have undoubtedly a major amount of hype behind you already. Our campaigns have been short, swift and targeted, all the time hit and run to avoid your identity being uncovered without our planning. Hit and run – He banged the desk three times to emphasise each word.

- So we're gonna get you guys round to a stylist, get you sharpened up, nice clothes, professional look – He made a square film director's frame with his fingers looking through it at them in turn – And then we'll turn you loose on the morning shows and then the late night chat shows. The two Scattish Doctors….And their human Zerox Machine – He swept his hand through the air in an arc – I can see it now –

Mike Rossi then opened a folder on his desk – This list of patients up to last week…….There is at least two thirds of them haven't been on any TV yet. I think we'll contact them and tie up some of your appearances with them; it'll be a nice touch –

- Yes a nice touch – Tony Rossi took over – The artists and their work – Again he waved his hand in an arc over his head – I can see it now. Maybe we could get some of the upcoming patients to go on with you too, that opens the door to a before and after appearance – He nodded.

- Yes – chipped in Mike Rossi – Two for the price of one. I can see it now – He gazed off into the distance.

Nolan smiled at Dr Mike. Dr Mike shifted uncomfortably in his chair. They chatted for a while about marketing strategies, billboard ads, radio jingles and advertising in the upscale press.

Mike Rossi abruptly stood up and handed a folder to Nolan – This has all your appointments for stylists, shoppers, photographers, etcetera. We've liaised and collated with Annie, so we'll get all of that done without affecting your work – he held out his hand which they both shook in turn.

Tony Rossi slowly rose to his feet and shook Dr Mike's hand then Nolan's – I was speaking to a good friend of yours last night Sam –

- Oh really – remarked Nolan.

- Yes, Salvatore Marchesi offered his warmest regards to you, when I told him I was meeting you today – He smiled.

Nolan's face went white – Oh yeah……tell him…..eh….em….. The same to him……- He muttered turning round and headed out the door, Dr Mike in tow.

- Next time we meet, you'll be famous – Mike Rossi shouted after them.

The following week was a hectic, non-stop series of hairdressers, makeup artists, photographers, scenesters. Both Doctors felt like pop stars, their chemistry clearly on show in the photographs taken. A myriad of advisers and stylists came and went, sometimes talking to them, often around them, as if they weren't there.

All the time Nolan took to this like a fish to water, meanwhile Dr Mike often had to be cajoled into wearing a designer suit, or even an eyebrow waxing.

Over the next few weeks, the two Doctors spent all their time between stylist appointments, pre-op consultations, collecting DNA material, and actual surgery. A frantic, hectic schedule was required to build the brand, define the brand.

Each day as they entered the clinic, Bored Receptionist, Grumpy Chinese Anaesthetist, and Annie would oooooh and aaaaah, as they confidently strolled in. Nolan had always had swagger, however, the change in Dr Mike, no matter how reluctant a subject, was completely transformative. The slightly slovenly, untidy, down-on-his luck librarian-meets-mad professor look had gone, to be replaced by quite a handsome, chiselled, British Gentleman.

Gone was the bird's nest hairdo, replaced by a floppy Hugh Grant style cut, gone were the unkempt eyebrows, now razor sharp neat. The dirty, broken Harry Potter glasses had been replaced with a modern contact lens. Even his affectations of modesty only encouraged the girls all the more, was causing even Nolan to cast an envious gaze whenever they were in female company.

The Rossi's influence spread far beyond merely looks, Dr Mike was now in the Chateau Marmont bungalows, whilst celebrity realtors scoured the Hills looking for their dream homes.

Also part of the Rossi plan was that the Doctors' attractiveness was attainable. Once they had explained that celebrity appeal increased dramatically when the subject was single and perceived to be available, Nolan explained this to a tearful Madison, happily terminating their relationship.

Whilst daytime was for work and image cultivation, night time was for Hollywood parties. The account managers at Perfect 10 worked hard, ensuring that both Nolan and Dr Mike were at every party, event launch, and happening in Hollywood. This was to increase exposure of the brand, and also put them on the inside track for future clients and work. The Doctors also used these situations to swell the ranks of their contacts within the service industry, garnering contacts they would have found impossible. Both carried small sample bags in their pockets, still harvesting the cocktail sticks and cigarette butts very discreetly themselves.

Nolan, naturally, took to this very easily, Dr Mike, however, although enjoying the trappings of swift success, was clearly not at ease with his new persona.

Chapter 9
L.A.Sun

Nolan stares at the closed curtains with the sun creeping round the edges. It's morning. It's another sore head, dry mouth, morning. Despite all his best efforts, and no matter how much better he felt, he kept lapsing into drunken nights. It would always start with good intentions, light sushi at dinner, no alcohol. Turning down the offers of starters, bread accompaniments, intermediate courses, sweet courses and pasties, he would finish the meal with an Americano, no milk, no sugar. On leaving the restaurant, he felt like a God. Fit, sparsely fed, sober but drunk on his own ego, Sam Nolan cut a sharp figure stepping out in Hollywood nearly every night.

Some nights his will power would extend, and he would stay sober and be in bed by ten, particularly those nights preceding surgery. But other nights, his insecurities would creep in, particularly with regard to Dr Mike. Dr Mike's stock had very much risen since his transformative styling and new hairstyle. In fact, Nolan had begun to notice when they attended social events together, the crowd or the principal characters would inevitably gravitate toward Dr Mike. The nicer girls would also be drawn to him. Dr Mike's naivety and innocence of all things Hollywood was like a magnet. This infuriated Nolan, as this was the one trump card he had always held in their relationship from the very beginning. Dr Mike's new found confidence was also grating on Nolan. Last night was one of those nights which had started well at Kristal, a new Champagne and Oyster Bar on Melrose, which had been hosting a 21st birthday party for the local Congressman's brat of a daughter, invites to which had been arranged for the two Doctors by Perfect 10. Numerous pointless exchanges with dull guests and their oyster-laced breath was taking its toll however. Nolan hated seafood, so avoiding the food was easy; however after three sparkling waters whilst listening to the Congressman's wife's medical aspirations for all three of their children, he could take no more, and grabbed a glass of champagne from a passing waiter's tray. A further couple of glasses got him past the Congressman's wife's inane ramblings and affections, and he spied Dr Mike reclining at the bar with the two best looking women at the party. He cursed under his breath, made his polite excuses and headed off to the bathroom. As he crossed the floor, he made sure the Congressman's wife wasn't watching, he changed direction and headed over to Dr Mike at the bar.

-.......And it was at that point I simply asked for my car keys and to hell with the consequences! – Dr Mike stopped and looked at Nolan as he approached laughing.

- That was such a laugh that night – Nolan joined in awkwardly.

- Em…...okay Sam……excuse me….where are my manners…- He looked at both women in turn before continuing – this is my good friend and partner, Dr Sam Nolan – he gestured to him, shooting daggers with his eyes.

- Good evening ladies – he kissed each of their hands in turn, causing them to blush and simper.

- Helllllloooo Dawktah Nolan – began the taller girl on Dr Mike's arm.

- I thought I recognised you earlier – began the other girl, almost cooly and offhand.

She was an athletic, good looking woman in her early thirties, short bobbed hair, immaculately dressed, and with almost a casual indifference to Nolan's presence.

Nolan immediately hailed a young waiter with a full tray of drinks, distributing the glasses. His inhibitions were reduced due to the previous champagne intake on his empty stomach, and this situation did not improve with a further three glasses in short time. Dr Mike was clearly unimpressed with his actions and slightly drunken demeanour, and conveniently scuttled across to another faceless group of socialites with his paramour, leaving Nolan with the athletic blonde.

- Bet you didn't know who I am – began Nolan with a slight slur.

- Bet you don't know who I am – retorted the blonde. This caught Nolan off guard, however, he was used to getting his own way, and wasn't going to let some upstart, no matter how good looking, interrupt his narcissistic flow.

He began to study her facially; the neat smooth brow, no evidence of filler, the symmetrical wide blue eyes, leading on the elegant curve of a perfect nose. Ear lobes perfectly aligned with the nose. A tanned, unmarked neck led gracefully up to a perfectly rounded chin, und upward to the most perfect mouth he had ever seen. Catching Nolan in examination mode, she shook her head and walked off, startling Nolan, and before he could get any words out, he felt slaps on the back from a David Bowie clone he had worked on and his stocky companion. By the time he had shaken hands and introductions made, he looked round, but she was gone.

The rest of the evening Nolan could not recall, although brief memories of photographs with the Congressman's family and introductions to future clients popped into his head.

He opened and closed his eyes several times just to confirm the hangover was real, then leant over to the bedside cabinet for a half-drunk bottle of Evian, which he downed in one. He sat half upright, breathing heavily from his exertion of drinking the water. As he replaced the empty bottle to the bedside, out of the corner of his left eye he noticed a jewelled high heeled shoe on the bedroom floor. At first, he couldn't focus properly, but after concentrating, confirmed indeed that it was a female shoe. His eyes darted about the floor in the gloomy half light. He spied a small clutch bag on his dresser, guarded by the oriental dragon statue. He further noted a small bolero jacket further over on the floor – Now that's definitely not mine – he thought to himself.

Just as he began to sit straight on, he felt a small gentle movement to his left. Slowly he moved his head round until he established there was a large lump under the sheet, and very probably, a woman in his bed. Or he hoped it was a woman. He gingerly lifted the sheet at his side a couple of inches, and silently swung his legs round onto the floor. He felt around in the gloom on the floor and eventually found his underwear which he pulled on, stood up, then tiptoed over to the windows where he parted the curtains slightly, letting the light flood into the room on the floor just in front of the bed.

Again, whoever was under the cover stirred slightly.

With the additional light source, he scanned the floor looking for further clues.

The bolero jacket had an Armani label – At least it wasn't one of the waitresses – he sniggered to himself, relived that he hadn't had to offer a free set of Jennifer Aniston cheekbones in return for a night of passion.

The other shoe was just beside the en-suite door. The distance between the two shoes indicated they had been removed in a hurry. Nolan began frantically scanning his memory for the slightest of details, but could remember nothing after shots at the bar with Bowie and his mates.

He began studying the hair just protruding the side of the pillow when the girl shot upright, causing Nolan to start.

- I'm so sorry – she began, clutching the sheet to her chest.

It was the short haired girl that had walked away from him earlier last night.

- Em ….no….it was my fault…….I should be getting the coffee on instead of daydreaming here….it's just I'm a little………tender….. -

- Well I'm pleased to meet you Little Tender – she extended her hand – My name is Ashley Hill –

Nolan shook her hand consciously aware of her just-up bed head Bardot-esque glamour in stark contrast to his hunched, creased boxers, hangover look.

- Delighted to meet you Ashley - he blushed - I'll just go shower up downstairs, so, eh, um, please feel free to use the facilities – he pointed to the ensuite – or just stay where you are, and I'll go organise some orange juice and coffee – he retreated walking backward awkwardly out of the room, and just as he started to close the door she winked at him suggestively.

All cleaned up and his mojo restored, Nolan efficiently moved around the kitchen, setting out cups and glasses, straightening chairs and removing clutter.

He looked up just as Ashley stepped off the last stair, her outline bathed

177

in backlight from the sun shining through the stair window.
She walked straight past Nolan over to the huge window with LA
spread out in the distance.
- That is some view – she stood in silence for a few moments before
Nolan interjected offering coffee.
- I'm just trying to work out where my house is from here.....I can see
that group of houses there – she pointed aimlessly into the distance –
and I can see that.....whatever it is, and that......- her voice drifted off.
Nolan handed her a mug of coffee. Even in last night's clothes, no
make-up, and dishevelled hair, she exuded glamour.
- So, Ashley, I'm afraid to say I was a little over indulged last night, and
my memory is a little fuzzy. I was kinda hoping you could fill in a few
blanks for me? – He smiled.
- You've really no recollection at all? – She retorted.
- I remember meeting you and your friend with my business partner, Dr
Mike, I remember later you daring me to eat oysters which I hate – she
laughed and covered her mouth at this point – I suppose you don't
remember being sick in your mouth and sprinting across the dance floor
to the restrooms either? – She giggled.
Nolan covered his eyes with his left hand and shook his head slowly.
- And presumably you don't remember your Saturday Night Fever
dance routine when 'Stayin Alive' came on either? – She laughed
louder.
Nolan lifted his other hand to cover his complete face – Aw no. I did? –
He dropped his hands and stared at her.
She strolled over to him, put her coffee cup next to his on the table, and
draped her arms around his neck.
- I was bored there anyways, Sam. I don't do average, I don't do
normal. And one thing I learned last night, Dr Sam Nolan, is that you
are not boring – she lightly kissed his lips – you are not average – she
kissed his lips slightly harder – and you are certainly not normal – She
now kissed him fully before standing back a pace. She then broke from
her demeanour and happily grabbed her bag and shoes, just as the
doorbell rang.

178

- That'll be my cab, Sam. I'm gonna go freshen up at home. If you're free later, maybe we could go grab a burger somewhere. Come pick me up at 1780 Mullholland around 2 if you fancy it –

Before Nolan could answer, she blew him a kiss, swung her bag over her shoulder, then did a hop, step and jump to the front door, and in one graceful move, opened, exited, and shut the door.

Nolan bounded up the stairs to the upper landing window and looked out just to see the cab disappearing from view.

He smiled to himself. She did seem different. Plus, she wanted more Sam. Which was always a good thing. He tried replaying the previous night's events as he walked back up to the bedroom, and looked for evidence of sexual activity on the bedsheets, but could neither remember or find any stains. He concluded therefore that his drunken inability to perform sexually had possibly been misconstrued as a sign of restraint, valour and integrity. The accidental hero. He smiled.

By the time 2pm rolled around, he had changed outfits several times, before settling on a long sleeve thin sweater and classic Levis. He even deliberated for several minutes over which aftershave to wear.

- Hugo Boss to be the Boss – he thought to himself.

He skipped down the steps to the garage to be confronted with his trusty white Porsche 911, and the newcomer. A gleaming, sparkling, new blood-red Ferrari convertible. This had been part of a deal secured by the Rossi Brothers and Ferrari of West Hollywood providing both Doctors with the use of the most up to the minute Ferraris. Whilst Dr Mike had opted for the beautifully understated metallic grey four seater coupe, Nolan had immediately made a beeline for the ostentatious, in your face convertible. If ever their personalities were defined, it was with these cars. He knew however, he could never part with the Porsche, a lifetime of longing, all stemming from a poster on his bedroom wall in Edinburgh, back in 1979. A Porsche Turbo in white side on, with a typically seventies topless model stretched out on her back up the line of the car's bonnet, her white high heels and bikini bottoms matching the car. It had been swapped to him from a friend in exchange for the Star Wars Soundtrack LP. It took pride of place on his

179

bedroom wall, between the Clash and the Sex Pistols. His mother tut-tutted at the tasteful nudity, and his father always gave him a sly wink. He often wondered where she was now. Was she as impressed with the Porsche 911 as he was? Did she ever live that lifestyle? That poster, like the Clash one and the Sex Pistols one, had a profound effect on him. Nolan hopped into the Ferrari, pressed the 'launch' button (yes, seriously) and the V8 engine roared into life, shaking the very foundations of the house. The garage door opened up and the car rumbled out into the road, the noise with the hood down like a Panzer Division rolling down the street, before he planted the accelerator, which changed the engine tone to a squeal, and the car shot forward like a missile, leaving a cloud of exhaust fumes in its wake, and the garage door dutifully rattled shut.

After entering the Mulholland address into the car's navigation system, he followed the twists and turns through the Hills, all the while his New Order soundtrack constantly interrupted by the shrill electronic navigation instructions.

- Turn right..........straight ahead at the next junction.......turn left......-

A large chequered flag on the screen showed that he had arrived. All Nolan could see was a giant wall with a laurel hedge topping off the last four feet. He crept round slowly in the car, its engine gurgling, clearly unhappy with the low pace and low revs. As he rounded the corner, he saw the gateway to the property had a gatehouse with barrier. He drew up to the barrier to ask the guard directions, when he noticed the 1780 sign on the guardhouse. The guard came out and looked down on the sportscar.

- I'm looking for an Ashley Hill at 1780? Does she have one of the apartments here? – Nolan quizzed.

The guard laughed loudly – There are no apartments here Sir, but I assume that you are Sam Nolan? –

Nolan nodded affirmatively as the guard re-entered the guard house and opened the barrier. He casually saluted as Nolan rumbled past.

The drive was a considerable length as the Ferrari growled up the gentle incline, bordered by manicured topiary and immaculate borders. Every now and again there would be a small gap in the bushes where he caught a glimpse of even grander lawns and embellishments. Eventually he rounded the final corner into a large courtyard with a renaissance fountain in the centre where he parked up. He was still taking in the full glory of the mock Italian 1920's villa as he exited the car when he looked up to see Ashley standing on the balcony above the front door.

- I'll just be down – she disappeared.

Nolan wandered up to the two huge front doors which were open and gingerly stepped inside. He was greeted with a huge open hall flooded with natural daylight from a giant roof cupola. A circular balcony circled the whole hallway before terminating in an elegant wide staircase. The same staircase was now depositing a gorgeous Ashley Hill right in front of Nolan.

Dressed in simple denims and white blouse, her hair held back with a large white band, Nolan realised how naturally good looking she was. Working in an industry of manufactured and fake beauty, it always struck Nolan when he was confronted with actual natural perfection. He snapped back into the moment.

- Is this all one house? – He queried.

She nodded in reply.

- This is some pad – Nolan nervously observed, looking around.

- Yes it is. I just moved here six months ago. After a year of searching, I fell in love the minute I walked through that front door. I knew I would have it – she casually asserted.

- What did you say you did for a living? He enquired.

- I didn't – she playfully replied.

Sensing Nolan's slight bewilderment, she continued – When I signed up for the fourth season of 'Drumbeat', my agent secured the largest salary in history for a soap actress, and so I decided to invest in something longer term – she turned and swept her arm around – But you don't wanna hear all that now.......let's do lunch! – She grabbed his arm and led him out of the house. She was aware of the confusion on his face.

- No......Drumbeat.......agent?.......*soap actress?* – He was taken aback.

181

- You have heard of 'Drumbeat' right? – She quizzed.
The look of confusion on his face answered her question.
- You have a TV Sam? -
- I *have* one, I just don't really use it –
- Let me help you out. 'Drumbeat' is the most popular soap opera show in the United States at the moment. It is currently midway through its fourth and most successful series. I play Cassandra Blake, one of the principal characters. I have always played Cassandra Blake. I am currently considering several offers of movie roles, and according to my agent, 'On the launch pad to the most glittering of careers in the entertainment industry'. Okay? -
She took his arm and guided him toward the door. At the top step she paused and looked at the Ferrari gleaming in the sunlight. Her head tilted both ways while studying the car
– Really Sam? – She laughed and they walked down to the car.
Nolan checked his phone just before he entered the car.
– Call me – read the message from Dr Mike.
– Excuse me a second – he turned away from the car and began texting Dr Mike. A second after he had sent the message, the phone rang. Dr Mike.
- Aren't you forgetting something Sam? – began Dr Mike.
- No, I don't think so, there's no surgery until Sunday – he replied haughtily.
- Just the matter of a meeting with the guys from Ambulin? You know, the deal we've been working on for the last month? – Dr Mike sounded genuinely annoyed.
- Damn. I forgot. Well, that's kinda your deal, and you're the guy for the platelets anyways - he began.
- Not really the point Sam. They will be here shortly expecting to see both Doctors –
- They're reps Mike. They are there to sell to us. It's what suits us, not them. You'll be fine – he hung up the phone.
He then pressed and held the button to turn the mobile phone off. He entered the car and tossed the phone onto the back seat.

- Bad day? – She gently enquired.
- No, just the usual – He laughed and started to creep the car down the driveway, its convertible roof opening slowly.
It didn't take long to escape the city and head North up the coastal route. The sun shone brightly, and with the wind in their hair, it was a picture postcard moment. They shared jokes and memories, some good, some bad. Nolan could scarcely believe his luck. In a few short months he had gone from being threatened by Italian mob types and operating his business from cheque to cheque, to hooking up with Dr Mike, transforming the business into the premier Plastic Surgery in the whole of California, and now here he was in a brand new convertible Ferrari heading up the Californian coast with one of the most beautiful women in the world.
- Whatcha thinkin' Sam? – She drawled.
- Huh?-
- We had been talking solid for the last half hour, and you suddenly went quiet – she continued.
- Oh, just thinking about how things have changed for me lately – he looked at her for validation. There was a long pause as she stared at him intently. He kept looking back to the road, then back to Ashley.
- I like you, Sam Nolan – she began – You're weird, but I like your kind of weird. The fact you didn't have a clue who I was, despite the fact you have a business predicated on celebrity. There's just something………something about you…….- She leant over and kissed him lightly on the cheek and sat back in her seat, almost at a forty-five degree angle, leaning in the corner between door and seat. Her white blouse and hair blowing in the wind, she looked at him fondly over the top of her $400 tortoiseshell Rayban Jackie-O's.
Nolan took a mental snapshot – Not often I'm happy – he thought to himself.
- Let's go get an Ice Cream in Santa Barbara –

====0====

The daylight was long gone as the sleek Ferrari growled back up the driveway at 1780 Mulholland.

Nolan stopped the car right outside the front door, and as she turned to exit the car, Ashley turned and kissed him on the cheek.

- We must do this again – she cooed, running her finger down his nose. And with that, she exited the car and skipped up the steps.

Nolan had enjoyed himself. An afternoon in Santa Barbara had just been what he needed. He made a mental note to do this more frequently. He reached over into the back seat and retrieved his phone, restarting it in the process.

He sat there illuminated by the car's dashboard and comforted by the engine's low growl, punctuated by the multiple notification and voicemail alerts on his phone as it gained signal. Multiple messages, voicemails, missed calls, texts, emails. Nearly all from Dr Mike.

He opened the last text message. "I'll be at the clinic until you get there – this is URGENT"-

Muttering under his breath, he pointed the car down the drive and hit the navigation button for 'work'.

Negotiating the tight cornered streets, he soon began to recognise the landscape and surrounding buildings, before he realised he was at the filling station a mile from the clinic.

He soon reached the parking lot, and parked alongside Dr Mike's car. It looked surreal, the empty lot with only two gleaming Ferraris side by side. The clinic was fully illuminated, and he noticed the blinds in his office twitch as Dr Mike had obviously been on point.

He sighed and exited the car, and headed to the front door, where a clearly irate Dr Mike swung it open for him.

- Bad enough you dump the Ambulin guys on me, but this……..this……THIS! – he gesticulated wildly as they marched along the hallway to Nolan's office – I mean why have a mobile phone if you don't have the damn thing on……..when you're mobile! -

- Mike, I've literally just got all these messages and I've been up in the hills where I didn't get signal. I don't know what you're on about? – He quizzed sympathetically.

Dr Mike grabbed the TV remote and began selecting a stored programme. As he was about to press play, he took a deep breath and stepped back from Nolan.

- You remember the Princess Leia girl a few months back? The one that kept coming back again and again? Jamie something –

- Of course I do - his face reddened - She had the basics there, just the minor facial, the laryngectomy to get the voice right.......the attention to detail she had was incredible. Every last detail. Christ, do you remember how we had Marco at the funeral home get us the source Carrie Fisher material? That was not our finest moment...- He laughed – She was so desperate to get that part in the new Star Wars movie, the prequel....a youthful Princess Leia or something like that......- His voice tailed off.

- It wasn't the movie part she was after, Sam – Dr Mike hit the 'play' button on the remote.

A smartly dressed news anchor was on screen.

- "It was absolutely unprecedented scenes at Municipal Court in downtown Los Angeles today in the case of Loudon v Fisher. Jamie Ellis Fisher, the young woman who announced her arrival last week in the form of a legal claim to the Fisher Estate as the long-lost daughter of Carrie Fisher, given up for adoption at the point of delivery was in court alongside Billie Lourd, up to now the only known child of the deceased Hollywood Superstar. This bitterly contested hearing has lasted several days, and with over $25 million and future image rights, etc at stake, a very contentious situation. The judge finally ruled yesterday that a DNA test would be the only way to settle this expeditiously. As the court re-convened this morning, both the Plaintiff's and the Trustee's lawyers had been made aware of the results of the test, conducted the previous day. A hushed courtroom was packed to the gills with journalists and photographers, as the Trustees of the estate of Carrie Fisher stood to read the report. The entire courtroom erupted into bedlam and chaos as the Trustees' Lawyer confirmed that the DNA was a 94% match and beyond any reasonable doubt that Jamie Ellis Fisher was indeed the natural child of the former actress Carrie

185

Fisher. A tearful Billie Lourd barged past the legal team to hug her new 'sister' in tearful scenes that will be shared around the world. She said at the hastily-arranged press conference, that 'although I have lost half a fortune, I have gained a sister, and you can't put a price on that'-

The camera then focused on Jamie Ellis Fisher being escorted through the Paparazzi scrum when Dr Mike paused using the remote, leaving a burred grinning Jamie on screen.

- What the hell are we going to do? – began Dr Mike – The devious little cow! No wonder she was never away from here needing pumped full of DNA! –

Nolan's face reddened even more.

- I'm afraid DNA was not the only thing she was getting pumped full of at the clinic Mike – Nolan ruefully whispered.

- You have got to be joking me! – Dr Mike roared – You stupid, stupid, idiot! There's absolutely no doubt a conniving, scheming cow like that won't have got some compromising material or photographs of you two together to prevent us going to the police! I can see the lawsuits now! Patient Doctor privilege indeed! Seems you're the only one that got any privilege out of this situation! You disgust me sometimes! – His face was contorted in anger.

- Now just wait a minute – I'm just taking this all in and it looks like I've been used and abused too here Mike, and I am genuinely sick and upset about this – he apologetically mumbled.

- Yes! Sick and upset she got the $25 million and not you! Jesus Christ! I can see it! You're annoyed you hadn't thought of it first! – He threw the remote down on the desk.

- Always the bloody victim, Sam –

A now clearly angry Nolan puffed up his chest, picked up the remote control and began to walk threateningly around the desk toward Dr Mike.

- So pray tell, how would you explain to the police how we came by the Fisher DNA in the first place? - "Yes officer, we paid $2,000 to an embalmer at the Forest Hills Funeral Home to steal one of the deceased actresses' fingernails" - I'm sure that would go down great, we

186

wouldn't be in any trouble at all, oh no – Nolan threw the remote back at Dr Mike who was now cowering back into the corner of the room – Not to mention every bell-hop, waiter, cleaner, valet, driver, server, maid in this whole town. You think after we throw Marco at the Funeral Home under a bus that any of these people would give us anything? After building one of the greatest networks of underclass this city has ever seen? Don't be so bloody stupid! Accept it. She was smarter than us – He hung his head and let out a deep breath.

Nolan checked his phone. He was aware of Dr Mike's panting breathing. He had obviously given him a shock with his response. Dr Mike headed over to his office and slammed the door. Nolan let out a huge sigh.

The next morning Nolan slowly opened his eyes half way. The smallest chink in the curtains revealed the tiny particles of dust floating upward this time in the sunlight. He studied this intently for a few moments then turned sideways to read the clock. The dry mouth, the pounding head reminded him he had decided to have a drink after his confrontation with Dr Mike. He recalled going into The Montrose 'just for one' but details seemed vague after that. As he sat up in the bed, the extent of his sore head indicated it had been more than just a couple of drinks. He flicked on the television which was on a news channel. They were still jabbering on about the Fisher trial. Nolan reached for the bottle of Evian on the bedside cabinet and took a long drink. As Jamie's face came up on screen, he toasted her with the bottle. The show then cut to commercial. Nolan half closed his eyes and let out a long sigh. He had meetings with Dr Mike at 2pm so he at least had a couple of hours to straighten out.

Just then, the sound from the commercial caused him confusion, he suddenly opened his eyes and then turned up the volume with the remote.

- "Here at the Sunnydene Clinic Dr Novo and his team of specialists will help you with the look you desire. Dr Novo has over twenty year experience in cosmetic enhancement, and had recently undertaken surgical work for several celebrity and not-so-celebrity clients" - Dr Novo was an aging bald man in his sixties with a silver/grey goatee beard and a face from a nightmare. A creepy, smiling Dr Novo now gave way to a terrible Prince impersonator who Nolan recognised immediately.

- Damn it! – Nolan slapped the bed.

"Prince" then leaned over to Dr Novo who proceeded to highlight the areas of the subject's face. "Debbie Harry" then wandered on from the other side, and Nolan recognised her as well. The details for the clinic then flashed up on screen in an identical font and style to the Sunnyside Clinic.

Nolan reached over and picked up his mobile phone and called Dr Mike.

- Hello? – He answered second ring.

- Hi Mike, em, this is gonna sound a bit strange, but was there anyone else at the Roslin Institute or on your roadshows that would be able to replicate what we're doing? –

- Never in a million years......why do you ask? –

- That idiot who we did the Prince cheekbone restructure, and the crazy bitch who actually thought she was in Blondie have both just appeared in an ad on TV with some crackpot surgeon under the title "Sunnydene Clinic" and it all looks very much like our ads, our graphics, all designed I think to confuse them with us. They're even passing off the work we did as their own –

- Right. I'll go research this right now. You get the surgeon's name? –

- Yes – Novo, and its "Sunnydene" Clinic. I'll be there in half an hour – he hung up.

An hour later Nolan entered the clinic, nodding to Bored Receptionist, but Annie was blocking his path.

- What's all this Sunnydene crap that's all over the TV and billboards Sam? –

- It's nothing. Just a tribute act. I'm just away to discuss with Dr Mike how we deal with it – he pointed down the corridor.

She moved sideways clutching folders to her chest, allowing him to pass.

As Nolan entered his office, a clearly pensive Dr Mike was in the patient chair fidgeting.

Nolan dumped his phone and keys on the desk.

- Well it turns out Dr Novo is an Albanian, Alessandro Novotchelik. Been in the US about five years, running a small practice in Michigan, but has just popped up here. The clinic was formerly rented by AdAstra, a window cleaning business, but according to the lease application to the City, they took it on only three weeks ago. The tradename Sunnydene hasn't been registered or even applied for.

Prince was Naseem Attah, a Pakistani kitchen worker. We did his cheekbone realignment, brow lift and chin implant. The job was good, but I think without the Prince DNA, you wouldn't have known. He was angry when we wouldn't do the next stage without money in advance. That was six weeks ago.

Debbie was Jane Atwell, waster daughter of Hollywood socialite. At the interview she had confessed to the gym addiction for the last year, and had been to see Blondie play at the Hollywood Bowl. Some nut in her group said she was a dead ringer for Debbie Harry, and that was what she had fixated on. She was maybe 20% when she came into us, the lipo, nose job and eye tuck with a healthy dose of Debbie DNA probably got her to a 70%, clothes and make up would complete the illusion. She booked in for the hairline adjustment and the breast reduction, but when the booking payment didn't come in, Annie chased her up but never got an answer –

Nolan leant back in the chair, hands crossed, looking at a clearly anxious Dr Mike.

- Well, they're coming right at us. Even on the drive over, I heard the ad running on KRQR. Annie says there are billboards now too. Just a matter of time before they start working the networks too. So, this guy has seen our business model, imitated everything including the name, fallen in with the two disgruntled losers we had previously done work on, and passed all of this off as his own creation. How does that make you feel Mike? –

- I……I…..dunno, it's not very fair…….rather underhand….. – Nolan started to ramble - He's a snake. Thieving snake. It wouldn't matter that he couldn't do the Digital DNA procedures, even his average surgical work could pass, as the people want to believe. It's all off our backs…….He brings nothing to the table except imitation…….We'll be viewed as a collective…….Our triumphs benefit him……He could probably run for a year or so trotting out substandard work before being rumbled, and in the process tarring us with his unprofessional brush. Sunnyside/Sunnydene……nobody would know or care about the difference – it's all that celebrity surgery place. Well he's got me angry. Bloody angry –

- What do we do Sam? – Dr Mike sat forward in his seat.

Nolan looked out the window far into the distance, then swung round and pointed directly at Dr Mike – I don't know – He looked left and right, then grabbed the phone and punched in a number aggressively.

- Hi Jane, it's Sam over at the Sunnyside Clinic. I know its short notice, but do you think Mike and Tony could squeeze us in for a very quick meeting today? We have a bit of an emergency, and it needs the brothers' cool heads to sort – he looked up at Dr Mike. After a pause of several minutes, Jane had answered – They'll give us 30 minutes at 5? That'll be great. Cheers – he hung up the phone – I can't believe they're copying so blatantly. I'm sure the Rossi Brothers will have come across this kind of situation before – Nolan stood up and made motion to leave the office – I'll just get you at Perfect 10's office at 5? – He queried matter-of-factly.

- Where are you going? – Dr Mike looked incredulous.

- Things to do and all that……. - he sheepishly answered.

- You're just here! We have two massive situations between the Fisher Fiddle and this tribute act stealing our business, and you want to clear out and go bang your actress girlfriend who you met two days ago? – Dr Mike was wide eyed – Fine. Go. I now know where I stand. Where this business stands – He strode out of the room and slammed shut his own office door.

Nolan went to open Dr Mike's office door but froze his hand above the handle. All that would happen is they would argue some more, and another hour of his life would be wasted.

He weighed it up. An hour arguing with Dr Mike, or an hour in bed with one of the best looking women he had ever seen? – Tough choice – he laughed to himself.

He shrugged and headed to reception. – Can you remind Dr Mike we have an appointment at 5pm? He knows where – he said to Bored Receptionist, who didn't look up from her computer screen.

Once out in the parking lot, he pulled his phone out and text "on way". He fired up the car and sped off.

At 4.55pm sharp, a freshly groomed Nolan was shown up to the Rossi Brothers' waiting area, where he once again admired the view of their secretary and her well-proportioned posterior. Dr Mike was already seated, flicking through some celebrity magazine. Nolan nodded acknowledgement but was ignored. Mike Rossi then came out of the lift and they rose to greet him. Handshakes and formalities concluded they headed into the main office where Tony Rossi was already seated, intensely studying a computer screen.

- So, our hottest guys in Hollywood needed an urgent meeting, Tony - began Mike Rossi jokingly.

- Well, it's usually about money or the lack of it – quipped back Tony Rossi.

- I'm afraid it's a bit more serious than that – said Nolan, and began to relay the events of earlier that day and all they knew about Dr Novo and the Sunnydene Clinic.

Dr Mike handed over a flash drive with the TV advert, which they inserted to the desktop and proceeded to watch. Nolan leant over and pointed out the principal characters.

- This does seem very specific, very targeted - began Tony Rossi – Is there any chance anyone else in your organisation could be connected to these people? – He pointed at the frozen image on screen with the heel of his glasses.

- No, no, - began Dr Mike. We're pretty sure it's all come from the two disgruntled patients. We believe they've somehow hooked up with this unknown Plastic Surgeon somewhere and he's identified that he could probably use them as advertising for his own practice off the back of our work on them, copy the image and branding, and hope that some customers either get confused and book him by mistake, or some go there anyway thinking he's an alternative to us –

Both Rossis' sat back in their chairs and considered. Mike Rossi leaned forward and spoke quietly.

- You guys are the hot ticket just now. We're on an upward trajectory, and our measured path will ensure that you get to where you guys want to be. We've worked hard, as have you guys, in making sure that your brand is known in this town. All the advertising, TV appearances, radio shows, PR, reps, billboards, parties, etcetera, etcetera, has been specifically targeted and applied where required, and I think we're all happy with the results, but the last thing we need is some upstart thief. I say thief, because that's what he is, wandering in from the sidelines and hitching his wagon to our express train. What we will do is reach out to the guys doing the ads and the promotions for this lot, and make them aware that unless they cease and desist, there's no work forthcoming from the Perfect 10 agency. We'll also put pressure on the guys over at this TV channel also to drop the ads, or again, nothing from Perfect 10. The billboards are the easiest. I know Jimmy at RiteScreen personally, so a call there ends all that. A communique around all Magazines, Radio & TV channels that if they promote this imitation organisation may render them liable in any future legal action should also remove any prospect of them using alternative channels for promotion. We have contacts in every other PR agency in this town, so if anything pops up, we'll slam it shut – He delivered in a calm, even voice, with just the hint of menace.

- That's fantastic – Dr Mike and Nolan looked at each other smiling.

- And this Sunnydene Clinic……- Tony Rossi looked over the top of his glasses – 6340 Emerald…….I think that's those dumpster units that Stan Zweig has……- He continued scanning the computer – Yes it is. I'll put in a call to him and see if he can 'discover' a flaw in the lease or give them notice. Stan's a good guy. Knows which side his toast's buttered – he began making notes on a notepad.

Mike Rossi sat back in the chair and looked directly at Nolan, causing him slight unease.

- And of course we'll give Dr Nolan's good friend Salvatore Marchesi a call to let him know about all this. I'm quite sure that he can arrange for a couple of his operatives to call into the Sunnydene Clinic and make Dr Novo aware that all our business interests are being compromised by his activities……..he does have a way of ensuring his message gets across…….– He stared directly at Nolan, who felt the dark eyes bring right through him.

- Is that absolutely necessary?..... I mean the measures you've already laid out seem pretty exhaustive and comprehensive…..surely we don't need to visit him? – Dr Mike meekly offered.

- This guy is stealing your business, Mike, our business. Do you have an objection to direct confrontation? Would you two rather go talk to him? – Tony Rossi growled at them, slightly irritated.

- No, no, no…….- Dr Mike shot a nervous sideways glance at Nolan, who looked at the floor.

- Good. Hopefully this time next week this joker will be gone. Now anything else we can do for you two? – Both Rossi brothers smiled and leant forward.

The doctors made their exit, profusely shaking hands and nodding in deference, before the sanctuary of the lift gave them respite. Dr Mike let out a huge sigh as the door closed.

- I can't believe you're OK with Dr Novo getting a visit from some hoods – began Dr Mike angrily.

- Me? You seemed to be fine with it all up there….'no, that's fine Mr Rossi'….- Nolan mimicked his voice – Listen it's dog eat dog. They're right. This guy is stealing our business and by extension he is affecting the income of all those connected with us. So what if Dr Novo gets a visit. He should have thought of this before ripping us off. The Rossis are right. We should have gone round ourselves and sorted the little creep out – Nolan was fired up.

Dr Mike shook his head and looked at Nolan incredulously. The lift doors opened and they spilled into the lobby.

- I'll see you at the Cematra fundraiser tonight? – queried Nolan.

- Yeah whatever – said Dr Mike who walked straight out of the building and jumped into a waiting cab and sped off, leaving Nolan standing behind the revolving door.

Chapter 10
The Cocktail Queen

- Is everything all right with you two? – queried a nervous Annie craning her neck around the door.
- Yeah just a little difference of opinion – Nolan muttered.
- It can't be easy for him, Sam. You're currently on every newsstand and TV programme. It doesn't matter where you go, you and Ashley are there. When did you last spend time with him? –
- You're right – Nolan got up from his desk and gently ushered past Annie before crossing the corridor and knocking on Dr Mike's door. He didn't wait for a response before entering.
A pensive Dr Mike was intently studying his computer screen.
- Listen, Mike, I'm sorry about things lately. I've been too caught up in all this Ashley stuff – He gesticulated in the air – And it's just for once, I'm feeling better about myself again. I'm easing off the drinking, no more late nights, and I've even had a couple of emails from Sarah! She's so excited about meeting Ashley, I think it could be a way for me to start building all those broken relationships again –
Dr Mike continued to stare at the computer screen, oblivious.
- I'm fitter, healthier, and happier than I have been in years, and it's all thanks to you. I would never have met Ashley without you, and would never have had this lifestyle without you. We *need* each other Mike -
Dr Mike's eyes shifted over to Nolan scornfully then back to the screen again.
- C'mon – he walked round to Dr Mike and put his arm around him.
Dr Mike continued to stare at the computer screen which Nolan could now see displayed the day's appointments.
- Our first appointment is in fifteen minutes – Dr Mike handed Nolan the file as he got up and headed for the coat stand where he put on his white coat and headed into Nolan's office where the files had been neatly laid out on the desk.
Nolan followed him through, and sighing heavily crashed down in his chair.

- So who we got today – He began looking at the first file just as Annie entered the room.

Annie beamed a huge smile – First in today is Adam Joffrey, a second hand car salesman from San Francisco who has already spent over $50k on surgical procedures elsewhere in town to replicate the look of his hero, Marilyn Manson. He's 40 years old, divorced, and owns a small chain of second hand car outlets in the Bay Area -

Nolan looked at the photograph in the file before holding it up to Dr Mike whilst screwing up his face.

- Who? – Asked Dr Mike – studying the photograph.

- Marilyn Manson – Annie replied – He's a popular singer in a Goth band –

- I hate the ones where we uglify rather than beautify – started Nolan before turning the photograph back round – and I certainly wouldn't buy a car from this freak. Only in California………urgh. He has his tongue split in half. What does he actually want us to do? –

- He's looking for liposuction to the face and neck, and for us to create the correct contour of his forehead by receding his hairline by about an inch, some cheekbone implants…….and of course he will need our signature 'special ingredient' – began Annie before being cut off by a loud sigh from Dr Mike who was now looking at the floor. Annie continued.

- Your 10.30 is Abbie Huntinger, a 34 year old soft porn actress who goes by the stage name of Danni Divine. Her initial enquiry was for some 'general enhancement' and a 'sprinkle of you guys' celebrity fairy dust' – Annie rolled her eyes before continuing – she feels she wants more of a curvy retro look, more Marilyn, more Jayne Mansfield, etcetera, etcetera – She proffered a photograph of a neat forties styled dark haired, large bosomed girl in lingerie. Nolan meanwhile had brought up Danni Divine.com on his computer, and half turned the screen so the others could see. There were mainly tasteful underwear and lingerie photographs, but the contact section suggested she was probably a high-class prostitute.

- Maybe we could use some of the Marilyn DNA – offered Dr Mike.

196

- You can tell from that website she's a hooker? – queried Annie.
- Yeah it's pretty clear Annie. All tasteful photographs with just a hint of nipple in a see-through bra, those come-to-bed looks in the lingerie photos, taken on an actual bed, and of course the 'On the Town' photos taken at various bars and restaurants where she's on the arm of more mature men. It's all pretty obvious she is available at a price – Nolan leaned forward to give a boudoir photograph greater scrutiny.
- Well I guess you would be the person to know – retorted Annie, causing them all to laugh.
- I'd go with Dr Mike on this one. Pump some silicone into her backside, hips and breasts, and give her a good old shot of Marilyn, you know, some of the stuff Bruno got for us -
He sat back from the screen – so who's our eleven o'clock? – Dr Mike was pouring through the contents of the file, a broad smile on his face – It's your John Lennon guy Simon Walker –
- Excellent. We took the samples off the hat, right? This one is cut and dried. The guy is already 90% of the way there and looks just like him already – began Nolan.
- That's the problem – he's looking for 100% - stated Dr Mike
- And he's at the right place to get to 100% - announced Nolan triumphantly.
They concluded their pre-op meeting, and as Dr Mike shuffled off to prepare, Annie shot Nolan a concerned look to which Nolan responded by swatting away an imaginary fly.
Just then, Bored Receptionist came into the room with a large important looking envelope.
- I had to sign for this for you – she glumly stated before handing to him.
The envelope bore the CBS TV logo and Nolan opened it with a wide grin on his face. Annie and Bored Receptionist turned to leave.
- Wait! Don't you guys want to see the next reality TV star? – he quizzed.
They stopped in their tracks and turned around simultaneously with a look of shock on their faces.

197

Nolan held up the bundle of paperwork.
- This is my contract for the newest series of *"I Would Do Anything for Fame, But I Won't Do That"* starting on CBS this fall – he said in a TV announcer voice.
- Oh my god! – Annie looked dumbfounded, and even Bored Receptionist broke into a smile. Annie shimmied around the desk and gave him a hug – You know these shows are designed to humiliate you, right? – Nolan nodded just as Annie gasped and raised her hand to cover her mouth – What about Dr Mike? So much for keeping a lower profile! –
- It was the Rossi Brothers who organised all this. They felt it would raise our public profile – He gave "public profile" air quotes – but Dr Mike didn't want to know. Said it was infantile and pointless. Both Rossi Brothers and I tried to persuade him but he walked out of the meeting. Ashley thought it would do me good, for me, to do something like that –
Both Annie and Bored Receptionist rolled their eyes at the mention of Ashley's name.
- Besides, if he doesn't want to become a household name then that's his lookout – Nolan asserted smugly.
- You are aware of the nature of the show aren't you? – began Annie as Bored Receptionist began scanning her iPhone for video clips - I mean it can be pretty debasing. I watched all of last season and some of the challenges I think even you would find quite daunting. I mean a show that's predicated on desperate Z listers and wannabes being defied to push to the limits what they would do for a trickle of celebrity...........Hollywood's got some pretty desperate people, Sam -
- I've never actually watched the show – he began, now a little nervous – But the Rossi Brothers told me it is number two in the viewing charts last season, and with the calibre of contestants like myself for this season, looks set to become the number 1. I have a teaser photoshoot next week, and they're gonna be running ads to build the hype –
- Oh my god....oh my god.... Oh my god... -
Bored Receptionist held up her phone to let both Nolan and Annie see a

clip of the show where various contestants were swallowing small shot glasses full of live wriggling baby eels on the pretext that it was a Japanese delicacy and this was for a Japanese TV advert. Most were pressing ahead but failing to conceal their disgust or throwing up afterwards as the audience howled with glee. Nolan looked decidedly uneasy as Bored Receptionist then scanned to the next clip showing an ageing Hollywood cinema star who Nolan recognised but could not name, preparing to take part as an extra in a gay porn film orgy scene, when he was clearly 100% heterosexual. The clip alternated between fuzzed out gay sex scenes and a look of outright disgust and revulsion on the actor's wizened old face, as the audience once again howled with glee at his very real discomfort.

- My favourite was the final two years ago when the guy who heads up the house band on Jimmy Fallon was up against Dale Owens from *Pets Win Prizes* when they had to prepare a Christmas Meal containing their own faeces for their families on Christmas Eve.....- Bored Receptionist had tears of laughter running down her cheeks, as Annie also laughed along – Wasn't that also the season where all the contestants had to give hand jobs to random homeless guys on Wilshere Boulevard? – asked Annie – Yes and didn't Angie Van Nuys use a disposable surgical glove!!!! – They both shouted in unison before collapsing into fits of laughter.

Nolan meanwhile looked slightly uncomfortable – I'm sure I can deal with anything that's put in from of me – he asserted.

- You're going to have to – said Annie shooting a sideways glance at Bored Receptionist causing them both to convulse into more extreme fits of laughter.

Dr Mike stuck his head round the door – Just when you're ready Miss McDonald and Miss Reed, Mr Adam Joffrey is in reception – He nodded and gestured for them to leave the office as he entered and sat alongside Nolan. The girls continued giggling as they headed down the hall until they abruptly stopped.

- That's them met Mr Joffrey – stated Dr Mike with a smile playing on his lips.

A few minutes later, Adam Joffrey was seated in front of both Doctors. A tall, gaunt approximation of Marilyn Manson replete in black with heavy black makeup.
After introductions, Adam Joffrey began to outline his ambitions.
- You guys are probably thinking I'm a good enough Marilyn, right? - both Doctors looked at each other and nodded approval – But I'm a 100% guy – he rolled his black loose shirt sleeves up to reveal a cluster of Devil/Pentangle/Occult tattoos covering both arms – I've spent thousands of dollars at Marilyn's own tattooist to get exactly every tattoo replicated in every detail. The clothes I wear are all either bought at auction from his own personal collection, or from the very stores in town where he holds accounts. I've even gone as far to get the clerks in these stores to text or email me with copy receipts so I can see what he's been buying so I can replicate his wardrobe – the two Doctors looked at each other nervously – This is all you know, confidential, right? – He queried.
Absolutely – said Nolan – Doctor/Patient privilege – said Dr Mike drawing an imaginary zip across his mouth.
- Yeah because I wouldn't want anyone to get into trouble that I have all these clerks and bellhops all over town giving me the lowdown on his every move and purchase. I guess what I'm trying to say is that I feel about 95% and until I had heard about you guys, thought that would be as far as I could feasibly go, but I saw the David Bowie guy at the Rainbow a few weeks ago, and because I had seen him before, I knew he was a 95% guy too, but you made him 100%. So basically, what I'm looking for you to do is take cranial and facial measurements and adjust me accordingly. I suspect my cheeks need probably taken in a few millimetres and my chin is a little short. Fill or lipo my face until you get the proportion correct. If you can also measure the relative distance between top lip, nose & hairline, and make any adjustment via a nip/tuck or graft to make sure that dimension is correct – he leant forward and stared at both Doctors through his asymmetrical coloured eyes.
Both Doctors found this quite unsettling, however, they gave Adam

Joffrey assurances along with a fairly hefty quote for the work which he immediately accepted, and left the office to arrange times and dates with Annie.

- Should be pretty straightforward with some lipo, a facelift, cheekbone implants, and a shot of Mister Manson's DNA – began Dr Mike.

- Better make sure we get the correct Marilyn DNA, I'd hate to see him pop out of a wedding cake and sing to the President – laughed Nolan.

- I'm more concerned about the correct Manson......I wouldn't want to be around when he comes round with a swastika on his forehead and a raging homicidal impulse – replied Dr Mike causing them both to chuckle.

- Marilyn Manson goes to the Brick Shelter nightclub on Sunset quite a bit. I'll email Danny the manager that we have a 'fan' looking for some 'material'.

Nolan began punching out an email on his computer.

Annie buzzed through to let the Doctors know that she was bringing Abbie Huntinger into the office.

Moments later, the door opened, and Annie ushered her into the room. Nolan rose from his chair to greet Abbie Huntinger. A reasonably attractive woman in her early thirties, fuller figured, hair immaculately coiffed in a 1940's style, heavily made-up, bright red full lips and jet black eyes. She removed her fur coat which Nolan took and hung on the office coat rack, to reveal a very tight period correct black rockabilly dress with plunging neckline. Nolan smiled to himself as he returned to his seat and nodded acknowledgment to Abbie Huntinger, then looked at Dr Mike, whose face was frozen. He sat there staring straight ahead as if in a daze. Nolan leant over and snapped his fingers directly in front of his face, as Abbie Huntinger simpered to herself.

- Wakey, wakey – began Nolan as Dr Mike sat upright with a start.

- I...I....I...do apologise – he stuttered, blushing.

- So Miss Huntinger....... - Nolan began studying the file - ....what exactly are you looking to achieve here? – He looked up over the top of his glasses.- Well...... – she cooed in a breathless, soft, Texan drawl – I was hoping you wonderful gentlemen could spinkle some of that

magical fairy dust you seem to possess all over lil' ole me.....-
- But what specific surgery do you require Miss Huntinger? – quizzed
Nolan – I mean you look fantastic – he motioned his hands toward her –
your physique looks in perfect proportion, your face is very attractive,
and from a plastic surgeon's perspective, I can't see much that we
would have to do –
- That's very kind of you Doctor Nolan – she almost whispered – But if
you would allow me to use your rest room – she gestured to Nolan's
private bathroom.
- Of course. Be my guest – he motioned to the bathroom as she tottered
over on her high heels. As the door closed he turned to Dr Mike.
- What the hell is wrong with you? Sitting there not saying anything?
What's the matter? – He hissed.
- Sorry. I just.......I dunno. Sorry – he sat up in his seat and
straightened his collar.
A few minutes later, the sound of running water in the bathroom
stopped and Abbie Huntinger stepped though the door, noticeably
shorter due to no high heels, wearing a surgical robe, and having
removed all her makeup. She walked up to the edge of the desk,
stopped, and dropped the robe to reveal herself fully nude in front of
both Doctors.
Nolan sat back in his chair whilst Dr Mike's glazed expression caused
his mouth to open.
- As you can see, Doctors, when primped and preened with two hours
of preparation, I can achieve fairly close to aesthetic perfection, but
without the girdle, the push up bra, the foundation, the other Max
Factor cosmetics, the $250 hairdo, I can appear almost normal, ordinary
– she cupped her breasts – these beautifully enhanced specimens were
the work of the great Dr Alfred Stevenson over at Bel View Clinic, but
that was twelve years ago, and I'm afraid to say, are in need of some
TLC – she turned half round to reveal her buttocks and rear thighs – and
these – she ran her hand down her rear thigh – are now starting to show
early signs of cellulite. In essence, Doctors, what you see in front of you
is a thirty-four year old Abbie Huntinger. I want you to see a twenty-

202

four year old Danni Divine. It really is that simple – she stood astride with her hands on her hips.

Nolan looked at Dr Mike who was now in some kind of shock, staring directly at Abbie Huntinger. He rose from his seat and rounded the desk to help her re-apply the surgical gown and escort her back to the bathroom. Once she was inside, he leaned back against the door, only to see Dr Mike still frozen in posture and expression.

- C'mon Mike – he waved his hand in front of his face and snapped his fingers – And…..back in the room! –

Dr Mike shook his head slightly.

- Sorry. Not quite with it today – he began to make pencil notes on the file.

- Still, should be straightforward enough, with breast uplift, lipo to the thighs and a general facelift all topped off with a shot of Jayne Mansfield, Marilyn Monroe and Jane Russell. I think I'll let you lead on this one, Mike –

- Em, yes, OK…..- Dr Mike rose from his chair and went to escort Abbie Huntinger out as Nolan gave a smile to her as she tottered out of the room.

Nolan rose and went to prepare for surgery. He could hear the excited tones of Simon Walker bidding farewell to his tearful girlfriend in reception, as Dr Mike and Annie fretted around them. Nolan jumped in surprise as Chinese Anaesthetist barged past him and began making preparations for theatre. He turned back into Pre-op and greeted a clearly nervous Simon Walker.

- Ah-ha! Beatle Boy himself – he extended his hand and shook hands warmly – Well Simon, we are all ready to go at this end, myself and Dr Mike are clear on your objectives, and I'm just going to take a couple of photographs of you just now – he produced his mobile phone and snapped a clearly anxious looking Simon Walker – Just for the 'before' section of your file –

Nolan headed off to theatre and Dr Mike headed to prepare the Beatle DNA.

A few minutes later Chinese Anaesthetist wheeled an unconscious

Simon Walker into Theatre and with Annie, lifted him off the gurney onto the operating table. Nolan began to make black pen marks at the side of his eyes and on his nose as the girls connected his vital monitors. Dr Mike appeared with a large syringe. It was literally the Money Shot, he thought to himself.

Nolan checked over his instruments, looked up at everyone in position awaiting his signal.

- Let us pray -

His hand hovered over the surgical instruments before alighting on the hi-fi remote and the opening chords of The New York Dolls filled the Theatre.

He began to work diligently and methodically, gently cutting the skin along the guide lines he'd drawn next to Simon Walker's left eye, before Dr Mike lightly folded the skin edges inward using Dermabond liquid stitches as a temporary hold as Nolan prepared to suture. They moved on to the right eye, the laser levels switched on to ensure perfect symmetry, then as Nolan finished up, Dr Mike began the tiny incisions into the nose bridge. The large computer screen suspended from the ceiling had a large side profile of John Lennon along with a zoomed in section of the nose with millimetre dimensions overmarked in every direction. As Dr Mike carefully peeled back the epidermis layers, Nolan began to manipulate the cartilage implants which would form the Lennon nose shape. They went in one by one, each time Nolan using the laser measurements to ensure match with the on screen template. An hour later, all were in place, and neatly stitched. Dr Mike applied three localised Digital DNA injections, and they were done. The last resonant crash of Jerry Nolan's cymbal echoed in the Theatre as they powered down and Simon Walker was wheeled away to post-op.

- Time for a late lunch? – Nolan enquired to which Dr Mike shrugged his shoulders – Why not – they went to disrobe and clean up.

As they left the surgery into the bright sunshine and headed towards Nolan's Porsche, Dr Mike looked around the parking lot almost mockingly – What? No Ferrari today? – - No, Ashley has it today. To be honest, it's not as good as the 911. Sometimes you have to stick with what you know is right – he opened the door and slid inside.

Twenty minutes later they pulled up at DiSanto's on Melrose, a trendy nightclub bar which catered to the late risers, serving brunch all day. The valet roared off in the car as they took a patio table on the main thoroughfare behind a wall of fake ivy. Nolan ordered Lattes and Avocado Toasts for both of them, and they both sat back in the late afternoon sunshine in their sunglasses. A mixture of Socialites with their toy dogs, Urban Hipsters with their laptops and headphones, Hungover Studio Executives and Z-Listers filled the tables all around. A pretty waitress delivered their Lattes, causing Nolan to have a second look as she walked away.

- So Saturday will be our finest moment at the AAPS awards, Mike. We'll finally get the recognition we deserve – he patted Dr Mike on the back, grinning.

- I've been overdue that validation a lot longer than the last few months, Sam – Dr Mike replied coolly. Nolan looked to his eyes for any sense of humour or friendliness, but the sunlight made sure his Raybans were two pools of black.

- Yeah, I guess you're right, but it did take the two of us to make this baby – he smiled, to which Dr Mike cocked his head slightly and made a small grunt of acknowledgement – You bringing anyone with you? –

- Not sure yet – replied Dr Mike, again without any warmth.

- What about that cute little Ethicon rep or the Rossi Brothers PA? Did you not have drinks with both of them recently? – Nolan grinned broadly, hoping this would be infectious.

Dr Mike didn't reply, staring off into the distance sipping his Latte. Just as Nolan was about to confront him, the cute waitress deposited their food. They began to eat in silence.

As they finished their food, a paparazzi photographer cycled past on the sidewalk and took several rapid fire photographs of them before cycling away at full speed. The small commotion caused several in the restaurant to look over at them before resuming their chatter. Nolan smiled to himself as he thought of another celebrity magazine cover. Dr Mike looked at the ground in disgust.

Just as the check arrived, both Doctor's phones began to ring simultaneously. They both answered at the same time, and removed their sunglasses to look at each other. There was a problem at the clinic. They sped along the 101, hypothesising what the issue could be, although an excitable Annie and Bored Receptionist were not the greatest communicators, even at the best of times.

The Porsche pulled into the clinic parking lot where Nolan's space had the 'Superstar Parking Only' sign, and purposefully strode into the clinic where a clearly agitated Annie awaited them.

- I've had the Anaesthetist give him another shot to keep him under, but you really need to see this – she hurried them down to the post op. They entered the room where Chinese Anaesthetist was carefully monitoring a drip. Annie reached above the bed and pulled the inspection lamp over Simon Walker's face. The tucks around the eyes were perfect, and the swelling almost gone, the scars faded. The nasal cartilage implants were magnificent, a faithful reproduction of John Lennon's famous profile. However, the face was not that of John Lennon. It was like a melted, twisted version. Dr Mike covered his eyes with his left hand – It wasn't Lennon's hat you bought – he turned and headed into the DNA lab. Nolan cursed out loud – Bloody 100% feedback my arse! Keep him sedated.....I'll be back shortly – he headed for his office.

Annie followed him – What if his girlfriend comes in for him? –
- Tell her anything. Just keep him sedated till I get back – he opened the safe in his office and stuffed wads of $100 bills into his jacket pockets – And tell Dr Mike to be ready! – He rushed out of the clinic and into his car, and sped off out of the lot.

Driving along the freeway, he kept banging the top of the steering wheel whilst cursing. He exited for downtown and headed towards Highland. After three sets of traffic lights, his destination was in sight. He drove up to the valet and jumped out of the car. Standing in the busy street, he looked up at the huge illuminated sign above. 'Hard Rock Café Los Angeles'.

He entered the foyer to be met by a pretty blonde Maître'd.

206

- Hi there – he looked at her name tag – Jo-Anne, can you tell Shane Price that Dr Sam Nolan is here to see him? – He smiled.

She picked up the phone and whispered into it, looking up at Nolan directly – Mr Price will be down to see you straightaway, Dr Nolan – A few minutes later Shane Price appeared – Hey! Dr Sammy Nolan no less – he boomed causing everyone around to look. Nolan looked uncomfortable as Price hugged him and stood back to look Nolan up and down.

- Celebrity definitely agrees with you my friend! Come on up to the VIP and we can have a little afternoon chaser – he began to lead Nolan through into the bar.

- No......I want to speak to you through here – Nolan pulled him towards a deserted side booth bar. Shane Price looked confused as Nolan forcefully manoeuvred them past the velvet curtain. They stood just inches apart in the middle of the floor.

- Listen Shane, I'm going to need a favour from you my good man –
- Anything Sam, you know I'm your guy – he replied.

Nolan leaned even closer. Their noses were almost touching. Nolan could smell the garlic and whisky on Shane Price's breath.

- You trust me, don't you Shane? – To which Shane price nodded hesitantly – You see I have a small problem, and you my friend are standing here with the solution – he placed his hands on Shane Price's shoulders and turned him so he was facing four large glass cases on the wall behind them, each containing a Beatle Jacket from the Sergeant Pepper album sleeve.

- I......I....I....don't understand.....you want to join the Beatles? – He nervously quipped.

- Yes Shane, I do. I want to join the Beatles, but only for today. I want you to give me John Lennon's jacket - Nolan pointed to the long yellow satin coat.

- But....but ....that's our most expensive item......it's irreplaceable.......I.....I.....would get fired......-
- It's only for a couple of hours, Shane, and I'll have it back to you, good as new. After all, you said you could trust me? – Nolan held his

hands out.

- This is different Sam. It's not my place. What if some of the bigwigs found out? I'd be fired –

- But you don't tell the 'bigwigs' that Marchesi shakes you down every month? That they run massive bar tabs that are never paid, that they openly deal coke in your bathrooms through black aftershave guy? Their curiosity never seems to run to those things, Shane? – He smiled.

- It's all very well stealing the odd celebrity item from the valet or used glass for you Sam. I don't mind our people doing that for you Sam, but this is different. Jesus – I mean that jacket is worth millions – he pointed at the card below the cases that showed that Hard Rock Inc had paid $2m several years previously.

Nolan reached into his pocket and produced a huge wad of $100 bills. He held it up to Shane Price's face – I can take this money to Salvatore Marchesi and tell him I want to borrow that jacket, or I can give it to you. Either way, I get the jacket. The difference is, what do you get Shane? –

A clearly sweaty Shane Price took the wad of bills and stuffed it into his pocket. He pulled a chair over to the jacket case, and lifted the walkie talkie from his belt.

- Hi. It's Shane. I have the guy from Head Office here to take the Lennon coat to the insurers as per their request. Disable alarm 22 while I take it out –

He re-holstered the walkie talkie and climbed up to the side locks on the case just as the little red lights went out on it. He lifted a bundle of keys from his belt and opened the case. Nolan strode over and Shane Price gently removed the coat from the dummy and handed it down to him.

- See you in a couple of hours – Nolan patted a miserable looking Shane Price on the shoulder and strode purposefully out, Sergeant Pepper's jacket over his arm.

====0====

The white 911 roared into the Sunnyside Clinic, and Nolan leapt out and into the reception. Bored Receptionist blocked his path as he entered.

- This is Claire Mitchell – she began – Simon Walker's partner – Nolan spun round to see a neat, pretty girl anxiously looking up at him. Her eyes immediately went to the brightly coloured jacket over his arm.

- Oh is that for Simon to dress up to surprise me? –

- Eh……something like that – Nolan nodded and hurried down the hallway.

An hour later, the samples had been cross-referenced and checked. They were also confirmed to be nothing like the material taken from the eBay hat. Annie had been despatched to return the jacket, Bored Receptionist was assigned to preoccupy Claire Mitchell with her recent Cancun holiday snaps, and finally Dr Mike began to administer a small injection in each of the surgical areas. The anaesthetic was reduced to a minor dose, and Nolan began to examine the now dissolving secondary sutures. By the time he had examined each in turn, a circa 1968 John Lennon lay before them.

Nolan looked up at Dr Mike who looked ruefully at the patient and walked away. Nolan removed his mask and headed down the hall.

The squealing of joy and tears of Claire Mitchell was still audible in the background as Nolan entered Dr Mike's office and sat in the consulting chair. Dr Mike continued to look out the window as the sun was setting, with his feet on the desk.

- That was close – began Nolan. Dr Mike didn't reply.

- The good thing is, at least we know that the later dosage becomes the more dominant – he said enthusiastically.

- That's because I trebled the dose – said Dr Mike in a monotone, only visible to Nolan as a pair of legs coming out from the back of his high backed chair.

- Trebled? – Nolan nervously enquired – you've done that before, with the sheep and that, right? –

- No, I haven't Sam. I haven't tried or trialled half the stuff we've been doing here. There could be massive lawsuits and legal problems waiting for us down the road, but hey, as long as Sam Nolan has his Ferrari and his movie star girlfriend, then what the hell, right? – He replied calmly.

- I think that's a bit harsh, Mike, I mean, we're 50/50 all the way? –
- Yes 50/50 on all the bad stuff too. I didn't think it would turn out like this.......–
- Turn out like this? – Interrupted Nolan - As a negative? What are you on about? This is everything we've ever wanted! You are finally getting recognition and proper financial reward for your work! I remember you at that crappy convention hall in LA, peddling your theories to geeks and half wits. That was never going to work Mike, and you bloody know it. Christ, you make more now in a week than you made in the last ten years! Just enjoy the bloody thing without all your stupid moralising and ethics. This is the modern world. We have insurances up the backside to cover for idiots and lawsuits, and the Rossi Brothers will make sure anything bad goes away....... –
- That's another thing – Dr Mike calmly interrupted – I don't like those Rossi Brothers. Shady isn't even the word. Telling me what to wear, who to be seen with, what parties to go to? I'm a Doctor, not a Rock Star –
- You're wrong. We *are* Rock Stars! This isn't Edinburgh General Hospital Mike, this is Hollywood, and we're Rock Stars enjoying the success of our first album –
- Maybe it's time I went solo – muttered Dr Mike under his breath.
- What was that? – quizzed an agitated Nolan.
- Nothing. A rude word. Next question –
- I can't believe you sometimes. We're sitting here on a goldmine, about to be recognised by our peers as well, at the AAPS awards on Saturday night. Can't you just switch off and enjoy it? Think of it. Getting the most prestigious recognition of what we do from our peers in front of our peers? Anyways – he put his feet on the other side of Dr Mike's desk – Who you taking? You've been very quiet on that front....-
- Ach I don't know if I'll even go.....-
- Don't be stupid. Some people would give anything to be in the

situation we're in. Besides The Rossi Brothers think......
- Would you shut up about The Rossi Brothers – bellowed Dr Mike uncharacteristically.
Nolan got up from his chair and headed back to his office, slamming the door behind him.
Annie stuck her head into Nolan's office.
- Everything OK? –
- Absolutely. If by you mean having an ungrateful clown as a partner, then yes. Everything is OK – He looked up and smiled sarcastically.
- As your procedure on Simon Walker overran, the photographer from NBC for your TV headshots is in reception. I've explained about a surgery overrun but he said he would wait. He's had about four lattes, but says he has to deliver the photographs to the studio tomorrow morning –
- Okay, show him in. I'll go splash my face with some water – he headed into the bathroom.
A few moments later, Annie showed a slightly effeminate middle aged man into Nolan's office.
- This is Kim Anderson, Sam for your headshots for NBC – she then retreated as he shook Nolan's hand.
- A man called Kim? – joked Nolan.
- No stranger than a man called Lindsey, or a woman called Charlie – he replied deadly serious.
- I'm sorry – said Nolan grinning broadly – just joking with you.
- Right. Can I set up here and use this wooden panelling as our background? –
- Of course. Go for it – Nolan began checking himself in the mirror, licking his hand and flattening a rebel hair.
He heard muffled voices in the corridor outside his room and the door began to open before it was pulled shut. Annie was preventing Dr Mike from coming in. He could see the shadows on the other side of the opaque glass interact before a 'For God's sake' from Dr Mike and he stormed off down the corridor. An overrevved start of a Ferrari FF and screeching exit from the clinic parking lot accompanied by honking

horns of other irate motorists indicated that indeed Dr Mike had left the building.

The photographer looked at him inquisitively, but Nolan simply shrugged his shoulders and gave his best profile.

A glittering Gaumann Theatre in downtown LA was resplendent in the dusk half-light, not quite the Red Carpet event of the Emmys or the Oscars, but a massive date in the image driven LA plastic surgery world….The American Association of Plastic Surgeon Awards. Or 'The Plastics' as some wag had dubbed them years before. Sunnyside Clinic of course was the talk of the town, their rise from a mid-range inauspicious lower Hills third choice clinic to a world leading innovative powerhouse was there for all to see, and with numerous examples of their celebrity look a like work filling the daytime TV chat shows, and in plentiful evidence tonight, it was clear a new bar had been set in the world of plastic surgery.

Nolan had hired a limo for the night, keen to enjoy the evening, despite Dr Mike's mood swings. The limo was now gently cruising along, Ashley in the opposite seat from Nolan, quaffing Bollinger. The Clash on the sound system. Nolan checked his reflection in the privacy screen. Both of them were groomed to perfection, sleek, elegant, and cool. Mike Rossi always quoted the line from 'American Beauty' to him – *"In order to be successful, one must always project an image of success"*. As he caught both their reflections, there was no doubt they were indeed projecting that image. Ashley in her sequinned rose gold ballgown was every inch the modern film star, every pore exuding confidence and beauty. She smiled at Nolan. He checked himself out for the umpteenth time. Black dinner suit by Armani, crisp white shirt with tartan bowtie, just for that added edge of sassiness. The cuffs of his shirt just the right distance of projection past the jacket sleeve, held together with Tiffany cufflinks. The ultimate power couple, he thought to himself as the car drew up at the theatre. Normally there would be mild interest in this event, but given the level of celebrity associated with the Sunnyside Clinic, the paparazzi were out in force. How many of the celebrities attending were in fact the real person, no-one will ever know, given the exceptional quality of the Sunnyside Clinic's work. Ashley alighted from the limousine first, to a barrage of flashes, closely followed by Nolan, who lifted his hand in acknowledgement. He spied the Rossi Brothers and their significant others waiting for them inside the foyer.

The Rossis greeted them warmly, and they headed into the auditorium. Hundreds of tables were arranged with illuminated floral sculptures between, and a subdued delicate light hung over the hall, concealing its sheer size. It appeared almost fairy like, with the central podium on the main stage the very epicentre of this religion. Many people were already seated, and Nolan saw a Freddie Mercury, a Charlize Theron, a youthful Ronald Reagan, a Buddy Holly, and at least two Rachels from Friends. Annie and her boyfriend were already seated at the table, and she mouthed a 'beautiful' to Nolan.

- Look upon his work, ye mighty, and despair – Mike Rossi patted him on the back – How do you feel seeing all this Sam? –

- I'd be happier seeing Dr Mike here – he replied – He's never late for anything – he looked left and right.

- I know. Tony said he'd started to become a bit problematic. Sometimes Sam, there's just some people you can't please –

- Well he's not raining on my parade. Not tonight -

Just at that moment, there was a commotion at the entrance to the hall, with much oohing and aaahing as camera flashes illuminated two silhouettes at the top of the entrance steps. Nolan looked up to see a very dapper Dr Mike pause on the top step with a peroxide blonde Danni Divine. She looked every inch the 50's American pinup, with an extremely low cut tight red and white sequinned dress revealing her plentiful assets. Dr Mike gave a facetious bow and waved away those around him as they swaggered towards the Sunnyside table, leaving a crowd of turning heads in their wake. - Good evening Sunnysiders and Rossis! – Dr Mike announced as he found his seat at the table. The

213

greetings, air kisses and hugs were conducted.

Nolan noticed a strong smell of whisky from Dr Mike as they shook hands. Danni Divine also appeared to be under the influence.

The evening began, and the meal was served under the glittering imitation night sky. They were attended at their table by a George Michael, who repeatedly thanked Nolan and Dr Mike every time he served their food, much to the delight of the rest of the table. Dr Mike's flippant, slightly drunken manner was irritating Nolan. Every quip, every answer, every motion, grated on his nerves. He was also thumping back the champagne with whisky chasers.

- C'mon Mike.......easy on the vino eh? We have a speech to give, and that's at least a couple of hours away –

Dr Mike simply had his glass topped up by George Michael and smiled at Nolan whilst raising his glass in mock salute to him. Nolan shook his head and returned to a conversation about pet cats with Ashley and Jane Rossi. Annie shot him a look of concern.

The evening continued through the several courses of food, Dr Mike's quips and laughter getting louder and louder. Even Tony Rossi leaned into him and whispered some kind of restraint. Nolan sipped gingerly at his wine. A knot of tension sat in his gut as he observed the scale of the audience, and the antics of Dr Mike.

The awards ceremony began to fanfare, as a tanned Angelina Jolie and Dr Benjamin Streicher PHD took the stage. As they worked their way through the minor awards, Nolan thought it strange how they didn't appear to be nominated for some of these. Mike Rossi must have read his mind and leaned into him.

- Couldn't have you winning everything, Sam – he winked conspiratorially – You guys would wipe the floor with everyone. Innovation? Check. Performance? Check. Improving the Industry? Check. The big one is the one you want Sam, believe me –

The awards then drew to their climax, as Angelina and Benjamin had the lights dimmed and adopted a sombre tone.

- If you're lucky, once in every lifetime comes along a visionary, a pioneer. Someone not afraid to take chances. Someone who has been told No! many times. These people are truly the future – began Angelina.

- Tonight we are extremely fortunate, because we have not one person who fits into that category, but two – Benjamin stated to rapturous applause.

He continued when the applause died down - We have seen right here in Hollywood in the last twelve months, history being made right in front of our very eyes – Angelina leaned into the microphone then retreated.

- A concept so challenging, so unbelievable, so..........*Hollywood*! – Benjamin stood back and swung his arm to point at a giant projection screen behind them which carried the Digital DNA logo.

A short film ensued showing aerial and tasteful shots of the Clinic, interspersed with professional photographs of Nolan and Dr Mike. The film then cut to before and afters, tastefully cut with tearful images and overwhelming happiness. The music then moved from Pan Pipes to the start of Guns 'n' Roses 'Welcome to the Jungle' as various clips from TV chat shows, daytime reality shows and new reports ran into each other, showing chaos, tears, angry spouses, emotional reveals, and incredulous reactions. The film finished with two Brad Pitts identically dressed at a red carpet event shaking hands and pointing at each other. They were truly indistinguishable. As the music and images faded back to the Digital DNA logo, the entire auditorium erupted in cheering and applause.

- Without further ado, Ladies and Gentlemen, the AAPS award for outstanding achievement and contribution to science, goes to……….. – began Benjamin as the drum roll began.

- Dr Sam Nolan and Dr Mike Richardson, Sunnyside Clinic, Hollywood, California! – completed both Angelina and Benjamin in unison to deafening cheering and applause.

Nolan stood up and took the adulation of the crowd, as did a slightly unsure and drunken Dr Mike after prompting from Danni Divine. Nolan headed up the three steps to greet Angelina and Benjamin, Dr Mike slipped on the second step on his ascent, and an audible 'ooooh' went up from the crowd as he recovered and joined the group at the podium.

215

Nolan accepted the award and put an arm around Dr Mike and leant forward to the microphone.

- On behalf of myself and Jack Daniels here (audience laughter) – Dr Mike shrugged off his arm – No seriously, folks, this is one of the proudest days of my life. Years of hard work has finally paid off (Dr Mike puzzled expression) and we have now in Hollywood, a world leading, innovative surgical centre of excellence. Already we have began to develop and study techniques and variations of our unique procedures that will benefit not just our cosmetic desires, but for the greater good of humanity as a whole – He held the award aloft and moved sideways to allow Dr Mike to the microphone.

- I would also like to......um.......eh......just say..........eh....umm............none of this would have been possible........um..........eh......ah......- just at that moment he stumbled against the podium knocking Angelina Jolie off balance, and Nolan caught and steadied them both. Just as Dr Mike re-asserted himself and leant forward to continue into the microphone, Nolan leant in and pulled it over to himself.

- Well, thank you very much Jim Beam – and headed off the stage to applause.

Dr Mike's face went scarlet as he muttered vague insults at Angelina Jolie and Benjamin Streicher and stumbled off the stage. Nolan was still standing at the table, his arms in the air taking the adorations of the audience, as Dr Mike grabbed Danni Divine and banged into Nolan heading out of the auditorium, also connecting with several other guests and tables in his quest to reach the exit.

The Rossi Brothers continued clapping but looked nervously at each other, and Annie rushed out behind Dr Mike.

Nolan however, basked in the moment. This was his time.

Chapter 11
I Hate the Rain

A humming lawnmower drills through the darkness. Slowly but surely Nolan begins to open his crusty eyes. A slow, deliberate rub to remove the sleep glue allows focus on the outline of the full length window, masked by heavy drape curtains. The sunlight beams round the edges, like an unopened treasure chest. It takes a moment or two as he studies the particles of dust slowly making their downward journey in the rare shafts of sunlight which escape the law of the curtain. The dry mouth, the churning stomach, the light headache, all add up to an all too familiar conclusion. As he peers into the gloom, he realises it's not his untidy bedroom at the back of his house, but the cavernous master bedroom of Ashley's Hollywood Hills mansion.

Over what looks like a massive expanse of deep pile carpet, he can just make out his suit from last night draped over a Louie IV chair. He falls back onto the pillow and reaches out his left arm but it falls on empty bed. Ashley is there, but the bed is so vast, and Nolan clings to the edge like a lifebelt. He drags himself to his feet and staggers over to the window and pulls the heavy curtains apart. The sunlight roars into the room causing Ashley to moan and Nolan to shield his eyes. The gardens below are beautifully manicured and stretch off into the distance. The humming and buzzing of assorted garden machinery drift in the distance as Nolan stretches then stands hands on hips. A Mexican gardener waves up at him, just as he realises he is stark naked, and retreats into the en suite bathroom.

A shower and shave later, and Sam Nolan is re-booted again, fit for the modern world, his hangover washed away down various plug holes in the extensive en suite bathroom.

As he returns to the bedroom freshly groomed, he notices the AAPS award on the dressing table, replete with Ashley's bra from the previous night draped over it. He smiles at the memory and flicks on the TV to see his previous night's triumph laid out. Fortunately the report makes no mention of Dr Mike's state or his exit. The Rossi Brothers will have seen to that, he thought to himself. He leapt on the bed alongside Ashley causing her to sit up slowly.

- Here's the King and Queen of Hollywood –

He pointed at the TV as last night's footage showed them outside the ceremony, Nolan with the award aloft in one hand, his other round Ashley's waist. She peered through half shut eyes, smiled and kissed Nolan gently on the cheek.

Nolan checked his almost out of power mobile phone. At least no messages from Dr Mike.

After a day of recovery, it was back to business on Monday morning. Nolan sat in the Ferrari inside his garage watching the sectional door open. He gunned the V8 engine out onto the street, negotiates the two left turns, and heads directly into slow moving traffic on the freeway. No cursing of luck today as he turns up the music on the radio. It's a sunny 88 degrees, clear blue sky, he's driving a new Ferrari California, and he's just left his Hollywood Starlet girlfriend in his Hollywood Hills house, heading to his multi-million dollar business.

He allows himself an inward smile of contentment. Before long, Junction 46 looms ahead and he takes the long sweeping curve and just catches the red light at the junction.

He looks up at the same billboard he's seen for the last thirteen years. But today is different. It's the first time his own face is on that billboard.

"You are just two blocks from where your dreams can come true" ran the strapline, with a photograph of an airbrushed Nolan and Dr Mike outside the clinic, grinning.

He turned the car slowly as the light changed and cruised down to the clinic, loving the attention the car attracted. He waved to everyone whose head turned as it growled along the road. He pulled up in the lot, and after parking, took a step back to admire the car before heading in.

He removed the AAPS award from his bag and positioned it carefully on Bored Receptionist's counter. She didn't look up.

Annie blocked his progress in the corridor with a clutch of files. Nolan skipped toward her, pirouetted and kissed her hand.

- Numbnuts in yet? – He nodded his head towards Dr Mike's office.

- No. I tried to calm him after the awards, but he was fully vested in that buxom floozy. He gave me the shoo shoo with his hand, which was the end for me. And no, he's not in yet –

Nolan took the file pile and threw them on his desk. As he hung his jacket, he reflected that things indeed were on the change. Clean and sober first thing on a Monday morning at the clinic. A neat, organised workload. In before Dr Mike. All new concepts.

He buzzed through to Annie.

- Let me know when Dr Mike's in. I'll start going through these meantime –

He fired up his computer and opened the first file.

Randy Warhol. Female impersonator/Drag Queen. Real name Dan Stirling. He studied the professional photographs of an exceptionally deceptive man, who would easily pass for a woman. Compared to most drag queens he had encountered, Randy Warhol didn't appear to revel in the obvious fakery. He continued through the file. He/she had already undergone gender reassignment, and had recently completed a six month course of estrogens and other assorted female hormones. A topless photograph revealed a set of small, bud like, small pert breasts, probably more associated with a fifteen year old girl rather than a twenty eight year old former construction worker. He studied the photographs in detail, and was impressed with the quality of the outcome. Randy Warhol was looking for small buttock implants and the Sunnyside magic to complete his/her look. Perfect candidate he thought to himself as he googled the price of buttock implants elsewhere in LA. Funny, he thought, this will also be another first. Female DNA into a male subject.

Second file was Maria Lindos. A wealthy Hollywood socialite, she was known as the Black Widow, due to her propensity to target wealthy studio executives/actors in the final stages of life and harvest the reward upon their demise. A veteran of many a contested will in LA courtrooms, she was a regular of the tabloids and Hollywood gossip columns. A tall Amazonian woman, she exuded glamour and strength at the same time. The file indicated that the matter in hand was so personal, she could only relay to the Doctors themselves, and despite requests for even a hint of what type of work was required, she divulged nothing. Nolan studied her photographs, some of which were vintage glamour shots. She appeared perfect in every detail, very much in the Farrah Fawcett Bionic Woman mould. Perhaps some of her frame had started to feel the effect of gravity, maybe some skin tightening required? Intrigued, Nolan looked her up on the computer and was surprised to see she had a Wikipedia page. Born to a poor family in Eastern Europe, she had come to America as the wife of a serviceman stationed in Germany at the time. The marriage lasted as long as her green card application and she then took up with a George Anderton, then a mid grade New York photographer, who had taken many of her early shots, leading to catalogue and soft porn work. It was when Anderton moved to Vogue as their US Photographic Editor, that her career took off. Once established as Vogue's No.1 model and celebrity hanger-on, Anderton was then discarded for flamboyant Boston Mayor Dan 'Blackie' Black. Black was a 70's left-over, parading as a wannabe gangster, and Maria Lindos was more than happy to be Bonnie to his Clyde. When he disappeared after the Horton Bridge financial scandal, she was very much the public face of his office, and as the grieving girlfriend, gained much publicity and sympathy until he was found in New Mexico and returned to Boston in disgrace, tried and sentenced to twenty years. She then appeared to move to the West Coast, and after a tempestuous affair with the married aging actor Ron Ducati, became more settled and targeted single or widowed wealthy men. Now past her 50th year, she had now focussed on wealth rather than celebrity. The most recent entry had her as the wife of ex-MGM studio boss Jimmy Kennedy, an 85 year old multi-millionaire, whose family fought tooth and nail to prevent her being named as the main beneficiary in his will.

According to Wikipedia, this case was still ongoing.

Third file was Ramos Di Santis. A small Mexican man, well-presented, clean shaven, slightly sinister looking. Apparently not keen on surrendering much information, other than a desire to have some Brad Pitt/Leo DiCaprio/Ben Affleck Hollywood A-Lister work. Keen to break into modelling. $5k deposit already paid in cash and keen to undergo at the earliest opportunity. Nolan brought up various A-Listers on his computer and propped Ramos Di Santis's photograph alongside. A few minutes later, he had decided on a 90's George Clooney. He then checked the DNA database to confirm that there was indeed, George Clooney material samples in the clinic. Some fillers and a small tuck at each earlobe and that should be an easy $25k, he thought.

Nolan looked up at the clock. 10.28am. He buzzed through to Bored Receptionist.

- Is Dr Mike in yet? –

- No – she answered with just the right amount of disinterest – and there's a Randy Warhol here for you as your 10.30 –

- Okay have Annie bring her along –

Annie gingerly steeped into the room with a very small Randy Warhol. Nolan greeted her and offered up a seat.

- Annie, if you wouldn't mind filling in for Dr Mike? –

He motioned to the chair at his side, where she dutifully sat.

- So Randy, I've looked over your file and your notes, but I'd like to hear from you what you want us to do – he sat back in the chair forming a cradle with his fingers.

- I would like you to complete my look, Doctor Nolan. I've studied your work, particularly those who have used the media to further their careers, and I can say without hesitation, that your work here is undoubtedly the best I have ever seen. The detail and proportionality is unrivalled –

Nolan spread his hands wide and nodded graciously.

- As you can see from my photographs, my bust line is improving, my facial features are as near to my goal as I can get, but sadly no amount of Jazzercise or Aerobics can get my ass the way I want. I only seem to end up with a muscular thin man's butt. I think that if you could add a small implant in each cheek, create the proportionality that you are clearly so good at, and give me that zing that you seem to give all your clients –

- In the nicest possible way Randy, Can you please lift your skirt and show me your backside? –

Randy complied, and Nolan walked round to investigate. He gently pulled down her panties to reveal a clearly male bony posterior. Annie looked over quizzically. He ran the tip of his pen down each side.

- Yes, we can get you sorted out –

Nolan said as he returned to his seat and indicated for Randy to pull up her clothing. He turned his computer screen towards Randy and asked

- Which one of these is your desired look? I prepared this earlier from your notes and concluded this is where you're looking to get to –

A series of photographs of young girls covered the screen. Randy hovered her finger over two in particular.

- So Edie Sedgwick or Kylie Minogue –

stated Nolan, turning the screen back toward himself and searching the DNA database. The search revealed they had Kylie DNA but not Edie. Keen to avoid another eBay debacle, Nolan began to turn the conversation to a Kylie orientated one.

- There's no doubt you're in the mould of both, but surgically I think the best outcome will be either a hybrid of the two, or based on the Kylie model. Your physique is probably more suited to her particular form, and that's where I think I can guarantee the best result –

- You're the boss, Dr Nolan –

- Thank you – they rose together and shook hands.

- Annie will get you scheduled – he gestured with his hand and they left the room. He reached over and buzzed reception.

- Any message from Dr Mike? –

- No – was the stern reply.

He checked his mobile. Various messages from his new found friends, but nothing from Dr Mike. He shot off a text – Are you remembering we have consultations this morning? –

The phone rang. He grabbed it quickly, all his pent-up anger ready to be directed on Dr Mike.

- That's Caroline at American Express. Says she needs to talk to you as a matter of urgency – droned Bored Receptionist.

- Put her through – he snapped.

- Dr Nolan, this is Caroline, your Senior Account Executive at American Express. How are you this morning? –

- Fine. I'm sorry to be so curt, but I am between surgeries at the moment. Is this something that could be best handled by email? –

- I'm afraid not, Dr Nolan, as I simply need your verbal authorisation on a recent transaction. Your account is over its authorised limit, and as valued customers we are more than happy to increase your limit…………-

- What do you mean over limit? – interrupted Nolan – that card has a $20k limit –

- That is correct Dr Nolan; however a transaction this morning for over nine thousand dollars has tipped you slightly over –

- Nine thousand? This morning? –

- Yes on the card used by Dr Michael Richardson. A charge of $9,087 at Le Monde Hotel in West Hollywood at 10:06 this morning –

- Are you sure?.......yes……of course….yes…..please authorise and proceed…..-

The rest of the call was taken up with verifications and authorisations which Nolan impatiently hurried through, agreeing with everything. Once the call was over he banged the receiver into its cradle and looked up Le Monde's number. He dialled it, punching each number viciously into the keypad. After the inevitable multiple choice menu, he eventually managed to get the Manager on the line.

- Ah Dr Nolan. A pleasure to speak to you. What can I do for you today? –

- Hello. Yes. I'm calling about a transaction on the Sunnyside Clinic's credit card for about nine thousand dollars that went through this morning? I believe the card was used by my partner, Dr Mike Richardson? –

223

- Let me see.........let me see.........ah yes. I can see here that Dr Richardson stayed here the last three nights in the Executive Suite. He used the bar and kitchen extensively during those three days, and had a small gathering last night until the small hours. He checked out with his companion at 10:06 this morning, Sir –
Nolan hung up the phone. Annie stuck her head around the door.
- That's Maria Lindos here now.....will I bring her in? –
Nolan held his hands up and gestured approval. He sat back in his chair, deflated.
Maria Lindos entered the room only as a six foot Amazonian ex-model can. Immaculately attired and her makeup to perfection, Nolan rose from his seat to shake her hand in a slight daze, a combination of his last telephone call and the vision of perfection in front of him. Annie moved into the seat next to Nolan.
- Thank you for seeing me, Dr Nolan – she began in an accent with a slight Eastern European tinge – But I did say in my request that this matter was so confidential that I was only prepared to discuss it directly with the Doctors – she shot a sideways glance at Annie.
- I'm afraid Dr Richardson is unavoidably detained today, and Annie is helping me with the clinic's caseload. I can assure you, her experience and confidentiality is second only to mine – He leant forward with his most concerned face on.
- I see. Then I assume neither of you will have any issue with a signature on this non-disclosure agreement? – She fished a plastic folder from her Louis Vuitton bag and proceeded to remove a sheaf of papers and place them on the desk – You see, what I am going to ask of you requires complete confidentiality, and I must stress that this issue cannot become knowledge to anyone outside of this room –
Nolan turned the papers round and quickly scanned them.
- There is a space at the bottom for you to put your name, signature and date – She handed over a Mont Blanc pen.
Nolan signed and dated.
- Annie, I'll understand if you don't want.......... – he began.
- Are you kidding? – She snatched the papers from him and completed.

224

Maria Lindos checked them, straightened them on the desk and put them back into the folder, and into her bag. She crossed her legs and began.

- You may or may not be aware that I have been married five times. You may or may not be aware that my current husband is ninety five years old, and whatever your opinions are on the matter, I do genuinely love him. I have been with Jimmy for nearly fifteen years, and we have had a wonderful time together. He is my true love, my true soulmate. Despite the forty year gap in age, we get on so well, like the same things, and think the same things. Unfortunately, in those fifteen years, he has deteriorated to the point where I suspect he may not have too long to go. When we first met, and the early years of our marriage, believe it or not, Jimmy was quite virile and active, and we had a normal sex life. Inevitably, that side of our relationship has now become non-existent, and it was Jimmy himself who insisted that I make alternative arrangements for my needs to be met. Over the last couple of years, I've met someone who he approves of, and who he accepts as his natural successor to look after me. I appreciate this is a very unusual situation, but I am aware of several other people who have entered into relationships of this sort, although usually the family are not receptive to this type of arrangement. Jimmy has met Leon several times, and we have even been on several holidays together. Leon loves Jimmy as much as I do, and that's why I got in touch with your clinic. I saw on the daytime TV just how precise and detailed your work was, and in particular that episode of *Good Morning LA,* where the audience could not tell apart two of the celebrities and their Sunnyside Clinic copycats. The job you had done was so good, even a full studio audience and the hosts could not tell them apart. So this got me thinking. One of the greatest regrets in my life was that I didn't meet Jimmy earlier, when we could have had a more productive life together, without the constraints of his age and his various medications. So when I met Leon, my initial attraction was that he was simply a younger version of Jimmy. Same tastes, same mannerisms, same wicked sense of humour. When I saw that show, I then went online and saw your website and all the positive energy that you guys have created in this town, I got Jimmy and Leon together, and suggested that maybe you guys were the very people who could perhaps transform Leon into a younger version of my beloved Jimmy? Not ridiculously younger, but maybe look around fifty ?

– She looked anxiously at the shell shocked faces of Nolan and Annie.

- Wow. That's quite a story. How old is Leon? – quizzed Nolan.

- He's thirty-eight –

- And quite willing to age himself for you? And be someone else? – asked a clearly shocked Annie.

Maria Lindos reached into the file again and produced several photographs of Jimmy Kennedy back in his Hollywood cinematic heyday, and a number of profile shots of Leon. Nolan held them up side by side and began to study through a magnifying glass. After a few minutes, he handed the images back.

- I'm fairly certain we can do a number of minor procedures on Leon that would get you the desired look, however I'm going to put it back onto you, that we would require a legal document that is signed by both Jimmy and Leon that they are perfectly happy with this arrangement – Annie looked at Nolan in horror.

- I knew this was the place to go. Thank you so much Doctor Nolan – she shot a steely look at Annie.

- Annie, if you could get Mrs Lindos booked in as soon as possible with both Jimmy and Leon as well, and I'll get the framework legal document emailed out in the next couple of days – He rose and kissed the back of Maria Lindos's hand, causing Annie to roll her eyes.

They left the room, and Nolan hurriedly reached for his phone and called Dr Mike. Straight to voicemail. He flicked onto Danni Divine's file on the computer and dialled the mobile number shown. Also straight to voicemail. He left a message asking her to call as soon as possible. He looked up Dr Mike's number at Chateau Marmont and called. It rang out.

He started to think where he himself would go after having a wild few days at Le Monde. Probably Vegas he mused or more like Dr Mike, a

quiet retreat in somewhere like San Diego, but probably with that hooker in tow, more like Vegas. He called Perfect 10.
- Hello would it be possible to get a word with Mike or Tony please? It's Dr Nolan at Sunnyside Clinic –
- Please hold Dr Nolan, I think Tony is available –
A few minutes later Tony Rossi came on the line.
- How's my award winning quack? –
- Not too bad, Tony. Listen, sorry to be brief but I'm between consultations just now. I was wondering if you guys had heard from Dr Mike since the awards ceremony as he hasn't shown up for work –
- Hahahaha. I'm not surprised. He was buried deep into the bosom of that tart he brought to the event. Relax. I don't think he was even that pissed off when he left. Probably too focused on getting into her pants. He's away drinking and letting off steam with his new girlfriend. You especially should empathise with that! – He laughed again.
- Yeah you're probably right. Listen, sorry for bothering you. If he checks in with you guys can you please let me know? –
- Sure. Now don't over work. Take a leaf from your partner's book and go let your hair down with that girl of yours. You won the award. You're number one. Enjoy it at the top Sam. I've seen plenty who don't appreciate where they're at, and by the time they do, it's too late –
- Yeah thanks – he hung up feeling slightly better.
Annie appeared at the door.
- That's Ramos Di Santis in, Sam. You good to go? –
- Sure. Bring him in –
Ramos Di Santis entered the room and shook his hand and sat down curtly. Leaner and more athletic than his submission photographs, he was a good looking man in his early fifties, well-dressed, Rolex on the wrist. His outward appearance however, was made slightly comical by his oversize moustache, which almost looked like a film prop. They discussed several small procedures, with Nolan showing the George Clooney photographs, and a demonstration of the clinic's new software showing the effect of the proposed surgery on a headshot of the patient. Nolan showed him the end result, with the moustache replaced by

medium length stubble, to which Ramos Di Santis seemed happy,
although as he was so sullen and unwelcoming, it was difficult to tell.
The $25k fee was agreed along with the procedures to be carried out
that week on Wednesday afternoon.
Once he had left, Nolan grabbed his coat.
- I'm off to try and find Dr Mike –
He grabbed the printout with Danni Divine's home address and his
mobile phone and hurried out the door. Once out onto the street, he
sped along Pine and headed round the short sharp bends that led toward
the Chateau Marmont. Ten minutes later he pulled up outside the
bungalow. He jumped out of the car and walked smartly through the
leafy gate and up the path to the front door. He rang the bell and looked
through the glass panel to the side. Reminiscent of his apartment back
in Edinburgh, it was typical Dr Mike. Unpacked boxes with jackets
strewn over them. Numerous pairs of shoes piled up at the side of the
room. Two or three rings later, it was apparent no-one was home. He
circled the property, and climbed the wall that surrounded the outside
deck and Jacuzzi. A few empty wine bottles sat on the table, a few
magazines lay on the ground by a chair. The Jacuzzi murmured away on
standby. He went window to window lifting his hand to the glass to
peer in. Every room the same story. No sign of anything untoward in
the piles of chaos in each room. He headed out via the resident's garage.
The Ferrari was not there.
He retreated to the car and then plumbed Danni Divine's address into
the satellite navigation.
The address was a penthouse apartment in a slightly dubious downtown
area. Nolan studied the area around as he drew up, and decided to park
a couple of blocks over where there was a heavier traffic flow.
He headed across a couple of streets, dodging the traffic until he arrived
outside the lobby of The Palm Palace Apartments. It had seen better
days. A grimy intercom revealed 'Danni' with a love heart was in 26C.
He buzzed up several times without reply, before giving up and
returning to his car. It was too late to return to the clinic, so he headed
for Le Monde.

On arrival, he asked for the manager, it turned out it was the muscular guy with the weak effeminate voice that they always laughed at.
- Hi there, I called earlier today about my colleague, Dr Mike Richardson? –
- Ah yes. What can I do for you Dr Nolan? –
- I'm afraid Dr Richardson appears to have gone missing. I'm desperately trying to track him down as we have some very important medical matters to be dealt with at the clinic, and he is not responding to the regular methods of communication. Did he say anything about where he was headed? –
- I'm afraid not, Dr Nolan. He arrived here with his partner on Thursday, and stayed in the suite until the awards on Saturday. They sent for room service in that period, and according to the door key swipes, they did not leave the room during that period. They returned a little after 11.30pm on Saturday night with what I can only politely describe as 'hangers-on', most of whom appeared to be more familiar with his partner, rather than Dr Richardson himself. They racked up the majority of the bill in food and drink between then and 4.47am on the Sunday morning, at which point most of the entourage left. Breakfast for two was ordered and delivered to the room at 10.34am, and they checked out at 12.04pm. They left in Dr Richardson's grey Ferrari which had been in the hotel car park since their arrival. I'm sorry I can't tell you anything other than that – the manager looked sympathetically at Nolan.

Nolan thanked him, slipped him two $20 dollar bills, and headed out to the hotel entrance on the street, where he looked up and down the road. The birds cheeped in the afternoon sun. He headed back to his car and the clinic.

That night he cruised around the streets of downtown and their usual haunts in West Hollywood, looking for just a glimpse of a grey Ferrari. He drove past Dr Mike's and Danni Divine's apartment at least six times, hoping for a chink of light, a sign of life, without success. Exhausted, he returned home.

The next day at the clinic, between appointments and work, he dialled round various hotels, restaurants, bars; in fact anywhere he remembered he had been with Dr Mike. He knew he was a creature of habit, and wouldn't probably go anywhere unknown to him. All without success. As the last client left he clinic, Annie stuck her head around the door to see Nolan with his head in his hands.

- Don't worry about it, Sam. He's just away blowing off steam –
- That's what Tony Rossi said too. And Ashley. And Bruno. Only thing is, he's not the type of guy to actually blow off steam! That's my worry. Oh, and the small matter of Ramos Di Santis tomorrow morning – he covered his face with his hands.
- What's the problem with Ramos Di Santis? – She queried genuinely.
- Hello? Just a matter of the correct treatment of the Clooney DNA. Don't want him looking like Amal Clooney. Or Mickey Rooney. Or Hong Kong Phooey – he laughed but in a self-pitying way.
- But I know how to prepare it – she answered meekly.
Nolan drew his hands down from his face.
- What did you say? –
- I know how to prepare the DNA. He showed me several times. There's also a Simpsons notebook in the top drawer of his desk with all the various calculations. All he does is simply calculate three main factors based on the patient's readings prior to surgery, and then he takes a percentage guess as to how much the patient already looks like the target –
- That's it? The big bloody secret that he keeps from me, he tells you without the slightest hesitation? Here was me thinking it was beyond us. All that time it was simply formulaic? Christ, you and Chinese Anaesthetist can ably assist with the surgical side of it, what do we need him for? – He stood up confidently.
- You need him to keep your feet on the ground. You're like a song writing partnership. Each person brings something different to the table. The end result is the mix of those elements. You take 50% away, it doesn't work – She said softly.
- It's him who has chosen to take himself away from us, Annie. Anyways, be great experience for the clinic to see if we can do it

without him. Be like old times, eh? - He walked round the desk and put his arm around her and kissed her forehead.

- Nice early night and we'll make a new George Clooney tomorrow morning! – He closed the door behind him as they left the office. A more confident Nolan strode out to his Ferrari and roared off into the night.

The Cult's 'Spiritwalker' blasts into the room causing Nolan to wake with a start. He sat up in bed and through half-closed eyes grabbed the remote and turned the music to a more bearable level. He loved no hangover mornings. These had now become the norm rather than the exception. No foul taste in the mouth, no memory loss from the previous evening, no thumping headache, no unbearable thirst. The alarm had been set to KRQR for 7am, and he sprung from bed as he remembered his new protocols of running, exercise and healthy eating that Ashley had installed in him. He padded through to the dressing room where he selected his designer sportswear and trainers, then headed to the kitchen for a pre-workout fruit smoothie. He prepped the fruit meticulously, and then studied it as the blender mashed it into a pink blob. He drank hungrily direct from the mixer, then put on his headphones and headed off on a tour of the neighbourhood. He gently paced through the leafy streets in the sunshine, nodding to fellow joggers, gaily stepping out of the way in an exaggerated fashion for dogs and single women, as the music powered him through. He climbed through his well-worn route, and then started the descent that would eventually return him home. His wrist monitor ensured his pace was constant, and bleeped whenever he slackened. Just as he turned into Jasmine Drive, he stopped suddenly, his heart pounding. There was the large blue BMW. He couldn't remember the number plate, but just its menacing presence. He studied the car for any sign of life, but the windows were so black he couldn't even tell if there was anyone inside. He slowly resumed his jog, the wrist monitor bleeping like crazy as he had interrupted his progress, and crossed over to the opposite pavement from the blue BMW. He studied it's immaculately polished exterior, again, looking for signs of movement within, but it just sat immobile in the early morning sun. He reached the bottom of Jasmine and had a cursory glance over his shoulder as he turned into his own street, home just a block away. After showering and prepping for the day ahead, he jumped into the Ferrari and opened the garage door. Rather than turning right to the freeway, he turned left and headed up toward Jasmine Drive. The BMW was gone. He stopped, U-turned and headed back to his normal route. Could they be watching him? He dismissed the thought. Must have been a similar car. BMW's are not uncommon in Beverly Hills he thought. He corrected himself for being so paranoid. As he immediately came to a halt in the morning rush traffic, he hit Dr Mike's number on the screen. It rang out for several minutes before he hung up. The traffic started to move again and before he knew it, the sign for exit 46 loomed up ahead.

He parked up in the lot, and strode confidently into the clinic, nodded to bored receptionist, and headed down the hall where he could hear the sounds of preparation in the theatre.

A happy, joking Annie and Chinese Anaesthetist came out through the doors and greeted Nolan.

- I've taken the liberty of bringing in the relief nurse Jane to help out as Dr Mike's not here – he said introducing the small red-haired woman who shook his hand.

- Yes of course, I remember Jane – he lied.

- Dr Nolan – began bored receptionist, - Ramos Di Santis is in reception –

- Send him along – he headed back into his office.

Di Santis entered shiftily without knocking, taking Nolan somewhat by surprise, however any discomfort he may have had dissipated with the large white envelope he handed over with $20k in cash. He thanked him, then ushered him out of the room across to Annie who went to prepare him for theatre.

Nolan opened his safe and put the money in it. He straightened up,

232

rubbed his eyes, and donned his gown for surgery. He moved into pre-op where the patient was being wheeled through into theatre. He scrubbed up, washing carefully, and realised this was his first surgical procedure without Dr Mike in quite a long time.

He dried his hands and held them up for Jane to apply his gloves. As he entered the brightly lit theatre, Annie stood at the ready beside the sound system.

- What are we in the mood for today? – She asked in a slightly suggestive way.

- Classical today – he stated quietly, strangely recalling the many procedures with Dr Mike, laughing, jumping around, and clowning with body parts.

Annie hit the play button and Schubert's Ave Maria filled the room. She headed out the side door to the freezer room. Nolan followed her as she began to run her finger across the rows and rows of small drawers.

- I'm watching this bit – he said, his breath showing in the freezing temperature.

He looked up to see Jane and Chinese Anaesthetist staring through the glass at them.

Annie found the Clooney DNA sample and pulled the small sample bottle from the drawer. She carefully placed it under the examination lamp and began to draw a small quantity up the syringe. It was then that Nolan noticed she was glancing over at Dr Mike's Simpsons' notebook. A series of small squiggles and Dr Mike's childlike handwriting caught Nolan's eye. Annie finished drawing the sample from the bottle and returned it to the drawer. She winked at Nolan and they headed back out to the small room with the large radiation warning symbol on the door. She switched on the lights and handed the syringe to Nolan.

- Here. Hold this. I'll go get his BP and stats – she headed out of the room.

Nolan looked at the small computer screen with the prompts for information. Apparently seven key indicators of the patient's current state, and Dr Mike's program would calculate the angle, speed and duration of the microwave dose that the donor DNA required. Annie burst back into the room with her scribbles on an Ethicon Sutures notepad. She punched in the several measures, and hit return. Within a few seconds, the sample chamber lit up and the door popped open. Annie placed the sample inside the chamber and closed the door. A countdown clock appeared on the screen and began counting down from twenty. A second countdown at the side in red showed seven minutes, forty-two seconds. Annie gently tugged his sleeve and pulled him out of the room where she closed the door behind them.

- On you go with your work – she pulled him gently through back into the theatre - I'll go back through for it once we need it. Now. Come on. What do we do here......ah yes. Two small cheekbone implants, and minor tuck under the ears to tighten it all up – she gesticulated for Nolan to start.

Nolan pulled the mask up over his nose and mouth, adjusted the position of the overhead light, picked up his scalpel, checked the blade, and began to cut to the gentle introduction of Tchaikovsky's Nutcracker Suite.

Two hours later, he laid down the scalpel, just as Jane and Annie began to hover the digital measurement laser over Ramos Di Santis, checking symmetry. The machine hummed as they pulled it left, right, up and down his newly sculpted features. Nolan looked up at the large monitor screen above them. One by one, green ticks appeared down the left hand side.

- You've done it again, Sam – beamed Jane – only 0.03mm variation. You're better than the machine itself! -

Nolan held up his hands and tilted his head in mock humility.

Annie then returned from the DNA laboratory with the syringe now full of the spun Clooney DNA which she began to inject at the points of surgery. Nolan headed out to clean up.

- I'll check on him in an hour – he shouted back over his shoulder.

He cleaned up and headed to his office where he checked his phone and email. Nothing from Dr Mike, but there was 30% off at Ralph Lauren, and he did need a new sports jacket. Opening a can of soda, he dialled up Dr Mike's number. Straight to answer phone. His previous called numbers were a jumbled combination of Dr Mike's mobile, bungalow number at the Chateau Marmont, Danni Divine's mobile number, and house number.

He rotated through all four again, no answer at any of them. Then it occurred to him. He looked through his contacts until he found Andrea at West Hollywood Ferrari.

- Hi Andrea, it's Sam Nolan at the Sunnyside Clinic here –
- No there's nothing wrong with the car –
- I just remembered that you mentioned there was a tracker device fitted to these cars in the event of them being stolen?
- Excellent. Well I'm afraid to say I'm a little concerned about my partner in the grey FF. I've been calling him for a couple of days and I'm not getting any answer. His neighbours haven't seen hide nor hair of him either, and I was wondering if you could tell me where the car is? –
- I appreciate it's highly irregular –
- No, I am fully aware of our obligations regarding discretion; however these cars are supplied as a pair contractually to the business, so I'm asking you as the business owner, to source the location of the car? Seeing as I'm liable for any damage to it –
- I see. So you need to get in touch with Ferrari USA head office who will source the car and give you the exact positioning –
- No, that's fine. I have a couple of small things to do here and I'll swing into the dealership in about an hour –
-I see. Not until tomorrow. So I could pop in first thing tomorrow morning? What time do you open? 10am. I'll be in at ten -
- No, *thank you* – He hung up with a satisfied grin.

Now all he had to do was decide how he would confront Dr Mike. Good cop or bad cop?

A tricky one, Too hard on him might send him running away again. Too soft and he might start regaining a conscience. And that would never do in this business, he thought.

He finished the soda, and scrolled through deleting unwanted advertising emails. Annie had obviously cleaned and screened the enquiry email account, as they were only a couple of very recent emails. Just at that moment, an email arrived from the clinic's lawyers, a copy of the agreement for Maria Lindos. He forwarded on to Annie.

Feeling better and more in control, he sent Ashley a text with a love heart, then donned his white coat and headed back to the theatre.

The huge smile on Annie's face as he walked in told him the procedure was a success.

As he approached the patient, it was obvious it was George Clooney's face on the patient.

He smiled at Annie.

- Looks like we managed without him after all - he grinned.

- I've got a small errand to run just up the road, but you guys can go clean him up now and bring him round. He's all paid, so take the photographs and send him on his merry way. That agreement for Maria Lindos is also in on email, so give her a call and see if she can come in with the husband and the lover tomorrow afternoon – he laughed, noticing the look of confusion on the faces of Jane and Chinese Anaesthetist. He waved goodbye and headed out to his car. His phoned bleeped indicating a text message.

He fished the device out from his jacket pocket, hoping for a message from Dr Mike, but it was from Ashley.

- I miss you. Come home now –

Another text message followed quickly afterward. He looked again, but groaned when he saw Dan Phillip's name.

He put the phone back in his pocket, hopped into the Ferrari, and headed off to Ashley's house.

Chapter 12
Close To Eden

Bang! Bright white light slams into Nolan's brain. A clearly happy and bubbly Ashley has pulled back the curtains letting the sunlight burn into his hangover.
- C'mon sleepyhead. You told me you had to be at the Ferrari dealership at ten, and its 8.45 now –
He eased out of the bed, wincing in the light and padded across the bedroom carpet, stopping only to peck her on the cheek, and on into the shower room. After a cleansing shower and shave, the transformation is almost complete. Selecting a crisp white Armani shirt and club tie, he then began to peruse the various suit offerings in his temporary wardrobe in Ashley's oversize walk-in closet. He opted for the Hugo Boss crepe wool everyday tailoring, the beautiful symmetry of the garments hang perfectly when worn due to the unique lightweight wool weave, that's even suitable for 100 degree days in California. He slipped on black Gucci loafers and then descended the sprawling staircase like a God. He pecked Ashley on the cheek and gently squeezed her thigh as he exited, causing her to hold onto his hand and begin to drag him back. She fired the come to bed eyes at him, and just for a moment as he caught a glimpse of her exposed thigh through the slit in her dressing gown, he almost considered staying. Instead, he retreated playfully, extricating his hand from hers, and he fired an imaginary pistol at her as he left through the door.
He jumped into the Ferrari, being careful to ensure that the roof did not automatically open, which would disturb his newly-coffered hair. He checked him self in the rear view mirror, and headed down to the Ferrari dealership of West Hollywood.
En route he made his now routine circuit of calling Dr Mike and Danni Devine's various numbers, all without answer. On arrival at the garage, he was met by an enthusiastic receptionist, clearly aware of who he was. She called through to the manager, and as usual, he had to wait.

He sat at the well-appointed reception area with a Cappuccino, noting that the Sunnyside Clinic was on the front page of one of the pointless lifestyle magazines on the coffee table.

He smiled to himself and continued to sip his coffee. As he studied the huge complex showroom, it struck him just how many people were actually working there. Every glass office, every counter had at least one employee squirreling away. Perhaps working was the wrong term, he thought to himself. They were certainly present, but aside from much staring at computer screens and carrying immaculate folders from room to room, there did not appear much industry, or actual selling of cars. In fact, he was the only customer. Thirty-odd employees to the one customer, and yet he still had to wait.

His concentration was broken as the pretty young receptionist offered to show him through to the manager's office. – Anyone ever tell you that you look like Princess Grace? – He asked.

He was shown into a bright glass office on the mezzanine level, minimalist in its appearance. Probably minimalist in its output too, he sniggered to himself.

- Good Morning Doctor Nolan. I'm Eddie Barclay, the manager here – he extended his hand, which Nolan shook then sat.

- I believe you have some concerns about your partner? –

- I do indeed Eddie. I haven't been able to contact him for a few days now, and as he isn't the kind to do something like this, I am quite concerned –

- Have you contacted the Police? –

- That will be my next port of call, however, when I remembered your rep telling me about the tracking system, I thought it was a perfect way to check on him without raising any alarms unnecessarily, and not to panic anyone – he added with sincerity.

Eddie Barclay handed him an envelope.

- This contains a PIN number and a web address which will enable you to track the whereabouts of the car. It is valid for seventy two hours which should be long enough for you to find it. It is very unusual for the company to give these out, and I ask that you use your discretion in this matter -

238

- Thank you very much Eddie – Nolan began to rise – You have been most helpful, and you can be rest assured of my discretion, and also the continued patronage of the Sunnyside Clinic, which is also more than grateful for your help in this matter – he shook hands and exited.

A smiling Sam Nolan placed the envelope in his breast pocket before entering the car. He dialled Perfect 10 as he got into the car, but both Rossi Brothers were unavailable.

His phone calendar bleeped to remind him of the meeting with Maria Lindos and her two lovers. He deleted two texts from Dan Phillips while he cursed under his breath. He checked the time, and threaded through the streets toward the Clinic.

He eventually drew into the car park where a gleaming black Rolls Royce was parked in his spot. The 'Maria' number plate gave the game away, and he smiled ruefully as he entered the clinic.

- I know, I know, I'm slightly late – he said to Bored Receptionist as he purposefully strode up the corridor, to where Annie was exiting his office.

He mouthed 'thank you' to her and burst into the room.

- I'm sorry, I'm sorry – he took off his jacket and turned to the three people all seated in his room – Now then, Maria, I know, you must be Leon and you sir, must be the great Jimmy Kennedy – he shook their hands in turn, noticing the clear look of bewilderment on the face of Jimmy Kennedy.

Annie knocked on the door and entered with a folder containing the legal agreement. She laid it on the desk and left.

- So Leon, I'm going to start with you – Leon was tall and gangly set, looking slightly uncomfortable in designer clothes which Maria had clearly bought for him.

- I need to know, and according to that document – he pointed to the folder on his desk – that you are 100% with the procedure that we are about to undertake. Based on the volume of enhanced genetic material that we are going to inject into you, it is going to have the physical effect of ageing you to around fifty years of age. I need to know that you are fully aware of this? – Nolan sat back, arms folded.

239

- No, I'm good, Dr Nolan. I have talked it over at great length with Maria and Jimmy, and we are all in full agreement –
Nolan turned to face Maria Lindos, who was sitting closer to Jimmy Kennedy, holding his hand.
- Mr Kennedy, I take it then that you are also confident with the procedure we are about to embark on? The taking of a sample of your DNA and using it to help mould Leon here into a younger version of yourself? –
Jimmy Kennedy didn't respond. He continued to stare blankly across the floor.
Maria Lindos leant over and began to whisper in his ear.
Slowly recognition appeared in his face and he nodded gently.
They continued to discuss the procedure, the recovery times, the basic pros and cons. Nolan moved the computer screen to allow them to view the proposed work with its before and after at the end. As the conversation continued, Nolan began to have deeper doubts about the whole thing.
Annie knocked again to bring in coffee for Maria and Jimmy. Nolan stood to his feet.
- I wonder if I could maybe get a word in private, Maria? – He pointed toward the door and led her into the dimly-lit pre-op.
- I'm not sure if I can go ahead with this, Miss Lindos. Jimmy clearly has advanced Senile Dementia. I've watched him the whole time you guys have been in, and he's absolutely no idea where he is or what's going on –
- Exactly Dr Nolan. That's why we have to progress now. Any further delays might simply be too late – she implored.
- I'm not sure if I could state in a court of law that he was of sound mind and in full control of his faculties –
- Nobody is asking you to state in court, Dr Nolan. He'll be fine once it's done. Don't worry about it – - And what if we scoop up some of the very DNA that has caused his dementia? Won't Leon have something to say about that being shot into his system? –
- Listen – she hissed angrily – We're all set up here to go today. I've

240

agreed to pay your exorbitant fees. You have Jimmy for the DNA. You have Leon ready and willing to be operated on. I've agreed to pay your fee. The nurses and staff are all here. We're ready to go at 2pm as arranged. Now you're gonna be the problem? What else would I need to do to get you to just get on with it? – She glared at him.

Unsure if this was a sexual come-on or not, Nolan seized his chance. His head bowed - Well if you were to pay the fee today, now, in cash, I'll go ahead – his eyes looked up to see her reaction.

- Why didn't you just say – she grabbed a set of scrubs from the hook on the wall and thrust them into his chest – You get on with the job, and I'll go to the bank –

She turned and left the room, Nolan following sheepishly behind her. She tottered into the office and kissed Jimmy on the cheek and whispered into his ear.

- I'll be back in half an hour or so – she said to Leon, as he stood up – It's time – she turned and left.

Annie entered the room, and with a curt nod from Nolan, gently led Jimmy Kennedy through into one of the small consulting rooms to prepare a sample to be taken.

Chinese Anaesthetist and the nurse whose name Nolan couldn't remember led Leon through into pre-op.

Within an hour, the theatre was set. A sedated Leon lay on the table, images of a younger Jimmy Kennedy covered the wall screens. Maria Lindos comforted Jimmy in Nolan's office.

The newly prepared Digital DNA lay in three small syringes on a stainless steel tray.

Nolan held the scalpel up to the light, checking the clean blade, as Annie hit the play button, and music filled the theatre.

Three hours later, the final dimensional checks carried out, Nolan removed his mask and returned to his office, leaving the clean up to the staff. He slumped down in his chair, tired but satisfied. He put his feet up on the desk and opened a cold coke from the fridge.

He lifted the mobile phone from his desk, and after deleting a couple of messages from Dan Phillips without even opening them, he checked his emails, however no response at all from Dr Mike. He dialled the now routine sequence of numbers, again, all unanswered or to voicemail. He hung up. He lifted the sealed envelope from the Ferrari dealer and opened it with the letter opener, very smoothly, as only a surgeon could. He admired the almost invisible tear in the paper before removing the letter.

He typed the web address into his browser on the computer, entered the PIN number as instructed, and was relieved to see the car details and registration plate (CUT 1) of Dr Mike's grey FF. Moving through the menu options, he arrived at 'Locate'.

He hit the option, and a spinney circle came up as the North point indicator flickered over the map of California. After what seemed like ages, the needle settled on the Trump Hotel in Las Vegas.

- Ah-ha! Bloody predictable – he thought to himself.

He then followed the instructions on screen to download the app to his mobile phone.

Once complete, he called the Trump Hotel and asked to be connected to Mike Roth's room. After the receptionist reported no-one under that name, he concluded they were clearly using aliases. He asked for the valet. After what seemed like an age he was connected to an elderly man. He refused to give any information on the car, but his old man obfuscations and poor excuses had more or less confirmed that the grey Ferrari FF was in their lot. Nolan hung up.

He then messaged Ashley that he had located the car and was going to Las Vegas to confront Dr Mike. He told her not to worry, but he would be home very late, given the four hour drive each way.

He then called Perfect 10 to let the Rossi brothers know he had located Dr Mike, however they were both unavailable.

Very strange, he thought to himself, as they were usually all over their new golden boy.

He checked his watch. Four-thirty. He could make it to Vegas for about 9pm. He pulled on his jacket and went to check on the patient.

He entered post op, and Maria Lindos was at Leon's bedside, crying. Annie was scuttling around the room organising. Jimmy Kennedy was

242

in a chair looking into space.

- Oh Dr Nolan…..- she whimpered – It's beautiful. Such a good job. You really are the best in the business – she kissed Nolan on the cheek – Aren't they Jimmy? – She questioned Jimmy Kennedy, who turned to look on hearing his name.

- I said they're the best in the business, aren't they? – She tried again. Jimmy meekly nodded his head and continued to look into space. Annie and Nolan exchanged nervous glances.

- Well I'm heading off now, and if I could get a minute, Annie? – He made his excuses and amid the adulation, thanks, and large brown envelope of cash from Maria Lindos, he headed down the corridor whispering to Annie.

- I've found Dr Mike in Las Vegas – he hissed – I'm heading up there now to get him sorted out once and for all. I've left messages with Perfect 10. If any of the Rossi's phone here instead of my mobile, get them to keep trying me as it could be the signal in the Desert –

- Okay. Good luck – she patted his back.

Nolan headed out to the car, gleaming in the afternoon sunshine.

He put the Trump Hotel address into the navigation system. Four hours eighteen minutes it read.

- Challenge accepted – he set the car mode to 'Sport' and roared out of the car park.

After a fairly uneventful drive that included a tour of some of his favourite teenage albums, the sun was beginning to set as he saw the twinkling lights of Las Vegas ahead at the end of the long straight. Emboldened, he gunned the engine and raced down the outside lane at over a hundred miles per hour. He slowed as he passed the 'Welcome to Las Vegas sign, and began the slow cruise down the strip toward the Trump Hotel. He checked the navigation. Three hours fifty-two minutes.

The car growled it's way along the strip, turning heads as it passed, dodging in and out of other supercars and limousines, until he reached the left turn at the end of the strip.

He crept round the corner, just then, the Trump Hotel loomed up ahead

243

of him, its golden luminescence caught in the dying sunlight.

He pulled up outside the lobby, where an elderly black valet came to take his car.

He established that 'George' was indeed the hopeless valet that he had spoken to earlier. He left the door open, handing the car over, and headed into the lobby.

The brash, golden interior took him a little by surprise; however, he scanned the area for any evidence of Dr Mike or Danni Devine before heading into the hotel bar. He pulled up a leather barstool and ordered a light beer.

He took his drink and wandered over to the deck overlooking the swimming pool, and put on his sunglasses to allow him to thoroughly check all the sun bed bodies by the pool, without being reported. Satisfied neither of them was there; he finished his drink, laid the glass on the counter and headed back to the main door.

George was sitting in the valet station with all the keys behind him.

- Hi George. I'm afraid I've left a couple of things in my car that I need. I am so sorry – he held his hand up in apology.

George lifted the Ferrari key from the back board, and Nolan could see there were another four similar Ferrari keys. He ambled around as if to head to the lot, but Nolan blocked his path.

- No, no, no, I am such an idiot, George. Just tell me where it is in the lot, and I'll just pop over for it –

- Ah'm not really meant to let anyone in there Sir……but if you're happy enough just to in and out, well, you're car is on the second level space number 57. If you see the other valet over there, jus tell him George said it was owkay – he handed him the key just as Nolan slipped him a $20 note.

Nolan took the key and smiled – I'll be back before you know it – and headed off to the multi-storey lot.

Once out of sight of the valet and bellhops, Nolan jogged into the car lot and began on the ground floor walking up through the ranks of parked cars, scanning left and right. He made his way up to the second level, where he saw his own car, and another red 356. He walked briskly on until the third level, where he spied the grey FF on the back wall.

He quickened his pace up to the car, and leaning round the back to confirm the number plate, he then looked inside the car, which was immaculate. No cups, cans, debris. Also no evidence of any jackets or hand luggage.

Once back in the lobby, he approached the reception desk, where a pretty girl named Andrea greeted him warmly.

- I know you - She cheekily wagged her finger – Doctor Nolan…….delighted to meet you. Now what can we do for you here at Trump Hotel? – She tilted her head.

- Now that you mention it – he lowered his voice – I'm trying to find my partner, Dr Mike Richardson. He is here – he looked left and right then leaned in conspiratorially – in a delicate romantic situation, if you know what I mean, and I've been trying to contact him for the last few days without success. Now I know he's here, as his car is in the lot, but given the circumstance, I suspect he has checked in under an alias. Would you mind terribly checking for me? – He gushed charm and gave his pained, concerned expression.

- As you are no doubt aware, hotel privacy policies prevent me from doing that……..But seeing as it's you, Dr Nolan, I'll see what I can do. Now what is that car registration number? – She smiled.

- It's C-U-T-One – he replied with a smirk.

- Of course it is – she replied smiling, before tap tap tapping the keyboard.

- Here we are…..they are checked in as Mr & Mrs Ramone. Room 2820. Do you want me to call them? –

- Yes please. If you could ask them to come to the reception urgently as there has been an emergency? – He shrugged in suggestion.

Andrea called.

- It's just ringing out. In fact, the room key hasn't been used in the last 36 hours. I'll call security to go check. You can go with them if you want? –

- Yes, lovely, thank you. By the way – he handed her a business card –

That mole on your cheek? I can sort that out in no time. If you're in LA anytime soon, give me a call –   He headed off to the elevator with the security guard, leaving Andrea looking puzzled whilst rubbing her cheek and checking her reflection.

They arrived at the room door where the guard knocked firmly. Just then the Hispanic maid came ambling past pushing a trolley.

- When were you last in here – he pointed at the door.

She pointed at the 'Do Not Disturb' sign on the door handle – Not since Monday –

The guard knocked once again, and then asked the maid to open the door.

She swiped her card and they entered. Nolan was impressed with the large suite, but it was as if no-one was there. He began opening and shutting drawers, wardrobes, doors.

- Looks like they gone – said the maid – hope they paid the bill –

She turned to Nolan but he had already left and was striding purposefully back to the elevators.

He stopped in at the reception desk again and asked Andrea to call him should Mr Ramone return. He called Ashley to let her know he was heading home.

Once ensconced back in his car, he headed back along the now garish, brightly lit Vegas Strip on his way out. It had completely come to life as the daylight had gone. He scanned the crowds looking for a familiar face, more in hope than expectation.

Once he passed the airport, the traffic thinned and he sped up, anxious to get home and regroup. He sped through the dark desert, stopping only to refuel. He drove in silence, conceiving of all permutations of Dr Mike's behaviour. As he passed the sign of thirty miles to Los Angeles, he became aware of the flashing lights of a police roadblock ahead. The few cars on the road queued to a slow crawl, and traffic in both directions was directed into a slip area where two officers were checking the cars' trunks and occupants. Nolan popped a mint in case there was any residual beer breath. Eventually the Highway Patrolman pointed Nolan's car over to two officers who approached his car.

The larger more experienced looking cop leant down to his window - Good evening Sir. Sorry to inconvenience you at this time, but we are conducting a lock down of all roads in and out of the city and checking for a very dangerous individual. You may or may not be aware of Diaz 'The Jackal' Rodriguez, the head of the infamous Mexican Gulf Drug Cartel, who escaped from FBI jail three weeks ago. There had been a confirmed sighting of him in West Hollywood a couple of days ago, and given he is number one on the World's Most Wanted list, we are checking all traffic , whilst searches are going ahead all over the city – The other officer walked around his car shining a light.

- There's not really anywhere in this car to conceal anyone – Nolan joked.

- Indeed. Very nice car it is as well, sir. If you wouldn't mind just having a look at the photograph of Rodriguez, and let me know if you have seen him at all on your travels? –

- I'm sure I haven't. I'm just returning from a business trip in Las Vegas………. - his voice tailed away as the officer held the photograph up.

Nolan went white and took the black and white prison mug shot photograph from the cop and held it under the vanity light of the car.

- Yes indeed. A very, very, dangerous character. Drugs, Trafficking, Gun Smuggling, and a best estimate is that he is responsible personally for the death of over three hundred people -

Nolan sat transfixed in silence.

- Wha……what…..who……ummmm - his hands were visibly shaking holding the photograph.

A photograph that was of Ramos Di Santis. A bit grainy, and the hair was different, but unmistakably Ramos Di Santis. The very man he had operated on the day before.

The policeman's voice snapped Nolan out of the shock.

- I wouldn't worry yourself unnecessarily Sir; he has only killed business rivals, fellow gang members, and those who might have something on him. Nothing for you to worry about – he took the photograph back, and they waved forward the next car.

247

Nolan drove on, dumbfounded. He pulled over and checked his telephone. Two messages from Dan Phillips which he instantly deleted, and seven in a row from Annie.

"Get to the clinic NOW", "Sam drop whatever you're doing and get here NOW" and the like. He dialled the Sunnyside number, but the line was dead. He dialled Annie's mobile but it was engaged. He sent a text message that he was indeed on way.

He hammered through the sparse late night traffic and exited at junction 46 as he done for so many years. As he sat first in the queue at the stop light, he gazed up at the billboard which had an advert for a cruise holiday.

- Just what I need – he thought to himself, his concentration shattered by the honking of the horn of the car behind indicating the light was now green. He gave the finger in his rear view mirror and turned down toward the clinic. Just as he looked down from the mirror, a figure was in the middle of the road immediately in front of him.

He swerved violently to avoid, and in the process clipped several cars parked by the side of the road, removing his own wing mirror. He heard the sickening sound of the Ferrari scrape along the other cars. He stood on the brakes and wrestled with the steering wheel to keep it straight, before the car came to a halt. He exhaled heavily, and then looked up in the mirror to see a crumpled figure lying in the road. He leapt out of the car and went to check on the body. He was certain he had managed to avoid hitting them, but he couldn't be 100% sure.

As he arrived bending over the figure lying in the road, he thought he recognised the suit the victim was wearing. He then saw the walking stick lying in the road. He gently slipped his arm under the torso to turn him over, all the time mouthing platitudes and words of comfort. As the head turned, mumbling incoherently, he realised it was Jimmy Kennedy. He checked him for any injuries, and satisfied he hadn't been hit by the car, he helped him to his feet. He was clearly distressed and agitated. Nolan helped him walk slowly and gently along the road and eased him down into the heavily damaged passenger side of the car. Once seat belted in, he walked round to his beautiful glossy undamaged side of the car.

248

Before entering the car, he looked around the deserted street. No-one was about, no cars had passed, and it was eerily quiet. All he could hear was the distant stream of traffic over on the 101.

He drove along to the clinic, all the while trying to reassure his passenger. As he pulled into the parking lot, a clearly distressed Annie was standing on her mobile phone at the front door anxiously looking all around.

There was a look of absolute confusion on her face as Nolan drew up in the damaged Ferrari with Jimmy Kennedy in the passenger seat.

She hung up the phone and ran straight in Nolan's arms sobbing.

- Hey, hey, hey……….it's alright. Now what's happened? –

She was heaving heavily with sobs, and he was finding it difficult to understand her.

- Take your time, Annie. Calm down. It's OK, I'm here now –

- I…I….I…was just on the phone to Ashley when you came in…..I tried……I tried to call you…..- She began sobbing heavily again.

- It's alright. I'm here now – he rubbed her back.

- Sam….I tried The Trump in Vegas, Le Monde, Montrose, everywhere for you……..- she sobbed.

- That's probably why your phone was engaged when I tried to call you back – he replied, which caused her to start crying heavily again.

- Sorrryyy…….sorrryyy……….It's Mike………-

- What about Mike – he ears pricked up.

- He's……he's……he's…….- she broke down crying again leaning against the car. She lifted her right hand and pointed to the clinic front door.

Nolan turned his head to look then ran into the building.

The reception was fine; he walked smartly up the corridor and looked into his office. His office looked normal other than the Apple Mac computer was gone. He crossed the corridor into Dr Mike's office where again the room looked fine, but again the large Apple Mac was gone. He opened the top drawer of Dr Mike's desk but the Simpson notebook was gone. He then noticed the flicking of a light on and off in the laboratory through the crack in the door. He opened it fully to reveal a completely trashed room. The large 3D printer was gone. The centrifuges were gone. The large piece of equipment Nolan had dubbed 'The Black Microwave' had gone. All samples, all testing equipment was smashed into an unusable state.

Shattered Petri Dishes and flasks lay all over the floor. Half of the LED light panels in the roof were flickering or completely broken, the dim light and flickering creating tall shadows on the walls, emphasising the hellish state of the room. He walked through the untouched pre-op and into the theatre. Again the theatre was untouched, although the small computer housing that stored the dimensions for facial matching was gone.

He looked left into the cold store. The lights were off, but he could see numerous warning lights glowing and flashing. The control panel on the exterior was flashing red indicating the safe temperature had been breached. As he came closer, he realised the door was ajar, and he stepped inside and switched on the light. Every tray of samples had been opened and spilled over the normally spotless stainless steel workbenches.

Every freezer door was open, and all the warning lights were flashing almost in unison.

Samples lay all over the floor, the surreal nature of the scene highlighted with sample labels with 'Elton John', 'Winston Churchill', 'Beyonce' and others scattered about. The computer that catalogued all the samples was gone. Samples in mid transfer and analysis lay on the floor.

Even in this hellish scene, Nolan laughed inwardly thinking of Tom Hanks DNA mixing with Martina Navratilova. Lady Diana with Will Smith. You might have been a Prince mixed with her, but not so fresh now, he thought looking at the sample staining the floor. He stood hands on hips surveying the damage laid out before him.

He turned and as he was about to leave the theatre, he noticed on the scheduling board, 'Sam Nolan' written in red pen, and an envelope held vertically in place by a scalpel stabbed into the centre.

He recognised the writing as that of Dr Mike, and tiptoed over the

250

debris and broken glass to retrieve it. He pulled the scalpel out and carried the letter back to his office where by force of habit, he slit the top opening neatly with his extra sharp letter opener.

He sat back in the chair and crossed his feet on the desk.

'My Dear Sam. Please accept this letter as my notice to quit the Sunnyside Clinic with immediate effect. In the beginning, it was great to see an old friend like yourself, and I heartily enjoyed our initial escapades and scrapes. I always knew you sailed a little bit close to the wind, but as I felt what we were doing was to a higher purpose, I tolerated your assorted vices and various peccadilloes. As usual, though Sam, you ended up making a mess of everything. All my time at the clinic, I diligently worked away on my own projects, aside from all the celebrity nonsense and mental cases. So, after my final humiliation at your hands at the Plastic Surgery Awards, I felt I have progressed enough with my work to branch out on my own. I knew that an amicable split with you would be impossible, I have talked with and met with both Jane and Sarah, and they also confirmed the pattern of your behaviour during your last 'amicable split' from them.

You will obviously be upset with the state of the clinic, but I had to ensure that you would not continue with this circus, as this would devalue what I am about to undertake.

You see, Sam, what I discovered was that a measured dose of one's own DNA after surgical procedures accelerated the healing and reduced the downtime, as it did with all our clients and their look a like obsessions. Procedures with little or no downtime. So I'm finally getting my wish. You should take pride too, that your input helped me get to a place where the Digital DNA will be available to everyone, and change the way that surgery is performed forever. Kidney transplants, heart by-passes, all manner of life saving surgeries. Now there aren't many people that can say that. You never know, you could be Sir Sam Nolan.

Now, before you start feeling sorry for yourself, take a think about what you have. You have a multi-millionaire gorgeous girlfriend. You live in Beverly Hills. Your clinic will survive; a chancer like you will always survive. You told me once that people's belief and their sheer will for something to be true or to work, is 90% of the way. You'll trade off our past, and I don't mind at all. I've also taken the liberty of depositing half a million dollars in the Clinic's business account. Just to cover the damage and you and the staff's loss of earnings for a short while. I've got what I need, and I'm back off to Edinburgh with Danni to start a new life there. Now before you think of following me, or sending any of your goons or their friends, please be aware I took several photographs of that poor unfortunate without half her face, the one that you had hacked to pieces and left in the cold store. Your genetic material was all over (and in) her. I also took several samples of *her* DNA and had them lodged along with the photographs, with my lawyers both here and in the UK, along with details of their current whereabouts of her remains.

Should anything happen to me, or I receive any funny phone calls, threats or intimidation, they are under instruction to send everything to the Los Angeles Police Department, along with your contact details.

So, all the best Sam. Who knows, we may meet again.

Dr Mike Richardson'

Nolan leant back against the wall. Outfoxed by Dr Mike. Who would have thought? He stumbled over the damage and headed back out to the parking lot, where a distressed Annie was attending to the various small cuts and abrasions to Jimmy Kennedy's face. He sat in the passenger seat of the Ferrari side on with his feet on the ground.

She looked up as he approached - What's happened Sam? –

Nolan looked at her tear streaked face with smudged black mascara.

- Turns out Dr Mike was using us all along. He had been working on a side project that needed the facilities we have here along with the revenue we raised to fund some 'good of humanity' thing. When I got to Vegas, they had checked out of the hotel and left the car in the lot – he held up the letter – And he's left me this little love letter – He looked down at the ground.

She continued to comfort Jimmy Kennedy – What does Jimmy have to do with all of this? –

252

- I nearly ran him down at the junction at the off ramp. He was wandering about in the middle of the road. I swerved, and well, - he pointed at the damaged side of the car.

- I suppose I'd better go phone Maria Lindos. She'll be worried sick about him – Annie stated as she straightened up and headed into the clinic to get her phone number – make sure he's OK Sam –

Nolan crouched beside Jimmy, gently rubbing his arm, and after a few minutes, Annie exited the Clinic staring at her mobile phone.

- I.....I....I....don't .....understand..... – she quizzically looked at Nolan – the maid took the call and said that both Mr Kennedy and Ms Lindos were at home, and we must be mistaken. She wouldn't let me talk to Maria........- she dazedly headed toward Nolan, who stood up and took the mobile phone from her and dialled the last number.

- Hello, yes. It's Dr Sam Nolan at the Sunnyside Clinic, I had Ms Lindos, Mr Leon Bruce and Mr Kennedy at our clinic earlier today, and it is urgent that I speak to them. A matter of life and death –

He continued to argue with the maid on the phone, until eventually he lowered the phone from his ear and handed it back to Annie.

- She hung up. Said it was too late to wake Ms Lindos or Mr Kennedy, and that Leon Bruce had left yesterday for good to return to his home in Cleveland – he stared at Annie – We've been had again. She had us sign the confidentiality agreements, pass Leon off as Jimmy Kennedy, safe in the knowledge he'd pass a DNA test, and poor old Jimmy here – he pointed to the old man sitting in the car – was either gonna be bumped off or simply cast loose with his dementia. He'd end up dying in a ditch somewhere and just be another homeless bum fatal statistic – his shoulders dropped.

- What are we going to do with him, Sam? – sobbed Annie.

He walked round to the driver's door and lifted his mobile phone off the seat. Twelve missed calls. Just as he went to view the callers, a rapidly braking car drove into the parking lot with its lights on full beam, causing Nolan and Annie to shield their eyes as it drew right up beside them. It was a very clean, very shiny, blue five series BMW. Both front doors of the car opened simultaneously, and Nolan recognised both

253

DaLuca and Williams. They moved swiftly to Nolan's side and gently but firmly escorted him to the back doors of the BMW.

- Don't worry Annie – he shouted – Just look after Jimmy. I'll be back tomorrow morning –

He ducked his head as he was ushered into the back seat. He wiped the sweat from his brow.

- I'm sure your assistant will lock up your business and your car – growled Williams.

Nolan sat in the centre of the rear seat, head in hands, rubbing his eyes.

- Déjà vu Dr Nolan – quipped DaLuca who looked at him in the rear view mirror – This time we're going for a longer ride –

Nolan looked up sharply with a look of horror on his face.

- Not that long – laughed DaLuca – Mr Marchesi and a few of his friends would like a word, but they're at a friend's house. A little further out of the way – he continued to study Nolan, while Williams spoke very quietly into his mobile phone.

Some 50's beatnik jazz played quietly in the background as the car glided up Mulholland Drive. He watched the road signs and housing become less frequent, until they were a car alone, twisting and turning on the narrow elevated roads. Nolan reckoned they were somewhere around Angeles National Forest. This did not fill him with confidence. Eventually, after what seemed like an age, the car turned off the road onto a well maintained driveway, illuminated with ultra modern low level lighting. The car pulled to a halt at a sentry box and gate, where the guard pushed the button to raise the gate. Nolan spied the reverse spikes countersunk into the driveway as they drove over. The car snaked along a considerable length of drive before pulling up at the car port of a flat roofed ultra modern house of many split levels. Williams exited the car and opened the door to allow Nolan to exit.

Two other men stood at the door as he entered, both had earpieces fitted. They nodded curtly to Williams before he returned to the BMW, and it slunk away back down the driveway.

The younger of the two men at the door smiled to Nolan – Follow me, Sir – and headed down the dimly lit hallway.

254

They came to a double set of oriental carved doors set in an obscured glass wall. Nolan could hear voices in the room, and was aware of movements behind the glass.

The doors opened and Nolan was ushered inside.

The air in the room had a whiff of cigar smoke, and contained four men sitting. Nolan nodded to Marchesi, and then turned to his right where a man he did not know was sitting at an ornate desk. The man raised his glass to Nolan and smiled.

He continued to scan round the room to his left where both Tony and Mike Rossi were sitting at either end of a long sofa.

- Good Evening Dr Nolan, or should I say Good Morning? – ventured Mike Rossi.

A clearly frightened Nolan sat on the smaller couch after prompting from Marchesi.

- Dr Nolan. I'm fairly sure you know why you're here. After all, you haven't responded to any of Phillips' calls or emails. You knew he would kick it up the chain to us, right? After the unpleasantness of the last time you defaulted, I thought we had a pretty clear understanding of how it would work going forward – Marchesi stopped in front of Nolan, his hands spread wide. He continued talking walking away – And yet, because you're now in with the high fliers and the Hollywood elites, you don't pay your bills. This gentleman here – he gestured to the older grey haired man who Nolan didn't know – is Don Giordano. It is only by his good grace, and the word of the Rossi Brothers here, that we have not taken a firmer route in recovering our debt. Phillips called you several times over the last week to let you know that your line of credit had now stopped, as you were now over the one million dollars. We had continued to let you run with this, as your payments up to last month were always on time, and always an acceptable percentage of what we asked for. Now, the Rossi Brothers inform me that your partner has done a runner, and this may impact on your ability to earn. We are aware your bank accounts are a little short, and even by our best estimates, you cannot pay us. We don't know what you were getting up to in that clinic of yours, and we don't really care. What we do care

255

about, is our money. We calculate you have maybe half of it in your various accounts and cash. It is only through the excellent work you did on my wife and the personal vouch for you from the Rossi Brothers, that we can again offer you a solution to your situation. Don Giordano's girlfriend would like to have some of your miracle surgical work. If you can provide the excellent standard of work as you did to my good lady, we are more than happy to write off the remaining half of the debt – Nolan looked shell shocked.

- I take it your partner Dr Mike's input is not necessary for this? – Marchesi queried.

- No – Nolan lied.

- Calm down. Shouldn't be too hard if I can find another 'donor' – he thought to himself, his eyes flitting left and right as he tried to formulate a strategy. – Another Nadine, another victim from the Sunset Strip that no-one would miss. Messy, but necessary – he thought.

- Are you sure? - Asked Tony Rossi –

- Yes it's fine. I have an alternative technique that I can implement without Dr Mike's involvement – he said quietly.

At that point Don Giordano rose and opened the doors to allow an athletic, pretty, middle aged woman in sportswear to enter the room.

- This is Donna – began Don Giordano.

- Very familiar – said Nolan – So who is it you'd like me to replicate? – She turned over a photograph and held it up to Nolan.

It was a photograph of Ashley Hill, Nolan's girlfriend.

74 **E** Ethicon — Noble Gas	75 **N** Nip — Inert Gas	76 **Su** Suture — Inert Gas	77 **P** Punk — Metalloid	78 **Ma** Magnolia — Metalloid
84 **T** Tuck — Carbon	85 **Su** Superstar — Noble Gas	86 **Zn** Blood — Carbon	87 **F** Fox — Noble Gas	88 **Wi** Jane — Noble Gas
94 **Da** Mob — Post Transition Metal	95 **Ss** Sputnik — Post Transition Metal	96 **Cl** Sunnyside — Heavy Metal	97 **Sp** Sex Pistols — Urban	98 **St** Genetix — Inert Gas
105 **Ma** Ciccone — Urban	106 **Lu** Cindy — Carbon	107 **Wa** Watson — Urban	108 **Jt** Thunders — Urban	109 **Cr** Crick — Noble Gas
115 **Sh** Dolly — Urban	116 **Rn** Roslin — Heavy Metal	117 **Lv** Genes — Noble Gas	118 **V** Mania — Noble Gas	119 **F** Ferrari — Inert Gas
125 **Aa** Courtesan — Post Transition Metal	126 **He** Avoidoid — Inert Gas	127 **Ny** Dolls — Urban	128 **Ho** Tinseltown — Urban	129 **B** Allergan — Urban